Bad Things

R.K. Lilley

Bex,
So happy you're
enjoying TJ's train
wreck of a love story :)
XOXO.
R.K. Lilley

This book is dedicated to all of those who have gone through the utter heartbreak of watching a loved one suffer the disease of addiction. It is the most helpless feeling in the world. My heart goes out to you.

BOOKS BY R.K. LILLEY

IN FLIGHT (UP IN THE AIR #1)
MILE HIGH (UP IN THE AIR #2)
GROUNDED (UP IN THE AIR #3)
LANA (AN UP IN THE AIR NOVELLA)
BREATHING FIRE (HERETIC DAUGHTERS #1)
BAD THINGS (TRISTAN AND DANIKA #1)

Danika hasn't had an easy life. Being insanely attracted to bad boys has never helped make it easier.

One look at Tristan, and every brain cell she possessed went up in smoke. This man was trouble with a capital T. It was a given.

She knew better. Bad boys were bad. Especially for her. Considering her history, it was crazy to think otherwise. So why did crazy have to feel so damn fine?

For as long as she could remember, Danika had been focused on the future with single-minded purpose. Tristan came along and taught her everything there was to know about letting go, and living in the present. She fell, hard, and deep. Of course, that only made her impact with the ground that much more devastating.

Bad Things is about Tristan and Danika, and their train wreck of a love story. This series can be read as a standalone, or with the Up in the Air trilogy

Bad Things is a full-length novel, at roughly 105,000 words.
This book is intended for ages 18 and up.

CHAPTER ONE

THE BEGINNING
DANIKA

I had the strangest shiver of premonition rock my body the first time I heard Tristan's voice. I heard it from a room away, as he said something offhanded to my boss, Jerry, and still I knew somehow that he would change my life.

I had an unruly armful of clean laundry and five dogs crowding my legs in my boss's cramped laundry room, when I heard the front door open, and two men chatting as they entered the house. I wasn't alarmed. It was a chaotic sort of house, with all sorts of people coming and going at all hours of the day, *and* I recognized the sound of Jerry's voice instantly.

The other man that spoke was a stranger, but his voice was deep and it sort of rumbled through the house until it reached me. I had an instant and positive reaction to it. I had mixed feelings about men in general, having a rather sordid past with them as a whole, *and* having recently gone through a nasty breakup with a real piece of work. My ex had been an out of work, pothead loser, and he hadn't been the first loser that I'd wasted my time on. Still, I knew right away that I adored the sound of that deep, masculine voice.

I dropped the pile of clothes into the clean laundry pile in the clean corner of the room. My laundry skills were negligible, to put it nicely. I worked for Jerry and his ex-wife Beverly, as a live in nanny/housekeeper/dogwalker/poolgirl/gardener/whatever they needed me to do. It was well understood that I pretty much sucked at the housekeeper part of that arrangement, but it seemed to work for us all. I'd been working for them for two years, and we were going strong. Beverly and Jerry, dysfunctional exes, and awesome co-parents that they were, had become my closest friends and two of my favorite people on the planet.

I was dressed like a slob in too short black cheer shorts and a washed out gray UNLV sweatshirt, my straight black hair pulled into a rough ponytail, and not wearing a scrap of makeup, but I went to meet the newcomer anyway. My five favorite animals on the planet dogged my steps as I padded down the hallway.

Jerry's back was to me as I turned the corner from the hallway and into the black, stone-lined entryway, the stranger facing me. I saw at a glance that the stranger was young, sexy as hell, and straight-up Trouble with a capital T.

I knew trouble when I saw it, it being a very old friend of mine. Trouble for me was this nasty little self-destructive streak that I'd never quite been able to shake. A theme song even played in my head when I felt the big T getting close. *Four Kicks* was that song, and it cranked up to full volume with my first glance at him.

He was tall, and built like a linebacker, both muscular and massive. He wore a tight black T-shirt that showcased every starkly muscled inch of his chest. His tattooed arms were folded across his chest in a casually attentive stance, but his presence commanded the room.

His face was handsome, with clean, even features that were dominated by pale golden eyes. He had a straight slash of a nose, with a rounded tip that would have brought him from handsome to pretty boy if he wasn't so damned big, and full lips on a wide mouth that popped killer dimples at me as it hitched up playfully. Those dimples were pure big T. His pitch-black hair was cropped short, with dark stubble lining his jaw. His easy smile was playful, but still managed to be sinister. It was a heady combination for someone who was on a first name basis with the big T.

Jerry turned to see what the other man was smiling about. He was a middle-aged man, short and balding, with a slight build. *His* face was far from handsome, with close-set eyes and a big nose, but I thought he had one of the best smiles in the world.

"Danika," Jerry said with that world-class smile. "This is my buddy, Tristan. He's going to be crashing on the couch for a few days. He's...uh...between residences."

I mentally groaned. Bev was going to kill him. One glance at Tristan and I knew he wasn't just a buddy. Jerry had a spotty history with helping out what he always thought was the latest rising star. He had big dreams of managing the next big rock band, and he took those dreams to extremes. He and Bev were both technically attorneys, but she was the only lawyer in the house that you could call employed. Jerry was too busy collecting unsigned bands to practice law.

I gave Jerry a pointed look. "Bev is going to string you up. She said that if you brought home one more out-of-work musician, that she was going to kick you out, and then *I* would get upgraded to a bigger room."

He grimaced. "Now, now, don't go jumping to conclusions. Tristan has a job. Look, he's not even carrying a guitar."

I eyed Tristan up. "What's the job?"

Jerry answered for him, which let me know that he was full of it. "He's a club promoter."

I rolled my eyes. "Is that the best you can do? That's Vegas code for *unemployed*, Jerry. My pothead ex-boyfriend even calls himself a club promoter, and I don't think he ever even

3

leaves his house. You need to think up something better before Bev gets home."

Tristan laughed, not looking even slightly offended by our exchange. "I *am* a club promoter, and I do also happen to be in a band," he said in a low, sexy drawl.

Oh lord, I thought, *Four Kicks* by Kings of Leon playing at full volume in my head as I heard his voice at close range. And I tried to pretend that I hadn't even heard that sexy as hell laugh. I knew that we were going to be a dangerous combination. Bad things were going to happen if we spent too much time around each other.

"Don't let Bev hear you say that," I warned him. I was really just trying to help Jerry out. I didn't want him to get into trouble with Bev again, and he never seemed to have a clue just what would set her off, even though it was always very obvious to me.

I sighed, knowing that this wouldn't be easy to fix. I tensed as I heard the loud garage door opening across the house. Bev's house was a huge, rambling, ranch style house, but the garage door was so loud that it always announced her presence.

I gave Jerry a stern look, sometimes feeling like his mother, even though he was forty-five, and I was barely twenty-one. I pointed at him. "I know what we need to do, but you're going to owe me. I hate lying to Bev." It was true. I was nowhere near nonchalant about the deception I was about to undergo, and I wanted him to know it. Beverley was my hero. No one had ever helped me as much, or been as supportive of me, as she had. Plus, I just liked her. She was my closest friend, and I'd developed a serious case of hero worship for the successful, forty-eight year old woman.

"Tristan is a friend of *mine*," I told them. "Do not mention the words club promoter, or band. He is a plain old out of work student, and crashing for *one week* on the couch. We met at UNLV last semester. Got it?"

Jerry nodded, giving me a grateful smile. "You're the best, Danika. I owe you."

He sure did. I looked at Tristan, who was giving me that playful smile of his, as though we hadn't just barely met.

"You're a sassy little thing. I like that," he murmured, just as Bev and her boys rounded the corner that led from the garage and into the main living area.

Ivan and Mat caught sight of me and the dogs swarming at my heels and rushed me with huge whoops. Ivan was an unabashedly diabolical eight-year-old, and Mat was a precocious six-year-old, and the two of them combined were more than a handful, but I loved them to *pieces.*

Mat went straight for a tackle to my midsection, while Ivan caught the biggest dog, Mango, in a bear hug. Mango was a tan-colored bloodhound. She was nine years old and left a trail of slobber in her wake. She was a terrible guard dog. We were all convinced that if the place was robbed she'd just see it as an opportunity to lick more faces.

Mat squeezed my waist so hard that he drew a little grunt out of me. The second biggest dog, Dot, took exception to the rough handling. He growled menacingly at the six-year old. He was a big black Belgian Shepherd, and none of us had any doubts that he was a good guard dog. A little too good, in fact. He'd taken to being my own personal protector, even against the other inhabitants of the house, and that included the boys.

I shushed Dot, hugging Mat back. He was a skinny blond kid with gorgeous blue eyes.

"You said you'd make us cookies when we got back!" Mat told me excitedly.

I nodded. "Okay. You gonna help me make them, or you want to go play while I cook?"

"Play!" he shouted. I didn't know if it was Mat, or being six, but the boy had a serious volume control issue. It just made me laugh.

"Okay. I bet you'll be able to smell when they're done."

"Yes!" he shouted, even louder, then took off for his room.

Ivan straightened, looking around at all of the adults and pursing his lips. He had light brown hair, was tall for his age, and had soft brown eyes like his dad. He was a funny kid. He had moments of being a shameless brat, but just as many moments of absolute charm. "I want to play, too, Danika, but I'll help you if you really, really need me to."

I smiled at him. "I got it covered, buddy. You go on and play."

He took off, never saying a word to his dad or to Tristan. Typical eight-year-old, only paying attention to the one making cookies.

Beverly and I shared a look. She gave her boys a laughing eye roll before heading the same way they'd gone, towards her bedroom. She'd barely spared Tristan a glance. It wasn't a good sign.

"Jerry, a word," she called out, still moving toward her room. It didn't bode well.

He swore under his breath, but followed her.

I headed over to the kitchen. I felt Tristan following me.

The house was set up with an open floor plan. It was huge, but the entryway, living room, dining room, kitchen, and family room all shared one massive space, so it was a straight shot into the kitchen once I got around the giant L-shaped sofa that dominated the living room.

The house was a strange combination of shabby chic, leaning way further in the direction of shabby. Beverley was very successful as a worker's compensation attorney, and she came from a rich family, so money wasn't an issue when it came to the house. It was colossal, and in one of the nicest gated communities in Vegas, but the house was lined with outdoor carpeting and the furniture was in desperate need of an update. The only saving grace in the house was the spectacular artwork that she collected. Words couldn't even express how much I appreciated her fine eye for upcoming artists, but they were the *only* saving grace when it came to the house's aesthetics.

I understood why she didn't update a lot of it. New carpet would be ruined in just a few weeks by her unruly dogs and crazy kids, and the dark green leather sofa had the entire back gnawed off. I couldn't imagine a new sofa wouldn't receive the same treatment.

I had to unlock the latch that had been installed on the side of the refrigerator before I opened it. Mango liked to eat sticks of butter when it wasn't latched tight…

I pulled out a plastic tube that was filled with chocolate chip cookie dough. I heard a clear, disappointed groan behind me.

I turned to look at Tristan, arching a brow at him. "What? You don't like chocolate chip?"

He shook his head at me, still showing off one dangerous dimple in a half smile. I really wished he'd put those dimples away. They were counter-productive to my peace of mind.

"You're joking, right?" he asked pointedly.

I had no idea what he was talking about. "Um, about what?"

"Cookie dough out of a plastic tube? Pre-made?"

I shrugged. "It's easy and fast, and they taste fine."

He shook his head again. "Show me to your baking supplies. I can't stand by and watch this."

I scowled at him. "You're bossy for an out-of-work houseguest," I told him.

"I have a job. Several actually. But yeah, I'm bossy. Now show me to your flour."

I kept scowling, but I was walking from the kitchen and into the walk-in pantry while I did it. I waved a hand at the area that kind of held the baking supplies. The pantry was hardly well organized, so he would probably have to dig around to get everything he needed for cookies.

I left him to it, going back into the kitchen to pre-heat the oven and grease a cookie sheet. I put out a large mixing bowl, measuring cups, and any other incidentals I thought he might need for baking. It was the least I could do if he was actually going to do the baking.

I shrugged out of my sweatshirt, suddenly warm. It was a hundred and ten degrees outside, but you wouldn't know it by the way I normally froze inside of the A/C'd to death house. It wasn't normal for me to get so warm inside for no reason at all.

I was wearing a thin white tank and sitting on the counter when Tristan strolled back into the kitchen, his arms full of baking supplies.

He set them on the counter near the mixing bowl, lining them up neatly. His biceps bulged with the smallest movement. It was fascinating.

"Salt?" he asked me, his brow raised.

I blinked, trying to process what he'd said.

I pointed behind me after a few awkward moments.

He moved towards me without a word, and I saw my folly then. The cupboard I'd pointed to was directly behind me. I should have just grabbed it for him.

He didn't seem to mind, moving uncomfortably close to me to reach behind me. His upper chest got so close to my face that I could smell him. He smelled divine, so divine that I closed my eyes for a second to take it in.

He had to reach up, so his hip grazed my inner thigh as he shamelessly moved between my legs to get closer.

I gasped.

"Sorry," he said, backing up, the salt in his hand. I saw his eyes flick briefly down my body before he turned away, setting the salt beside the other ingredients.

"So you're the nanny, huh? You are *not* what I pictured when Jerry said he had a live-in nanny."

I glared at his back. "What did you picture?"

"I don't really know. I didn't have a clear picture in my head. I just wasn't expecting someone like *you*." He turned his head to flick me another unreadable glance.

I gave him a very unfriendly look, offended, and a little wounded. "What is that supposed to mean?"

"Nothing bad. Quit giving me evil eyes. Nannies just don't usually look like you. You're like what Hollywood would cast to be a nanny to add sex appeal to a movie. You're sexy. Really sexy. Don't play coy. You know you're gorgeous."

I stopped glaring, but I was wary of the compliments.

"Relax, okay?" he said, studying my face. "I'm not hitting on you, and I won't. What are you, like eighteen? Way too young for me. I'm just stating facts. Normally women don't appreciate other women as hot as you underfoot."

I was glaring again. "I'm twenty-one, and Bev is my best friend. I've been working for them for two years."

He threw up his hands, giving me an apologetic smile. "Sorry. I'm not trying to be a dick. It just surprised me that you were the nanny Jerry was telling me about. He gave me no hints that you were, well, hot."

"How old are *you*?" I asked him, still smarting from the too young comment.

"Twenty-six."

"That's not that old," I told him.

"I know. Just too old to be dating eighteen-year olds, or even twenty-one year olds. Frankly, though, I'm bad with women my own age, too, when it comes to relationships, which is why I don't do them."

I couldn't help it. I had to ask. "So what do you do?"

"Hookups. Brief, casual hookups. How about you?"

I shook my head, pursing my lips at him. I couldn't quite believe that we had jumped to this already. He was a man to be careful of, to be sure. "I do relationships. No exceptions. Never had a casual hookup in my life."

He sighed, measuring some flour into the mixing bowl. "Well, I guess that makes things less complicated. We'll be friends, then." He shot me a sidelong smile that was downright irresistible. I thought that this was one of the strangest conversations I'd ever had, being that we had just met. Only, it didn't feel like we'd just met. He spoke to me like he'd known me forever, and it was hard to refuse anything he said in that low voice of his.

I nodded, giving him my own, rather begrudging smile. "Okay, friends, since we'll be living under the same roof for the next week."

"Okay, then. My first job as your friend will be to show you how to make the best chocolate chip cookies in the world."

CHAPTER TWO

Tristan walked me through every step of the cookie making process, and I pretended to pay attention, but that attention kept wandering to his spectacular arms while he worked. I barely kept my composure when he used the mixer, and I watched his ripped arms vibrate with the movement of it.

"Did you catch that, Danika?" he asked me with a smile.

I shook myself out of it, looking at his face. "Huh?"

He shook his head at me, his smile widening. I found my eyes focusing on the shadow of a beard lining his jaw. I'd never found the unshaven look so attractive before.

"You're a little troublemaker," he told me matter-of-factly, going back to his cookie dough.

"*Me*?" I asked, and I wasn't sad when he didn't respond. We didn't need to get into a conversation about Trouble.

He spooned little balls of his dough onto the cookie sheet very precisely. He slid the pan into the oven, setting the timer.

"Do you like to go out?" he asked me as he washed his hands.

I couldn't seem to take my eyes off his hands. "Go out?"

He dried his hands and approached me, stopping just short of my legs. "Yeah. Go out. Like to bars and clubs and parties. What do you like to do for fun?"

I opened my mouth to answer, but my mind was pretty blank. Fun? What did I do for fun? I kept busy, that was for sure, but was any of it strictly for fun?

"I swim with the boys a lot. And I walk the dogs."

He blinked at me, and I wanted to smack my own forehead. I sounded like a weirdo, even to myself. "You swim with the boys and walk the dogs? When was the last time you went out?"

I mulled that over, quickly coming to the conclusion that I would not admit how long it had been since I'd 'gone out'.

I was saved from having to even attempt to answer by the swarm of dogs that invaded the kitchen. They had all followed Bev into her room, but had apparently finished saying their hellos.

Dot moved between Tristan and me, letting out a little warning growl, and taking his place to guard me.

Tristan studied the dogs, his hands moving to his hips as he took them in. "Are you going to introduce me?" he asked.

I couldn't help it, my lip curled at him in a smirk. "You want me to introduce you to the dogs?"

He shrugged, that easy smile of his in place. "If you don't mind."

I pointed to Mango first. "That's Mango. She'll slobber on you, and get on top of you when you're sleeping, but she's the sweetest dog in the world."

He nodded, moving to stroke his hands over the big dog. She was putty in his hands.

I pointed to the next dog, a little, black and white lhasa-apso. "That little one is Pupcake. She's the easy-going one, and the boys' favorite." He had her rolling onto her back in seconds.

I pointed to the spotted brown coon hound. "That one is Coffeecup. He's the youngest, and he and I are working through some issues."

He laughed at the name, stroking the dog. Coffeecup licked his face, and he didn't bat an eye. Son of a bitch. "Dare I ask

12

about the issues, or is it a touchy subject?"

"It's touchy," I told him. The wild dog was driving me up the wall bonkers lately, and I didn't want to explain all of the reasons why.

I pointed at Dot, who was nuzzling into my dangling leg. "This is Dot. He's the guard dog of the bunch."

Tristan nodded, bending down to pet the dog, his hand not an inch away from my leg. Shockingly, Dot let him, his tail wagging, no snarl in sight, close proximity to me and all. *What the fuck?*

"How did you do that? Dot never takes to strangers."

He wiggled his fingers at me. "Haven't I told you? I have magic hands."

I rolled my eyes.

He straightened, pulling a pack of cards out of his pocket. I couldn't believe I hadn't noticed them. I'd been enjoying how he fit into his jeans rather intently...

He shuffled the cards. I could tell by the way he handled them that he practiced a lot. His hands were big, which made the deft movements of his fingers more impressive, and more distracting.

He fanned the cards out, smiling at me. "Pick a card, any card."

I arched a brow at him sardonically. "Are we really doing this? Card tricks?"

He nodded, his smile widening. "See, skeptics are my favorite. So much more room to blow your mind."

I rolled my eyes, but I picked a card, extracting it carefully, keeping it turned away from him. I almost rolled my eyes again when I saw that it was the Queen of Hearts.

"I want a new card," I told him.

He just laughed, shaking his head. "Just memorize it and put it back."

I did, making sure he couldn't see it.

13

He started shuffling the cards again, not even glancing down. "I've seen this trick before," I told him.

His brow furrowed, and cards started shooting from his hands, going everywhere. "Hm. You have?" he asked.

I nodded, uncertain if throwing the cards everywhere had been part of the trick.

He whistled loudly. "Mango, bring her the card."

I glanced down at the dogs, totally lost. "What the...?"

Mango had a card in her mouth, and I bent down to her, holding a hand out.

"Don't eat cards, silly. That's even worse than a stick of butter..." I trailed off as I pulled the Queen of Hearts out of her mouth.

I straightened, thrown for a loop. I raised my wide eyes to Tristan's smug ones. "How on earth did you do that?"

He wiggled his fingers at me again. His magic hands.

"Jazz hands are hardly an answer," I told him.

That had him doubled over laughing, and me smiling, because I already loved the sound of his laugh.

"Seriously, how did you do that? How in the world did you have Mango in on the trick?"

"Magic hands is the only answer you'll ever get out of me. So, can you still say you've seen that trick before?"

I just shook my head, trying hard to figure out what all he had to have done to pull that off.

"Those are some...fun dog names." He startled me out of my thoughts.

I shrugged. "The boys named all of them except for Mango. I thought they did a pretty good job. They're funny kids."

I turned my head as Bev called my name, approaching the kitchen with a smile. She turned that smile on Tristan as she got close. She was a tall, slender woman, with cornflower blue eyes and reddish blonde hair. She was forty-eight, but I didn't think she looked it, her pale skin showing just the faintest signs of aging. Her features were attractive, her figure trim, and she was always dressed impeccably.

"I'm so sorry, Danika," she told me. "I didn't realize this was a friend of yours. I feel so rude, storming off without introducing myself. I thought, well, I thought he was another of Jerry's... projects." She swept her hand in the air, as though to wave the idea away.

I didn't think I'd felt so shitty about myself in years as I did staring at the apologetic curve of her lips.

"But anyway," she turned to Tristan, holding out her hand. "I'm Bev."

Tristan didn't hesitate to smile back, taking her hand. "Tristan."

Bev looked at me. "Jerry tells me you met him last semester. Why is this the first I'm hearing of it?" she asked, smiling. Bev's smile was all open charm. No one in the world would have guessed she was a lawyer by that smile.

I shrugged, feeling defensive and guilty as hell. "Nothing to tell. He's just a buddy. He'll only be staying for a week, I swear."

She waved that off. "Don't worry about it. Stay as long as you like, Tristan. Any friend of Danika's is a friend of mine. So where and how exactly did you guys meet?"

"We had a class together," I answered, shooting Tristan a glance.

"What class?" she asked, as persistent as you'd expect from an attorney.

"Psychology," I threw out.

"English," Tristan said at the same time.

I shot him a very unfriendly look for contradicting me.

He grinned at Bev, totally unfazed. "Both. We had two classes together, actually. Danika was nice enough to share her notes with me."

Bev shot me a fond look. "She *is* meticulous."

I smiled back at her, vowing to myself that I would never lie to her again, no matter the reason. Damn Jerry.

"I was just trying to get Danika to go out to a club with me tonight," Tristan told Bev.

I blinked at him, wondering what the hell he was doing.

"She seems to think that walking the dogs is what a twenty-one year old should be doing for fun. I think she needs to get out more. Will you help me convince her?"

Bev looked at me, her brow furrowing. "You know, Danika, I can't remember the last time you went out. Tristan has a point. You're twenty-one. You *should* be having more fun."

If looks could kill, Tristan would have dropped dead on the spot. He'd managed to get *my* Bev on his side in under a minute. I couldn't quite believe it.

He just smiled back at me, unfazed by my look of death. "It's settled then. We'll go out tonight. There's this new club at the Cavendish casino. It's great. You'll love it."

I glared at him for a solid minute before I spoke. "You just want me to drive your sorry ass. You probably don't even have a car."

I felt a little silly as both Tristan and Bev began to laugh.

"You two seem to know each other well," Bev gasped. "How have I never heard a word about Tristan before this, Danika?"

I shook my head, but Tristan spoke before I could. He put his hand over his heart, giving me a heart-stopping smile. "That hurts my feelings, Danika. Don't you ever talk about me?"

He was enjoying this little charade, but I sure wasn't. "Nope," I said curtly.

"Oh, Danika, you have to go out. I insist. Go have a good time. I don't need any help with the boys tonight."

I grimaced. "I have things to do."

"Like what?" Tristan asked.

"Well, for one, I need to walk the dogs."

"Okay. Let's go do that now. I'll come with."

I rolled my eyes, fully realizing that I was acting like a ten-year old. "Fine, but you have to walk Coffeecup."

He shrugged. "Sounds great."

"And I have to clean the pool," I told him.

"Oh, don't worry about it," Bev said.

"I'll help," Tristan said, being strangely persistent.

"And I have to finish the laundry."

Tristan shrugged. "We'll get started after the cookies are done."

"You don't have to do that today, Danika," Bev tried again. "I can get to the laundry myself tonight, and the pool can wait. You could use a night off."

"We'll knock those chores off in an hour, and she'll still have plenty of time to get ready," Tristan said.

The oven timer started to beep, and he went to check on his cookies. Bev and I just watched him, not saying a word, as he put on oven mitts and slid the cookie sheet out of the oven. It was a strange and riveting sight; a ripped man at home in the kitchen. Baking fucking cookies. This man was so much Trouble...

He studied the delicious smelling cookies for a long moment, then gave me a sidelong smile. "A perfect batch. You two have to try these."

I curled my lip at him. "I'm watching my figure."

His eyes flicked shamelessly over my body. "And you're doing a damn fine job of it, but you can eat a cookie."

"Who could turn that down?" Bev asked.

Who indeed? I thought resentfully.

He was too bossy for my taste, or at least, I told myself that.

"So what chore do we need to tackle first?" Tristan asked, while he slid a few still hot cookies from the sheet and onto a plate.

"Dogs," I said absently, still distracted by his ease in the kitchen.

He nodded, bringing the plate over to us. "The cookies will be cool enough to eat in a minute. You're eating one, and then we'll walk the dogs."

I reached for a cookie, completely enticed by the smell. I was usually really good about dieting since I had to maintain my figure for dancing, but even I couldn't resist the lure of his divine smelling cookies.

He swatted my hand away. "I said one minute, Danika."

I glared at him for at least a solid minute.

He only smiled. He offered the plate to Bev first. She took one, thanking him.

I folded my arms over my chest, and just looked at him. I was trying hard to talk myself into refusing to eat a cookie, just to spite him, the bossy son of a bitch.

He flashed a dimple at me, his golden eyes filled with mirth, and had the utter nerve to grab one with his own hand and hold it up to my lips.

I took a bite, the smell and his charm irresistible to me. I closed my eyes, groaning as I chewed.

I heard Bev making a similar noise. The man was *not* all talk. His cookies were as good as he claimed. It was just the perfect flavor combination of salty and sweet, and the texture was perfect, not too gooey, but melt in your mouth soft. I barely had to chew.

Finally, after taking my time with the first bite, I opened my eyes to look at him. He was still smiling at me, his hand still holding the cookie to my mouth for another bite, but there was heat in his eyes now.

I grabbed the cookie out of his hand, taking another bite. He nabbed one for himself, taking a huge bite. I watched him chew, transfixed by the hard line of his jaw as it worked. Finally, I made myself look away, finishing my cookie with slow, savoring bites.

The boys rushed the kitchen right as I was finishing, and

Tristan handed them cookies and paper towels, introducing himself.

He was at ease with the kids, and they seemed to take to him instantly, just like everyone else had. The man was like a charm grenade.

I gathered the dogs' leashes from the laundry room, slipping into flip-flops and heading to the front door.

Dot saw the leashes first, and rushed to the door, tail wagging. Bev had a huge backyard, but the dogs still loved their walks.

I got them all ready, intending to leave whether Tristan joined me or not. I didn't need help, and I didn't quite understand his need to keep me company for my chores.

He caught up to me as I was slipping out the door, holding it open for me. He held a hand out to me as we got outside, and I handed him Coffeecup and Pupcake's leashes.

We were just moving onto the sidewalk when he asked, "So tell me about your issues with Coffeecup."

I sighed. "Why?"

"Why?"

"Why on earth do you care about my dog issues?"

"Because I'm curious, and I think it's adorable that you have 'dog issues'."

That drew a small smile, and an answer, out of me. "He's rambunctious. He's made it his mission in life to try to rush out the front door every time I have to open it for any reason. He's gotten loose in the neighborhood three times this week."

He shrugged. "It's a quiet neighborhood. It's not like there are cars speeding around here. It's gated. What's the big deal?"

I grimaced. "It's a big deal because of the chicken lady."

That surprised a laugh out of him. "The chicken lady?"

I laughed too, knowing how ridiculous it sounded—how ridiculous it *was*. "Yes. The *crazy* chicken lady."

He had to stop walking, he was laughing so hard. "Okay. You have to tell me this story. What exactly is a crazy chicken lady?"

I shook my head, but I told him. "Well, there's a community stable in the center of the neighborhood. Residents can rent out stalls. Most of the stalls are used for horses, but this one lady uses them for her prize chickens."

He arched a brow. He had a way about him that was so hard for me to resist, especially the way he gave me every ounce of his attention with single-minded focus. I drank up that attention as though I'd been starving for it.

I really needed to get out more.

"Prize chickens?" he asked.

"Yes. She has prize chickens. She lives right by the stables, and as far as I can tell, spends most of the damn day there. She lets them roam the stables while she's there, so they're loose a lot of the time….completely unprotected."

He started laughing again. "Oh no," he said, seeing where the story was headed.

I nodded. "Oh, yes. I've timed it. Coffeecup can get to the stables in under two minutes, and nab a chicken just seconds after that. He's taken out three of her chickens just this week alone."

"Taken out?"

I nodded. "He eats them. He has their necks snapped before I can catch up to him, and I'm a fast runner."

"That's messed up."

"Yes, *I know*. This is why Coffeecup and I have issues. Crazy chicken lady goes ballistic on me when she loses a chicken. Bev has to pay her fifty dollars every time it happens, but that's no consolation to crazy chicken lady, since the damn chickens are her life."

We started walking again, but we were both smiling..

"Well, if he gets loose while I'm around, I'll catch him before he can murder any chickens. I promise."

"He's really fast," I warned, not believing for a second that he could catch the crazy dog if it got loose.

"So am I."

I just shook my head, laughing.

CHAPTER THREE

We got through my chores in record time. Tristan even folded laundry with me. I thought he was bizarre...and really kind of sweet.

Within short hours of meeting the strange man, I found myself rifling through my closet, looking for Vegas club gear. The dirty Vegas club scene was *so* not me, but I still found myself excited about going out. Tristan was just...fun, and I was excited for fun. The candid conversation that had set us up as friends right off the bat eased any reservations I might have had about hanging out with someone like him.

I didn't have a lot of friends my own age. I'd adopted most of Bev's circle of friends as my own, and besides myself, the youngest of them was thirty-two. I felt comfortable with older people. I attributed that to Bev. Being around her had just always been so good for me; so safe. She was mature, and she knew how to be healthy. She was stable, and I *needed* stability. I clung to it. And people my age living in sin city rarely belonged in the same sentence with stability. I knew that Tristan was no exception, he likely didn't belong in the same *book* with stability, but still, he was hard to resist.

I was staring at my closet full of clothes for a good five minutes when Bev found me. It was a well-stocked closet, thanks to Bev's frequent hand-me downs. Thank God we wore the same size, and I couldn't complain, but I just wasn't sure *how* to dress. The Vegas nightlife was pretty diverse; I could get away with wearing jeans, or go fully decked out, but I just couldn't decide what I *wanted* to do. I didn't want to look like a slob, but I really didn't want to look like I was trying too hard.

Bev gave a brief knock on my door before she came in—her usual routine. She had a black silk halter dress draped over her arm. I recognized it as one she'd worn several times before. It was one of her favorites. It bloused out, and banded at the hips. I'd tried it on for fun once, and I knew it was flattering, in fact, it was gorgeous, but maybe too dressy for a club night out with a guy I barely knew.

Still, I coveted that dress.

I bit my lip, and she gave me a 'look'.

"If you wear this, I'll give you a free pass at anything you want in my closet at a future date of your choosing," she told me.

Just like that, she had me. Her closet was mind-boggling, and way above my pay scale.

"Thank you," I told her.

She smiled and winked at me, clearly pleased with my agreement.

I showered and did my hair and makeup first, letting the steam from the shower smooth out any small wrinkles in the dress. The top was pure silk, held at the neck with Swarovski crystals. The fitted skirt was a silky looking material, but it had elastic, so it had stretch, and I could still dance in it, which was a must. I didn't love to go clubbing, but I did love to dance.

I eyed the way out of my price range dress as I blew out my hair, letting it fall straight—a black waterfall down my back. Black was always a good bet for me. It brought out my ivory skin and pale gray eyes. My mother was half-Russian, half-Japanese, and I supposed my features were a mix of both. That was only a guessing game, though, really, since I'd never known what the other side of that equation consisted of.

I lined my eyes carefully in black, and smudged a smoky dark gray shadow onto my eyelids. I was liberal with the mascara, and used a dark maroon lip stain, but that was all. My skin tone didn't need, and couldn't handle foundation.

I was still wearing just a towel when Bev breezed into the bathroom with me. She and I hadn't had privacy boundaries for years, and I only smiled at her as she barged in on me after a cursory knock.

I started shaking my head as soon as I saw the jewelry box in her hand. She didn't own any cheap, costume jewelry, and I would be terrified if I borrowed something expensive and then lost it. The sad fact was I could never afford to replace even her cheapest piece of bling.

She completely disregarded the headshake, opening the box to show me a pair of earrings. They were huge, pear shaped, diamond studs, two carats at least. "They latch on tight, Danika. There's no way you'd lose one, and that dress begs for diamonds."

"I can't, Bev. I just can't. And I think I might already be overdressed. Tristan is probably just going to wear a T-shirt and jeans, anyway."

"You're wrong there. I saw him. He's already ready, and he's looking sharp."

I smirked. I loved it when she went all old school on me. "Sharp? Like a pencil?"

"Sharp, like dressed up, you smart ass."

"What's he wearing?"

"Black slacks and a blazer over a black T-shirt."

"Sounds a little Vegas douchy. The T-shirt with a suit, I mean. And isn't it a little hot for that?"

She shrugged. "Wait until you see him. Call it whatever you want, but he looks edible."

I laughed. "I can't believe you're encouraging me to go out

with him. Lucy will have a field day, harassing you about it. Hell, she'll harass us both."

Bev pursed her lips, and I grinned, knowing that she was going to go into Lucy mode. She did a spot-on impression of our psychiatrist friend, Lucy.

"Jumping from one relationship and straight into another is a symptom of your love addiction, Danika," she said, her voice pitched low.

I sighed. "He really is just a friend, no funny business at all, but I doubt she'd believe that if she got a look at him."

Bev nodded. "I believe you, but I have a feeling she'll have something to say about it."

I started getting dressed, completely unfazed by Bev's presence.

I heard a big sigh behind me as I was slipping the dress over my head.

"I'd give anything to have tits like that again. I had to tape mine up to wear that dress, I shit you not."

I laughed. "I remember. I helped with the tape. You looked fabulous, though, which is all that counts."

She grimaced. "I remember my braless days, though. Now that's fun. You're smarter than I was. You rarely go without a bra. I never even owned one until my late thirties."

I shrugged. I was only a small C-cup, but I didn't feel comfortable without a bra. The only time I went without was when a dress demanded it, and that rarely ever happened, since I hardly ever dressed up.

I adjusted the dress around my hips, then straightened the neckline. It was one of those dresses that felt good, and looked better.

"Your red shoes," Bev said.

I nodded, knowing which shoes she was referring to. She'd given them to me after wearing them herself to four different events. They were open toed stilettos with a four-inch heel. I loved them, and though they weren't comfortable, they were hot, and I could dance in them fine, which was all that mattered.

Bev tried to talk me into the earrings, but I held strong. This wasn't the prom, and I was already decked out.

I felt like hot stuff as I strode out into the living room, but I stopped dead when I got a load of Tristan. If I was hot, he was scorching. The worst part was, I would have bet money it had only taken him minutes to get that way.

His slacks and blazer were nice. I didn't know a thing about suits, but his looked expensive to me, and it fit him perfectly, hugging his build so that no one could doubt that he was buff. It looked like a custom suit, especially considering his size, though I couldn't have said for sure, and I found it unlikely, since he was a 'club promoter'. I was pretty sure that was one of those jobs that never had an actual pay check.

Black was his color, to be sure. It brought out his tan skin, handsome features, and his golden eyes. He hadn't shaved, but somehow the black stubble on his jaw and his short black hair went just right with the suit. He looked sinister, and drop-dead gorgeous.

He grinned when he saw me, and I tried my hardest to stop checking him out. I already knew he looked good. I would only embarrass myself by ogling him.

"I'd like to say several things," he began, "but since we're just being friendly, may I just say that you look *very* nice."

"Thank you," I told him, still trying hard not to check him out. He shifted, shoving his hands in his pockets, and my eyes went to his chest, fascinated with the way that the material pulled there. "You look very nice, too."

His grin deepened, and his dimples made my own self-destructive music play at full volume in my head. "You like to dance?"

Oh, God, please say he doesn't dance, I thought. *Please, please, please, say he's not good at it.* "I do," I said, my tone flat.

He wiggled his brows at me playfully. "That's good. So do I. We'll have to see if you can keep up."

I folded my arms across my chest, arching a brow at him. "I can go all night."

He touched a hand to his forehead, looking pained. "Tease," he murmured, opening the front door for me.

Either Bev or Jerry had been nice enough to shut the dogs in back so they wouldn't be rushing the front door as we left.

"Am I driving?" I asked. I didn't really want to drive my beat up, 98' civic to the strip, but I was pretty sure that was our only option, since Tristan had clearly driven to the house in Jerry's car.

"Nope." He pointed to a black sedan that was idling at the curb. "I'd hate to make the twenty-one year old act as the designated driver. That's blasphemy. My friend is going to take us. He owes me a few favors."

He opened the back door of the car for me, I slid in, and he shut it behind me, climbing into the passenger's seat.

A skinny, brown-haired guy sat behind the driver's seat. He wore black-framed eyeglasses. He was handsome, in a hipster sort of way, with even features, and dark eyes. I thought he could have been a year or two older than me.

He flashed me a friendly smile as Tristan made introductions. "This is Kenny. Our friends love nicknames, though, so we call him Pancakes."

"Pancakes?" I asked.

Kenny rolled his eyes. "It's stupid."

"We call him that because he's a nice guy. No matter how brief the hookup, he'll always make a girl pancakes in the morning."

It was my turn to do some eye rolling. "Aren't you a bunch of charmers."

Kenny grinned, and Tristan laughed.

"What about you?" I asked Tristan. "You don't even make them pancakes?"

"If they're around in the morning, sure. I'm not opposed to cooking."

"Do you have a nickname?"

"Tristan is the only name I answer to," he said.

Kenny shot him a wide-eyed look. "The guys call him Tryst, like with a Y, but he hates it."

"That's adorable," I said, instantly liking the way it made him glare. He was way too smiley, most of the time. "Tryst. A nice way to call you a man-whore. I like it."

Tristan turned in his seat to look at me. "You are not allowed to call me that."

I shrugged at him, grinning. "How on earth could you stop me?"

He grinned right back. "Trust me, I'll think of something."

Of course that only made me curious about what he would do. "Sure thing, Tryst," I told him.

He shook his head. "Don't make me get out of my seat."

"What will you do?"

He thought it over. "Let me try again. It's obvious threats only encourage you. If you can refrain from calling me that, I will cook you breakfast."

"I don't like pancakes," I warned him.

"I'll make you anything you want. Consider me your short order cook."

"Is this offer good for only one breakfast?"

"I'll make you whatever you want, every morning I stay at the house."

"Deal," I told him quickly. After tasting his cookies, I wanted whatever he was cooking. "But I'm very picky. You'll have your work cut out for you in the morning."

He just smiled. "I look forward to it. I'm going to blow your mind."

I crossed my legs, looking away, my mind veering far from the thought of food.

"So you two aren't....dating?" Kenny asked Tristan, shooting him a glance.

"We're not, but don't get any ideas.   None of you knuckleheads are allowed to go near her. Spread the word."

"What sort of caveman reasoning is that?" I piped in, agitated. I certainly had no intention of dating one of his obviously immature friends, but I sure as hell didn't think he should have a say in it.

He flashed those damned dimples at me, so charming that I wanted to hit him over the head with my purse. "Just looking out for my friend. You're the relationship type. None of the guys you're going to meet are. I'm looking to save you a headache down the road."

"How sweet," I murmured, wondering what I was getting myself into with this crowd. "We meeting all of these charmers tonight?"

"I don't know who will be there," Tristan said, looking at Kenny.

Kenny shrugged. "Who knows? Cory is working the bar, so my guess is there will be a turnout. Not many of our friends will turn down free drinks at one of the hottest clubs in town, but Jared is the only one I know for sure will be there."

"Nice," Tristan said, sounding pleased. "Jared is my baby brother. You'll love him. Everybody does. You have any brothers or sisters?"

A tight fist gripped around my heart at the question. I hadn't been expecting it, and it was a subject that my mind tended to shy away from. "I have a sister."

"Older or younger?"

"She's two years younger than me."

"She live in town?"

I bit my lip. "I don't know. I haven't heard from her in years."

"Why the hell not? You have to keep in touch with family."

If only it were so simple. "She hates me, actually. I couldn't get her to talk to me if I tried."

"Why?"

"Because I'm a shitty big sister. Are we done with the interrogation?"

"My bad. I didn't mean to be nosy."

"So don't be. Just drop it." I felt bitchy, but being a bitch was better than rehashing painful old baggage just to appease his curiosity.

He put his hands in the air to signal that he would stop. Even agitated, I couldn't help but study those big, sexy hands.

"Sorry," he said, sounding sincere. "Sorry. I will drop it. To make up for being so rude, I'll pick up your tab for the night."

I gave him a level stare. "You know the bartender. It was already going to be free, wasn't it?"

Those damned dimples came back in force. Even in the darkness of the car, I could see the twinkle in his golden eyes. "Have I mentioned that I like sassy women? Yes, the tab was going to be covered either way. How about I help you with your chores while I stay at the house? Will that make up for me being so nosy?"

I studied him, knowing that, friends or not, being in close proximity to him for a prolonged period of time would not be good for my peace of mind. Still, I just couldn't seem to resist. I enjoyed being around him, Trouble or no.

"It will. You're my chore bitch for the week," I told him. A happy smile overtook my face as he threw his head back and laughed.

"She owns your ass," Kenny said, laughing.

Tristan gave me a sideways smile that could only be described as mischievous. "I can think of worse things."

R.K. Lilley

CHAPTER FOUR

It was mid-summer, and the air felt like a hair dryer as Tristan handed me out of the car.

"You're kind of a gentleman…for a man-whore," I told him so only he could hear.

That startled a laugh out of him. "I try," he told me, not sounding at all offended.

Kenny had valet parked, so we were inside of the Cavendish Casino in a few short steps. Cool air blasted me as we stepped inside, a stark contrast that had my nipples hard as rocks in a heartbeat.

"Brrr," I said.

That made Tristan steal a glance at my nipples.

I heard the perverted bastard mutter, "Fuck," as he looked quickly away.

"Pervert," I said softly.

Of course that made him smile.

He grabbed my hand, pulling me with him as he started to walk at a fast clip across the marble of the grand foyer that led into the casino.

"Slow down," I snapped at him. "Have a little sympathy for a girl wearing four inch heels."

He glanced down at my feet, shaking his head. "I'm sorry.

On behalf of men everywhere, thank you for wearing sexy fucking shoes. I'll try to remember not to walk too fast."

"Thank you for not minding that I can be a pain in the ass," I told him, thinking how sweet it was that he was so accommodating.

"On the contrary, I love that you tell me what's on your mind. I'm not good at guessing games, and I find it refreshing that you just tell me what you're thinking. I hate sulking, Danika, and you're no sulker. Give me shit, hell, yell and scream at me, just as long as you let me know where we stand."

I blinked at him, thrown for a loop. "I can do that. I'm actually very good at that."

"Yes, you are. I love that about you."

"And I love that you love that about me," I told him, meaning it. And boy did I. I loved a man that could take a little honesty. My ex had been a whiny bitch who was always protecting his fragile little ego, so my brand of honesty had never been the order of the day. Tristan was a nice change of pace, to say the least.

I took in our fancy surroundings as we strode slowly through the casino portion of the Cavendish property. "Where did Kenny go?" I asked as I noticed that the other man had disappeared.

"Not sure," he said, looking around. "He'll meet us at the club, though. It's not far."

Decadence, the club, was intimidating. There was a long line to the entrance as we approached. My first thought when I saw a line like that was to head in the other direction.

I slowed, but Tristan just pulled lightly on my hand, heading straight for the front of the line.

The huge, stern-looking bouncer didn't even check our IDs, just nodded us through the door, no expression on his face.

"You know him?" I asked Tristan.

He nodded, pulling me along.

33

I found myself quickly distracted. The club was breathtaking. Long couches flanked numerous indoor pools that formed one huge circle, a huge waterfall the center of it all. Nearly every pool had its own bar. It was by far the most impressive club I'd ever seen, but one huge shortcoming stood out to me right away.

"Where's the dance floor?" I asked him.

He waved at the pools. "This is the lounge, though you can sure as hell dance here if you want." He pointed at a large arch that led into a darkened room. "That's the dance floor. And as you can see, there are bars everywhere. We just need to find the one our friend, Cory is working at to get hooked up with free drinks."

A few bikini clad women frolicked in one of the nearby pools. They were giggling loudly enough to draw attention.

"I didn't bring a swimsuit," I told him.

He glanced at the pools, looking surprised at the idea. "I didn't think of it. If you want to swim, I'll find us some suits. It's up to you. Let's get a drink, dance, and then decide."

"How are you ever going to find a random hookup, if you spend all your time with me?"

He just smiled. "You let me worry about that."

I hadn't really been worried about it. Not at all, in fact. There was something about him, and it wasn't just his size, that seemed to command every room he walked into, even this one. *Charisma*, I thought.

By the looks women were shooting him, I knew that he wouldn't have to look hard to find anyone. Hell, showing up with a woman on his arm would probably only make him more appealing to this crowd.

"Am I like your wingman tonight?" I asked, as a particularly bold blonde gave him a thorough once over.

He seemed to like that idea, his smile widening unabashedly. "Wouldn't that be ironic?"

"Why is that ironic? Because I'm a woman?"

His mouth twisted, and he stopped to study me. "I'm not sure I should answer that. It's not a...friendly answer."

"Well, now I *have* to hear your explanation.   What's that supposed to mean?"

He sighed. "You asked for it. Don't say I didn't warn you."

He leaned in close, speaking into my ear.   We were just outside of the room that held the dance floor, so it wasn't so loud that I couldn't have heard him. I thought he was just doing it for dramatic effect.   "It's ironic that I'd use you for my wingman, when I want to fuck *you* more than any of the women here."

"Oh," I said eyes wide on him as he pulled back.   "That was sweet, you silver-tongued devil."

He laughed, and I couldn't help but join him. Those dimples, and the clear admiration in his eyes, were a potent and irresistible combination, and his shameless flirting didn't raise any red flags for me.   On the contrary, I thought he was too much fun.

"What are we drinking, sweetheart?" he asked, tugging me back the way we'd come.

"Hey!   Where are we going?   I thought we were going to dance!"

"I just spotted my friend at that bar over there. Time for some free drinks. Lady's choice."

"Something with tequila," I told him.

"Now we're talking."

We approached one of the bars near the club's entrance. A good-looking blond male bartender grinned when he spotted Tristan, holding up his hand in a small wave after he'd handed two martinis off to a man in a suit.

"Hey, Cory," Tristan said as we drew close.   "This is my friend, Danika. Danika, this is my friend, Cory. Tell him what you'd like to drink."

I shook the man's hand, immediately taking a liking to him. I thought that was because of his easy-going smile. He was handsome, but more than that, he just had one of those faces that made you want to like him at a glance, with kind eyes and a sweet smile. He was wearing a white dress shirt with the sleeves rolled up, and I could tell he was built. He was thinner than Tristan, but he still obviously spent some time at the gym. If I had been on the lookout for a man, which I emphatically wasn't, Tristan's friends would have been some prime candidates.

"Nice to meet you, Cory," I told him, not even having to raise my voice. I thought that was something you must only get in the really nice clubs, since all the ones I'd been to before I'd have had to yell to be heard.

"Nice to meet you, Danika. What can I get you to drink?"

I shrugged, biting my lip. I wasn't a big drinker, so nothing specific came to mind right off the bat.

"Something with tequila," I said.

"Shots or cocktails to start?" he asked, looking between me and Tristan.

"Let's start with a shot," Tristan said, his hand going to the small of my back to usher me onto a padded, high-backed bar stool.

We watched Cory as he mixed the shot. The only bottle I recognized was tequila.

"What's he making us?" I asked Tristan.

"Hell if I know. Something with tequila."

Cory made a production out of pouring the shots, sliding them to us with a smile. "Diablo shots."

I laughed. "That sounds ominous."

Cory wiggled his brows at me. "Oh, it is. Go for it."

"You aren't having a shot with us?" I asked him.

"I'm working."

"At a *bar*," I added.

He didn't say another word, just grinned while he poured a third shot. He held it up to us in a toast. "This one is for the mysterious hottie on Tristan's arm tonight! You're a lucky bastard!"

I glanced at Tristan, and we were both smiling as we took the shot.

I just about choked as liquid fire went down my throat, but I got it down.

Tristan laughed at the look on my face as I set the glass down. "You didn't like it?"

I grimaced. "It was a shot. I didn't know I was supposed to like it. I sure as hell *felt* it. Isn't that what matters?"

Cory answered, already busy pouring the next round. "Feeling it is the point. Good shit, right?"

I nodded. I was already a little light-headed, which meant that tiny shot had been pure alcohol.

I watched Tristan's big hand as he picked up his re-filled shot glass. He held it up.

I grabbed my own, watching him.

"To sarcastic women who aren't afraid to tell it like it is!" Tristan said, holding the shot glass up to his mouth, and tipping his head back.

Oh, I like this one, I thought, watching his throat work as he swallowed. A sexy man who liked sarcastic women...

I downed my own shot, blinking rapidly as it made my eyes water. I met Tristan's eyes. "I hope you're strong enough to carry me home if I get too blitzed. I'm not used to drinking like this."

He flashed me those dangerous dimples. "Sweetheart, I could carry two of you home."

I rolled my eyes, setting my shot glass down for another round. "I'll bet you've done that before."

"Done what?" he asked, looking thoroughly confused.

"Carried two women home."

Tristan waved Cory off as he started to pour another shot. "I think that's enough shots for the moment. We'll take two margaritas on the rocks. Make mine a double, and one of your raspberry ones for her."

"Make mine a skinny," I added.

"No fucking way," Tristan interjected.

I shot him a look.

"No fucking way," he repeated. "You don't need a skinny anything. You, my dear, are skinny enough."

I glared. "Are you saying I'm *too* skinny?"

He laughed. "No, I'm not. As determined as you are to take offense, I was giving you a compliment. You look great. As a matter of fact, you look amazing. You don't, however, look like you need to be counting calories."

"Well, I look this way because I *do* count calories."

"*Well*, give yourself a night off."

Cory was already sliding us the margaritas, and already buzzed, it was pretty easy to take his advice, and just drink.

"I'm feeling awfully pretty," I told Tristan as I finished the glass.

He choked out a laugh, setting down his own glass. "Well, you are pretty, so that's good."

"It's a drunk thing. I know I'm drunk when I feel real pretty. What's your drunk feeling?"

He thought about it for a moment, rubbing at that sexy stubble on his jaw. "I guess I know I'm really shit-faced when I start to think I'm invincible, or that I'm exempt from consequences. But yours sounds better. My new term for getting drunk has been officially changed to 'feeling pretty'."

"Feeling pretty, huh?" Cory called out from behind the bar. "Don't think we won't be giving you shit for that one!"

Tristan shrugged, not looking at all bothered by the notion.

Cory pointed to a spot behind us, and I turned to see Kenny approaching. There was a tall young man with black hair next to him who looked uncannily familiar, though I had to study him hard for a minute to figure out why.

It was only as Tristan rose and embraced the black-haired one that I realized that they must be related. The other man was much thinner than Tristan, though they were of a height.

Tristan was grinning as he made quick introductions. "Danika, this is my little brother, Jared. Jared, this is my friend, Danika."

Jared smiled as he leaned in close to shake my hand. The dimples ran in the family, and Jared used them almost as lethally as Tristan did. His wrists were layered with black and silver bracelets, and I saw that his arms were inked with full sleeves that disappeared into the arms of his black T-shirt. The brothers definitely shared a love for tattoos.

"Nice to meet you," Jared said, and I saw the piercing in his lip as he spoke.

"You too," I told him.

"How do you know my brother?" he asked, propping his arm on the back of my chair.

"He's crashing at my boss's place. We met earlier today, actually." It felt weird to say that. I felt like I'd known him for a lot longer than a day already.

"Wanna dance?" Jared asked.

"Hey now!" Tristan said, throwing an arm around his brother's shoulder. "I've been waiting all night to dance with her. You don't just get to walk up here and cut in!"

He was smiling as he said it, which let me know he wasn't serious, but serious or not, Jared backed off instantly.

"Of course, bro!" Jared said. "It just seemed like a waste to me, that she'd be sitting in here, instead of dancing in there."

Tristan finished his drink and set the glass down hard on the bar. He shrugged out of his suit jacket, draping it over the back of his chair. I tried not to stare at the sight of him in his tight black T-shirt, and the display of tattoos on his hard muscled arms, but it was distracting.

"By God, you're right!" he declared. "Let's go, Danika! We've wasted precious dance floor time drinking!"

CHAPTER FIVE

Tristan didn't waste any time after that, pulling me straight into the chaos of the dance floor. House music was playing, which wasn't always my favorite, but I could work with it. Whatever the DJ was doing had a good beat, which was all I needed.

I smiled as Tristan moved in front of me, facing me to dance. It was a mischievous smile, because I knew, just absolutely knew, that I was about to blow his mind.

I didn't do the Vegas bump and grind thing that people called dancing. I was a trained dancer. I'd trained in ballroom, salsa, hip-hop, and club dancing. Hell, I'd even trained in belly dancing. Although my obsession was hands-down ballroom, I had my club freestyle down to a science.

I started with one little hair toss just to get his attention. I raised my hands above my head, and began my own scintillating version of a gyrate.

The floor was crowded, but I had just enough room to work. I put one hand on his chest while I twisted my hips. He was dancing, and the man had some moves, but his jaw went a little slack when he got a load of mine. He recovered quickly, though, and swiftly made his best effort to keep up with me.

I went for it. Shaking, popping, stepping, and twisting. We danced until I felt sweat dripping down my spine, and then we danced some more. Tristan was right there with me the whole time, and as I laughed and spun and just let loose, I tried hard to identify what I was feeling just then. After a time, I realized that I was just having fun. I couldn't remember a time when I'd enjoyed myself more. I danced often, to train, and to stay in shape, but I never did it for fun. *This* was fun.

Tristan was flirty, but he never crossed a line, never brushed up in ways that a man might try if he was making a move on a woman. I felt a strong attraction to him, I think any woman would have, but I appreciated that he'd said friend, and he seemed to mean it. I wasn't sure even *I* could have resisted him if he'd been hell bent on seduction.

The house music melded from one beat into the next, heavy on the bass. I couldn't tell how many songs we danced for, but I was a sweaty, happy, hot mess by the time Tristan finally dragged me back into the lounge.

"I win. You quit first," I told him.

He sent me sidelong smile. "Was it a competition? I didn't know. Let's just get a drink before we head back out. I'm nowhere near quitting."

The guys were just where we'd left them, and Cory slid us waters as we walked up.

"Shots," Tristan said.

Cory grinned. "More Diablo coming right up."

"How long were we out there?" I asked Jared.

"A long time," he said, checking the faceplate on his phone. "Over two hours."

I laughed, grabbing my water for a long drink. I'd known we'd been out there for a long time, but I'd never have guessed two hours.

"My turn?" Jared asked, watching me with a very interested glint in his eye.

"Hell no," Tristan answered for me. "Danika and I have a competition going tonight. We're dancing 'til one of us drops."

I had no problem with that. I had a competitive nature, and I just *knew* that I'd be winning.

"You do realize that I can't carry you home..." All four men laughed, and I'd have been lying if I said that I didn't enjoy the attention of four good-looking men.

Cory slapped five shots down on the bar, and we shot them. I'd barely set my glass back down before Tristan was dragging me off again.

We were back at it the instant we stepped out on the floor. I could tell right away that he was feeling more flirtatious this time, moving closer to me, his hand at the small of my back.

"You making a move on me?" I called out to him, but I wasn't pushing him away.

I was relieved when he shook his head. His smile was innocent enough, but I thought there was a hint of something else in his eyes.

"Just dancing, sweetheart."

I dropped low, really low, and shook my way back up, my hands just brushing his thighs as I rose.

"You making a move on me?" he called out with a laugh.

I shook my head at him, giving him a wide-eyed, innocent look. "Just dancing, sweetheart."

It was on after that. He'd caress my hip. I'd counter that by a turn and an extra little arch of my back, just brushing up against him. He'd curse loudly, but we kept dancing.

I was actually giggling when he finally pulled me back into the lounge. I couldn't remember the last time I'd giggled.

"I'm conceding, but only because I think you'd go until we both passed out, just to prove a point," Tristan told me as we walked.

"All I heard just now was 'blah, blah, blah Danika wins'."

He stopped, shaking his head and laughing. "I like you," he told me.

I wrinkled my nose at him. "I like you, too, platonic friend of mine."

We were both grinning like fools as we rejoined the group.

Cory served us another round. Kenny and Jared immediately started making cracks when they saw that Tristan was drinking a margarita.

"He drinks those to feel pretty," Cory made sure to add. "True story."

"Real men don't drink margaritas," Jared told me, waving his bottle of beer.

I pointed at the bottle. "That will give you a beer gut."

Jared grinned, lifting up his shirt to show me some very nice abs. "Hasn't been a problem so far."

I was a little too tipsy not to give him a very big smile for the very nice show.

Tristan slapped a hand onto his brother's shoulder, leaning in to say something in his ear. Whatever it was wiped the smile from Jared's face. He let his shirt drop.

"Give us a minute," Tristan said, moving a few feet away.

They had a short, hushed conversation before returning to us. Tristan's face was very blank, but Jared's looked slightly flushed, perhaps with temper.

"So are you in this band that Tristan claims to be in?" I asked Kenny.

Kenny beamed at me. "Yes, I am. All four of us are, plus one of our buddies who isn't here tonight."

"What kind of music do you play?" I asked.

"Rock."

I wasn't surprised in the least. "So who plays what?"

"I'm bass, Jared is lead guitar, Cory is drums, Tristan is lead vocals, and our friend Dean is rhythm guitar."

I shot Tristan a look. "Gee, the lead singer of a rock band. I'm shocked. I never would have guessed." Sarcasm dripped from every word.

He seemed to find that funny, which was good. I'd much

rather have him think I was funny, than be offended by my sense of humor.

"So when and where do I get to see you play?" I asked, turning back to Kenny.

Kenny's brow furrowed. "I'm not sure. Dean is setting up some gigs for us. Of course you're invited, whenever that happens."

"So what are your day jobs?" I asked, figuring they all had to have one.

"As you've seen, Cory is a bartender, and I'm a valet parker on the weekends here. Our friend Dean is a blackjack dealer. And Tristan and Jared are both in the club promoting business."

"They get paid to party," Cory added.

I couldn't seem to keep my two cents in. "All I think when I hear club promoter is drug dealer, or unemployed."

Jared grimaced.

Tristan just laughed. "You're coming to the next club party I host," he said, pointing at me.

I shrugged, giving him a sassy look. "Don't threaten me with a good time..."

All four of them seemed to find that hilarious. I flushed with pleasure. I could get used to this kind of attention, especially since it was coming from four hot guys.

"Danika works for Jerry," Tristan told them.

"We love Jerry!" Kenny said.

"She's the *nanny*," Tristan added.

"Holy shit," Jared muttered.

"Did not see that coming," Cory called out, his back to us as he mixed a drink.

"Not what I was expecting," Kenny mused.

"Why is that so surprising to everyone?" I asked, baffled that all four of them had had the same reaction to my being a nanny.

"I had you pegged for a model," Jared said.

"Tristan *loves* to date models," Cory called out.

"Fuck off," Tristan told him.

"We're not dating," I stated firmly.

"I would have guessed dancer," Tristan told me, as though he hadn't just told Cory to fuck off. Typical guys...

I pointed at Tristan. "This round goes to Tristan. I'm a full-time student, and a nanny, but I *am* an aspiring dancer, not that I ever have the time." I returned his smile, utterly charmed by it. "And the model thing is very flattering, guys, but I'm a little short for that."

"Not for Vegas modeling," Jared pointed out.

"You're what, five-eight?" Kenny guessed. "That's tall enough."

"I'd guess she's five-seven," Tristan mused, "and she *is* tall enough, but I'm betting she's never even tried modeling, especially of the Vegas variety. Not your scene, right?"

I curled my lip at him. "You don't know me that well. Quit pretending you're an expert."

"Am I wrong?" His brows shot up with the question.

"You're not," I grudgingly admitted.

I blamed the alcohol when he gave me a smug smile, and my reaction was to stick my tongue out at him.

He grabbed my hand, pulling me back out of my chair. "Just for that, we're going for another round on the floor."

"You're a glutton for punishment," I told him, but I followed easily enough.

The music had changed to Top Forty remixes, and something slow and sultry with a heavy beat had overtaken the room.

Uh oh, I thought.

My eyes narrowed on his as he pulled me flush against him, sliding one sneaky knee between mine. "What are you doing?" I asked pointedly.

"Just feeling the music. What happens on the dance floor, stays on the dance floor, and I really am just dancing with you, I swear."

I can live with that, I thought, moving against him, letting the music take me over for another intoxicating spell.

We danced close, but he still didn't cross any lines. We kept our lower regions very carefully apart, though our chests rubbed together more than once. I didn't know what it said about me, or my previous relationships, but I didn't think I'd ever been more turned on in my life as I was just from dancing with Tristan. My breath came out in little pants, every inch of my skin overheated, and not just from exertion.

"You're absolutely positive that you don't hookup? Not even one really awesome night together before we settle down to being friends?" His voice was a rasp in my ear that made me shiver from head to toe.

I shook my head with no hesitation. It wasn't that I wasn't tempted; I just knew that I would feel like shit in the morning, if I did something like that. I wasn't someone who could handle sex without commitment. I never had been.

"I'm positive," I said into his ear.

"No friends with benefits, either?" he asked hopefully.

"The friends with benefits thing never works."

He pulled back to meet my eyes. "I agree," he said, though he didn't look happy about it. "That never works. Someone always ends up getting hurt. Sorry, I just lost my mind for second. That was an asshole thing to say."

"It's okay. Just don't let it happen again." I smiled while I said it, and there was no anger behind the words.

I just wasn't sure how many times I could tell him no and mean it. I wanted him, and I wasn't dense enough to deny it to myself.

"I'll try my best," he murmured.

CHAPTER SIX

I knew before I'd even opened my eyes that I had a raging hangover. You couldn't go from hardly ever drinking, to losing count of your drinks in one night, and not feel it, and *Lord* did I feel it.

I checked the clock and groaned out loud when I saw that it was seven a.m. That's how I knew that my hangover was truly heinous; it had woken me up after only three hours of sleep.

I sat up reaching for the glass of water I kept on my nightstand. I drank the entire glass, even though drinking was the last thing I wanted to do, because I knew that getting rehydrated was the best way to recover from the hangover.

Dot, who'd been sleeping in his own doggy bed near the foot of mine, moved to my feet. He put his head on his paws, and looked up at me. I couldn't decide if he was giving me a sympathetic look or a condescending one.

My door opened, and Mat peeked his head inside, grinning. "Good morning, boo," he said, using the nickname he'd given me when he was four.

"Morning, peeka," I told him, using my own nickname for him.

Mat was always the first one awake, but everyone else quickly followed, usually due to the noise he managed to make. "Everybody else is still sleeping," he said in a whisper that managed to be louder than outright speaking.

"I figured," I said with a rueful smile. He always woke me up first, since I cooked breakfast. "Whatcha want for breakfast?"

"Blueberry pancakes, please!" he nearly shouted.

I winced and held up a hand. "Coming right up, but I'm going to need you to stay nice and quiet this morning, okay?"

"Got it!" he said in a slightly quieter voice. "Will you turn on cartoons while I wait for my food?"

"Of course, bud. I just need to go to the bathroom, then I'll be right out."

I used the restroom and made my way to the living room, Dot dogging my steps.

Mat was sitting on his kid-sized couch on the floor, Pupcake in his lap. He was staring in confusion across the room, and as I stepped into the room, I saw why.

I padded quietly across the room, switching on the TV and finding a channel with some cartoons. Mat fixated on the television, and I walked quietly over to the shirtless hunk of a man that was sprawled out on the sofa. I was so fuzzy headed that I'd forgotten he was even crashing here.

He was lying on his back, a pillow pulled over his face, and another one draped over his lap. He'd completely kicked off his thin blanket. I could just make out that he was at least wearing boxer-briefs, which was good, but the rest of him was all tanned, bared, tattooed skin.

Not good, I thought, taking him in. I'd had no doubts that he would look good naked, and I certainly didn't need to see just *how* good.

Even at rest, I could see the hard ridges in his abdomen. And his arms. *Jesus.* His arms were huge, which was kind of a thing for me. I thought they might have been bigger than my waist, and for sheer perverse reasons, I wanted to measure them to see if I was right. And the tattoos...God, the tattoos. I didn't have a bit of ink, but I loved his. He didn't have full sleeves, like his brother, but he wasn't too far off. His arms were covered with intricate designs, and it wasn't all black, either. I loved all the color. It stood out startlingly against the other black ink, as though the black was just there to frame the color.

I told myself it was totally necessary as I reached out and touched his bare shoulder. I nudged him, and if I enjoyed the feel of his muscular flesh, what was the harm?

"Tristan," I said quietly, nudging him again. My hand stayed there, and I tried to shake him a little, but he was too big for that...

He started, pulling the pillow off his eyes and blinked up at me. "Fuck, Danika, it's early."

"He said a bad word, boo!" Mat called out, clearly affronted.

"Fuck, sorry," Tristan said, then winced.

I couldn't hold back a grin. "You can use my bed to sleep it off. This living room is about to turn into a war zone, and I need to make some blueberry pancakes."

"Is that what you want for breakfast?" he asked, sitting up.

I backed away like he was on fire. Which he kind of was...

"Huh?" I asked him, totally distracted by the sight of that perfect body, practically naked, and moving around. I went to the gym often, and I stayed in good shape myself, but I didn't think I'd ever seen a body so perfect in my life.

He stood up, and I took another step back. He started to move around the couch, and something he was doing finally snapped me out of my trance.

"Why are you still holding a pillow over your lap?" I asked.

He sent me a wry smile, bending down to pick up his duffle bag, which he'd set behind the couch. "Can't you guess? I'll give you a hint; the first word is morning, and the second rhymes with hood."

I blushed, feeling stupid. "Oh...well, you can use my bathroom, and you can stash your bag in there, so it's not in the way."

"Okay. Thank you. Just give my five minutes, and I'll cook breakfast for everybody."

I waved him off. "Go back to bed. I've got it. I know you must be feeling rough."

He sent me a rather stern look. "Give me five minutes. I said I'd cook for you. I'm cooking. And you have to be feeling just as rough."

"I'm fine. I've got this."

He pointed at me. "Don't go near the kitchen until I get back." He strode away, and I made a face at his retreating back, though I was secretly pleased, and still shamelessly checking him out. I'd seen what he could do with cookies. I wanted more.

Normally I just had a Greek yogurt for breakfast, but hungover and hungry, I was already planning to indulge.

I sat down on the couch when I heard the shower in my bathroom turn on. There was plenty that I needed to do, but I just sat there for a solid five minutes, my mind on Tristan in the shower.

He was back out quickly, wearing a fresh white T-shirt and jeans, his short hair still wet from his shower.

"Come keep me company while I cook," he said, tugging me up from the couch.

"So bossy," I muttered.

He completely ignored that statement, pulling me into the kitchen. He cupped my hips, lifting me onto the counter exactly where I'd sat to watch him bake cookies.

He moved away before I could do more than gape at him.

"So Mat wants pancakes for breakfast. What do you want?"

I opened my mouth to tell him I'd just take that, but he spoke again. "I know you don't want pancakes. We need something salty and greasy. Let me whip us up some hangover food."

I had to make a conscious effort to close my mouth. "You

read my mind," I said.

He had the sheer gall to wink at me. "No. I've just been hungover enough to know just what to do. So tell me why Mat called you boo? Is that a nickname?"

"Yes." I didn't elaborate.

"That's adorable," he said opening the refrigerator and studying its contents. "Where did it come from?"

"I don't remember when it turned into an actual nickname, but we used to play peekaboo a lot. He named himself peeka and me boo, and it stuck. Two years and counting."

"Well, boo, how does bacon sound?"

"Bacon sounds great, but you can't call me boo."

"Why not?"

"Because you're not a rapper, and I'm not your shorty."

He laughed, a low, deep rumble that made muscles in my stomach tighten. "You're just making me like the nickname more. Here's the plan, buttery biscuits, scrambled eggs, bacon, and some hash browns. Oh, and some blueberry pancakes for the kids. Any objections?"

"That sounds amazing," I said, meaning it. "But it'll take forever."

He shrugged. "It'll take how long it takes. What's the rush? You got a date?"

I sighed. He was stubborn, to be sure. "Can I help?"

"You can entertain me while I work."

"If you have this handled, I should probably go work on some chores."

"If you want bacon, you'll keep your ass right where it is while I cook you breakfast."

I did want bacon. "I can't believe we stayed out that late," I said, thinking back to the night before. I'd never stayed out that late dancing, and I'd never had a night fly by so fast.

"We going again tonight?"

"Are you joking?" I asked.

"No. Didn't you have fun? Let's do it again."

"You're batshit bonkers."

"Sure am. And I want to take you dancing again. What do you say?"

"We barely got three hours of sleep last night."

"So we'll take turns getting naps in later, if the kids need watching. What do you say?"

He was giving me his most irresistible smile, his dimples making me want to slap and/or kiss him senseless. I held out for maybe five seconds before I was smiling back at him.

"No funny business," I told him.

"No funny business," he agreed. "I took care of that in the shower. Should tide me over for a solid two hours."

I blushed. I hadn't even known I had any blushes left in me. "What happens after two hours?"

He stopped what he was doing, setting an egg down to give me his full attention.

He gave me a once-over that was borderline indecent, then went back to cracking eggs. "I might need to take another shower."

That shut me up for a while. I watched him work, studying the myriad of tattoos on his arms, and the ones that showed through his white T-shirt. As he mixed the pancake batter, the stark muscles in his arms working, I thought that I'd found my new favorite hobby—watching Tristan cook anything at all.

"Bev has this really great frilly pink apron," I told him. "What would I have to do to get you to wear it while you cook for me?"

"You don't even want to know, boo," he said.

That effectively shut me up again.

Within ten minutes, he had the kitchen smelling divine. I moaned as the aroma of sizzling bacon reached me.

His gaze flicked to me, then quickly away. "Tease," he muttered.

He had the pancakes done first, prepping a heaping plate for

Mat.

"You realize that he's six, right?" I asked, eyeing up the huge plate.

"Does he like bacon?" he asked, ignoring my comment.

"Yes!" Mat shouted from the living room.

Tristan handed off the plate, and I brought it to Mat in the living room. Bev didn't care if they ate on their little couches. The dogs always picked up any scraps they happened to leave behind.

By the time I got back into the kitchen, Tristan had a biscuit breakfast sandwich waiting for me. He handed it to me with a paper towel, then took a huge bite out of his own.

The smell of the eggs and bacon had me salivating, and I tore into the sandwich. I had to close my eyes with the first bite, chewing very slowly to savor every second of it.

"What do you do to food to make it taste this good?" I moaned.

I opened my eyes when he didn't answer me. He was staring at me with a look in his eyes that made my toes start to curl.

He set down the uneaten half of his sandwich, striding out of the kitchen.

"Where are you going?" I called to him.

"I'll be back in five minutes," he called back.

I wasn't sure if I was pleased or appalled when I heard my shower turning on.

CHAPTER SEVEN

TRISTAN

I turned the shower on, giving myself a good berating while I stripped down and got inside. I'd never been the guy that had to have a girl just because she was a challenge. I hated that guy, in fact. I usually thought that guy was a douche bag with little to no redeeming qualities.

I liked to keep sex in a separate category from all other parts of my life. Things just worked better that way, for all parties involved. I didn't do the girlfriend thing, and the fuck-buddy thing was full of land mines.

So why couldn't I stop thinking about being inside of Danika? She'd been crystal clear about the fact that she didn't do the casual thing, and now that we were officially friends, that was off the table, anyway. *But God, the body on her.* And that face. She was one of the most beautiful women I'd ever seen, and she didn't even wear makeup half the time. And she walked around in a skin-tight tank top and tiny shorts most days, confident about her body in a way that drove me wild. I even thought her personality was sexy. She didn't put on airs. She never tried to play it cool. She let me know what was on her mind before I had to wonder. I'd spent years dealing with chicks who thought it was cool to keep a guy guessing. I was fed up with that shit. Danika was like a breath of fresh air. A breath of fresh air that I didn't get to fuck.

If I'd been smart, I would have found a quick hook-up the night before, at the club. Then I wouldn't be stuck jacking myself off in the shower every time Danika looked at me funny.

Yes, I definitely should have found a quick hook-up last night, I thought, yet again. That was what I normally did at clubs...I'd never spent five hours dancing with a girl that I knew for a fact I wouldn't get to sleep with.

I stroked my rock hard cock, thinking about her rosebud mouth, and her striking gray eyes. And her shapely little body. Her waist was so tiny I could have spanned it with my hands, but she had the sexiest curves...and the way she walked. I could have guessed she was a dancer just by the way she swung her hips as she moved. Even her voice made me hard. She had a soft, steady voice, her tone even, as she gave me shit about whatever she pleased.

I fisted my cock hard, stroking, once, twice, three times, before coming hard into the air.

It would have been embarrassing how fast I got myself off, if there'd been anyone else there to witness it.

I thought I'd gotten it out of my system until I walked back out into the living room and saw her bending over in those damned tiny shorts. Fuck me, was I in some trouble...

We didn't end up having to take turns taking naps, since Bev took the boys out for the afternoon. We both crashed for three hours, me on the couch, and Danika on her bed.

I ended up cooking everyone enchiladas for dinner, just to watch the look on Danika's face as she tasted them.

When I'd realized that I couldn't move into my new apartment for a few weeks, even though the lease on my old apartment was already up, I hadn't known things would turn out like *this*. Still, I wasn't complaining. I couldn't remember a time when I'd had more fun.

I wore a dark, collared shirt and jeans for our night out. Few clubs were as strict with their dress code as the Cavendish resort, and Cory wasn't working, so we couldn't afford to go to Decadence.

Danika came out in tiny black satin shorts, and a crimson blouse that hugged her breasts in a way that made my mouth water. She was wearing the same fuck-me heels she'd had on the night before, and it was official—she had killer legs.

"Fucking A," I said, not bothering to watch my language, since the boys were already in bed.

"You're not so bad yourself," she said, tossing her hair as she gave me a sassy grin. "Is Kenny our chauffeur again?"

I nodded. "Let's wait outside for him. If he had to ring the bell, that might wake the boys, and then there might be hell to pay."

It was a bit of a challenge to get out of the front door without the dogs getting loose, but Danika managed it like a pro.

"So you don't have a house, *or a car?*" she asked, as we made our way to the curb to wait for Kenny.

I smirked. She didn't pull punches, that was for sure. "I have a car. I loaned it to a buddy, who needed to drive to L.A. for a few days."

"That was nice of you," she said.

I shrugged. "It's not a big deal, especially since I have friends like Kenny, who will drive me around."

"Kenny is a sweetheart," she said, sounding like she meant it.

I felt my jaw clenching, though I knew it was unreasonable to be jealous.

"He's a guy in a band. Don't trust *any* of us," I warned, my voice harsher than I'd intended.

She shrugged. "You all seem safe enough to me, as long as I'm not stupid enough to date any of you."

I felt a wave of relief at her dismissive tone. "Exactly."

We ended up going to a club that ironically enough was

called Tryst. I shot Danika a warning look when Kenny told us where we were headed. The look said 'say a word, and I won't cook you breakfast again'.

She seemed to get the point, but her grin was infuriating.

"You getting us free drinks at this place?" she asked.

"Yes," Kenny answered. "Our buddy Doug is working one of the bars tonight."

"Do you have connections at every club in town?" she questioned.

"Just about," Kenny conceded. "When you're trying to promote a local band, you tend to get to know a lot of the people working the clubs."

"I'm sure it doesn't hurt that you guys seem to go out every night, too," she shot back.

Tryst was packed. Still, the bouncer at the door recognized us on sight, and let us in with one small nod. Getting in was always half the battle.

We found Doug at one of the main bars in the club. He nodded when he saw me, waving me over. His bar was so packed that I had to shoulder my way in.

"Got you guys a table," he said into my ear, voice pitched low. "And bottle service. It's your lucky night."

I grinned. "Thanks, man."

"Sure thing. It's not like you've never hooked me up. Who's that fucking hottie you walked in with?"

My grin wilted a little. "My friend, Danika. She's off-limits."

He sighed. "All the ones that look like that usually are."

A VIP hostess showed us to our seats, courtesy of Doug. She was cute, and shot me some very inviting looks.

I smiled, not really considering it. I'd invited Danika out to dance, and by God, we were going to dance, even if I *was* jonesing for a hook-up.

Danika gave me a mischievous smile as we slid onto the cushioned VIP bench.

"So where did you learn to cook like that?" she asked. "Those were the best enchiladas I've ever had, and enchiladas are one of my favorites."

I smiled, thinking of my mother. "My mother taught me to cook. You should try *her* enchiladas. They put mine to shame, especially since I was missing some of the ingredients for pico on top."

"Does she live here in Vegas?"

"Yes. In fact, I'm due for a family dinner soon, and I'm going to make you come with me."

Her eyes widened. "You want me to meet your parents?"

My face stiffened a little, but I didn't let it show. It couldn't be a sore subject if I didn't allow it to be.

"I want you to meet my *mother. I've* never met my father. He left the second my mother told him she was pregnant. Never bothered to look him up."

She nodded, her eyes searching my face. She swallowed. "We're in the same boat, my friend. I've not a clue who my father is. My mother would never tell me a thing about him."

I blinked, a little taken aback. It was selfish, but I felt comforted by the thought that she and I had both experienced something so painful. It made me feel less alone, and so connected to her in ways I couldn't remember being connected to anyone besides family since I could remember.

"No wonder we get along so well," I finally responded. "We have more in common than we'd realized. Is your mother in Vegas, too?"

She shrugged, one side of her mouth jerking down. "I'm not exactly sure. She and I never really got along. We don't keep in touch."

I'd learned my lesson when I'd asked her about her sister, so I didn't ask her why on earth she didn't know where her mother was, though I was curious as hell about it.

"So what's a good day for you to come meet my mother?"

She smiled, the clouds in her silver eyes clearing. "So you're not asking, but telling me, that I'm going to meet your mother?"

I gave her a rueful smile. "I'm letting you pick the day, at least. You have nothing to worry about. You two are going to love each other."

"If she's anything like you and Jared, I can't imagine we won't get along."

That brought my mind to my baby brother. It didn't matter that he was an adult, he'd always be my baby brother. I'd have done anything for him, anything at all, but I knew that he was a little upset that I'd told him that he couldn't ask Danika out. We had very strict brother rules about dating the same woman, but since I wasn't dating her, he thought it was unfair that I'd warned him off. Still, whether he understood it or not, I thought he'd respect my wishes.

The waitress brought out our bottle service, and I saw Danika's eyes widen. I made a note to myself that I owed Doug big time.

"I'm impressed. Grey Goose bottle service. You've got some pretty good connections, for a homeless guy."

I laughed, already mixing dirty martinis for us.

"Just how dirty do you want this?" I asked, wiggling my eyebrows suggestively.

That surprised a giggle out of her, and I thought that was my favorite sound. It was just so uncharacteristic for her, and I loved to be the cause of it.

"I'll take it as dirty as you can dish it out."

I felt myself growing hard. She'd gotten the better of me, yet again.

We had two drinks before hitting the floor.

I was a good dancer, but I had absolutely nothing on Danika. The girl could move. And her dancing wasn't just about the sexy. I thought that every move she made was filled with talent and beauty. It was a Top Forty dance mix tonight, and she knew the words to every song, frequently matching her moves to the words in cute little ways, flipping her hair, or holstering air guns at her sexy as hell hips.

I bummed a cigarette off Kenny when I saw him where he was chatting up some guy in the corner.

"Do you mind if I smoke?" I asked Danika as I returned to our table.

She was looking at her phone, but she glanced up briefly to shake her head. She didn't look happy.

"It's not a habit," I reassured her as I lit up. "I only smoke when I drink."

She laughed. "Well, from what I can see, you drink every night. How is that not a habit?"

I smiled ruefully. She did have a point.

"Who are you texting?" I asked, trying to get a look at the screen on her phone.

Her lip curled in distaste. "No one important. My ex won't leave me alone, but I've learned not to text him back, even if it's just to tell him to go to hell."

I felt a totally unreasonable surge of anger move through me at that. "Want me to kick his ass?" I asked, not even close to joking.

She laughed, shaking her head as she put her phone back into her tiny clutch. "No. He'll give up eventually."

"What did his text say?"

She rolled her eyes. "He says he loves me. But he sure didn't love me enough not to cheat on me."

My gut clenched and my fists curled. "How long ago was that?"

She made a dismissive motion with her hands. "Almost a month now."

My eyes widened. "You haven't even been broken up for a month?" I couldn't have said exactly why, but that bothered me. A lot.

"We're ancient history, as far as I'm concerned. One strike and you're out. I don't know if it was the first time he cheated on me, but it was the first time I caught him, and once was enough for me. I wouldn't take him back if he were the last man on earth. I'm 'if he caught fire, and I had a glass of water, I'd drink it slowly and watch' done."

Even out of sorts, I had to stifle a laugh at that visual.

I heard the faint noise of her phone dinging at her even in her purse, and I wanted to punch somebody.

She got it out again, checked the screen, then put it back.

"You let me know if he keeps it up, and I will make sure he stops."

She sent me a sideways smile that made me want to kiss her. "You're sweet, you know that?"

I shook my head. I'd never thought of myself that way. Not even a little.

"What do you say we hit the floor again, boo?" I asked her, after we'd both had two more dirty martinis.

Her perfect little nose wrinkled at me. "Don't call me that. That is such a weird nickname for a grown ass man to be calling me."

"So what should I call you?"

"Danika."

"That sounds so formal. I can't call you by your name *all* of the time."

"Then call me something sweet. Like sweetheart, or hell, I don't know, pudding."

"Pudding?" I laughed.

She nodded. "It's sweet, and I like the way you say it. You can't call someone pudding and not sound sweet on me.

"You're just messing with me, aren't you?"

She shook her head. "No. I sincerely want you to call me pudding. I think it's adorable."

"You're drunk," I noted.

She shrugged. "So? I'd still like to hear you call me pudding."

"You won't say so in the morning."

"Then I give you my drunk permission to ignore whatever the sober me tells you. You should like the drunk me better, anyway, because I like you more than the sober me does."

I couldn't really argue with that. "Okay, pudding, let's dance."

CHAPTER EIGHT

DANIKA

We quickly developed a pattern, and five days later, we'd gone out dancing nearly every night.

I was a restless person. I always had been. I found myself constantly thinking of the next step, calculating what was to come, or even ten steps ahead. I rarely found myself living in the moment. Tristan did that for me. He brought me back to the moment nearly every second I was in his company. It was an addictive kind of feeling, to know, just know, that whatever was going on right now was worth attending to. I didn't have to look forward with Tristan. I lived in the present, and I loved it.

"Are you getting sick of my hangover sandwiches?" Tristan asked as he handed me one.

"Abso-fucking-lutely *not*," I said, taking my sandwich from him.

As I thought about it, I wasn't sick of one thing about him. We'd been inseparable since nearly the moment we'd met, and it was far from getting old.

"I actually have a promoting gig tonight," he told me between bites. "So you get to see me work. It's this new club, over off Paradise. You'll finally get to meet Dean."

"I can't go," I said, recalling what day of the week it was. "I have a thing tonight."

He stopped eating, watching me. "A thing?"

I shrugged. "A weekly thing."

"Care to elaborate? Is this a date type of thing, or a girls' night type of thing?"

I blinked at him, caught off guard by the idea of it being a weekly date. *What on earth had I said that would make it sound like it was a date?* "It's a girls' night."

"Where at?" he asked, taking a bite.

I studied him, wondering what was going through his mind. "It's here at the house. Why?"

He shrugged. "I thought maybe I'd swing by after I'm done tonight and join you. You're meeting all of my friends. I can return the favor."

"It's a girls' night, so..."

He shrugged. "I'll finagle my way in."

"We won't be partying until four in the morning, so you'll still be out by the time we're done."

His eyes narrowed on me. "Why don't you want me to come to this thing?"

I poked a finger into his chest. That only served to turn his glare into a smile. "You aren't invited. Don't sweat it. It's just a small, quiet get together. You'd be bored to tears in five minutes."

"What time does it start?"

"Early. And it ends early."

"Do you all sit around and talk, or like watch chick flicks?"

I sighed. "We sit around and talk and drink cocktails. There's not a thing about it you'd be interested in. Just go and do your usual routine tonight. Don't worry your pretty little head about it."

That lit his face up with his most sinister smile. "I feel like you're daring me to come."

I shook my head. "You're a whack-job, you know that? I am

most definitely *not* daring you. I'm warning you off."

That had his eyes narrowing again. "You're hiding something from me. I'm going to ask Bev what this is all about.

I lifted my chin. "Go for it. She'll tell you what I just did. Girls only. No boys allowed."

He sighed, finally looking resigned about the whole thing. "Fine. What about tomorrow night? We on for tomorrow?"

I smiled, relieved that he was done pressing the issue. I really didn't want Lucy to get a load of him. She wouldn't believe for a second that he and I were purely platonic. Hell, even I didn't really believe it.

"We're on," I told him.

"Any plans for today?" he asked, taking the last bite of his sandwich.

"I told the boys I'd swim with them after breakfast."

"You said you'd swim with us for four hours!" Ivan called from his couch, where he was scarfing down his blueberry pancakes.

"I said four hours or until you said uncle," I called back. I took a huge bite out of my sandwich, stuffed but unable to throw it away.

Tristan snagged the last bit out of my hand, eating it.

"Lucky for you, I have swim trunks packed," he said after he'd washed the bite down with a long drink of his water.

"Oh, darn. I was hoping you'd have to borrow a bikini from me. That would have made my day."

He laughed. "You'll have to remember that the next time you win a bet."

Tristan was competitive. In fact, he took the term to a whole new level. He could turn anything into a challenge, from eating breakfast, to being the dogs' favorite, and he liked to gamble with it. Always. Even my mundane life was never dull, with Tristan around.

"Oh, I will, now that you've put it on the table."

"Whoa, whoa, whoa," he said, waving a hand as though to

ward the notion off. "It's not on the table unless you have something just as big to wager on your end."

I pursed my lips, thinking. "I'll come up with something by the time you pull some new competition out of your sleeve."

"How about letting me sleep in your bed?" His expression was perfectly innocent, the reprobate.

"Excuse me?" I asked, wondering if I'd heard him right.

"No funny business. If I win our next wager, I get to sleep in your bed with you, instead of on the couch. I repeat, no funny business. If you win, I'll wear one of your bikinis for a humiliating swim session. It'll have to be here at the house, and with the boys gone, since I can guarantee I'll be exposing myself."

My mind went crazy for a minute, picturing that very vividly. I'd never thought that cross-dressing could be a turn-on for me.

"Oh no, boo," he uttered softly, watching me. "Don't get that look on your face. Are you trying to *kill* me?"

I snapped out of it, swallowing hard. He'd won our little tiff over the nickname boo. I'd given up. He'd wanted to call me that more than I hadn't wanted him to. I was secretly even beginning to think it was cute.

I pointed. "You can change first. I need to get the boys' swim trunks out for them."

He strode out of the kitchen and towards my room. I wasn't surprised when I heard the shower turn on less than a minute later.

I fished out the boys' swim trunks and left them to change. I nearly walked into Tristan as he stepped out of my bedroom and into my path.

I looked up at his face, trying hard not to stare at his bare chest. The sight was mouth-watering. "The boys are getting ready," I told him. "Now I just need to change. I only need a minute. Can you wait out by the pool, in case they jump the gun and rush it?"

He just nodded, turned, and walked away. I had the supreme self-control not to watch him do it.

I was a big fan of one-piece black suits for pool time with the boys, but I didn't even consider it just then. I fished out my only string bikini. It was bronze, with a gold cover-up, but I left the cover-up in my drawer, knowing I'd be swimming the entire time.

I was reaching out to open the sliding glass door that led to the pool when I remembered sunscreen.

I grabbed a tube of forty-five SPF out of the bathroom, catching Mat as he was racing through the hallway.

He stood still, but tapped his foot impatiently as I helped him put it on. "I coulda been in the pool already, boo," he whined.

"Well, we don't swim without putting sunblock on first, so no you couldn't have," I told him sternly. I wasn't one to indulge whiny moods.

He glanced at me, and snapped out of it almost instantly. "Can I go now?"

I nodded, waving him off. "Go for it, peeka."

Ivan came barreling down the hallway, and I gave him the same treatment. He stood patiently, knowing the routine.

"Is Tristan going to live with us for very long?" he asked.

"Not very long. Just another week or two. How come?"

"I like him. He's a good cook, and he's funny."

"Can't argue with that," I told him, then waved him off.

I took a minute to pull my hair into a messy ponytail on top of my head, and carefully sun-blocked my face in the mirror. I went outside to keep an eye on the boys as I spread it over my body.

Ivan and Mat were already in the pool as I stepped outside. Tristan was poised at the edge of the pool, watching them attentively. I had a brief moment to take in the awesome sight of Tristan shirtless in broad daylight before he looked at me.

I slipped on my gold framed shades, then bent to rub the

sunscreen into my thighs. I propped my foot on one of the carelessly strewn lounge chairs to cover my knee and calf. Slowly, I gave my other leg the same treatment. I straightened, rubbing it onto my shoulders, and arms.

I began to walk towards Tristan as I slathered it onto my stomach.

I handed him the bottle when I reached him.

I saw his throat work as he swallowed hard. He was wearing shades, too, but I could still read his expression well enough.

"Want me to get your back?" he asked.

"Yes," I said, caught off-guard. I'd forgotten to do my back. I'd meant for him to use it for himself, but he made a good point. I turned around.

The first touch of his slick hands made me jump. He rubbed the sunblock on, and I was very conscious of the fact that I loved his hands on me. And he hadn't even begun...

After he'd covered my shoulders and back with tantalizingly light touches, he began to rub and massage, focusing on my shoulders. I just about melted beneath his fingertips.

"Mmmm," I hummed as he worked at a tense spot on my neck.

"I see you rubbing this spot all the time. You're tense. You should let me work on you."

"Are you a massage therapist, too?"

"No, but I have strong hands, and they're at your service, whenever you like."

Boy, did my mind go crazy with that statement, running wild with the things I'd *like* him to do with his hands.

His hands moved down my back, rubbing deep into my muscle tissue. He worked to the sides of my waist, kneading. I moaned when his arms circled me, his hands working on my abs. I felt his chest just brush against my back, and instinctively I leaned into him.

"Boo, why is he touching your belly?" Mat shouted with typical six-year old volume control basically loud enough to alert the entire neighborhood.

That snapped me out of it. I straightened, moving away from Tristan. "He was helping me put on sunscreen, peeka."

I didn't look at Tristan again until he spoke. "Can you get my back?" he asked, his voice hoarse.

"Yes, of course," I said, moving to help him automatically. I paused for a long moment, staring at his back on full display.

I thought that there couldn't be anything on earth sexier than a strong back as I began to work the sunblock into his skin, relishing the feel of his firm, resilient flesh. I kneaded at his shoulders, trying to copy what he'd done to me, as I studied his myriad tattoos.

There was a golden dragon on his shoulder. It was intricate, and every detail looked precise and perfect, even in the direct sun. It was beautiful. I made a note to ask him about it. Later.

He moaned, and I kept rubbing, working down his back, slipping my hands to his sides. I could scarcely believe it, but he felt even better than he looked.

I was careful to keep my chest from touching his back as I reached around to rub his abs. It was only fair...and I was dying to know how they felt. I'd never touched six pack abs before.

I shut my eyes, leaning into him, as I kneaded at his hard flesh.

"Now you're helping him put some on his belly, boo?" Mat shouted.

"Yeah, peeka," I said, flushing hotly.

I stepped away from Tristan, handing him the bottle of sunscreen so he could finish putting it on.

I didn't look at him, taking a few brisk steps, and diving into the pool.

CHAPTER NINE

We both made a good show of ignoring those brief moments of contact, but I couldn't seem to get my mind off how good he'd felt, or how amazing it had felt to let him touch me.

We swam for hours, playing and frolicking in the water.

Tristan was great with the boys, throwing them around the pool just how they liked.

He lifted a giggling Ivan above his head before dropping him into the water.

Ivan resurfaced, laughing. He pointed at Tristan. "I bet you can't do that to Danika!"

"You *bet* me?" Tristan asked.

"I dare you!" Ivan said.

Tristan arched one sassy brow, sidling over to where I was working with Mat on his backstroke. I yelped as he gripped his big hands around my waist, lifting me before I could think to put up a fight. He didn't throw me, as he had Ivan, but lifted me high, thrusting his head between my legs, and settling me onto his shoulders.

I scrabbled for a handhold, trying to grip his too-short hair, finally settling for a hold under his chin. My thighs clenched hard around his neck.

"What are you doing?" I asked him.

"Ivan dared me."

"You can't say no to a dare, can you? Even if it comes from an eight-year old?"

He shrugged his shoulders, jostling me until I clutched him harder, screeching.

"I guess not," he said.

"I dare you to drop her!" Ivan called, the little traitor.

Tristan didn't hesitate, lifting me by the hips, holding me high over the water for a brief moment, then dropping me.

I came up sputtering and glaring.

He just smiled.

I started thinking hard about how to get even.

The sliding glass door opened, and Jerry leaned out. "I'm running errands, boys. Anyone want to join me? I might just be getting ice cream while I'm out…"

Mat was climbing out of the pool before Jerry had even finished. Ivan paused for a moment, considering. Finally, he chose ice cream, bolting out of the pool.

Jerry waved at us as the boys ran inside. "I've got them for the afternoon, so, have fun."

I waved back, still plotting about how I could dunk Tristan under water. He was just so big…

Jerry ducked back inside, and we were left alone.

Tristan smiled at me, leaning back, and propping his arms up along the side of the pool. He sank low, watching me, and I saw my chance.

I glided over to him, trying hard to look perfectly innocent. I moved close, getting right up in his personal space.

He watched me, swallowing hard.

I slid my arms around his neck, brushing my hands over his hair. I leaned in very close, and his breath caught, but he didn't stop me.

I straddled him, hooking my legs behind his knees.

"What are you doing, Danika?" he asked roughly, looking

almost panicked, but still, he didn't stop me.

"I'm daring you," I began, gripping the backs of his massive arms, "to go under!"

I took his legs out from under him, yanking his arms away from the side of the pool.

He went under, but then again, so did I.

The maneuver also had the troublesome side effect of shoving his face between my breasts.

He didn't come up right away, instead wrapping his arms around my waist and keeping his face right where it was. When he stood, he took me with him. I laughed as he began a wet motorboat between my breasts. I yanked at his short hair to no avail.

He finally tilted his head back, laughing up at me.

We both stopped laughing abruptly as he lowered me, and my body slid along his. There was a brief moment of contact between my sex and his. He was hard. We both gasped.

I pushed away, and he let me, taking a step back himself.

"Bad idea," I said breathlessly.

"Yeah," he agreed, running a hand over his wet hair.

"Guess we're done here. You can shower first," I told him, since we were sharing a bathroom.

"Thanks," he said, lifting himself out of the water with one smooth move. He wrapped a towel around his hips as he moved toward the house.

"Just let me know when you're done. I'll wait out here."

He was already at the door, sliding it open. He kept his back to me as he gave one short nod.

I stayed in the pool, trying not to panic. So we were attracted to each other. It didn't mean anything. We were two grown-ups who could control ourselves.

I didn't even want to have sex. Sex had never been good for me. For me, at its best, it had been a way to stay connected to someone that I wanted to feel intimate with. It was a sad fact that if I really wanted to get off, I had to take things into my own hands, and not just when I was single.

I had no idea why I couldn't seem to keep my hands to myself when it came to Tristan. It was a new problem for me. I felt hot and bothered as I never had before. I decided to make a short appointment with my vibrator in the very near future. It could only help.

I swam laps, trying to blow off steam, and give Tristan enough time to shower and change.

I was breathless and exhausted when I stopped. I started as I saw that Tristan was standing over the pool, dry and dressed in a white T-shirt and some gray athletic shorts.

"Shower's all yours," he said, watching me, his expression blank.

"Oh. Thanks."

I moved to get out of the water, and he met me at the steps with a towel.

"I'm going to go workout," he said as I dried off.

I just nodded. He'd made good use of Bev's home gym in the short week he'd been staying at the house.

"Feel free to come and join me."

I nodded again. "I might. I need to wash the chlorine out of my hair, and do a few things first."

"Sure," he said, walking back into the house.

I couldn't tell if he was out of sorts, or just in a quiet mood.

I showered, and changed into a comfortable T-shirt and some shorts. I started to head to the home gym when I changed my mind, turning around.

Maybe Tristan was on to something with his frequent showers.

With kids underfoot, I kept my vibrator at the back of the drawer in my nightstand, wrapped in a sock that was wrapped in a T-shirt. It was very well hidden, since I did not want to have a conversation about *that* with the boys.

I shut and locked my bedroom door, turned on some music, slipped out of my shorts and panties, and grabbed the neglected toy out of my nightstand.

I sprawled out on my bed, closing my eyes. I pictured Tristan as I set to work on myself with the small vibrating wand.

I pictured his massive arms as I worked my T-shirt up, cupping my breast. I visualized his sinister smile as I kneaded the flesh around my nipple. I was already wet. I thought of his golden eyes as I pushed the wand inside of me, shivering in pleasure as the vibrations rocked me. I pulled it out and moaned as I touched it to my clit, imagining his body, with those perfect abs, and that ripped chest. I remembered that brief touch of his erection against me, pushing the toy inside of me.

It usually took me a long time to relax and let go enough to come, but I wasn't having any trouble just then, my race toward the finish faster than I could ever remember. I was letting myself relax into a climax when there was a knock at my bedroom door. I tensed.

"Danika?" Tristan called.

I closed my eyes, letting that deep voice wash over me.

"Yes?" I answered breathlessly.

"You coming?"

"Yes," I nearly moaned.

"What's taking so long?" he questioned.

"Almost there," I gasped.

There was a long pause from the other side of the door. "What are you doing?" he asked, his voice rougher now.

I didn't answer, something about that rough tone setting me off. I grabbed a corner of my blanket, biting it to stifle my moans as I climaxed.

"Can I come in?" he asked.

I heard him try the door.

"I need a minute," I told him, just lying there, my heart still racing.

"Okay," he said, almost too quiet for me to hear.

I was decent but flustered when I finally opened my door.

Tristan was just standing there, hands on his hips, eyes on the floor. He looked up, then craned his neck to look into my room.

"Everything okay?" he asked.

"Yes," I said, mostly meaning it. I did feel more relaxed than I had.

"We working out?"

"Sure. Let me just tie my hair back, and grab my shoes. I'll meet you there in a minute."

He startled me by tipping my chin up with his finger.

I blinked at him.

"You look different."

"What do you mean?"

He hummed low in his throat, and I about lost it. It was the sexiest noise I'd ever heard. "Fuck, Danika, I know that look. Were you taking your own version of a 'shower' in there?"

It took me a while to catch his meaning. My cheeks flushed red, but I was too stubborn not to meet his gaze squarely. I firmed my jaw, leaning away from his hand. "And what if I was? You think you're the only one that needs a 'shower' every once in a while?"

He seemed taken aback by that. "No. I didn't—I don't think that. I'm sorry, you just caught me off guard. That's...way too fucking hot. Excuse me." He turned around and started walking back down the hall.

"We still on for a workout?" I called to his back.

"Hell yes," he called back.

I grinned.

I was jogging on the treadmill for a good forty-five minutes before he said another word.

He dropped down from doing a long round of pull-ups that I pretended I wasn't counting.

He approached the front of my machine, studying my face.

"So, um," he finally spoke, clearing his throat, "how often do you need to, uh, take a 'shower'?"

I sent him an arch look, but my heart was pounding harder at his question. "Is this a *friendly* conversation?" I asked, breathing hard, from the workout, and the question.

He smiled his most troublesome smile. "We're friends, aren't we? Of course it's friendly."

"No funny business?"

"None at all. Just pretend I'm one of the girls."

Unbidden, my gaze ran down his body. By sheer force of will, I returned my eyes to his face. *One of the girls, my ass...*

"I don't need to do it often," I admitted. "Nothing like what you need to do. I go weeks without needing to. Hell, sometimes I go months."

He grimaced. "That can't be healthy."

I hitched my shoulder up in a shrug, keeping up my steady pace.

"Anything in particular that made you need a 'shower' today?" he asked, watching me closely.

I glared. "That is *not* a friendly question."

He sighed heavily, turning away. "My bad," he muttered, heading to the free weights.

We hadn't gotten much sleep the night before, and I found myself laying down for a nap by early afternoon, since Jerry and the kids were still out and about.

I was just burrowing into the covers when there was a soft knock at my door.

"Yeah?" I called.

Tristan poked his head in. "Hey. I was going to take a short nap, too, before I go out. Mind if I stay in here with you, since the living room will be overrun by the kids pretty soon..."

I watched him. "No funny business?"

"No funny business," he agreed. "I'll stay on my side of the bed."

I snuggled into my pillow, almost at peace with the fact that I could never seem to tell him no. "Okay. Night, Tristan."

The bed moved as he climbed on the other side. I shivered as I felt him getting under the covers with me.

"Sweet dreams, boo," he said quietly.

I smiled, my eyes drifting closed.

I woke up as my bathroom door opened. I blinked up at Tristan, who was fully dressed for his night out. He wore a crisp navy dress shirt with dark-washed jeans.

The sleeves of his shirt were rolled up; the collar unbuttoned enough to show a distracting amount of his throat.

"Aren't you going to be hot?" I asked.

He grinned, approaching the bed. "Aren't I, though?"

I rolled my eyes.

He startled me by bending over and placing a soft kiss on my forehead.

I gave him wide eyes as he straightened. "What was that?"

"That was a 'have a nice night, friend' kiss."

I pursed my lips, sitting up. "Do you kiss Cory or Kenny on the forehead?"

He just smiled. "I would, if they were as gorgeous as you. I'll see you later, boo. Have a nice night."

"You too," I told him as he walked out.

CHAPTER TEN

I started making snacks early for the girls' night. Those bitches could *eat*. Everyone would show up, say they weren't hungry, have two cocktails, and promptly pig out. I loved it, and I made sure we were prepared.

I prepared a mix of healthy and unhealthy comfort food. I made guacamole, but also put out some processed cheese dip that one of the girls loved. I put out plain tortilla chips, whole wheat pita chips, and plain old potato chips. I made pigs in a blanket, and baked some tater tots, but made sure I cut plenty of fresh vegetables. It was a diverse crowd of women that attended our girls' night every week, and we tried to accommodate them all. One thing they all indulged in equally, though, was Bev's cocktail of the week.

Bev joined me in the kitchen when she got home from work. She came bearing gifts in the form of bottles of apple juice, apple schnapps, and vodka.

I nabbed one bottle, inspecting it. "Apple juice, huh?" I asked.

"Indeed," she said with a grin, washing her hands. "Appletinis."

One of the best things about girls' night was that no one even considered dressing up. We all wore sweats or yoga pants. I had my favorite pair of pink sweat short-shorts on that read 'sassy pants' on the butt, and a red half-shirt that read UNL because the V had worn out.

Bev took less than five minutes to change into her own pair of sweats—a sight you only saw on girls' night.

"Jerry just called," Bev told me as she came back into the kitchen. "He and the boys are catching a movie. They won't be home until bedtime."

The doorbell rang, and Bev answered it with a ready cocktail in hand, all of the dogs following closely on her heels.

It was Lucy. Lucy always showed up early. She sort of ran this thing, though she'd been reluctant at first. Our girls' night had, over time, turned into a weekly group therapy session. Lucy had argued at first that it might not be the best idea to have therapy sessions with her friends, but, when she'd seen how much we all apparently needed it, she'd become more enthusiastic than any of us about the whole thing.

We'd even affectionately named the event. 'Fuck Anonymous', because it was anything *but* anonymous, had been going strong for over a year now, and I wouldn't change a thing about it.

Lucy and Bev embraced, kissing cheeks, and Bev handed off the cocktail.

Lucy studied the bright green liquid in the martini glass. "This is either tasty, or wicked," she murmured. She was a petite black-haired woman in her early forties. She had a pretty face, with dark eyes that always seemed to be crinkled up with laughter.

"It's a little bit of both, I think," Bev said.

Lucy came into the kitchen, where I was laying out the food, paper plate buffet style.

I set down the plate in my hand to give her a big hug.

"How are you, dear?" she asked as she pulled back. "You look great."

I glanced down at my sloppy ensemble, wondering if she

could be joking. "Um, thanks. I'm doing good."

Bev went back to bartending from the small bar in the dining room, pouring and then bringing me my own bright martini.

I thanked her, taking a tiny sip. My brows shot up. "That's tasty."

Bev went back to the bar, pouring herself a glass. She held it up. "Cheers ladies. Fuck anonymous!"

"Fuck anonymous!" I said, raising my glass.

"Fuck anonymous!" Lucy called, smiling.

I took a long drink, then went back to stocking the buffet.

The doorbell rang. Bev answered it with another green martini in hand.

It was the neighbor, Sarah. She was a short, plump, white-haired woman in her sixties. She had a plate of her famous peanut butter cookies, as always.

Bev handed her the cocktail, and took the cookies.

They embraced, and Sarah took her usual spot on the sofa in the living room.

"Fuck anonymous," she called out sweetly, before taking a big drink.

Jen, another neighbor, arrived next. Jen was a blonde, Barbie doll housewife with a great personality and a beauty pageant smile. She was the only one of us that never resorted to wearing sweats, even for girls' night. She wore an emerald green sheath with mint green stilettos.

"I matched the drink of the week. What are the odds?" We all laughed.

She'd brought a huge box of chocolates, and we added it to the paper plate buffet.

"Fuck anonymous," Sarah said quietly, taking a drink.

Harriet and Sandra arrived together.

Harriet was an attorney, like Bev, though her firm was smaller. She was thirty-nine, and she had dark hair and nondescript features. No one would know at first glance that she was a closet sexpot.

Sandra was Harriet's neighbor. She was a small brown-haired, brown-eyed woman with a somewhat austere demeanor. She was an assistant at the art gallery at the Cavendish resort. It went without saying that after two drinks she'd start going on about how hot her boss, the hotel's owner, was. I'd seen pictures of the twenty something billionaire playboy, and I couldn't really blame her.

Olga showed next. She was a retired gymnast/acrobat with a heavy German accent. She was older, with a bit of overdone plastic surgery that made it hard to tell her age. She could drink the lot of us under the table.

Candy was the last to make an appearance. At thirty-four, she was the closest of the group to my own age, though there was still a thirteen-year gap between us. She worked in a burlesque show on the strip, and was a dead ringer for Betty Page, hairstyle and all.

"Hello Hookers," she called loudly as she took her martini glass from Bev, giving her an air kiss. Her hair and makeup were fully done, but she was wearing Betty Boop PJ's, and kitty slippers. "I'd like to start tonight, if no one objects. I need to vent."

"No objections here," Lucy said, looking around.

I moved into the living room, Dot and Pupcake following me again. They always followed Bev around for a while right when she first got home from work, but some or all of them eventually made their way back to me.

"Sounds good to me," I said. I sat down on the loveseat with Bev and took a big drink of my martini.

Everyone sat. There were plenty of seats, with spots for six on the sectional, the loveseat, and two extra recliners. The living room wasn't pretty, but it was comfortable. The dogs lounged around the room, as though they were in on the discussion.

Candy was the only one who didn't sit, tapping a kitty slipper, her hand on her hip.

"Okay, here goes," she began. "I'm frustrated—no, you know what, I'm pissed, at George! I just don't think that he even attempts to understand me, and sometimes, a lot of times, I feel like he just tries to be contrary, like he's just looking for reasons to shut me down."

Lucy's brow furrowed as she studied the other woman. "Okay, you're frustrated that your partner doesn't understand where you're coming from—"

"I don't think he even tries to understand," Candy burst out.

Lucy nodded calmly.   "I can see how that would be frustrating. I think we can all relate to that, on some level, but can you give us some specific examples of why you're feeling this way?"

Candy downed her martini, and Bev was up to take her glass for a refill before she continued.   "Well...you all know I'm bisexual. George knows it. He's known it from the start, but he won't let me be with other women. He actually had the nerve to say that he would leave me if I hooked up with someone else, even if it was a *woman*!"

"Are you still monogamous?" Lucy asked, her tone very neutral.

Candy blew out a frustrated breath.   "Yes. We're *living* together now, but I like to be with men *and* women. George is talking marriage, and part of me is thrilled by that, but another part of me can't imagine not having sex with a woman for the rest of my life. It's not fair of him to ask that of me."

"Well, you may just have to choose, Candy."

"But that's not fair. I'm attracted to men *and* women."

"I understand. And that's fine. Only you can decide what you want to do, and how you want to prioritize your relationships. You did agree to monogamy with George. If I recall, it was your idea. What he's asking you to do—to not have sex with other people, is no different than what any partner asks in an exclusive relationship—"

"But I'm *attracted* to *women.*"

Bev brought Candy another martini.

Candy thanked, her, taking a long drink.

"I understand that. I really do. Do you think any monogamous relationship doesn't face those same challenges? It's a commitment for everyone to deny those other potential attractions. If you married George, you may never have sex with another woman, but that's what marriage is. If George says he won't tolerate you having sex with other women, you either need to adhere to that, or break it off."

"Most men would be thrilled that I liked other women! Most men think it's hot! Why does he have to be different?"

"I don't know. And you're right, many men would like that. But you chose George, and he's been clear about what he wants. What he's asking of you is not unreasonable, but it's also not unreasonable if you decide that you can't make the sort of commitment that he wants."

"Well, fuck. This is hard. I was hoping you'd just tell me that he was an asshole."

Lucy gave her a very understanding smile. "You know that's not what I do."

"Yeah, I know. A girl can dream. Okay, I'm done with my rant. Who wants to follow that hot mess?" Candy sat down.

No one spoke right away, and Lucy's concerned, benevolent gaze swung to me. Dammit, but her understanding looks undid me.

"What about you, Danika?" she asked, as I'd know she would. "How are you doing? Where do you stand with your ex? Are you still broken up?"

That last question made me bristle a bit. "Of course we are! I caught a chick giving him a blow job in exchange for pot. It's not a complicated situation. It's very cut and dry. I'm not wishy-washy about it. I never want to speak to him again." It was the strangest thing, how something that had felt so awful just a month ago, didn't make me feel anything but annoyance just then.

She nodded, not looking at all surprised by my outburst. "And has he been trying to call?"

I sighed. "Yeah. It's calmed down to a few attempts a day, so I'm confident that eventually he'll stop trying altogether."

"And have you started seeing anyone else?"

"No. I'm determined to just be by myself for a while."

"That's good. Very good. Your last two relationships ended and began within two weeks of each other, and they both lasted two years, two very *impressionable* years. Jumping from one relationship and into another gives you no time to gain any perspective, especially at your age. I think it would benefit you greatly to remain single. We've gone over this exhaustively, but with your past, and your patterns, you strike me as a prime candidate for love addiction."

I tensed at the mention of my past. The room at large knew a lot of it, but I'd kept the really nasty bits from everyone except for Lucy and Bev. Those two were like a truth serum for me most of the time. I couldn't keep a thing from either of them for long.

"I hate that term," Candy said with a smirk.

Lucy waved her off. "I'll call it codependency, if that makes you feel better."

"It does."

Lucy ignored her, still focused on me. "You grew up with an addicted parent, and so far, both of the long term relationships you've been in, have turned out to be with addicts. Down the road, when you do start dating, I want you to be very careful about the men who you find yourself *very* attracted to, because of your history with addicts. The chaotic bad boys have not been good for you. You need to reprogram yourself to start looking for men that could be considered stable. Does that make sense?"

I nodded. It made way too much sense, and my mind shot to Tristan. *Chaotic bad boy...* She'd hit that one on the head.

She smiled warmly. "Okay, I'm done picking on you. Love you, girl."

I swallowed hard. "Love you, too."

"I love all of you hookers," Candy said loudly.

It eased the tension, and we all laughed.

Lucy looked at Bev. "And what about you? How are things with Jerry?"

Bev sighed heavily. "They're good. They've been pretty good for a while, but recently, when I'd thought he'd done another stupid thing, all of my anger just came back, as though all of our progress together had just disappeared, which made me realize that my anger is still very present."

Shit, shit, shit, I thought. I'd begun to feel like I'd made some sort of peace about having lied to her about Jerry and Tristan, but that guilt came flooding back in spades as I realized what she was talking about.

"And what exactly happened that made your anger resurface?"

Bev grimaced. "It was all a misunderstanding, but I thought he'd brought home another musician, which would have meant that he was out playing around with the band thing, instead of looking around for another firm, like he promised he would."

"Anger often lingers, just looking for ways to come out, but you're doing all of the right things. If you both *keep* doing the right things, that anger will slowly fade with time, instead of staying right under the surface."

Bev nodded.

"Anyone else have anything they want to talk about? Something to get off your chest?"

"My hemorrhoids are flaring up," Olga said loudly, her accent heavy.

I tried my hardest not to laugh, we all did, but as soon as I saw that Olga was grinning, I lost it.

"I can get you a referral for that," Lucy said.

"Not necessary," Olga said.

"Anyone else? Should we break for snacks and cocktails?"

"I don't think I'm attracted to my husband anymore," Jen said, smoothing her green skirt over her legs in a nervous gesture. "I have to stifle the urge to cringe away from his touch."

"You've been struggling with this for quite some time. Since your three-year old was born, correct? Has it changed recently? Are your feelings of distaste more acute?"

Jen nodded, her eyes wide. "I don't know what it is. He tries, he really does, but when I get even an inkling that he's going to make a pass at me, I want to run in the other direction."

"You say that you want to run in the other direction, but not that you do that. What is it that you actually do?"

Jen looked very vulnerable as she answered. "I just...do what he wants. I don't say anything. I just get it over with."

"Have you said anything to him about it? Does he know that you don't enjoy your sexual encounters?"

Jen shook her head, wincing. "I haven't said anything to him about it. I think he knows that I don't climax anymore, but he doesn't know that I hate having sex with him."

"Well, a lot of things could have started the decline in your sex drive, but I think I can tell you why it's suddenly gotten worse. Even though he may be clueless to the fact that you're finding sex with him distasteful, you're likely beginning to resent him for it. Have you considered telling him how you feel?"

"I don't know how. I'm afraid it would make him mad, or even hurt his feelings, if I told him that I've basically just been suffering his advances for so long."

"Hm. Maybe don't tell him all that. And certainly don't begin with that. You could just begin by telling him that your sex drive has gone away. How ever you open up the communication, though, the point is that you begin to talk about these things. Communication is an important component to all types of intimacy, even the physical kind."

Jen nodded, took a deep breath, then smiled. "I'll give it a shot. I vote it's time for cocktail number two."

I seconded that.

We ate, and drank, and talked for hours. As the therapy session wound down, the talk turned silly, as it usually did.

"Fuck. Ing. Hot." Sandra said, referring to the owner of the Cavendish casino, and the gallery where she worked. She looked like she was feeling awfully pretty. "He came into the gallery a few days ago, and I about had a heart attack."

"He *is* gorgeous," Candy said, toasting the air.

"No," Sandra said. "You don't understand. He looks gorgeous in pictures, but in real life, he will *blow your mind*. Once you've seen his eyes up close, you can never go back."

"You should make a pass at him," Candy said.

"*I'd* make a pass at him," Harriet said. "In fact, I wouldn't take no for an answer."

Sandra shook her head. "He only dates supermodels with legs that go up to their tits, or playboy models with tits that go up to their chins."

"Just go for it," Harriet said. "What have you got to lose?"

"Um, her job," I said, rolling my eyes.

Harriet and Candy were funny as hell, but not the ones to take advice from. Their brand of outrageous would not work for everybody. It backfired on *them* half the time.

"Dating the boss rarely turns out well," Lucy pointed out reasonably.

"I wasn't saying she should date him," Harriet defended. "I was saying she should bone his pretty brains out."

"Arguably an even worse idea," Lucy mused.

Sandra held up a hand. "Settle down everybody. He's not

interested in me, so it's not even a question. I just like to vent about how fucking hot he is."

"Amen, sister," Candy said, toasting the air again.

I raised my glass, as well. I could toast to that. "To hot men who we don't need to fuck to appreciate," I said.

I got a few startled glances for that unexpected outburst, but everyone toasted with me.

"Are you just speaking in general?" Lucy asked, tilting her head to study me. "That sounded a little specific."

"Oh, it's specific," Sandra slurred. "James fucking Cavendish is specifically the hottest man alive."

Bev giggled. *Uh oh*, I thought. She was tipsy if she was giggling. "Wait until you get a load of Danika's friend, Tristan," she said. "He could give Boss Cavendish a run for his money, and he and Danika have *crazy* chemistry."

"The fuck you say?" Candy inquired, looking very interested.

"Why you holding out, Danika?" Harriet questioned, her words slurred.

"Who's this Tristan?" Lucy asked, and I saw by the way she was studying me that she was already worried.

I hitched one shoulder up in a self-conscious shrug. "He's strictly a buddy. Bev is just drunk."

Bev nodded. *Very drunkenly*, I thought.

"Is he hot, though?" Olga asked, her accent even more pronounced now that she'd had a few drinks.

"He's very good looking," I allowed. "And he has a great sense of humor. And he's super tall, with biceps the size of my waist." I held my hands out in a circle to show them how big. "And he's really nice. And don't even get me started on his dimples." After about the second sentence, I started to realize that I was feeling *really* pretty. *Dammit, how many drinks had I had?* It was hard to count, when Bev was constantly bringing a new glass, and I had no idea just how strong the cocktail was.

"You sound like you admire him," Lucy pointed out. "But you

say it's purely platonic?"

"I'm attracted to him, and I love being around him, but I have every intention of *keeping* it purely platonic."

I must have sounded a touch defensive, because Lucy wasn't the only woman in the room that didn't look convinced.

CHAPTER ELEVEN

I was in the kitchen, replenishing the snack trays, when I saw that I'd missed three calls.

I'd left my phone on the counter, and I grabbed it, a little too eager to see who had called.

I felt a ridiculous amount of disappointment when I saw that they were all from my ex, or Daryl the Dickhead, as I liked to think of him.

It was silly to expect Tristan to call me, just because we'd been apart for a few hours. Lucy'd hit it right on the head about my co-dependency issues.

My phone dinged a text at me, and I was disappointed yet again when I saw that it was a text from Daryl.

Daryl: I miss you, baby. Why you ignoring my calls?

I felt my lip curl up in disgust. *The bastard had a nerve.*

I started to respond before I remembered that texting back, no matter what I said, only ever encouraged him.

Two things happened at once.

"Is that asshat bothering you again?" Candy shouted from the living room, right as the front door opened.

I looked up to see that Tristan had just walked in, and all of the women were watching me. That quickly changed, and I could have been happy that the potentially awkward conversation about my ex had been avoided, except that Tristan had apparently heard her comment, and although the women's attention had shifted to focus on him, his was very much focused on *me*.

"Who's bothering you? What's going on?" he asked, striding straight to the kitchen. He'd obviously taken Candy's comment way too seriously.

"Um, no one. Nothing's going on. Why are you home so early? Shouldn't you still be working?"

He shrugged, his eyes going to the phone still in my hand. "I ducked out early. Is it that asshole ex of yours calling you again? I'm seriously going to kick his ass if he doesn't leave you alone."

I set my phone down on the counter, folding my arms across my chest. I saw his eyes go to my bared stomach, and I was gratified as he swallowed hard before looking back at my face.

"The first time you've had a paying gig all week, and you ditch out? Are you like, *allergic* to work?"

I'd been trying to distract him from talking about my ex, and it worked like a charm, for all of ten seconds.

He laughed, moving into the kitchen.

He grabbed my phone off the counter before I saw his intent.

"So rude," I told him. "How would you like it if I started snooping through your phone?"

He didn't look up from my phone as he reached into his pocket and handed me his. "Go for it, boo."

"Boo?" Candy called from the living room, sounding amused.

I'd forgotten that we weren't alone, which said a lot about how much Tristan distracted me.

I set his phone on the counter, folding my arms across my chest, and giving him a very unfriendly look.

He didn't look up, scrolling through my phone. I saw his jaw clench right before he brought the phone to his ear.

Without another word, he strode out of the kitchen, through the dining room, opened the sliding glass door, and walked outside.

I followed him, wondering what the hell he was up to.

"Is this Daryl?" he said into my phone.

My jaw dropped.

He paused for a long moment, and whatever Daryl was saying was loud, because I could hear his voice from several feet away, though I couldn't make out a word of what he was saying.

"Who I am is the guy who is going to kick your fucking ass if you don't leave her alone. One more phone call, one more text, so much as a fucking email, and I will *find* you. Do you understand?"

He paused again, and I could hear that Daryl was yelling on the other end of the line. "It doesn't sound like you're understanding what I'm saying. How about I come over to your house, and we can talk about it in person? Hell yeah, call the cops. Cops or no, I can guarantee that I will mess you up before they can take me away. I'm a very close friend of Danika's, and I take my friendships very seriously. Now do you understand? *Lose her fucking number.*"

He paused for a long time before speaking again. "That's just fine. Fuck you, too, man, just so long as you leave my girl alone."

He hung up the phone, looking at me.

He sighed, striding to me. He pushed my face into his chest, hugging me. I melted against him, even pissed. I thought that was because I wasn't *really* pissed. It was more that I thought I should be pissed. What I *was* was completely infatuated. I didn't think I'd ever met a sweeter guy in my life.

He kissed the top of my head, murmuring, "Don't be mad at me, K? I just want to look out for you. I can't help it. You've put up with enough of that guy's shit. Let me take over. I'll make sure he never bothers you again."

"You aren't really going to beat him up, are you? That was just a threat, right?"

"Sure, boo," he murmured into my hair. "I won't beat him up, just so long as he never tries to contact you again."

Reluctantly, I pulled myself out of his arms. "You're impossible, you know that?"

He nodded, and gave me that dangerous smile. "I'm impossible, and you're irresistible. That's a great mix, if you ask me."

I rolled my eyes, heading back into the house. "Irresistible, my ass," I muttered.

He laughed. "Exactly," he said.

He laughed harder when he saw the writing on my butt. "Sassy pants, huh? Did you have those custom made?"

I shot him a very sassy look as I started to open the door. "You think you can just infiltrate a girls' night in? We'll see about that. I'm going to have you voted out."

He stopped me with a hand on my arm and a big grin. "Let's make a wager out of it. If the girls vote me out, I'll give you that bikini peep show you've been fantasizing about."

I raised a brow, instantly intrigued. *That would be priceless...*

"And if they don't vote you out, you get to sleep in my bed, no funny business."

He nodded. "No funny business."

I held my hand out to shake.

His big, warm hand enveloped mine.

"You're going to lose," I warned him. "I know these women better than you do. They won't be swayed by your pretty face and your slutty body."

I opened the door and walked inside while he was still laughing at me.

I went back to the loveseat and no sooner had I sat back

down than Tristan was sitting next to me, crowding so close that I had to scoot nearly into Bev to give him room.

Tristan threw his arm over the back of the couch, making himself very comfortable.

"Girls, this is Tristan. He thinks he can crash our girls' night. I told him it was girls only, no exceptions. Who wants to help me kick his ass out?"

My eyes narrowed when not one of them volunteered.

"I vote we keep his ass in," Candy said, giving him a very friendly smile. "I like his ass already."

I mouthed a few choice words at her.

"It's more of a friends' night than a girls' night," Harriet said. "We just don't have any men volunteering to join."

"What's the harm?" Jen joined in. "The more the merrier."

I couldn't believe it. They were turning on me. I opened my mouth to say something when Tristan spoke into my ear. "If you tell them it's a bet, I automatically *win* the bet."

"Fine," I bit out. "Let's take a vote. By a show of hands, who wants to let a man into our sacred girl ritual night?"

Everyone raised an eager hand in the air, except for Bev and Lucy, apparently the only ones who had my back.

I continued, even knowing I'd lost. It wasn't in my nature to just give up. "Who votes we keep our girls' night how God intended it, girls only?"

Me, Bev, and Lucy raised our hands. I didn't know if I wanted to laugh or kick him when I saw that Tristan was raising a hand. He knew that he had enough votes, even if he voted with me, the smug bastard.

And so he stayed, chatting up the ladies until nearly three in the morning.

Aside from the sting of losing a bet, I thoroughly enjoyed having him there.

He was funny, and charming, and for whatever reason, he gently deflected Candy, and then Harriet's subtle, and not so subtle come-ons.

Lucy shot me a few concerned glances in the beginning, but in the end, even she was charmed by Tristan's playful personality.

"You know, we usually call it a night by ten, eleven tops," I told Tristan, as he helped me clean up after all of the women had left. He'd even managed to shoo Bev off to bed, not letting her help with cleanup. She'd had enough of her own strong cocktails to take him up on the offer gratefully.

"Did I corrupt your friends?" he asked with a shameless smile.

A corner of my mouth kicked up ruefully. "Not as badly as you're corrupting me. I don't do the dirty Vegas club scene."

"I think I understand you a little better now, after meeting your friends. You're like a forty-five year old, trapped inside of a hot, twenty-one year old body. That might be why you can never really cut loose and just let go."

I took exception to that. "I cut loose all the time. We've been out dancing every night this week. What do you call that?"

He pursed his lips, which drew my traitorous eyes to them, even in a bit of a pique. "It's true you can dance. God, can you dance. And you're certainly able to go out and have a good time, but that just isn't the same as letting go. Even drunk until you feel pretty, you seem to stay in control every single second. I've yet to see you have a twenty-one year old moment."

"Well, excuse me for not being a total slutbag, like half of the twenties crowd in Vegas."

"It's probably a lot more than half..." he mused.

"Well, it isn't me. If that's your idea of letting go, I think I'm just fine how I am."

"I wasn't trying to offend you," he said in his most conciliatory tone. "And I absolutely don't mean that you should be sleeping around. I don't know how to put it into words, but I'd just like to see you acting carefree sometimes."

I stewed about that for a bit, as we finished cleaning up.

Perhaps he has a point, I thought.

I'd had an aimless sort of existence, growing up. My mother, a slave to the illness of addiction, had only ever lived in the present, which, I supposed, was why I had my eye determinedly on the future, which I knew was not the typical frame of mind for a twenty-one year old.

My sister and I had been tossed around ruthlessly by our mother's fickle way of life. She'd been so negligent that, in our teenage years, when she'd disappeared for a solid two weeks, social services had been alerted, which had led to an unfortunate turn of events. I had been so powerless, back then.

But not anymore. Nowadays, I had my own fate well in hand.

"Are you stewing about the bet you lost? Going to miss keeping that big, soft bed all to yourself? I'll bet you're a cover hog."

I rolled my eyes at him, but I couldn't contain my grin. I knew I should have been more worried about the fact that we were going to be sharing a bed, but I just wasn't. It was strange for me, especially considering we'd only known each other a week, but I trusted him.

It wasn't *his* fault that I was wildly attracted to him.

"I'm stewing about the fact that I won't get to see you wearing one of my bikinis," I shot back.

He laughed. "There's always the next bet."

We found ourselves out by the pool, past four in the morning, just lounging and talking. I thought that might have been my favorite thing of all about Tristan—that we could just talk forever, about everything, about nothing. There was never an awkward silence to be found.

"So tell me about this band. I know you're the lead singer, and I know what instruments you all play. Tell me the rest."

He snagged one of my bare feet. I started to kick him off, thinking that he was going to tickle me, but he didn't, just rubbing at the arch. It felt so good that my eyes practically rolled up into the back of my head.

"God, your hands," I moaned. "You are so good at that."

"I aim to please. What do you want to know?"

"What are you called? Who writes the songs? When can I see you perform?"

"The band is called The Escapists. Kenny writes all of the songs, composes all of the music. This band was his baby from the start. We've all been friends since the fifth grade, but I was the last to join up. They needed a singer, and I can carry a tune."

"You make it sound like you aren't that into it."

"I am. Now. To be honest, I wasn't at first, but the guys changed my mind. I think we have a shot at making it."

"Why do you call yourselves The Escapists?"

"It was the only name we could all agree on. I think it has a different meaning for us all. It makes me think of magic, which is why I liked it. Kenny relates to it because songwriting is his way to escape. It's his passion. The rest of the guys, hell, who knows, probably a drug reference for them. But regardless, the name just seemed to fit us all."

"What were you planning to do before you got started with the band? Did you go to college or anything?"

"I didn't. I was a bartender for a long time, and then I got into the whole club promoting thing, which has turned out to be lucrative for me."

"What about your card tricks? You live in Vegas, and you're obviously talented. I'm surprised you didn't pursue something with that."

He sighed, looking vaguely uncomfortable. "I did. For years, I did. That's not something you can get into without some connections. Connections I didn't have. Everyone in town can do card tricks."

"Not like you."

"Well, thank you for that, but any talent I have wasn't

enough," he said, switching to rub my other foot. "It's just a hobby, since I've found out very clearly that there's no money in it for me."

"That's a pity. I've seen some of the shows on the strip. You could've given some of those old guys a run for their money."

He laughed.

"So when do I get to see the band perform?"

"We should have a gig soon. Dean is supposed to be putting a few together, but I don't have any specifics. You'll know about it when I do."

"You promise?"

"I promise, pudding."

I grimaced. "Don't call me that."

He just laughed harder. "You told me you might say that, and that I shouldn't listen to you."

"I know, but I didn't mean it."

"I think I'll listen to drunk you, since she claims to like me more."

I threw my hands in the air, giving up, standing up, and walking inside.

"I'm going to bed," I told him.

I felt him directly at my back all the way to my room.

"Me too, pudding."

I shut the bathroom door in his face, or I'd swear he would have followed me in there, too.

I made sure he got his own set of covers, and set a pillow pointedly between us on the queen sized bed. He didn't try to stop me, thank God.

"Goodnight, boo," he said quietly, as we lay in the dark, backs facing each other.

"Goodnight, Tristan," I said just as quietly, closing my eyes.

I felt a hand on my belly, and stiffened.

Oh no, I thought, caught somewhere between a dream and

waking thoughts.

Please no, not again.

The hand began to inch down, and I whimpered, instantly feeling terrorized, because this had happened too many times to count, and I'd thought it was over forever now.

The hand disappeared at my whimper.

"Fuck. I'm so sorry, boo," Tristan said sleepily, kissing the top of my head, before he rolled over on his other side, facing away from me.

The instant I realized it was Tristan, I felt a wave of nearly overwhelming relief. That relief made me realize how profoundly I already trusted this man. We'd known each other for so short a time, but already I knew with certainty that he would never hurt me.

I rolled over, pressing my face into his back, happy to have him there—a comfort to me, rather than a terror.

CHAPTER TWELVE

We were hitting the club again the next night. We were out the door nearly the second after I'd put the boys to bed.

Tristan's friend Cory was pulling a shift at the Cavendish resort, and so we got decked out again.

We drank too much, and danced for hours, before changing into swimsuits and taking a swim in the warm pool beside the bar Cory was working.

Some brunette with huge fake boobs brushed against Tristan in the water, giving him a very bold look as we passed her.

I rolled my eyes. "So you're hot. That doesn't give her the right to act like a cat in heat about it."

"So you think I'm hot?" Tristan asked, letting those infuriating dimples do their worst.

I shrugged, giving him my steadiest eye contact. I could hide my drunk with the best of them. "You aren't much to look at," I said with a straight face.

He threw his head back and laughed, enjoying my sarcastic sense of humor, as always. It was one of my favorite things about him.

"You aren't much to look at," I said again, when he was done laughing, and just back to giving me a dangerously fond smile. "But your personality makes up for it, mostly."

He tugged on my hair, still grinning. "You are so damned cute."

I gave a heavy sigh. "Yes, I'm very cute. Adorable, really. I'm sorry you'll only ever know what it's like to have a cute *personality*."

He was laughing so hard by the time I'd finished that he was doubled over. I thought that I'd never wanted to kiss anyone so badly in my life. I restrained myself, just smiling affectionately at him as he straightened.

"Where have you been all my life, Danika?"

"Not skanking it up in enough bars to find you, apparently. Silly me, spending all my time working or at school."

"Silly you," he said softly, touching my chin. "Didn't you know I was out here, just waiting for a friend like you?"

My heart did a slow, painful turn in my chest. It was pathetic how easily he had me wrapped around his little finger. "Of course I didn't know. I'd have been dancing on top of every bar in town, instead of studying, if I'd known that."

He didn't laugh, as I'd intended, but leaned in close. "Tell me not to kiss you," he said, when his lips were a breath away from mine.

"Don't kiss me," I told him, my voice a breathless rasp.

"Mean it," he said, crowding me into the corner of the pool.

He tilted my chin up with his finger.

"I can't," I gasped.

The words had barely left my lips before he was kissing me.

I'd have been lying if I didn't admit that I'd spent a lot of time wondering what it would be like to kiss him, and even with all of the fantasizing, he didn't disappoint.

His kisses were drugging, his mouth hot and demanding, but his hands were gentle as he buried them in my hair.

I was lost. It didn't even occur to me to push him away. This was a bad idea, *but God*, I wanted him. I couldn't remember wanting to touch anyone so badly in my life.

Every touch showed me that he could barely restrain himself, and I loved it, his breath coming in hard little pants between kisses.

I wrapped my arms around his neck, pressing my breasts hard into his chest.

He pulled back briefly, gasping at that contact, before moving his mouth over mine again. The pleasure thickened, my blood beating in tune to the waves of need rocking into me.

One of his hands left my hair, stroking down my back. He gripped the back of my thigh, pulling it high on his hip as he moved against me.

I moaned as I felt his hardness pushing against me. It was only as we were grinding mindlessly against each other that I realized how fast things had gotten out of hand.

I wrenched free of him, and he let me.

"What are we doing?" I gasped.

"I don't know," he answered, looking stunned.

"That was stupid," I told him.

"That was stupid," he agreed, his rapt attention on my mouth.

"We need to get away from each other until we sober up some," I said slowly. "I think we're both feeling way too pretty right now."

He didn't say a word, but he got away fast enough.

We avoided each other for a solid hour.

I dried off, got dressed, and took a seat at Cory's bar. It wasn't smart, but I had another drink. I spotted Tristan on the other side of the room. He was smoking a cigarette, and talking to the brazen woman that had brushed up against him earlier.

I ordered another drink.

"Drinking alone tonight?" a familiar voice asked me from behind.

I turned, giving Jared a very big smile. "Not anymore," I told him with a vigorous toast.

He laughed, glancing behind me to nod at Cory. "I'll have

what she's having," he called to the other man. "So where's my brother?" he asked as he sat beside me. "This is the first time since I met you that you two weren't attached at the hip."

I nodded across the room, sneering when I saw what's her name laughing at something and touching his chest. "Unless I miss my guess, he's about to get lucky." I tried hard not to sound as upset about that as I actually was.

"He thinks I need to loosen up," I continued to Jared. "And I think he's a little *too* loose. It makes for an interesting friendship."

Jared flashed a stunning smile at me that was a close second to his brother's. "Dance with me."

I agreed readily enough, though I was more than a little disappointed when Tristan never even spared us a glance as we headed from the bar and into the next room.

Jared was a good dancer, but he was no Tristan, and he had even less trouble than his brother did getting right into my personal space.

I went with it, dancing close.

His hands gripped my hips. When he moved a thigh between mine, I angled out of his range, finding a safer position as I moved close again. He was determined, though, and we were dancing close, his face an inch from mine, within short minutes.

He leaned in to kiss me, his breath minty, and his lips half-tempting.

But hell, I thought, if I could resist full-on tempting, it was a breeze to turn down *half*. I turned my face away, and he moved his face into my neck, undeterred.

I giggled, his lips tickling me, before I pushed him back.

I shook a finger at him. "I don't know you that well," I chided.

He grinned a wicked grin. "Well, then, let's get to know each other better."

I rolled my eyes. "You and your brother are too much alike. Being man-whores must run in the family."

He laughed, un-offended. "We aren't that much alike," he said into my ear. "Tristan is strictly into hooking up. I'm the relationship type. In fact, I'm not all that crazy about being single."

"Well, I'm trying to be single for a while, though I'm not that crazy about it, either."

"Just let me know when that phase is over. I'd love to take you out."

"I'm not sure what your brother would think about that."

"It's not his business. You two are still just friends, right?"

I nodded.

"Well, friends don't get to tell each other who to date."

"What about brothers?" I asked pointedly.

"Brothers don't either, when they're being completely reasonable about it."

My mouth twisted ruefully.

"Just one date. At least give me that much. Let me take you out one night, whenever your dating ban is up. You don't have to decide right now, but at least tell me you'll think about it."

"I'll think about it."

We'd had our mouths at each other's ears for the entire conversation, and Jared took full advantage of that, nuzzling into the sensitive spot just behind my ear.

I pulled away, shivering.

I was certainly attracted to him, if not in the crazy, irresistible way I was to Tristan. But Tristan was a lost cause, and when I was ready to start dating again, Jared *was* dating material. I didn't know him well, but he was hot, in a skinny rocker kind of way, and he seemed nice and charming, if a touch forward.

"That's all I ask," he said, tugging me back into the bar, since we'd both stopped dancing several minutes before.

I didn't spot Tristan as we made our way back to the bar, and my gut twisted sickly. I shouldn't have been upset by the fact that he'd likely gone off somewhere to hook up with that skank.

I knew the score. He'd never been mine to lose. Not even close.

Still, I felt forlorn as the minutes passed, and he didn't show.

I wound up drowning my sorrows with another drink, and on a dare from the irrepressible Jared, I found myself dancing on one of the small tables that ran beside the pools.

I didn't notice that there was some guy sitting on the couch by the table until Jared was yelling at him.

I turned, my head notably fuzzy after that last drink, to find some creep crouched low, probably getting a pretty good look up my skirt.

I opened my mouth to tell the jerk off, but I was quickly distracted by the sight of Tristan descending on the man, murder in his eyes.

I stumbled back, shocked, as Tristan grabbed the man by the throat, nearly lifting him with just one hand.

A soft hand at my back had me turning to see Jared at my side. He held a hand up to help me down, and I accepted it gratefully.

"I'm sorry," he said into my ear. "I didn't see that piece of shit until after you'd started dancing."

I just nodded, accepting the apology, much more concerned with what Tristan was doing.

Security had become involved, separating the two men, who were both shouting obscenities at each other. I'd never seen Tristan like that, so angry and violent, and the sight was hard to look away from.

Jared tugged me away to my seat by the bar.

I searched out Cory, who was watching the altercation with wide eyes. I couldn't imagine he was happy to have his friend brawling at his job.

I was shocked when Tristan took a seat beside me within a few short minutes. He didn't look at me as he ordered a drink.

"What was that?" I asked him.

He shot me an annoyed look out of the corner of his eye. "That's what I'd like to know. What was that?"

"I was dancing. I didn't realize there was some creep on the couch. And I can't believe they didn't kick you out for attacking him."

Tristan opened his mouth to reply, but Cory distracted us both.

"Fuck. Holy fuck. Jesus, Tristan, here comes my boss. I hope to hell you didn't just get me fired."

I turned to see what he was talking about, and as a tall man with dark golden hair approached; my jaw went a little slack. I'd never seen a man so beautiful in my life.

He was slender, but not thin by any means. He was tan, with turquoise eyes that stood out like jewels even with the dim bar lighting. I'd seen pictures of the famous hotel chain owner, but Jesus, pictures did not do the man justice.

James Cavendish flashed white teeth at me in a charming smile, holding out his hand. I reached out my own automatically, still stunned that he was so...pretty? Stunning.

His warm hand enveloped mine in a comforting gesture. "I just wanted to offer my profuse apologies about what happened back there. That man has been escorted off the premises, and banned from the club. I happened to be visiting the club on business when I heard what had happened. Are you okay, Miss...?"

I swallowed hard, unnerved. "I'm, uh, Danika. And let me just say that *I'm* sorry. I was dancing on that table, and I probably shouldn't—"

"Now, now, Danika, I shudder to think that you'd be discouraged from dancing on tables after that. Don't let it be said that Decadence isn't the *best* spot in town to dance on a table."

I laughed nervously, not certain if he was joking or not.

The stunning man turned to address Tristan, who was

glowering at him.   James Cavendish didn't seem to notice, holding his hand out to shake.

"I'm James Cavendish, the club's owner."

They shook hands, Tristan looking confused.

"May I just say," James continued. "On behalf of my security, thank you for reacting so quickly. Please, let me know if we can do anything for you two, anything at all. Your drinks will be free for the evening, and I'll be sure to have the manager give you a voucher for a future visit. I'd hate to think that this unfortunate incident might discourage you from visiting the club again."

The charming, intimidating man continued on, graciously offering us comps, and making sure that we were well-settled, before moving on.

Tristan and I stared at each other with wide eyes after he'd gone. I was the first to start laughing, but Tristan joined in soon after.

I ordered shots, and Tristan gave me a searching glance.

"Don't you think you've had enough? You don't usually dance on tables..."

I stuck my tongue out at him. "At least I didn't choke anybody. I can't believe you didn't get in trouble for that..."

"I can't believe it, either."

"Were you *trying* to get arrested?" I asked him in my best drunk/lecturing tone.

He shrugged, which was infuriating. "I wasn't trying to get arrested, but I was willing to. No one gets to treat you like that."

I didn't know if I wanted to shake him, or hug him, the sweet bastard.

He reached over, snagging my hand. He linked our fingers, watching my face. "Are you okay? Was that...upsetting?"

That threw me. "I'm fine. I was mostly upset when I thought that you were going to get arrested, you crazy man."

He smiled. "I'd do it again in a heartbeat, even if they did arrest me.   You remember that, boo.   I've got your back.

Always."

I squeezed his hand, blinking back uncharacteristic tears, touched by his words.

CHAPTER THIRTEEN

I was in rough shape the next morning, to say the least.

I barely made it to the bathroom in time to throw my guts up into the toilet.

I felt my hair being messed with, but I couldn't summon up the will to turn and see what was going on.

"What the hell are you doing?" I bit out, before another wave of nausea hit me.

"Braiding your hair, boo," Tristan said, his big hand stroking my back comfortingly.

Even sick as a dog, I thought that was sweet. "I don't want you to see me like this. I'm disgusting." I punctuated that statement by further emptying out the contents of my stomach.

"Don't worry about me. You just let me know what I can do for you. You poor thing."

"Why don't *you* ever get sick?" I whined at him between bouts of throwing up.

"I weigh two twenty-five buck naked, sweetheart. I can handle a lot of alcohol."

Even nauseous and feeling disgusting, I took a moment to linger on an image of him naked. I wouldn't be human if I wasn't at least curious.

"That's not fair," I moaned.

"It's not. Can I get you anything?"

I shook my head. I thought my stomach might finally be empty, but I was afraid to hope for it.

"Why don't you try to sleep it off for a bit? I've got the boys and breakfast covered. Just go lie down."

I did. I was in no shape to refuse.

When I woke up again, I felt human, if only barely. I showered, and pulled on the first clean clothes I found.

The house was almost eerily quiet when I left my room. The only sign of life in the whole place was coming from the kitchen.

My stomach rumbled in a good way when I smelled what Tristan was cooking.

"I *need* one of those today," I told him, pointing at the hangover sandwich in his hand as I took my usual seat on the counter.

He brought it to me with a sympathetic smile. "Fresh coffee is brewing. I'll fix a cup for you when it's finished."

I thanked him, taking a huge bite, closing my eyes and chewing it slowly, enjoying every second of it, before swallowing.

I opened my eyes to find him watching me, his face carefully blank. "Where is everybody?"

"Bev and Jerry took the boys to the mall. It's Saturday, you know, not that we've been keeping track."

I devoured the sandwich, and then a cup of coffee, followed by two bottles of water. I felt like a different person when I'd finished it all.

"Thank you. You saved my life. I've never had a hangover like that before."

"Let's hope you never do again, either. How many drinks did you have last night?"

"I have no idea," I replied honestly. "But don't get all preachy about it with me. I got bored when you left to hook up with what's her name. I was just passing the time."

"Hook up with what's her name? What are you talking about? I didn't hook up with anyone. I spent half the night looking for you. Where did you disappear to, by the way?"

I glared at him. "I went and danced with Jared, and when we came back, you'd disappeared."

His brows drew together and his eyes were stormy as he replied, "I *disappeared* looking for you."

I studied his face, looking for a lie, but strange as it was, I believed him, and it scared me how relieved I was that he hadn't been hooking up. If I was this relieved that he hadn't, just how hurt would I be when he finally did? I knew it was coming. He'd given me more than fair warning.

"I have an idea," he said, moving around the kitchen counter, and into the dining room.

He opened up a drawer of the desk that ran along the far wall.

"That sounds ominous," I said, following him.

"On a scale of one to ten, how much do you like the last guy that you slept with?" Tristan asked me with an arched brow and a crooked smile, flashing those dimples at me. He used those things like a weapon.

"My ex? Negative five, since I'm feeling mellow right now," I said instantly.

He nodded. "Exactly. The last girl I hooked up with threw a drink at another chick for smiling at me, and the one before that started nagging me about my drinking after we'd hooked up *one time*. Sex turns women into nagging psychos, and it turns men into straight-up assholes. Now, how much do you like me?"

I wrinkled my nose at him. "Right this second? Well, this little speech is kind of annoying but I do *kind of* like you most of the time. I'll give you a solid five."

He just grinned, not at all offended. I don't think he would have known what to do with me if I wasn't giving him shit. "Well, I give you a *ten*, which averages our friendship out to a solid seven, making you one of my favorite people *of all time.* I'd like to maintain our average, so I say we make a list."

He had actually gotten a pen and paper out, and I made sure he saw me roll my eyes.

His grin just widened. "That's what I love most about you. I never have to wonder what you're thinking. It's all right there on your lovely face."

My scowl just deepened as I saw what he was writing.

'THE FRIENDS DON'T LIST' –
Because I like you too much to sleep with you

I sighed loudly. "What is the point of this? We don't need to write it down."

He straightened, giving me a look that made things low in my body clench in the most delicious way. His gaze was borderline obscene as he eyed me, top to bottom.

He swallowed hard. "*I* need to. God, Danika, even your feet are fucking sexy to me, and I like you too fucking much to screw it up. I want to be around you. I'd be sad if you we didn't see each other anymore, and I'm batting zero at the relationship thing. I'm a good friend, though, so yeah, I need a real clear 'don't' list, so I don't screw it up."

I smirked at him. "My feet, huh? My feet are really that sexy? You crazy horn-dog."

I didn't want a relationship with him, either. I knew that it would mean the end of us as friends, but knowing that he found me that sexy made me warm all over. It didn't make me feel dirty to have him look at me like that, it made me feel special. It was a novelty for me, to be sure.

He laughed and nodded, giving me really good eye contact. "Yes. It's a problem. I'm a man-whore, and you would tempt a saint. Let's find a way to keep our friendship safe."

I liked that, liked that he valued my company more than my

body. I nodded, finally giving him smile for smile. "Yes. That makes sense. Sex isn't worth it anyway. It never leaves me with anything but a need for a date with my vibrator, and that's if I'm lucky."

He groaned and slapped his forehead. "I need to get that image out of my head. That was cruel. Do you mean that your last boyfriend didn't make sure you got off?" He asked the question like he just couldn't help himself. I knew him well enough to know that he couldn't.

I laughed, trying not to make it sound as bitter as it actually was. "No. I'm saying that *none* of them did. They couldn't find a clit with a *map*. Selfish pricks."

He ran a hand over his face, and it went a little slack before he looked at me again. "That hurts me deep in my soul, Danika. I wouldn't do *that* to you. I'd make sure you came, first *and* last. I'd go down on you every time, if that's what you like. I'd lick—"

I held up a hand, giving him an arch look, though I was far from unaffected by his little speech. I wanted badly to see if he was really that good, but I shook myself out of it.

He grimaced. "Sorry, sorry. That was out of line. You can't tell me stuff like that. It makes me want to punch somebody and, well, do things to you that do not need to be spoken out loud. But it does prove my point about me needing a 'don't' list."

I nodded. It was becoming apparent that we both needed one. "Yes. Don't you worry about poor old me. I like my vibrator just fine. Better than any cock that's ever come near me, in fact."

He closed his eyes, lowered his head, and held up one finger as though he needed a moment.

I giggled, because I had been trying to torment him, and I saw by the oversized bulge in his jeans that I'd succeeded.

I snapped my fingers at him. "Okay, okay, let's get on with it.

Get started with your list."

1. No sex, no making out, no kissing.

"No getting off and thinking about you?" I asked. Yes, I was trying to torment him.

He held up that finger that made me giggle again. He looked like he was thinking hard for a long moment, finally shaking his head. "Nope. Can't do that. Sorry. It's like saying I won't get hard when I see you wearing a bikini. It would just be a lie. But I won't torture you with the details, I swear."

I nodded, still smiling. Teasing just never got old with him. He made it so much fun. He made absolutely everything fun. "The same," I told him. "I'll try not to be too loud when I cry out your name as I get myself off."

He shook his head, looking pained. "So jacked up," he muttered under his breath.

After a long pause, he started writing again without another word.

2. No getting jealous or complaining about who the other one is dating or hooking up with.

"That goes for you too, right?" I asked archly. "No hitting guys in bars for looking at me funny."

"I didn't hit him. I just choked him a little."

"Um, yeah, that sounds worse than punching. Not helping your argument."

He completely ignored that, writing.

3. We can hang out whenever we want, but we won't call it a date, even if we're doing date-like things

"Would oral be considered date-like?" I asked, just messing

with him, as usual. I'd never been able to have sexual banter with a man that didn't end up making me feel like shit. It was just the opposite with Tristan. For some reason, it made me feel warm and fuzzy every time.

He sent me a twisted grin. "I'm pretty sure that would be breaking the no kissing rule."

"Pretty sure leaves wiggle room."

He gave me a look that could only be described as longing. "I do love the way you wiggle."

I giggled.

He went back to writing.

4. No nagging.

"That counts for you, too. No telling me when I've had too many shots. That's for me to decide."

He sent me an exasperated look. "Well, if you drink enough shots that you climb on the bar to dance, and some guy grabs you, don't nag me for beating the shit out of him."

"That sounds like a clear violation of rule number," I pointed out.

"That's not jealousy. That's me being protective of my buddy."

I rolled my eyes. It was a fine line.

He started writing again.

5. Always remember that we like each other too much to sleep together, and that sleeping together will ruin EVERYTHING.

6. If the words 'I love you' are ever mentioned, it will be assumed that it is in a friendship type context.

7. No talking dirty, or talking about dates with your

vibrator.

He sighed, immediately crossing #7 out.

7. No talking dirty, or talking about dates with your vibrator.

"That one is just no fun at all," he explained.

I giggled. Only Tristan could make me giggle.

He sent me a warm smile.

"I named my vibrator after you," I told him with a smirk. "He's small, but he makes up for it by working hard."

He straightened, moving a little close to show me just how small he wasn't. I backed up to the edge of the table, and he followed.

He gave me his sinful smile. "I'm big like this everywhere. Don't make me prove it to you."

I rolled my eyes. "Every guy says that. It would be refreshing to meet a guy that just admitted to being average-sized, or God forbid, small."

He shook his head. "You want me to do something crazy. I see your game now. Not falling for it."

I couldn't hold back a smile, because I *had* been egging him on. The man was so outrageous, he'd do anything on a dare. I shrugged. "I'll never know, but in my imagination it's very clearly average, bordering on small. No way to change it."

He pursed his lips, his fingers going to the button on his jeans.

I slapped my hands over my eyes, running away and giggling like a kid.

He overtook me in seconds, picking me up easily. He flung me over his shoulder, heading to the back door.

I knew where this was leading.

"Put me down!" I screeched between giggles. "I just washed

my hair!"

"Every time you make me want to pull my dick out for you, for any reason, I'm throwing you in the pool. This is for the sake of our friendship, Danika."

I was already flying through the air before he'd finished talking. I heard him say Danika right before my head went under.

The bastard.

CHAPTER FOURTEEN

As though putting it in writing had somehow aggravated the situation, the sexual tension between us only seemed to get worse. Still, no one could say that we didn't try our best to stick to that stupid list.

I found myself at his mother's house for dinner the next day, which I found strange, and a little surreal, but he was persistent enough to talk me into just about anything.

She lived about forty-five minutes away, in one of the more rundown neighborhoods just east of the strip. Her house was big, but in rough shape at a glance, with huge chunks missing from the stucco, a disaster of a lawn, and two cars parked in the driveway that were missing tires.

I shot Tristan a glance. "She has two full-grown sons. Why don't you guys help her fix up the place?"

He'd been about to get out of the car, but he paused at that. His brow furrowed. "It's complicated. I've tried before, but her boyfriend takes it as an insult if someone else tries to make repairs to her house, even though he'll never do it himself."

"He sounds like a winner," I muttered, not quite under my breath.

As always, I was gratified to hear him laugh. My lips turned up in a happy smile. Not everyone could appreciate my brand of sarcasm, and I relished the fact that Tristan seemed to find it endlessly entertaining.

"He's...difficult, but I try not to make any waves. I learned a long time ago not to get between my mom and one of her boyfriends."

I thought that was telling, and I sent him a sympathetic look as we made our way to the house.

"I can relate to that," I told him quietly. "My mom once tried to kick me out of the house because I told one of her boyfriends that he wasn't my dad." I swallowed, finding it hard to tell him the story, for some strange reason. It wasn't as though it was a sensitive subject for me. "I was eight at the time."

He stopped and grabbed my hand, a world of understanding in his eyes. "I see more and more why we took to each other so quickly. We've been through a lot of the same things. It's...nice to have someone that just understands."

I squeezed his hand, losing myself a little in his golden eyes. "It *is* nice."

It felt like we shared a moment of perfect understanding, but it was short lived, as the front door opened, Jared poking his smiling face out.

"Hey!" he called out. "The food is ready. Good timing. Get in here." He popped his head back inside, rather reminding me of Ivan for a moment.

I liked Jared, but I didn't quite get him. He could be like a carefree kid at times, and almost too intense at others. I felt like I was missing some piece of the puzzle where he was concerned. He was so much easier than Tristan, in ways, but he worried me more, though I couldn't have said just why. One thing was certain; neither men were a puzzle that I expected to solve any time soon.

Tristan let go of my hand, which left me feeling a little bereft. I could admit to myself that I loved it when he held my hand. It made me feel so connected to him, for such a small contact.

He didn't leave me like that for long, his hand moving to the small of my back in a light caress that nudged me forward with him. "You're going to love my mother, but more than that, you're going to die for her enchiladas."

The house we walked into was crowded but colorful, the walls painted brightly, but a little too cramped with furniture and knick-knacks.

His mother was a surprise to me, for several reasons. She was young, or at least she looked very young. She could have maybe passed for Jared and Tristan's older sister, rather than their mother. The biggest surprise by far, though, was that she was very obviously Hispanic, with a thick accent. I'd always just thought of the brothers as big white boys.

"Mama, this is my friend, Danika. Danika, this is my mother, Leticia." He accented the name in a way I'd never heard him speak before, immediately showing me a touch of his Latin side.

I blinked, thrown for a bit of a loop.

Leticia was beautiful. There was a very obvious resemblance between the three of them. Their features all had a similar, striking cast, thought her eyes were black, and her skin was a few shades darker. Her thick black hair fell in heavy waves to her mid-back.

She gave me a smile, and it was lovely, but I noticed that Tristan must have gotten those dimples of his somewhere else.

She hugged me like family, kissing me on both cheeks. "So lovely to meet you, Danika. You may call me Mama, if you like. I never get to meet any of the girls Tristan spends time with. You must be special."

I caught Tristan shaking his head out of the corner of my eye.

"I wonder why I never bring any girls here...Really, Mama. Don't embarrass her."

"If she chooses to spend a lot of time with you, I doubt she's easily embarrassed," Leticia shot back.

I thought she had a good point.

"Dinner's getting cold," Jared pointed out from the doorway that led into a divine smelling dining room.

The table was small, but loaded with food.

"I'll do clean up, Mama," Tristan said, pulling out two chairs from the table, and nodding his mother and I into each, "since I missed helping out on all the prep."

"Gracias, mijomiho," she said, shooting him a very fond smile.

"Brown-noser," Jared muttered, from his seat directly opposite of me. I shot him a wry smile for that one. It's like he'd read my mind.

Tristan sat to my right, and for some crazy reason, I felt his big hand squeeze my knee after he sat down. I shot him a rather shocked glare, and he removed it just as quickly as he'd placed it there, his expression completely innocent. If he wanted to play the teasing game, I thought I had a distinct advantage. I wasn't the one that needed to jack off in the shower five times a day.

I shook myself out of that distracting thought process as everyone began to dish out the food. Leticia had a heaping serving on my plate before I could tell her it was too much.

The cheese enchiladas already had my mouth watering when Tristan spooned some black beans and rice onto my plate, and Leticia followed it with scoops of fresh pico de gallo, guacamole, and sour cream. Mother and son were tag-team overfeeding me, and I kind of loved it.

Leticia blessed the food, and I dug in eagerly. The first bite of the enchiladas had me closing my eyes, and I didn't even try to stifle my moan of pleasure. Enchiladas were my favorite, and these ones were a perfect combination of...everything. I thought it was the sauce that made it so perfect.

Tristan's big hand squeezing my knee again was what it finally took to get me to open my eyes. He was staring at me, and the look in his eyes was downright sinful. I swallowed, my jaw going a little slack with want as the hand on my knee caressed me, moving just a touch higher. I was wearing shorts, so it was skin on skin, and more than a little distracting.

I quickly snapped out of his little spell, glancing at Leticia and Jared. I was vastly relieved to see that they weren't paying attention to us, instead digging into their own food with gusto.

I took another bite, shooting him a glance. He was still rubbing my knee, and for some asinine reason, I wasn't pushing his hand away. Even more asinine, my left hand moved to cover his under the table, rubbing over his knuckles softly, then harder. I thought about touching him way more than I *actually* touched him, and so when I did, it always seemed to escalate way too fast. His hand was moving higher, and my own traitorous hand was only encouraging it, kneading his fingers harder into my thigh.

"So good, right?" Jared asked loudly, and I pushed Tristan's hand away, my face turning bright pink.

"So good," I agreed, meaning it, as I took another bite.

"The best," Jared added.

"Hands down," Tristan agreed.

I nodded, though I secretly thought that Tristan's had been just as good.

Leticia flushed with pleasure. "I have the sweetest sons in the world, don't I, Danika?"

I bit my tongue from making a sarcastic comment, playing nice instead. "They're both very sweet."

"A mother couldn't ask for more."

I was oddly touched when I caught the soft smile Tristan gave her for that comment.

Dessert consisted of stiff margaritas, which I thought said a lot. This family could *drink*, tiny mother included.

I was stuffed, and just a touch tipsy when the meal ended. I found myself lounging on a comfortable sofa in the TV room that directly connected to the kitchen, as Tristan and his mother cleaned up after dinner. I had a clear view of mother and son working in the kitchen together.

Jared joined me on the couch, sitting close, making a point to follow my gaze to his brother. "He's a good guy," he said quietly. "A good brother. He's had my back since I can remember, even if I was in the wrong."

"He's always looked out for you," I guessed.

"He can't seem to help himself."

"That's what big brothers are for," I explained.

Jared studied me. "You say that like you can relate. Are you a big sister?"

A familiar pain pinched at my chest. That pain never seemed to lessen. Time hadn't done a thing to numb it, which was why I supposed I did my best never to think about my little sister.

I swallowed hard, his prying not making me want to lash out, as it would have with Tristan. I felt no compunctions about lashing out at Tristan, but somehow I did with Jared. It felt like Jared and I were on equal footing, but somehow, even at his sweetest and most amiable, I always felt that Tristan had the upper hand, and in a way, that made it hard for me to open up to him.

I kept my eyes on Tristan where he was helping his mother in the other room, and my voice very impersonal. "I am. I have a younger sister, but I'm not like Tristan. I tried my best, but I was a shitty big sister."

I didn't look at him, but Jared sounded very sympathetic as he asked, "What happened?"

I shook my head, surprised that I actually answered the question. "Too much to go back from. She loathes me, and I don't blame her. We haven't spoken in years."

"Where does she live?"

"I couldn't say. She asked me never to contact her again, and I've respected that request." I didn't have words to express how hard that had been for me, to be utterly rejected by the only person in the world I'd considered real family. I'd loved her so much, but it hadn't been enough to keep me from failing her.

"How long ago was that?"

"Four years ago."

"Damn. How old are you?"

"Twenty-one."

"Me too," he said. I'd known his age, courtesy of Tristan, but Jared sounded surprised about mine. "So all of this went down when you were seventeen? How old was she?"

I swallowed, surprised that, of all of his probing questions, that one was the sorest wound. "Just fifteen. Just a baby."

"Don't you think enough time has passed for things to blow over? I'll bet she's not even mad anymore. You should try to find her."

I shook my head, not even considering the notion. Dahlia's rejection hadn't been about anger. It had been about betrayal, disgust, and contempt, and I didn't blame her for any of it. "It's not as simple as that." My voice was quiet, my tone final.

His hand clasping my own startled me enough to make me start violently, but I didn't push it away. I didn't look at him, because there was nothing on earth I wanted less than sympathy, and seeing it directed at me always inspired unpredictable results, but still, I let his hand comfort me for just a moment.

"I think you're too hard on yourself, Danika."

I'd heard that line before. Exhaustively, from Lucy, and Bev, and even a few times, Jerry. Everyone was always telling me that I was too hard on myself, apparently even people that I barely knew these days, thought so. If they were all right about that, I still didn't know what to do about it. I'd made some healthy changes for myself over the years, which had been largely instigated by the persistent Lucy, but I couldn't begin to know how to change something so fundamental to my nature. The fact was, I expected a lot from myself, and I was often disappointed.

125

Tristan turned, getting a good look at his brother and I, sitting close and clutching hands.   Of course he'd look just then, I thought wryly. I saw his jaw tighten, and knew he wasn't happy with what he saw.

Still, I was surprised when he strode right to us, his eyes boring straight into Jared.

"A word," he said through his teeth, then turned on his heel, striding out the back door.

Jared sighed heavily. "Well, fuck," he muttered.

He squeezed my hand lightly before standing and following his brother.

I could imagine what was going on back there. Tristan would be reaming his brother out for what he'd have taken as a direct come-on. And certainly his brother was capable of that. They both were.   But I didn't think that had been what Jared was about.   He was a genuinely nice guy, and I really thought he had just been offering comfort after asking a few too many awkward questions.

I'd told Jared that I would consider going out with him, when I was ready to date again, but I had to wonder if that was even an option.   I knew, just knew, that if I dated Jared, it would drive Tristan insane, no matter that he and I had firmly committed to just being friends. *What a mess*, I thought.

Leticia came to sit beside me.   Her eyes were on the back door, her brow furrowed.   I marveled again at how lovely she was as she turned her dark eyes on me.

"You aren't going to make my boys fight over you, are you?" she asked softly, glancing at the back door. It was sliding glass, but the brothers had moved out of sight right after they'd closed the door.

Her words struck me as a little hostile, but she didn't seem hostile, just concerned.

"I'm not." My words were soft, and even to my own ears they lacked any conviction. That made me defensive. "Tristan and I are strictly friends."

She shot me a sardonic look. She'd been sweet as sugar to me so far, but I saw the spicier side to her personality in that one look.

"You're a smart girl, but that's not a smart assessment. Strictly friends? Do you really believe that?"

My mouth twisted. "We're trying really hard to keep it that way. It's what's best for both of us."

She tossed her hair, and rolled her eyes. It made me smile. Who was *I* to knock a sassy woman? "Well, good luck to you, but I think you're fighting a losing battle. And God help you if Tristan decides he wants more. He's just like his father, and his father was *impossible* to resist, even when he was being a bastard. God, I loved that bastard. I named Tristan after him, in the hopes that he would be like that. His father could be callous, but...so charismatic. That man could get anything he wanted out of life. I wanted my son to be like that."

"You named him after his father that left you both?"

She did her little hair toss/eye roll. "I did, and I don't regret it. Tristan hates that I did that, but it makes perfect sense to me."

It did *not* make sense to me, and I was definitely siding with Tristan on that one, but I held my tongue. I didn't need to get into an argument with a woman I'd just met about something that was none of my business.

"And what about Jared? Did you name him after his father?"

"I did. I loved him, too."

"And did he leave, too?"

I knew I'd overstepped with that one, but it didn't seem to faze her.

"He stuck around for years actually. He was a very nice man. If you want to know the difference between the fathers, just look at the brothers."

That made me a little angry. I didn't think it was fair to compare Tristan to a man who had left his son with no father.

127

But then again, I had very similar baggage, so I *was* a touch sensitive about it.

"Has Tristan knocked up any girls, and then run in the other direction?" I asked, feeling riled.

She pursed her lips, sending me a sidelong look. "He hasn't. Not yet, anyway. You don't have to defend him to me. No one loves him more than I do."

"Then give him a little credit."

She waved her hands in the air, as though erasing the conversation. "Enough of the serious talk. I love my boys. That's all I meant. Don't make them hate each other."

"I would never—"

"Good. Then let's move on. Do you like mota?"

I just blinked at her, confused. "Mota?"

Hair toss. Eye roll. "Marijuana? Do you like?"

I shook my head vigorously. In my experience, only losers smoked pot, and so I'd always stayed far, far away from the stuff.

"Well, I like, so I hope you don't mind if I partake."

I shook my head again. "It's your house..."

The brothers were both smiling as they filed back into the house, which I found reassuring, but I was a little shocked when Leticia casually handed Jared a lit joint, and he just took it, thanking her.

Was this normal? Was I really such a prude?

She offered one to Tristan, but he waved her off, glancing at me.

"Don't deny yourself on my account," I said wryly, though I really didn't want him to. I hated the stuff.

He shook his head. "No, I'm good."

"What the hell was up with that move you made during dinner?" I asked him later as he drove us home in my junker of a car.

"Hmmm?" His tone and even his lying face were all

innocence.

"You know what. The hand on my knee. What was that all about?"

He sighed, dropping the act. "Fuck, I'm sorry about that. Just watching you eat with that look on your face... I lost my mind for a minute."

"You were being a tease. I'd recommend you not start playing *that* game with me."

"Is that a threat?" he asked, sounding all sorts of intrigued with the idea.

"It is. Don't start a war you can't win, my friend. In the battle of the teases, I would whip your slutty ass, you sex fiend."

He laughed so hard that he had to pull the car over.

"You know I'm right," I said, folding my arms over my chest.

He nodded. "I completely agree, but you know I can't turn down a challenge. Is that what you're doing? Making it a challenge?"

I shook my head. "No. There's no challenge. No competition at all, and I refuse to turn it into a bet."

He pulled the car back onto the street again, smiling and shaking his head. "That's a pity."

Dare I ask? "Why is that a pity?"

"Because I'd love to win *or* lose a bet like that. But you're right. It would be a stupid thing to do."

"*So* stupid," I agreed. We didn't say another word on the ride home, and I just knew that we were both thinking about how much we wanted to do something stupid.

CHAPTER FIFTEEN

We went a few days without managing to do anything stupid, but of course, that wasn't meant to last. The only surprising thing was, I was the first one to break open the stupid damn.

I woke up a few mornings later having the most graphic sex dream of my life.

It was Tristan's big hands on me in the dream, cupping my breasts and kneading, working down my belly, between my legs.

We were out in the pool, alone. Like most dreams, nothing quite made sense. Like, why were we skinny-dipping in the middle of the day? Still, my dreaming mind went with that eagerly.

I was lying on an inflatable lounge that we hardly ever used, because it was shaped in a huge circle, with the middle cut out, and the boys always found horrible ways to use it, like sticking each others' heads in the hole and dunking.

The hole was being used for an entirely different wrong way in my dream, though. Tristan filled the hole, his distracting torso spilling out of it as he used his mouth on me in the most distracting way.

I'd never had a guy go down on me before, and even in the dream my imagination was limited. He just nuzzled me there, his hands far more of a distraction.

I woke up with my panties around my knees, and my shirt pulled up to my neck. One of my hands was on a sensitive breast, kneading at it, the other fingering my clit with restless strokes.

It wasn't that I didn't care that Tristan was sleeping on the other side of my queen-sized bed, a big pillow all that separated us, it was more that I was too turned-on to let it deter me, and my sleepy mind told me that I could be quiet enough not to wake him. I'd gotten myself too worked up to stop, but I knew from experience that I needed more than my fingers to get myself off.

The hand on my breast reached over to my nightstand, opening the drawer very slowly, the finger on my clit still circling, again and again.

I tried not to make any noise as I fished out my vibrator, but the low vibrating sound that it made when I turned it on was louder than I could ever remember. Then again, I didn't have the luxury of turning on music to drown it out, as I usually did, with someone dead asleep in the bed next to me.

I gasped as I shoved it inside of me. I was wet from the dream, and it slid right in. I used one hand to hold it there, the hand from my breast moving to work on my clit.

My eyes were closed, my breath coming out in quiet little pants. They only opened as I felt the bed moving.

That movement should have made me stop, or panic, or do anything at all besides moan, shift the wand inside of me, and bite my lip as I glanced over at the gorgeous man moving towards me.

Stupid, stupid, stupid, I told myself.

More, more, more, my body screamed back.

Tristan made a guttural sound, low in his throat, and I couldn't hold back my own low moan.

I was under the covers, but so was he, so that hardly helped.

I didn't protest when he pulled them off both of us.

He moved close, crouched at my side, his knees a breath away from my hip and thigh. The look in his eyes was... intoxicating.

He bit his lip, and I felt myself clench around the wand in response.

My legs were splayed apart, and he moved to straddle one of my thighs, looming over me, but still not touching.

I watched him swallow hard, his eyes fixed on my hands.

I squirmed.

"Can I...help?" he asked hoarsely.

I couldn't even form the words to answer, just whimpering and shifting restlessly instead.

He took that for a yes. One of his hands covered the hand that held the wand, tugging it up my body.

I started to protest as it started to slip out of me, but his knee caught it, pushing it deep inside of me.

"Ohhh..." I gasped.

He moved my hand until I was cupping my own breast. He squeezed my wrist, which in turn made me knead harder at my pliant flesh.

"Pinch your nipple," he told me, licking his bottom lip. I felt my own tongue copy the motion as I obeyed.

My eyes, hungry to take him in, shot from his intent face, down his ripped torso, past the sexy V formed by the muscles at his hips, and to his heavy erection. He still wore boxer briefs, but they barely contained his jutting cock. I gyrated my hips, trying to get closer to his knee, and grinded the vibrator deeper inside of me.

"Mmmm," he moaned. "That's right, Danika. Perfect. Circle your hips just like that."

His other hand moved over the hand I had on my clit, not touching anything but the back of my hand as he took over the movements.

I circled my hips, while he moved my hand to circle my clit with just the perfect pressure.

He moved the hand at my nipple to my other breast, nearly touching my skin as he rubbed my fingers deep.

He cursed long and fluidly.

I caught movement at the bottom of my vision, and looked down to see his erection visibly twitch, pre-come soaking his boxers where they touched the tip of him.

"Tristan," I moaned.

I closed my eyes, a heady orgasm washing over me in lush waves.

"Danika," he rasped, his knee jerking up until it was no more than a whisper away from my entrance.

He moaned, long and low.

I didn't open my eyes again until I felt him moving away. The wand slipped partially out of me, and I pulled it the rest of the way out, hastily turning it off as I rolled over to look at him.

He'd flung himself onto his back beside me, his arm thrown over his eyes.

His breathing was harsh.

I swallowed, my eyes moving down his body. "Did you, um…?"

He sucked in a breath. His voice was low. "Please, don't ask. I haven't embarrassed myself that bad since I was a teenager."

I glanced down, the state of his shorts, and his words, telling me clearly what the answer was.

I lay down on my back, pulling the covers up to my neck. I was a little in shock about what I'd just done. What the hell was wrong with me?

My hormones had ignited, and I was pretty sure I'd lost some important brain cells in the fire.

"Fuck, what was that?" he panted.

"That was crazy," I gasped. "And stupid. Especially stupid."

"If that was your first attempt at winning the teasing war, I'm not sure if you just won or lost it all with one try."

In spite of myself, I giggled. "There is *no* teasing war. Get that out of your head. This is not a contest. This is a disaster that never needs to happen again."

"Seriously, though, if I wake up to that again, I'm not sure what I'll do, Danika."

"It won't happen again, so don't worry your pretty little head about it."

"And what if I...accidentally start jerking *myself* off in my sleep?"

"Stop it. You're incorrigible."

"And you are the queen of all teases. You know I'll never get that picture out of my head...Fuuuuck. Do you have any idea how much this messes with me?"

I sighed. "I think I have a pretty good idea, Tristan. Can we just...never mention this again?"

"I can try, but that doesn't mean I won't be thinking about it."

"Yeah, I know." There was no way *I'd* ever forget the look on his face as he'd helped me get myself off.

"Just let me ask you one thing, before I drop the subject forever."

I blew my breath out in a noisy sigh. "Go for it."

"What started that?"

"I was having a...sex dream. I think I can feel some sympathy for the wet dream thing guys have now."

"Was it about anyone specific?" he sounded more than idly curious.

"No," I lied through my teeth. "And that was more than one question."

"One more, I swear, and then I'm done. What was the dream about?"

"I was getting oral on a floatie in the pool."

He cursed fluently, and he didn't ask me any more questions.

R.K. Lilley

CHAPTER SIXTEEN

The next 'stupid' incident started with an unexpected package, a chicken murdering hound, and the dog chase from hell.

Ivan was at the table, working on his daily journal entry, and Mat was busy scribbling in one of his coloring books.

It was raining out, a summertime Vegas flash flood, but it was still hot as hell. I wore a thin white tank top, and my favorite sassy pants shorts.

I was just correcting Ivan's spelling when the doorbell rang. I shot an annoyed look at Jerry's closed office door. He and Tristan had been in there for hours, discussing supposed 'band' things, but it was the closest room to the front door, and I was right in the middle of lessons, so it seemed to me that one of them should answer it.

As though they'd read my mind, the office door opened, and both men stepped out, serious looks on their faces, as though they really had been discussing 'important business'.

Tristan opened the front door, greeting the UPS guy. UPS guy needed a signature, so Tristan stepped back, opening the door wider. Jerry moved in to sign.

My last thought right before all hell broke loose was how strange it was that no dogs had crowded at the front entrance as soon as they'd heard the doorbell.

136

One lone bastard of a dog shot straight from the hallway and out the front as though he'd been planning for just this moment.

"Coffeecup!" I shouted, pointing like a crazy woman.

Everyone just turned and stared at me, instead of at the dog I'd been yelling about. Perfect.

I grabbed a leash off its hook in the hallway by the kitchen, shoving my feet into a pair of Bev's running shoes. I was following that crazy dog out the door in less than thirty seconds.

Please let the chickens be locked up tight, please let the chickens be locked up tight, was a mantra in my head as I booked it across the neighborhood.

I was a fast runner. I went to great pains to stay in good shape, and jogged outside whenever the weather allowed. Which was why I was surprised when Tristan was suddenly running beside me, and then passing me.

I wasn't sure when he'd left the house, but I was sure it'd been *after* I had.

I saw a flash of spotted brown fur at the corner of my vision, and turned on my heel. We were still several house rows away from the stables, which meant we actually had a shot at saving some chickens.

Coffeecup hesitated at one house, sniffing out something, and I pounced, diving for him. The rain had already made his coat slick and wet, and he wriggled out of my arms before I could get the leash on his collar.

I screamed curses at him as I scrambled back to my feet, resuming the chase.

I nearly cheered as Tristan intercepted him in the muddy ditch that led up and directly into the stables. He gripped the dog's collar, hooting with laughter. We were sharing rather smug smiles as I approached, when Coffeecup pulled a ninja dog move and slipped out of his collar, darting for the stables.

Tristan tackled him, grabbing him around the chest to hold him back.

I dug into the mud for his collar, glaring at the stupid dog while I tightened it around his neck, one rung tighter than the last time, since it had apparently been loose enough for him to slip out of. I clipped the leash on, still catching my breath.

"You look like you couldn't decide whether you wanted to mud wrestle, or be in a wet T-shirt contest," Tristan said with a laugh, having to shout to be heard over the downpour.

I looked down at my sopping wet, muddy white tank top. He had a point...but *he* hadn't faired any better.

I pointed at him. "So do you! You look worse, in fact. I'm not the one on their back in the mud!"

I shouldn't have said it. It was too much like a challenge, and I should have known better than to offer Tristan a challenge.

His hands snaked behind my knees, pulling me down with him, until my bare knees sank heavily into the mud on either side of his hips.

"You son of a bitch!" I said, but I was laughing.

"I'm pretty sure saying that is a faux pas, now that you've actually met my mother."

"My bad. I take it back. Here, accept my sincere apology." As I spoke, I reached down, gripping a heavy handful of mud. I was giving him my sweetest smile as I smeared it on top of his head.

He gasped, and then gave me the most evil grin. "You're gonna pay for that," he said through his teeth.

I tried to get up, but one hand on my hip kept me straddling him. He had the advantage, with much bigger hands, and the huge gob of mud that he smeared over my chest far outweighed the bit I'd put on his head.

I gasped in outrage. "That was so much worse than what I did to you! So rude!"

He laughed, muddy hand going to my other hip. "Really? A handful of mud on your chest is worse than what you just did to my head?"

"Well, let's see," I said, diving for more mud. My target was no secret. I went for his face.

He caught both of my wrists, pulling them far apart, which brought our chests flush.

I rubbed against him, smearing as much mud as I could from my thin white shirt onto his. The motion of our chests rubbing together had our playful mood changing in a hurry.

He brought my wrists behind my back, pushing me down until my hips were crushed to his. As though they had a mind of their own, my hips moved, bearing down. My entire body seemed to shudder as I made contact with his obvious erection.

Our faces were close, and I couldn't have said whether it was him or me that moved first, but our lips met in a furious clash. He lay back, and I followed him down, moaning into his mouth as his tongue swept into mine, invading like he owned the place.

His kiss was insidious, seeping into every part of me. He took me over in a way I couldn't believe I allowed. A few seconds into the kiss, and I was ready to relinquish all control, which I'd have sworn was the antithesis of everything I was before I'd met Tristan.

He let go of my hands, his fingers sinking into my ass as he pushed his straining cock right into the center of me.

I'd never considered myself to be a particularly sexual person, but I was mindless in that moment, every part of me sexual, focused only on the heavy beat of desire in my blood— on having him inside of me.

I gripped one hand into his short hair, the other reaching down his chest, over his hard abdomen, and finally over his thick length, rubbing.

He panted against me, and I bit his bottom lip. He growled, delving back into my mouth.

God only knows how far we would have let things go but for a shrill scream that echoed to us from the stables.

139

I yanked back, looking around, totally confused for a moment as to where I even was.

Finally, the sight of my hand, my empty hand, where the leash should have been held, jarred me back into the problem at hand.

"Coffeecup!" I yelled, stumbling to my feet.

Tristan used his hands on my hips to help leverage me up, and I was off, sprinting towards the stables, hoping that I wasn't too late to save at least some of those damned prize chickens.

It was a massacre.

Feathers and blood made a trail that led me to right to the chicken murdering dog, who would still have been happily murdering away, if one parka-covered crazy chicken lady didn't already have his leash in hand. She was literally shaking with rage as I took the leash out of her hand. She pointed at me accusingly, as though I had been the one to behead—I counted one, two, three of her chickens. *Damn*, but he was efficient at murdering chickens. This had to be a record.

"I'm so so sorry—" I began.

"The home owners association will hear about this!" she cut in.

I nodded, my eyes wide, not sure how to handle her. We only ever saw each other when stuff like this happened, so I'd only ever seen her crazy side. As far as I knew, she was straight crazy chicken lady all the time.

"That dog is a menace!" she shouted.

I nodded again. I couldn't argue with that. I didn't point out that if she didn't let her chickens run loose around the stables all the time, they wouldn't make such easy targets for blood-thirsty Coffeecup. I knew from experience that trying to form any kind of defense only made her crazier.

Tristan approached right as she was storming off, still muttering curses at an ironically contrite looking Coffeecup.

"Well…" he said, running a hand over his muddy head. "That

could have gone better."

"You broke your promise, you know," I told him as soon as crazy chicken lady was out of earshot.

He raised a brow in question, trying ineffectually to dry himself off with his hands.

"You promised that if Coffeecup got out while you were around, you'd catch him before he murdered any chickens."

"Um, I did catch him. If you'll recall, I caught him back in that muddy ditch over there. You're the one that let him go again."

He had a point there.

"We broke half of the rules on our list back in that ditch," he told me as we made our way back to the house.

"I'm well aware."

"I think I know what the problem is." He sounded resigned, and troubled. I didn't particularly want to hear what had him sounding so serious.

"We're stupid and a little nuts?" I guessed.

"I've been celibate for too long, and now I'm taking it out on you. I need to blow off some steam, ya know?"

That stung. It shouldn't have, but it hurt bad. I was on board with the friend thing, but the idea that this attraction between us had more to do with his own sexual frustration, and nothing to do with how he might feel about me, well, it made me want to cry, which made me feel like a particularly stupid girl, and I *hated* that feeling. I liked to think that my head ruled me, not my heart, and being around Tristan played havoc with that idea.

"I think I'll go out tonight…by myself."

Ouch, ouch, ouch, I thought. "That makes sense," I said. "I need to catch up on sleep, anyway. This crazy clubbing schedule is not my thing."

"I'll still make you breakfast in the morning," he offered.

I grimaced, wondering if he would even be home in the morning. "Don't worry about it. I'll manage."

He snagged my hand, stopping our progress to look at me. I

squinted at him, rain falling straight into our faces. This was no place to have a chat.

"Are you upset?"

I shook my head. "Of course not," I said instantly, my tone dismissive.

I *was* upset, but I didn't have a right to it, so I refused to acknowledge it out loud. I had too much pride for that.

"How the hell are we going to go into the house like this?" I asked, changing the subject. "We're covered in mud. Maybe we should just stay in the rain, until it washes off."

"The backyard hose," he suggested.

That turned out to be a bad idea, even if it was our only option. Someone who you badly want to sleep with, but have decided that you won't, is not the person you want to hose down with water in a hot, hot rainstorm.

I was in a black mood after that, but tried hard not to show it. As I went through my daily chores, played with the boys, and put them to bed, I just felt...down and...sad. And as I realized how depressed I was feeling, that's when it occurred to me just how happy I'd been since Tristan had come along, hangovers and all. I'd been...giddy lately, the days flying by, as though in a dream, and it suddenly felt as though it was all crashing down on me.

What were we *doing*? Hanging out constantly and playing house? What did it mean? *Nothing*. Nothing at all. Well, except for one thing. I was a stupid girl, and I had feelings for a guy who was basically a walking hormone where women were concerned.

Tristan seemed to sense my mood, and he turned extra affectionate. Nothing blatant. No come-ons. Just a shoulder rub, a random kiss on the forehead, or a careless hand stroked over my hair, with lots of questions like, "Is everything okay? Are we cool?"

I gave answers like, "I'm just tired," and, "I need to catch up on sleep."

I never slipped up once, never told him that I hated that he was going out without me, and especially that I hated why he was doing it. I kept my pride, if nothing else.

Tristan was beyond sweet, helping me put the boys to bed, and even playfully insisting on tucking me in before he went out.

He wasn't going any place with a dress code, I noted, by his black T-shirt and jeans. Still, he looked too gorgeous to be real, and I hated how easy I knew it would be for him to find some random girl to fuck.

"Don't wait up for me," he told me with a wink.

I made sure he saw me roll my eyes. "I'll be asleep before Kenny even picks you up."

I didn't cry after he'd gone, but it was just as troubling to me that I had to make an effort not to. Eventually, I fell into a fitful sleep.

The sound of the bathroom door closing, and then the shower turning on, woke me.

My tired eyes found the clock. It was four a.m. Tristan was just getting home. I was suddenly wide awake.

I waited in silence when he finally finished his shower, walking quietly to his side of the bed.

"Did you get lucky?" I whispered as he settled in.

He froze, and then he was hugging me from behind, his voice a rasp in my ear. "You waiting up for me, boo?"

"No. I just woke up when you opened the door. So did you? Get lucky?" I held my breath as I waited for his answer.

He sighed. "I did. Hopefully I can control myself now. Our friendship is safe." He patted my hip comfortingly as he said it, like he'd done it for me.

He'd washed the other woman off him. Or at least, I didn't smell anything like that on him. But I still smelled the alcohol on his breath, and there was something about his voice, not a slur, but something more subtle, some sense of disconnect in his tone that made me think he was high, or at least very drunk.

I shut my eyes tightly, cursing the tears that bled down my cheeks.

It took me forever to get to sleep. I just lay there for a long time, calling myself every kind of fool.

CHAPTER SEVENTEEN

I woke up in black mood. I put on a good show for the boys, but I all wanted to do was curl up in a ball, and be alone for days. The fact that Tristan stayed in bed for most of the morning didn't help.

I was feeling...self-destructive was the best way to put it. I was finding it nearly impossible not to do something that would distract me from the fact that I was feeling tender, and wounded. I wanted to do something phenomenally stupid, like call my ex.

Which was why it was such horrible timing that Jared chose that morning to call me. I'd given him my number, in a friendly sort of way, days before. I'd saved his into my cell at the time, so I knew right away who was calling me.

We were outside, and the boys were playing in their tree house. They were playing the usual tree house game, where Ivan attacked the tree house with an invisible army, and Mat and I had to defend. This usually involved me sitting in the cramped little wooden structure, pointing out of the opening, and firing my finger at a worked up Ivan about every three minutes, while Mat did all of the ground work; basically spazzing out in a circle around the tree. Often, I found this highly entertaining, since the boys seemed to have a ridiculous amount of knowledge about warfare, courtesy of cable. Today, though, I was just phoning it in, pointing my finger, and shooting on cue with little enthusiasm. Luckily, it seemed to make no difference to a six and an eight year old.

I stared at my phone for a long moment when it began to ring, and I saw who it was, but I answered, wanting a distraction, even a self-destructive one. I supposed that Jared was a better option than my ex.

"Hello, Jared," I answered.

"Hey! Danika. Listen, I know you said you weren't up for a date or anything yet, but I was thinking we could just go to dinner. Just a friendly dinner, nothing fancy. How does that sound?"

It sounded like a date. *Did I care?* Not just then. I knew it was shitty, since he was Tristan's brother, but I wanted so badly to just be distracted for an evening. Distracted from Jared's *brother*, in particular. I told myself that would be enough to help me stop thinking about Tristan. Some corner of my brain even acknowledged that I also wanted badly to be able to tell Tristan that I had plans if he wanted to do something that night, or even if he didn't.

So I had a crush on Tristan? So what? It had developed quickly, and I swore that it would fade even faster.

Jared was still talking, his tone cajoling, as he tried to make it sound like he wasn't asking me out on a date.

"Sure. Yeah, I'd love to, but it will have to be a late dinner," I interrupted.

"Great. Perfect." He sounded pleased but surprised. "What time should I pick you up?"

I chewed on my lip as I thought about it. "Nine o'clock should be good, but I'd rather meet up somewhere."

"That works. Is there a place you'd prefer for dinner?"

"Chipotle."

"Um...that sounds very informal."

"It's not a date, right? Nothing fancy, you said."

He laughed, and it reminded me so much of Tristan that I wanted to cry.

"Fine, fine. That works. Aren't you close to the Beltz Mall? How about we meet up at the Chipotle over there?"

"Sounds good. I'll see you then."

I was just hanging up when I caught sight of the sliding glass door opening, a rough looking Tristan stepping outside.

He was the picture of remorse as he approached me, giving me an endearing smile that made my heart twist. "I slept in. I didn't mean to. I promised you breakfast. How can I make it up to you?"

I shook my head, waving that off and trying not to feel horrible about going out with his brother. All of my reactions were off when it came to Tristan. I should not have felt so broken up about the fact that he had slept with some random girl last night, and I should not feel guilty about spending time with his brother. But, strictly friends or not, I felt both.

"I am fully capable of making breakfast," I told him.

"I know, but I still wish I hadn't slept in. I *like* doing nice things for you. I like spoiling you. I like doing anything at all for you, as long as it makes you smile."

I looked down, pretending to study my phone, blinking back ridiculous tears.

"What would you like to do tonight?" he asked, moving as close as he could get to me through the opening in the tree house. "I'm getting my car back today, so we can go anywhere. I'll let you pick this time, and I'll drive. We'll go wherever you like and I'll treat."

I swallowed. "I have plans, actually. Maybe another night." It hadn't felt nearly as good as I'd thought it would to turn him down.

"Oh?" he inquired, still smiling. "Another girls' night so soon?"

"No, not that. That's not for a few days. I'm just going out...

147

with a friend."

"A friend? Just one? She can come with us, or I could tag along with you."

"It's...not like that. It's just a dinner thing, with a friend. Just the two of us."

His smile died, his brows drawing together, though his expression was still just curious. "Who's this friend?"

I shrugged.

"Is this a girl friend or a guy friend?" he asked, just as though he had the right.

I cleared my throat. "It's a guy, though it's not a big deal. Like I said, we're just going out to dinner."

He nodded, rubbing his jaw and looking at his feet. "It's not your ex, is it?" he asked quietly, his voice low.

"It's not," I rushed to answer, a little defensive because I *had* considered that idea, albeit briefly.

"Just a friend, huh?" he asked blandly.

"Yep."

"So why does it have to be just the two of you? That seems more like a date to me."

I felt my temper rise a bit. "What if it *was* a date? Would there be something wrong with that?"

He moved into the small opening, bringing his face close. I was sitting cross-legged, and his hand found my knee, squeezing lightly. "I thought you said you weren't going to date for a while? Didn't Lucy tell you that you should avoid that for now, and didn't you agree with her?"

"I thought we agreed we weren't going to nag each other? Wasn't that on our stupid list?"

"There's a difference between nagging, and expressing concern."

"Now you sound like Lucy," I said dryly.

"Who is this guy you're going out with tonight? Why have I never heard about these plans until today?"

I hated, absolutely *despised*, that he sounded like a concerned parent just then. "How about we add this to our list? I don't get to ask you about who you fucked last night, and you don't get to ask me who I go out with."

He looked around, eyes wide. "Watch the language. The kids."

The boys had moved on as soon as we'd started having grown up talk. They were currently wrestling with Pupcake in the sandbox by the fence.

"You should fucking talk," I pointed out sharply.

"I've gotten better, haven't I?"

He had a point. He'd improved his language around the kids faster than anyone could have predicted.

"Fine, I'll drop it," he said, his tone dark. "What time is he picking you up?"

"I'm meeting him somewhere at nine."

"That seems late. And he can't even be bothered to pick you up? You can do better, boo."

"You're an ass," I told him, taking exception to the bite in his tone. "It was my idea to meet up."

"Hiding him from me? You worried I'll scare him off?"

I let out a noise of frustration through my teeth, wanting to throttle him.

"Sorry. I *am* being an ass. I'm just feeling, I don't know… overprotective? The thought of you being alone with some strange guy makes me…worry."

"Well, don't. Where I'm concerned, *all* the damage has already been done. There's nothing left to protect me from."

He'd begun to back off, but at my words, he moved close again, studying my face, that big warm hand back on my leg. "What on earth does that mean?"

I blinked rapidly. I couldn't believe I'd said something like that, and to *him*. Already, there was sympathy in his voice, enough sympathy to have me blinking back tears. I *hated* sympathy, but was somehow always strongly affected by it. "It's nothing. Certainly nothing you want to hear about."

"I certainly do. *Please*. I want to know just what you meant by that. What damage has already been done?"

All of it, I thought. "Nothing," I said.

He didn't buy that for a second. "We're friends. You can tell me anything."

I mulled that over. Was that true? I was in a mood to find out. "Promise you won't feel sorry for me," I whispered, my eyes on the kids, making sure they were out of trouble, and out of earshot.

"I promise," he whispered back, his other hand reaching into the tree house opening and pulling at my shoulder to tug me further out. I let him, not even protesting when he had my legs out, his chest pressed against my bent knees. "Tell me."

I grimaced. "It's nothing, really. It's old news, and not even that big of a deal. It's just...you never have to be protective of me. I can take care of myself, and even if I can't, I know from experience that I'll survive it, whatever it is."

"I don't like the sound of that," he said softly, one of his hands moving into my hair.

Gently, he turned my head to look at him. "What the hell does it mean? Did someone *hurt* you? Are you talking about your ex? Do I need to go and hurt *him*?"

I shook my head. "He was a mistake, and a royal asshole, but no, that's not what I meant. Though you can't protect me from assholes, either. That's my choice to make. What I mean is that I'm not some innocent kid. I haven't been innocent in a very long time, so don't go thinking that you need to protect me, as though I am."

"Is that really what you think? That only innocents deserve protection?"

The bastard had pulled a Lucy on me. *Is that really what I thought?* As I considered the question, I realized that I did, at least as it pertained to me.

I was embarrassed by that realization, but it didn't change my thinking. My issues were too deeply ingrained for that.

I shrugged, turning my head to look away from him. He didn't let me, bringing his other hand to tip my chin up.

"Will you tell me what happened?" he asked, something in his tone making me think that he already *knew*.

"I will," I allowed, "but not right now. Okay?"

He didn't look happy about that, but he nodded, his hands dropping away.

CHAPTER EIGHTEEN

I didn't know who was more out of sorts after that.

I had effectively spread my black mood to Tristan, and we steered clear of each other for hours.

I was slipping my feet into my tennis shoes, getting ready to take the dogs for a walk, when Tristan approached me with a cajoling smile.

That smile was nothing but Trouble.

"I just got a call to do a promoting job tonight. Come with me. It'll be fun. You can go out with what's-his-name some other night."

I glared at him, snapping the dogs into their leashes.

He took Coffeecup and Pupcake's leashes, unfazed by my hostility. I let him, not speaking until we'd nearly circled the block. "I'm not changing my plans tonight."

"Well, how late are you planning to stay out? You could come by the club after you're done."

"Stop," I said quietly, my expression hard. "Why are you pushing this?"

"Are you really going to be out that late? What exactly are your plans?"

"Just stop!" I nearly shouted, angry now, at him—at both of us. "You don't get to go out and do whatever the hell you want, and then ask me about what *I'm* doing."

He gripped my arm just above the elbow, stopping me. "Is that what this is? Are you mad at me about last night? Is this *revenge*?"

"Why would this be revenge? *How* would it be revenge? We're just friends right? We're still sticking to that little list, right?"

He nodded, studying me. He looked worried. "You *are* mad at me. Fuck, Danika, I'm sorry if I hurt—"

"Don't," I interrupted him. "I'm not hurt. I'm just fine, but we need to establish some boundaries here. You can go fuck whoever you want whenever you damn well please, but you don't get to keep tabs on me, just because I'm a girl. That's not happening."

His jaw clenched, and he let go of my arm.

He didn't say another word about it, but if I'd thought he was in a foul mood earlier, it was nothing compared to the dark mood that conversation put him in.

He went out before I did that night. I was still getting ready when he left. He'd barely said a word to me—barely looked at me, since we'd walked the dogs.

He barely looked at me now, just hovered in the doorway of my bathroom while I put on makeup. "Be careful, boo, and call me if you need me."

He left before I could respond.

I wore cuffed navy shorts, and a sleeveless, magenta, bib style silk shirt. A pair of flip-flops made it a casual look. I twisted my black hair into a smooth chignon at my nape. Smoky eyes and soft pink lips was the extent of my makeup. I wanted to look nice, but I certainly didn't want to go overboard and give him the wrong impression.

Jared's reaction when he saw me was enough to make me flush in pleasure. "You look amazing," he said, swallowing. "You're so beautiful."

The brothers sure know how to make a girl feel good about herself.

Jared looked pretty good himself, in just a black T-shirt and jeans. He had the skinny rocker hunk look down pat. Aside from his build, he reminded me so much of Tristan that it made my heart twist just to look at him.

Dinner was friendly enough. I bombarded him with questions about the band I was so curious about. Everything about Tristan fascinated me, and the fact that he was in a band, and I'd met most of its members, but still hadn't heard them play, consumed an unhealthy amount of my thoughts. Tristan didn't share much about the band, but his amiable brother was more than happy to.

"Dean is putting together some gigs for us soon."

"Do you have to call them gigs? Isn't there a less douchey alternative to calling it a gig?"

He laughed richly, reminding me so much of his brother. "We have some *performances* coming up. Is that better?"

"Yes. Am I invited?"

"Of course you are!"

"Will you tell me when they're happening?"

"I will, though I'm sure Tristan will tell you first."

"Will you be sure to tell me anyway? In case Tristan doesn't..."

"Okaaay. Are you two fighting or something?"

"No. Why?"

"I just got that feeling. And just so we're clear...You two still aren't dating, right?"

"Still not dating," I said through my teeth, not sure how I felt about the whole thing. Nothing sucked worse than having feelings for someone who just may have been your best friend. Especially when that someone clearly didn't return those feelings.

"I'm sure you know this, but Tristan warned me—ordered me

rather, not to ask you out."

"I know."

"Normally I'd respect that, but if you two aren't dating...or hooking up, I thought that was completely out of line, so I ignored him."

"I know," I said with a smile, though something in my gut twisted at the notion. Would Tristan have warned his brother off if he wasn't *at all* interested? But then again, I'd always known he was attracted to me. He'd never made a secret of that.

"So I know *this* isn't a date," he continued with that engaging smile that ran in the family, "but maybe sometime, down the road, when you're dating again, we can go on a date."

"Maybe," I allowed, returning his smile.

"So there's this party tonight, some big house party. Wanna go?"

"I don't think so. I won't know anybody."

"You'll know me. And you'll meet some of my friends. Have you met Dean?"

"I haven't." I'd almost met the band's mysterious fifth member a few times, but it had never actually happened.

"Well, it's your lucky night. He'll be there. And this cool chick Frankie will be there. She's a tattoo artist, and she's getting her own reality show, so she'll be famous soon. I bet you two will love each other. She'll hit on you, because you're gorgeous, but that's to be expected."

"I don't think it's a good idea. Don't you think Tristan will be pissed if he finds out we we're hanging out? I went out of my way not to tell him who I was going out with tonight."

Jared shrugged, unconcerned. "Who will tell him? He's working tonight, so he won't be coming, and I can guarantee Dean won't say a word. If we run into anyone else, I doubt they'd make the connection between you and him. So he's still staying with you, huh? I can't believe his apartment isn't ready yet..."

155

That gave me pause. Not that the apartment wasn't ready, but the fact that I'd never given a thought to how long he'd been at the house, and some part of my brain had even forgotten that he was supposed to be leaving soon. Originally, he'd only been staying for a week, but that week had come and gone in a flash.

"We can just go for a little bit," he cajoled. "It's only twenty minutes away. I'll drive, and I'll bring you back to your car whenever you ask. It's a pool party. We can go swimming. I promise it'll be fun."

I *did* have a suit in the car, packed from my last excursion to Decadence.

"Do you mind if we just go for an hour or so?" I asked.

He took that as my capitulation, and his smile widened. "That sounds perfect."

We wound up somewhere to the west of the strip. And what he called a 'house party' was held in a gated estate that I don't think anyone could have called just a 'house'.

"I'm not sure exactly where, but someone told me James Cavendish has a place just down the street. Frankie, that tattoo artist you're going to meet, is actually good friends with him. The reality show she's starring in will be in his casino."

"Really?" I asked, impressed.

"Yes. And like I said, you're going to love her. She's a blast."

"Are you sure we're dressed for this?" I asked him as he pulled his black Mustang through a set of intimidating gates.

"Oh yeah. Half of these people will be wearing swimsuits, so we just might be overdressed."

I'd stuffed my bikini into my purse, but I glanced at his hands as we made our way past closely parked cars to the huge building at the center of the property. "Do *you* have a suit?"

He grinned. "Already wearing it, under my jeans."

"You had this all planned out," I observed.

"I had my hopes."

The place was packed, and the setup reminded me of a frat

party more than anything, which surprised me, considering that it was held at the biggest mansion I'd ever seen.

People were walking around in swimsuits, holding red plastic cups. I was instantly more at ease. My first impression of the place had been intimidating, but I could deal with plastic cups and a pool party, no matter the swanky location. Still, it was hard to even get through a room, there were so many people.

"How will you find anyone in this crush?" I asked Jared, having to lean into him and speak directly into his ear to be heard.

He shrugged. "Let's get to the pool. We'll either see them or we won't."

It took some searching, but Jared found me an empty room to change. Luckily, my small outfit fit into my purse. I was just debating about where to stash it when Jared opened the door a crack, peeking his head in. "Want to stash your purse in my trunk? We can just go around the house to get to the pool, so we won't have to swim through the crowd twice."

"Good idea," I said, following him.

He snagged my hand as he navigated us back through the crush of people.

Tristan held my hand all the time, but for some reason I felt like I shouldn't let Jared do it. I didn't protest, though, telling myself I was being silly.

We stashed my purse in his trunk, making our way toward the back of the house by way of a paved path.

I was surprised when Jared stopped us at the side of the house, pulling me into a darkened alcove. He pulled me close, and I didn't protest, closing my eyes and tilting my head back.

I let him kiss me, shivering as he ran light fingers along my bare back. He was a good kisser, his lips soft on mine. He wasn't forceful at all, just cajoling, and I found myself thinking about how Tristan's kiss had been, how it had demanded more from me that I'd known I wanted to give, and how I'd wanted to give more than I could afford to. Even thinking about another man the whole time, though, I could see that Jared knew what he was doing.

Still, it felt wrong, and I found myself quickly regretting it. This was Tristan's *brother*, and as much as I wished that I didn't, I had feelings for Tristan, and this was *wrong*. It was a nice kiss, but that was all. Just nice was nothing like what I felt for Tristan, which meant that the kiss, as meaningless as it was, was giving the wrong impression. I couldn't date Jared. It was naive of me to even have considered it.

I pulled back.

"I'm sorry," I told him quietly. "We shouldn't."

"I know," he said with a smile. "This isn't a date. Still, I had to try."

I rolled my eyes, less worried about leading him on after that statement.

"That came out wrong. What I meant was...I like you, a lot. I think about you way too often, and I'd like to spend more time with you. I won't try that again, not until you want me to."

I sighed, hating what I had to admit, but knowing that it was the only fair thing to do. "I don't think we can ever date, Jared. Tristan and I *are* just friends, that was the truth, but I do have feelings for him, which makes this wrong."

Even in the dim light, I could see his mouth tighten, and his brows draw together, but he nodded. "Okay. Okay, I understand."

"Please don't tell Tristan that I said that. He doesn't know."

"Of course."

We suffered through a long, awkward silence before he spoke again. "Do you still want to swim?"

"Yes. If you do."

"Yeah. I still want to be friends. All of the stuff with Tristan doesn't change that. We're friends, right?"

I smiled, which drew a small smile from him. "Yes, we're

friends."

CHAPTER NINETEEN

The backyard of the mansion was just as impressive as the front, and the pool was colossal. But it wasn't our first destination.

We fell into the line that led to the margarita bar. I was ready for one, after *that* awkward conversation.

"I'm so sorry—", I said.

"I'm sorry," Jared said at the same time.

We smiled at each other.

"I won't make this awkward," Jared said quietly.

"Good. Thank you. I hate awkward."

"Agreed," Jared said. As he spoke, a very pretty blond man clapped him on the shoulder from behind.

Jared turned to see who had grabbed him and grinned. "Mean Dean," he said, his tone laced with affection.

Mean Dean was gorgeous, in a pretty boy sort of way. In fact, I'd have said he was the prettiest man I'd ever seen, if I'd never laid eyes on James Fucking Cavendish.

Dean was just a few inches taller than me, and lean bordering on slender, even compared to Jared. I doubted he had a six-pack, like the brothers, but his face was his attraction. Almost white blond hair, tan skin, cornflower blue eyes, and the face of an angel would have made anyone do a double take.

Still, right from the beginning, there was something I didn't like about his smile.

He grinned at Jared, stepping closer to us. Someone behind us made a loud comment about him cutting into the line, but he pretended not to hear. "Glad you could make it, Diet T."

Jared stiffened at the nickname.

I raised my brows, instantly curious. These guys and their nicknames...

"What does Diet T mean?" I asked.

Dean turned a rather greasy smile on me. "Have you met his brother? Isn't Jared like the diet version of Tryst? Skinnier, less handsome, less smart, less talented. So we call him Diet T."

Jared looked uncomfortable, and just that easily, Dean went right to my shit list.

"And what's *your* nickname?" I asked Dean.

"I'm Mean Dean. And who are you, my lovely?"

"I'm Danika. Where does Mean Dean come from? It sounds like they went easy on you in the nickname department."

"I don't remember how the nickname started. So you're Danika... I've heard about you. Going out with both of the brothers, huh? I think I just thought up your nickname! We'll call you Number One, because you're the band's first groupie."

As he spoke, he gripped Jared's hand, and I saw a small baggie pass from one man to the other.

I was irate, for more than one reason.

"Quit being an ass," Jared muttered to his friend.

"Oh, relax. I'm only joking," Dean said.

It was pretty easy to see where the Mean Dean nickname had come from. He was a vicious motherfucker, but then again, so was I, if provoked. "You're awfully clever for a drug dealer," I told him, my smile sweet, my tone, not so much.

His grin only widened. "I'm not a dealer if I'm giving it away. Want some, Number One?"

"No thank you," I said through my teeth, stifling the urge to make up a rude nickname for *him*. *There's nothing more immature than name calling,* I told myself firmly. "So you're just a drug pusher, not a dealer? That's much better…"

Dean looked at Jared, still smiling. "She's feisty. I like that. When do I get my turn with her?"

"Sorry, I'm not into chicks," I told him, deadpan.

That killed his grin, and widened mine.

"She's got a point," a laughing female voice said from behind me. "Dean is almost pretty enough to interest *me*."

I turned to see a petite, black-haired girl with doll-like features. Her makeup was heavy, ran toward goth, and she was covered in tats, but it was obvious that she had a very pretty face, and a pretty smile.

"Finally going to take me up on my offer, Frankie?" Dean asked.

"I said almost, Dean. And almost isn't enough for me to deal with a penis."

Frankie held out a hand to me, giving me a very warm look. "Danika. Tristan told me about you. Nice to meet you. I'm Frankie."

I shook her hand, trying to smile, though I still wanted to punch Dean in the face. "Nice to meet you. Jared was just telling me about your reality show."

She wiggled her brows at me, her smile self-deprecating. "Hopefully it doesn't bomb."

"I'm sure it won't," I reassured her. "Especially if it's at the Cavendish Casino. That place is hot right now."

"Let's hope you're right. You've probably seen some of my work. I've done almost all of the ink on Tristan's back, and his arms. And I've done quite a bit of Jared's, too. Whenever he's done having a private chat with Dean, I'll show you."

I glanced over to where the two men had been, and saw that they'd moved several feet away, and were speaking quietly to each other.

"Jared's great, but Dean can be a pain," Frankie said, her voice pitched low.

I nodded. I thought that was putting it nicely.

"So do you have any ink?"

I shook my head, reading from her smile where she was going with the question.

"Is there anything you *really* want? I'd be happy to help you make all of your tattoo dreams come true."

I chewed on my lip. I had been thinking about that, especially recently. Something about staring at Tristan's tattoos way too often had made me start to want my own. "I've toyed with the idea of getting a little cherry blossom branch on my back."

Her grin widened. She clearly sensed a victory. "We'll have to work on that. I'll show you some of my designs that will blow your mind. You don't even have to let my camera crew tape it, though I'd love it if you did."

I blanched. "TV? I don't know…"

"It's not as bad as all that. Just think about it."

My eyes narrowed on her. "You do this all the time, don't you?"

She shrugged, a very engaging twinkle in her eye. "I love putting my mark on beautiful people. Call it a personal quirk."

"Tristan's ink *is* the best I've seen."

"Why thank you. Have you seen Jared's?"

"I haven't gotten a close look at any of it."

"But you have gotten a close look at Tristan's? Interesting…"

I shrugged, my mouth twisting wryly. "I don't know if interesting is the word. Frustrating would be more apt."

She laughed. She started to say something, but it was interrupted by some woman behind me loudly calling her name.

I turned to see a blonde woman descending on us. She was Vegas pretty, with hair bleached platinum blonde, a face that reminded me a bit of a Bratz doll, and bombshell curves that no one could have mistaken for natural. Still, she filled out her pink bikini in a way that would have made any straight guy look twice.

Frankie smiled at the woman, but there was a noticeable chill in her eye that hadn't been there before.

"Natalie," Frankie said. "Long time no see. What are you doing here?"

She pronounced the Natalie strangely, the a's made into ah's. I guessed that Natalie was one of those women that tried to make a pretty normal name sound exotic, but it just came out sounding a little stupid.

"Frankie, I can't tell you how I excited I was when I heard you were getting your own show! I've been dying to talk to you!"

"Oh yeah?" Frankie asked, disinterest practically pouring off her in waves.

"Well, I've been wanting to get a tattoo for ages."

"Really?" Frankie was clearly skeptical.

"And I think it would be great for my career to have it done on your show."

"Career?" Frankie asked.

"I've gotten into modeling," Natalie said smugly.

Only in Vegas, I thought. Natalie was a good three inches shorter than me, which made her unlikely model material, no matter how pretty she was.

"I take it you and Howard didn't work out."

Natalie shrugged. "We're still seeing each other. Nothing exclusive anymore, but he's been good to me, and I won't forget it."

"Sure, yeah." It was so obvious to me that Frankie couldn't stand the woman, but Natalie seemed oblivious to it.

Natalie's gaze sharpened on something behind Frankie, and I'd have sworn it turned predatory. "Is that Jared Vega?" she asked softly.

Frankie didn't bother to hide her eye roll. "It is."

"Is Tristan around? Those two are usually inseparable."

Frankie's smile was just a flash of teeth. "Nope."

"Damn. I needed to talk to him."

"You could always call him," Frankie offered.

Natalie flushed. "I don't have his number. Could I get it from you?"

"Sorry. Can't do that. I'll let him know you wanted to talk to him, if you want."

"Fine," Natalie said, her tone dismissive, then abruptly walked away.

"That was…interesting," I said, wondering what to make of the blonde woman. She hadn't been openly rude, just strange.

"Natalie wouldn't know how to be anything but self-serving. A lot of conversations with her end like that. When you're no longer useful to her, she just walks away."

"Hmm," I said.

"She's a gold digger. You know the type. What she said about her ex, Howard, says it all. That was gold digger code for, we're not dating, but I give him a blow job every time he pays my bills. Howard is almost sixty years old, by the way."

"Yuck," I said, watching the bombshell blonde approaching Jared and Dean. "She has to still be in her twenties."

"She is. And that's not even the worst of it. The whole story is just awful. She was Tristan's high school sweetheart."

That made my heart twist painfully in my chest.

"The fact that he won't date, that he only hooks up, is at least partially because of that twat," Frankie said.

That word made the side of my mouth kick up in spite of the way her statement made me feel. "Twatalie made him like that?"

Frankie threw back her head and laughed. "Oh, I like you. Yes, she did. Or at least, *I* blame her. Twatalie started seeing Howard when she still had Tristan's ring on her finger."

I went from mildly disliking Natalie to openly hating her guts with that one sentence. I couldn't have said which made me hate her more; the fact that she'd been engaged to Tristan, or the fact that she'd cheated on him.

"That twat," I said softly.

"Exactly," Frankie agreed.

We reached the front of the line, and a very friendly bartender got me two margaritas, and an entire tray of tequila shots for Frankie.

I eyed up the shots dubiously. "Please tell me those aren't all for you."

She shrugged. "For us. I don't like to drink alone. How hard do you think it will be to get Jared away from his pretty boyfriend?"

I glanced over at the two men. Natalie was gone, but they hadn't stopped talking quietly to each other. "They don't look like they want to be disturbed."

"Well, then, let's start without him. He'll find us when he's done."

We hopped into a shallow corner of the pool, setting the drinks on the edge.

She talked me into a tequila shot, and I downed it with a grimace.

"So I know that Tristan had to work tonight. Does he know that you're here with his brother?"

"He doesn't."

"Be careful about that. I know you aren't dating, but it feels… messy to me. Those two are close. It would be a pity to drive a wedge between them."

I sighed. "I know. I thought about dating Jared, but I've decided tonight that it's not happening. It just feels wrong. I don't want to come between them, and I don't want to lead Jared on."

"Have you told Jared that? He seems to be sporting a big crush."

"I told him. It was awkward, but he was very nice about it."

"He's the nicest guy in the world, but I worry about him."

That surprised me, but before I even asked, I knew what she was referring to. "Why?"

"I worry about both of the Vega brothers, but I especially worry about Jared. He's just too open to anything, you know? He doesn't seem to have a slow down button when it comes to drugs and alcohol. Neither of them do, but Tristan at least sticks mainly to the booze. I don't think there's anything Jared hasn't tried, and at some point, you can't just call it all experimenting."

"Does Tristan know?"

Frankie sighed, looking like a worried mother in spite of her age. "He knows. He'll be the first to say it's normal to try things. When you're smoking joints with your mother before you're twelve, it's hard to get perspective about it."

I grimaced. "I went to dinner at her house, and saw some of that. I'm a total prude about drugs, and I know they're grown-ups now, but that raised some red flags for me."

"Don't get me wrong, I love that woman to death, but that's just messed up, and it isn't even the half of it."

"Dean handed Jared a baggie of something the second he showed up," I told her, my voice pitched low, since Jared was approaching the pool.

"See now, that's the shit that worries me. Dean will get him anything he wants, with no thought to what's good for him. And I can guarantee that wasn't just a baggie of weed."

We dropped the subject as Jared joined us in the pool, and Frankie went over every piece of ink she'd done on his skin, which was considerable.

"Mama's boy," I teased him gently when she pointed out a tattoo for his mom that he'd done on his chest.

It was an anchor with the word mother etched into it. I thought it said a lot that he'd chosen an anchor to represent his mom, though to me it said something far different than what he thought it did. Lucy had trained me to look for signs of codependency, and permanently marking your body with the fact that someone was dragging you down was about as obvious as it got.

"Absolutely. Until the day I die, I'll be a mama's boy. She's my best friend."

In spite of my reservations, a little 'aww' escaped me at such sweet words coming out of a grown man.

"Tristan is a mama's boy, too, but not as bad as this one," Frankie told me, as she ran her hands down Jared's abs, tracing over the scaled dragon she'd done.

My brow furrowed as I studied the intricate dragon. It was golden, and so elaborate that I had to study it carefully to catch all of the details. It was a lot like one she'd done on Tristan's shoulder, but Jared's dragon had one extra quirk that made me roll my eyes.

"Is that dragon smoking a joint, or a cigarette?" I asked, my tone wry.

"Guess," Jared said playfully.

"Well half of it is in the water," I complained.

"Here." He hopped out of the pool, perching on the edge so I had a better view.

I moved close, getting between his legs to study the smoking dragon. "I can't believe you put a dragon smoking a joint on his stomach," I said to Frankie, my tone accusing, when I saw for certain what it was.

"I tried to talk him out of the joint. But he insisted. There's also a marijuana leaf on his hip, though that wasn't me. I explained to him that people almost always regret drug tattoos. When he's older, with kids of his own, he'll never be able to tell them to say no to drugs without looking like a hypocrite."

"I wouldn't tell them to say no. I'll be a cool ass dad."

"See now, everyone says that, until they have children," Frankie explained. "Your priorities will change, I guarantee it."

I glanced up at Jared when he had no response to her statement.

He was looking towards the house, an expression of frozen panic on his face.

I knew who it was before I turned to look. My hands fell from Jared's stomach, where they'd been innocently tracing a tattoo.

"Fuuuck, he's going to kill me," Jared said softly.

Tristan had arrived, and he was striding towards us with a look on his face I'd never seen before.

CHAPTER TWENTY

Tristan didn't even spare me a glance, his cold eyes all for his brother. The color gold had never looked so icy.

He barely paused when he reached us.

"A word, Jared," he said tersely, striding right past us.

Jared ran a hand over his damp, inky black hair, his expression tight. "Wish me luck, ladies," he uttered softly, before following his brother.

"This is an unfortunate development," Frankie said, watching the brothers stride away.

"He wasn't supposed to be here," I defended.

"You're right. I wonder how he found out about you guys being here together."

"You think he came here because someone told him?"

"He had a club promoting job tonight, right? Something compelling brought him here, and you and Jared showing up together is the only thing that comes to mind."

"But I don't even know anyone here. Who would have told him?"

"It looks like me and Dean are the only possibilities, and I didn't rat you out. I'll be getting hell for that later, by the way."

"Fucking Dean," I said darkly.

"Fucking Dean," Frankie agreed. "They've all been friends

since they were kids, but I can't stand Dean. He's always rubbed me the wrong way. He's just too slick. You'll notice he disappeared right before the shit hit the fan."

It was several minutes before Tristan approached us again, and this time it was without Jared.

"Where'd your brother go?" I asked him, searching the crowd. I saw no sign of Jared.

Tristan crouched down near the edge of the pool, looking meaner than I'd ever seen him.

"He went home. Can we talk, Danika?"

It was the tone he used, as much as the words that made a shiver of dread go through me. I'd never seen him like this.

I moved to the side of the pool, and began to climb out.

"Hey Tristan," Frankie called out, her voice friendly. "I didn't expect to see you at this thing."

"Hey, Frankie. It's pretty apparent that nobody did." As he spoke he helped me out of the pool.

"Do you have a towel?" he asked, his tone still as hostile as I'd ever heard it.

I shook my head, feeling a little numb.

"Are you cold?" he asked, solicitous even in a rage.

I shook my head again. It was hot as a hairdryer outside, and even the pool hadn't been enough to cool me off.

I didn't realize that we were leaving the party until Tristan called out, "Talk to you later, Frankie," as we walked away.

He snagged me a white towel off a huge pile of folded ones near the house. I wrapped myself in it, following him silently. I was torn between feeling guilty about going out with Jared, and being pissed about the way he was acting. He had no right, but I *had* as good as lied to him by not telling him who I was going out with.

I followed Tristan through the house and out the front door. He was opening the passenger door of a black Camaro before I spoke again.

"I can't take the towel," I argued, glancing back at the mansion. It seemed like such a trashy thing to do—to take advantage of the mysterious homeowner's hospitality.

His jaw clenched, and he just stood there, staring at me and holding the door open.

I got in, stealing the stupid towel.

He closed the door softly behind me.

He drove for a solid five minutes before either of us spoke.

"Is this your car?" I asked.

He gave one short nod as an answer.

The next stretch of silence was very nearly unbearable. I felt my heart pounding in my chest while I waited to see what he had to say. My thoughts were a little manic; going from wanting to chew him out, followed by the strong urge to apologize. The last thing in the world that I wanted to do was come between brothers, but on the other hand, I could argue that I wasn't coming between them, since Tristan and I were supposed to be platonic.

I was at war with myself, at war with my own innate logic, and my out of control emotions. Tristan had that affect on me.

"I just have two questions, and then I'll drop it." His rough voice in the darkness made me jump.

"O-Okay." I hated the weak thread of my voice.

"Was all of this because you were upset about last night?"

I cringed. That was just the question I hadn't wanted, because finding the answer required me to be brutally honest with myself.

"In part it was," I finally answered. "I wanted a distraction from you."

"Okay. I wish you had just told me that. Second question, are you really interested in my brother?"

I breathed a sigh of relief. That one I could answer honestly and easily. "Jared is great but I already told him I couldn't date him. I don't have those kinds of feelings for him."

172

Tristan exhaled noisily, then fell silent.

We didn't speak again until we were back at the house, and then only to say a brief goodnight.

Tristan slept on the couch, and I felt vaguely like I was being punished.

I tossed and turned all night.

He was gone by the time I was up the next morning. I stewed about his absence all day, especially since he didn't call or text me once.

I fell asleep quickly that night, exhausted from the bad night of sleep the evening before.

I was so relieved I wanted to cry when I found him sleeping on the couch the next morning.

Ivan and Mat had slept over at a friend's house down the street, and so the house was quiet as a tomb. I tiptoed away silently, letting him sleep. There weren't many mornings in the house where it was peaceful enough to sleep in, and it was a pity to spoil one of them.

I decided to go swimming. I shunned my black one-piece again, donning my bronze bikini. It was a silly thing to wear to swim laps, but my pride won out for that one.

I had lost track of the number of laps I'd done when I caught movement out of the corner of my eye.

I swam to the side of the pool, clinging to it as Tristan approached. He was already wearing black swim trunks. The look on his face could only be described as repentant.

He dove into the pool in a mouthwatering display, swimming straight to me. He crowded me against the side. "I was a complete ass the other day," he said quietly, earnestly. He kept moving close until we were nearly hugging. "Forgive me?"

I didn't even hesitate, just nodding as I watched him steadily.

He bent down, wrapping his arms around me.

I threw my arms around his neck, hugging him back.

His arms tightened until we were pressed close. He held me like that for a long time, no funny business, just good old-fashioned holding.

"Did you and Jared make up, too?" I asked into his ear.

He pulled back, and I was sorry I'd broken the spell. "We did. He was pissed at me, but we're good now. It didn't hurt that you'd already shot him down."

"He told you that?"

"He did. Is that true?"

"Yes. I already told you that."

He grinned his most troublesome grin—a mixture of joy, mischief, and the best dimples in the world. It was the smile that got me every time.

He swooped me up in a cradle hold, moving to the pool stairs. I should have seen it coming, but a shriek of surprise escaped my lips as he threw me back in the water with a happy laugh.

I came up sputtering. "You made me do a side flop. That hurt."

"You could always pay me back and throw me in."

It was stupid, but I tried. I only ended up pushing him in, and following closely behind.

He threw me over his shoulders. I shrieked and started slapping at him when he carried me to the diving board and started bouncing.

"You weigh too much to be doing that," I yelled at him. "We're going to break this thing!"

He threw me in, and I surfaced in a fit of uncontrollable giggles.

"You're out of control," I scolded him, backstroking away from him.

He followed with a wicked smile.

"What's gotten into you?" I asked him as he crowded me into corner of the pool.

He kissed me, and the world disappeared.

It was a hair pulling, legs wrapping, mouth bruising, earth *and* soul shattering kind of kiss.

I'd wanted him from the moment I'd laid eyes on him, but something integral inside of me changed with that kiss. I needed him, needed something that our relationship did for me, and I decided with that kiss to stop being such a pussy about it.

He curved his mouth over mine again and again, deep, sweet, drugging pulls that only made me crave more.

My arms were around his neck, my legs around his waist, before I even realized I had moved. I shifted until his thick erection was nestled in just the perfect spot.

His chest moved with an unsteady breath, a soft, rough, dark sound escaping from his throat and into my mouth.

I responded with a soft whimper, circling my hips against him. He felt so big, probably bigger than I'd have wanted to handle if I was in my right mind, but my right mind had gone on vacation for this.

One of his big hands moved to my ass, holding me in place as he grinded against me. The other moved up my side, and over my ribs, hovering just below my quivering breast.

With an impatient little moan, I reached down and pulled it up over my breast. He cupped my flesh, then kneaded softly.

He pulled back, but before I could protest, he was perching me on the edge of the pool, his head buried between my breasts. He peeled the material of my bikini aside with his teeth, sucking my nipple into his mouth.

I gripped his head, trying to get a good handful, but it was too short. "You need longer hair," I gasped.

He grunted, turning his head, kissing his way to the other side. His mouth was hot on me, and I writhed at the contact.

We were both panting when he pulled back. The second his head left my hands, I leaned back on my arms, trying to remember how to make my brain work again.

He gave me very steady eye contact. "I've been thinking," he began, his voice low and rich.

I nodded at him to go on, far past the ability to think myself.

His hands moved to my stomach, and he started rubbing and then kneading my sides and my waist. I trembled as he kneaded deep into the muscle tissue just below my navel.

"I have an idea," he offered, one big hand dipping to rub at my hip, caressing the flesh inside and down...

I let out an unsteady breath as his hand skimmed past all of the rest, and began to rub my inner thigh. I squirmed, my legs falling open for him.

"Do you want to hear it?" he asked, stepping away.

I just watched him as moved to grab one of the long floats that was lying along the side of the pool.

"Do you?" he asked, and I couldn't have guessed what he was asking about to save my life.

"What?" I asked.

"Do you want to hear my idea?" he repeated, pulling the float to me.

He showed no visible strain as he lifted me onto the rolling surface. He pushed me to my back on the inflatable plastic with a firm hand, and I gasped as water splashed into my lap, and onto my stomach with the movement.

"Yes," I said raggedly.

"I don't like relationships," he explained.

"You don't," I agreed.

"And you don't like casual sex," he continued.

"I don't."

"So let's try this. I get you off. That's all. It's perfectly innocent. You won't feel used, and we stay friends."

My brain felt too fuzzy just then to argue with the twisted logic he was using. My brows drew together, and I latched onto the biggest gap in his argument.

"What do *you* get out of it?"

He smiled his best smile, the one that ruined me for every other smile in the world.

I had it worse than I'd realized until just that moment.

"I've become obsessed with the idea of making you come. Ever since you told me that no one could get you off—"

"I said hadn't, not couldn't," I argued.

"What's the difference?"

"The difference is that you weren't supposed to take it as a challenge!"

"Well, ever since then, it's all I can think about. I've even been dreaming about it. And then the other morning, when we woke up like that..."

As he'd been speaking, I'd started to regain some brain function, but it went away again in a little puff of smoke when he mentioned that wake up session.

He swallowed hard, his hands moving to rub my stomach, water splashing over the sides of the float and hitting me in gentle waves with his movements. "When I helped you... pleasure yourself, well, I'd thought I was obsessed with it before that, but it got worse...Let me get you off. Don't worry about me. I'll go take a shower when you're finished."

"I'm not that easy to get off," I warned him. "I usually take a lot of time, and a vibrator."

He lifted one of my hands to his mouth, palm first. "How about a vibrating tongue?" he asked against my hand.

What he did next defied all explanation for me. He moved his tongue in fast, jerky little circles on my palm. He was so fast, in fact, that it felt like vibrations.

"What is that? What are you doing?" I asked, trying in vain to pull my hand free.

"Demonstrating what I'm about to do to your clit. Any objections?"

I couldn't think of one.

He'd made a pretty spectacular promise, but he didn't start

there.

He began rather innocently, his hands massaging the sides of my legs. Of course, his eyes weren't innocent. My bikini was askew, the triangles still pulled aside to reveal most of each breast, and his eyes were drinking in my dishabille.

He moved one hand to my inner thigh, shifting it so he could step between my legs as his huge hands worked on one lucky thigh.

"You have great hands," I told him.

"I'm here any time you need a masseuse," he reassured me.

"I need a masseuse."

He gripped my hips, moving his hips between my thighs. He pulled until his hardness was nestled against my sex. Between my bikini, and his swim trunks, the position left nothing to the imagination.

I moaned at the contact.

I could literally feel his reaction to that as his erection twitched against me.

"Are you going to be complaining to me about blue balls later?" I asked as he began rubbing my shoulders.

"I won't complain about any of this, hand to God. In fact, doing this to you has been on my bucket list for a couple of weeks now."

"I bet your bucket list is just full of chicks you want to go down on."

He had worked down one arm and was massaging my hand. I'd never realized how much tension I carried there until he was rubbing it out of me. My eyes almost rolled back in my head, it felt so good.

"Nope. Getting my hands on you was the only sexual act on that list."

"What else is on that list?"

"I'll tell you later. Now's not the best time."

I saw what he meant as he worked his hands over my ribs

R.K. Lilley

and down into my navel.

"You have the sexiest fucking abs I've ever seen," he told me, which made a thrill of pleasure run through me. I'd been complimented by a lot of men, but Tristan always made me *feel* it.

My heavy lidded gaze went to his six-pack. It was dripping wet and washboard tight. "You should talk."

He flashed a dimple at me for one brief instant before he took his mouth to me. Neither of us did much talking after that.

It was the most surreal barrage of sensations, with the sun on my front while I floated on the water, Tristan moving his hot mouth over me, his hands massaging me everywhere.

His hips pushed mine underwater as he kissed my throat.

I shivered, throwing my arms around his hard shoulders, trying him to keep him there.

He didn't cooperate, moving his lips to play at my collarbone, slipping down my body just enough to dislodge his lower half from mine, and bringing my hips back up above the water line.

I mumbled a protest.

"Sweetheart, I'm not a saint," he said against my skin, his words making delicious little puffs against my skin with each word. "If my cock stays there for long, it's going to try to find a way inside."

He nuzzled between my breasts, my top disappearing as though by magic. It just went poof, no sign of it anywhere that I could see.

He sucked one aching tip into his mouth, his hand moving to cup the other one firmly.

My entire body was trembling with anticipation by the time he made it down to my lower belly. Any self-control I may have possessed had long since evaporated.

I tried to push his head down further, tried to get his tongue closer to where he'd said it was going to go, but he didn't budge an inch.

I tried another tactic.

"Please," I said softly.

He chuckled against my hipbone, nuzzling there. "Please won't help you right now, Miss Over-thinker. This isn't about letting you stay in control. This is about making you lose your mind. *I* say when you're ready, and I plan to take my time getting you there."

I swallowed and licked my lips, watching his slow as molasses progress south. "No one's ever gone down on me before. You'll be the first."

"I know, and I plan to make it good for you. I've given it just a bit of thought..."

"Well, could you do it sometime *today*?"

"Demanding is an even worse idea than begging," he murmured into my skin.

I felt my teeth grinding together in frustration, but that didn't last long. His mouth moved to my inner thigh, making my jaw go slack. He sucked hard at the spot between my thigh and my groin and I just about screamed. He seemed to have insight into every sensitive nerve in my body.

He removed my bikini bottoms with his teeth, pulling each knot out slowly, torturously.

By the time his mouth made it to my sex, I was more primed than I'd ever been. I could literally feel the moisture seeping out of me, which was not how my body usually operated.

He pushed his shoulders between my thighs, my heels digging into his back as he bent low.

The position tilted my hips up, and brought his face close, until I could feel him breathing into the hot core of me. I held my breath.

He licked me, one deliciously long lap of his tongue, and my eyes rolled into the back of my head, my toes curling.

When he started circling my clit relentlessly with his impossibly fast tongue, I lost it, writhing and whimpering, pulling at his hair, trying to grip in vain, and finally settling for gouging at the top of his shoulders with my nails.

He slipped one big finger inside of me, groaning against my sensitive flesh as he pushed it in deep. He started up a smooth rhythm with his finger while his tongue worked its magic.

My vision went dark, then light, as the most delicious orgasm washed over me in voluptuous waves. It didn't stop for long minutes. Every time I thought it had stopped, another decadent tremor would wrack my body.

I fell apart and came back together again, my whole world thoroughly rocked.

CHAPTER TWENTY-ONE

"You need longer hair," was the first brilliant thing I managed to gasp, long moments after I'd finished.

He chuckled, nuzzling his face into my hip. "Longer hair. Got it. I'll add that to my to-do list."

"You do that," I ordered, trying with all of my being not to sound like I'd just had my world turned upside down. "I need something to grip."

"I need to go shower. Can you stand up? I don't want you falling asleep in the pool on me."

He helped me slip off the float, and I could stand, if only barely.

I didn't bother putting my bikini back on, just collecting the pieces while Tristan got out of the pool and wrapped a towel around his hips.

He didn't look at me again as he strode inside.

It was ridiculous, but I had the strong urge to beg him to hold me.

I dried off, and went to my bedroom to wait for my turn to shower.

I fell face down on the bed, feeling lethargic and fuzzy headed. I thought I could have slept for days, after that out of this world orgasm.

I heard the bathroom door open, and only realized as Tristan sucked in a gasp that I was buck naked on top of the covers, towel on the floor.

"Sorry," I mumbled.

He didn't respond, but I felt the bed move as he sat at my hip. My skin felt like it was on fire as I sensed him just staring at my naked back for a long time.

When he did speak, his voice was low and hoarse, and sent a shiver of pure pleasure from my head to my toes.

"I didn't get to rub your back. Time to finish your massage."

I nearly purred my assent.

His warm hand caressing the back of my thigh had me almost jumping out of my skin. He eased my legs open gently, and I could hear his breath coming out in hard little pants as he studied me.

He pushed a big finger inside of me, and I was still wet enough that it went in smoothly.

"I'm never this wet," I explained breathlessly, strangely embarrassed by it.

He groaned, pushing in a second finger. He started up a rhythm that had me close to the edge again shockingly fast.

"I can't come twice," I warned him with a whimper. "I never do. I'm not a..." I moaned, pushing with my knees to move against his wicked fingers.

He pressed himself against my side, throwing one leg over mine to keep my legs spread wide. I knew he'd jerked himself off in the shower, but he was hard as a rock where his cock dug into my hip through his boxers.

He bit down with just the perfect amount of pressure on the tendon between my neck and shoulder, and I came with a long moan of purest pleasure.

"You're not a what, boo?" he asked, a rough whisper in my ear that made me tremble.

My mind was blank. I couldn't even remember where I was,

let alone what he meant by that question.

"You said you can't come twice. You never do. And you started to say you weren't...?"

My mind grasped the conversation, if only barely. His big fingers were still inside of me, and it was hard to focus on anything else.

"I'm not a multiple orgasm kind of girl," I finished the sentence for him.

He chuckled into my neck, his fingers moving, pulling out, then pushing in again roughly. I didn't like rough, but I'd never had a rough caress feel so good before, and my hips circled, moving with his hand as he started up a hard rhythm.

I made a loud sound of protest when he pulled his fingers out, but he just flipped me onto my back, quickly pushing them in again.

His eyes on my body were mesmerizing. The look on his face was stark, his gaze hungry.

"You know I just take that as a challenge, right?" he asked, moving down my body, his intent clear.

"Where did you learn to do that?" I asked him.

"Do what?" His face hovered over my groin.

"That thing with your tongue."

"I'm not answering that," he said firmly.

That was fine, because I quickly forgot the question.

"You know, I can do that with more than my tongue," he said, and punctuated the words with his hand, the thrusts of his fingers turning into a rough vibration that blew my mind to pieces.

"You're so beautiful," he told me after I came down from my third glorious orgasm of the day.

"That was three," I told him, stunned.

He moved up my body, smiling as though *he* was the one that'd just gotten off three times.

He kissed me, pushing his body onto mine, his bare chest

184

pressing into mine, his stiff length nestling in just the perfect spot, rubbing it hard against me. If he hadn't been wearing boxers, we'd have been as good as having sex.

I could taste myself on him, but I didn't care, I couldn't get enough of his mouth, or his weight on top of me. Usually I hated that feeling, of a man's weight pinning me down, but I relished it when it was Tristan.

"I could do something for you," I offered as he broke away from my mouth and started kissing my neck, his thick hardness thrusting against me in a frustrated rhythm.

"No. This is for you. I still owe you a back massage."

I pulled his face back to mine, sucking at his mouth, my legs moving to wrap around his hips in a death grip. We both groaned as that pushed him partially into me, even through his shorts.

"You were so tight on my fingers. You felt so perfect."

I pushed against him, watching his face. "I want you inside of me."

He didn't even consider it, just shaking his head. "That wasn't the deal. The deal was, I get you off, not, I get you off, and then take advantage of you while you're good and sated."

"You're not taking advantage. I want you. All of you. Every inch of your cock buried deep inside of me."

He went glassy eyed, giving one last frustrated thrust against me before pulling away. "We'll talk about it tomorrow. I don't trust either of us right now. In the meantime, I owe you a back rub, so turn over on your stomach."

I rolled over, closing my eyes.

He worked on my back for several minutes with his gloriously strong hands, kneading deep into my muscles, taking his time, relaxing every inch of me. I was nearly asleep before he spoke into my ear.

"I forgot to tell you," he rasped. "All of my massages have a happy ending."

He surprised a giggle out of me, he was so outrageous, but the giggles quickly turned into gasps as he pushed his fingers into me, starting up a fast rhythm that took me over the edge yet again.

The last thing I remembered before drifting off was murmuring a soft, "Thank you," and feeling him gently kiss the back of my head.

My first thought as I woke up was that I'd never had such peaceful sleep in my life.

I could have gone right back to sleep, but I was quickly distracted by the fact that it was dark outside. As I realized this, I scrambled to my feet and threw on the first clothes I could find, nearly running into the living room.

Jerry and Tristan were sitting on the couch. Their voices were pitched low, and there was no sign of the boys, which meant I'd slept through bedtime.

"I'm so sorry, Jerry," I began. "I didn't mean to sleep the day away."

He waved me off with a smile, standing. "No worries, Danika. Tristan and I had it covered. Everyone needs a good nap every now and again."

"Did Bev already go to bed?" I asked, glancing toward the kitchen.

"Hours ago. She works early. I'm heading to bed, too. It's past midnight. Goodnight, kids."

I smiled at him. Usually when someone in their forties referred to younger adults as kids, it was condescending, but never with Jerry. I knew that he meant it as a term of endearment.

"Night, Jerry," I told him.

"G'night, old man," Tristan said, a twinkle in his eye.

"You think you're insulting me," Jerry shot back as he strolled out of the room, "but I feel twice as old as you think I look, so it's all the same to me."

I sat down beside Tristan, watching his hands.

He was shuffling a deck of cards, as he often did, the ritual seeming to soothe him. I was always impressed by how deft his big hands were, how lightning quick. My admiration had reached new heights earlier, when I saw the other ways those hands could work magic.

"I just found out that my apartment's ready," he said.

I stiffened, shocked by the news. I shouldn't have been. He had stayed longer than any of us had been expecting.

"Where's it at?" I finally asked.

"Not far from here. It's in Henderson, off Warm Springs, maybe fifteen minutes away."

"Oh."

"Yeah. Oh."

"Do you have any roommates?"

"One. Dean."

I tried not to make a rude face when I heard the name.

We shared a long, awkward silence. I didn't think either of us knew what to say, or where to even begin. For better or worse, things had gotten *complicated*.

I watched his hands as he shuffled his deck of cards, again and again.

"Nothing's changed, Danika. I'm still not ready to make you any promises."

I knew it said a lot about me that all I heard in that sentence was that he might be ready, *someday*, and that was enough for me. I'd fallen so hard, and so fast.

"Are you okay?" His voice was whisper soft.

I nodded jerkily, thinking that one over. I thought I might be a touch numb, my mind only focusing on the fact that, now that we'd been intimate in certain ways, I just wanted to touch him. Not necessarily in a sexual way. It was more that it felt like I

187

should have certain rights, and some of our reservations should have disappeared. I should be able to just walk up and hug him where he sat, since we'd done so much more than that just hours ago.

In fact, the longer we just sat there, trying to find the right words, the more I just wanted to just say fuck it and do as I pleased. Four mind blowing orgasms had messed up all of my priorities—those damned things had gone and made me lose my mind. Some part of my brain was still telling me, *no, stop, this isn't healthy.*

Too bad for that part of my brain, I didn't think I was capable of healthy just then; crazy was feeling too damn fine.

"It's past midnight, which means it's tomorrow," I said quietly.

He sighed heavily, bending forward. He gripped the deck of cards at the ends, then filed them onto the coffee table with one neat cascade. He'd done it from a good foot away.

"How did you do that?" I asked, my eyes going to his hard muscled chest as he leaned back, folding his arms behind his head.

"Like I've been telling you, my hands are magic."

We shared a brief, Troublesome smile. "I'm beginning to believe you."

He sighed again, breaking eye contact. "You sure we want to rush into this conversation? I don't see the harm in putting it off for a little longer."

I saw the harm. He was leaving soon. I felt a sense of urgency just thinking about it. If I was going to lose him, I wanted him to *remember* me.

I put a hand on his thigh, and saw the air clear out of his lungs with one harsh breath. I loved that one touch from me could do that to him.

I moved to my knees on the couch, leaning toward him.

His eyes were wary on me as I moved to straddle him, pushing my chest into his. I brought my face close, settling my weight against him. I circled my hips in a teasing move that made him groan.

He kept his arms behind his head, his jaw clenched hard. "You should know that I'm too weak to resist you right now, so tread carefully, boo."

"Who said I wanted you to resist?" I taunted, moving my lips to his throat. He smelled so good that I inhaled deeply before taking my mouth to the pulse in his neck.

"I want you so badly that I'd do just about anything to have you," he said roughly. "The only thing I won't do, though, is risk losing you. Can you promise me that if we do this, I won't lose you?"

I didn't hesitate, didn't think over the question as I should have. I wanted him, and I wanted him now. "I promise."

We kissed, a rough clash of our lips. He bit my lower lip, and I just about melted.

He thrust his hips forward hard enough to move us both to the edge of the couch, his cock digging hard into me through our clothes.

"Wrap your legs around me," he said raggedly.

I did, using the motion to grind my sex into his erection.

His hands gripped my hips, and he stood.

I gasped. "I love how big you are," I told him.

He flashed a dimple, bouncing me against him. "Not yet. But you will."

I punched his shoulder. It was a weak hit from that angle. "I wasn't talking about *that*. I meant that I love how you can carry me around as though I don't weight a thing."

"Sure you did," he teased, striding out of the living room.

He started kissing me again as we reached my room, closing the door behind us with his back, his hands moving to my butt, but he quickly made his way to the bed.

He dropped me onto the soft mattress, shrugging out of his shirt before I'd even stopped bouncing. I never stopped being in awe, and in lust with how amazing his body was. I loved the broad set of his shoulders, the chiseled cut of his abs. Even the definition in his collarbone was a turn on for me. And those arms…

My eyes followed his hands hungrily as they went to the waistband of his athletic shorts.

He paused there, arching a sassy brow at me. "If this is a striptease, you're going to have to reciprocate."

"Deal," I agreed, before he'd even finished talking.

He laughed, pushing his shorts down.

I gasped, my eyes widening when I got a good look at his jutting erection. I'd known he was big, I'd felt just *how* big, but just then it looked intimidating, it was so huge, nearly as thick as my wrist and arching up to his navel. I tried to reassure myself that it was just the lighting.

His mouth twisted ruefully when he saw the look on my face. "Don't worry, we'll fit."

I nodded, but I wasn't quite convinced.

He sprawled onto his back on the bed, folding his arms behind his head. "Your turn."

I nodded again, eyes still wide on his thick length.

My hand darted out, my fingers wrapping around him before he could see my intent.

He sucked in a rough breath as I gripped him.

My fingers could just touch, which alleviated some of my tension. At least I could grip him with one hand.

I pumped at him once with my fist, and a spurt of pre-cum escaped from his tip.

He pushed my hand away, cursing. "That's not in the plans tonight, Danika. My control is shot to hell as it is. Now, where's my striptease?"

CHAPTER TWENTY-TWO

I stood, sending him a wicked smile. I drew it out longer than he had, inching my shirt up slowly, teasingly uncovering my skin, inch by slow inch.

I tossed my shirt on the floor, cupping my breasts as I bared them. I was encouraged by the pained look on his face as I moved closer, my steps slow and sultry.

"You did say strip*tease*," I explained, biting my lip as I fondled myself, my expression taunting.

"I did," he bit out. "But you still need to keep stripping."

I did, pushing my tiny shorts down even more slowly than I'd peeled my top up.

"I love your body," he told me as I inched the shorts just below my hipbones. "It's perfect. You have the sexiest little hips in the world."

I practically glowed at the praise.   No one could do compliments like Tristan. He said things that put me on cloud nine for days, and I knew I'd remember those words long after this was over.

I gave one last teasing little shimmy before I let my shorts fall to the floor.

I moved to the bed, propping one foot up near where his feet were pointing. I touched myself, circling my clit, letting him see how wet he'd made me, when things like that usually embarrassed me. The usual shame associated with sex had disappeared for me, with Tristan.

"Come closer," he growled. "I can do that for you."

"I want to ride you first this time," I told him, ignoring his request.

"Fine, if that's what you want. Just get the fuck over here."

I giggled. Being teased made him grumpy, and I kind of loved it.

"First things first. Do you have any condoms?"

He groaned. "You aren't on the pill?" he asked, sounding annoyed, which annoyed *me*.

"I am, but you're wrapping it up for me anyway."

"Why? I'm clean, and I know you are."

I didn't feel like listing all of the flaws in his logic. "The fact that you don't want to wear a condom tells me that I want you to. Now where are they?"

"Fuck. They're in the side pocket of my duffle bag."

I found one easily. He had plenty, thank God.

I held the packet in my teeth as I climbed over him.

"I never ever ride bareback, Danika, if that's what you're worried about."

I decided not to point out that riding bareback was just what he was trying to do, which made it pretty unlikely that he *never* did it.

"Please, let's not argue about it," I told him when I'd moved to straddle his thighs, the packet falling from my mouth. "I'm not doing this without one. It's not negotiable."

He let out a noisy breath. "Okay. I'm sorry. I was being an ass. I just want us skin on skin so bad…"

I ignored that last part, opening the wrapper of the condom. I held the tip as I rolled it on, loving the feel of his hardness as it jumped in my hands. I stroked him a few times for good measure, before he waved my hands off.

"I'm not coming again until I'm buried inside of you," he groaned.

I loved the sound of that.

I climbed up his long body, rubbing my wet sex along his cock, readying us both to ease him inside of me.

I rose high on my knees to position him at my entrance.

I circled my hips in a sultry display before I began to impale myself onto his length slowly. He shut his eyes, and the look on his face was beyond gratifying.

I eased myself onto him, one slow inch at a time. There was no other way to do it, considering his size. I was slick with moisture, but I still felt a nearly painful stretch as I bore down on his length, the last few inches very nearly too much for me. I didn't let that stop me, though. I was intent on rocking his world, and a bit of discomfort wasn't going to hold me back.

His breath came in hard pants as I started up a relentless rhythm, my eyes on his face. I bit my lip as I pushed down hard enough that it felt like I'd bruised my insides.

I was gratified when I saw how fast I was taking him over the edge.

His neck arched back, and he almost shouted with his release.

I kept moving, riding out each spasm of his pleasure. Watching him lose it was almost as good as losing it myself.

His hands moved to my hips, and he looked almost angry as he met my gaze.

"Okay, that's not happening again." His voice was low and almost mean.

I was caught off guard. "What do you mean? Didn't you enjoy it?"

"Of course I did. You saw that. But that isn't happening again. I'd rather not get off at all than have you suffer through it, more concerned with impressing me, than enjoying this. It's not a fucking competition, Danika."

That threw me for a loop, and I found myself blushing hotly.

"Okay, new ground rules," he growled, dislodging me with two firm hands on my hips.

"New ground rules?" I repeated. "What do you mean?"

"No over-thinking this, first of all."

I knew exactly what he meant. I had been more in my head than in the moment, and whether we were dancing, swimming, or having sex, he could always seem to tell.

"Okay. Fine. What else?" I squared my jaw as I said it.

"I'm in charge."

"Excuse me?"

"Because I don't want this to be calculated for you."

"What do you want, then?"

"I want you to let go. I want you to submit. I want to make you lose your mind. I want you to be so far gone that the only word left in your vocabulary is my name."

A shot of pure heat ran through me. I licked my lips. "How are you going to do that?"

He rolled me onto my back, looming over me. His brow was furrowed, as though in deep thought. "It's really too bad we don't have any restraints around."

My eyes widened. He liked to find new and interesting ways to surprise me.

"Do you have some sort of fetish? How did I miss this before? Aren't there supposed to be warning signs for this sort of thing?"

He chuckled as he rose from the bed. My eyes stayed glued to him as he went into the bathroom, gloriously buck-ass naked.

"Are you going to find me some restraints, Master?" I called out.

"Oh, shush," he said, and I could hear the smile in his voice.

I just lay there for the minutes it took him to clean up and join me again.

My eyes widened into huge saucers as he set more foil packets beside me on the bed.

"One. Two. Three. Four…" I counted, wondering if it was even possible we'd need them all.

He smiled, a flash of his straight white teeth. "I was being conservative. I can always get more out of my bag, when we come up for air."

"Okay, now I know you're shitting me."

He laughed hard. "Such a pretty girl…such a dirty mouth."

I stuck my tongue out at him, and his face turned serious as he bent down to kiss me.

"I was serious, Danika. I've wanted this from the moment I laid eyes on you, and we're not stopping any time soon."

I tried to process that, but my mind wasn't working at top speed, as his mouth moved down to my neck, and his body slid hotly along mine. I could feel his sex, already rock hard again, rubbing hard into my thigh.

I snaked a hand down, wanting to touch him, but he stopped me with a firm hand on my wrist.

He pulled that arm up high above my head, then gave my second arm the same treatment. "I was serious about the restraints, too. If I had something here, you'd be tied to this bed already. You lost touching rights when you pulled that stunt back there."

"It wasn't a stunt—I was just trying to make it good for you—"

"You were keeping score, turning this into something ugly by taking your own pleasure out of the equation. That's not happening again. I'll be doing the touching from now on."

"You did the same thing, yesterday. You took your own pleasure out of the equation, too."

"You're lying to yourself if you think I didn't enjoy that just as much as you did, and I sure as hell wasn't *suffering* through it."

That shut me up, that and the fact that his mouth had wandered south.

Delicious shivers shot through me he made his way down my body with feather-light kisses.

"Are you going to let go for me, Danika?" he breathed against me.

"I'll try my best," I gasped.

"You don't have to *try*, sweetheart, you just have to submit," he murmured, right before he set to work on me in earnest. Somehow, his words had the intended effect, and I found myself relaxing into his hold. Even when his hands moved away from my wrists, I left my arms where he'd put them.

His mouth was relentless, his hands everywhere at once, rubbing, stroking, driving me wild, and making me weak.

I submitted to him, my restless mind went quiet and dark, and it was the sweetest feeling in the world to let him take control of it all.

Something inside of me, in the way I'd been shaped, made it so hard to change the way my mind worked, and the way it worked was *twisted*. I felt so much shame when things were out of my control, and that control had always included sex.

For the first time in my life, I trusted someone enough to take that control from me, I gave him that control willingly, and that trust healed something raw and aching deep inside of me.

He had me wet and quivering before he poised himself at my entrance, the heavy warmth of his body sliding over mine. He held my legs wide as he entered me, easing in much more easily than the last time.

"See," he rasped into my ear, "we fit just right."

"Yes," I gasped.

He began to move, slow, heavy strokes that had my hands flying to his shoulders, scratching mindlessly.

"I swear to God, I'm finding something to tie you up next time," he grunted, gripping my hands back above my head firmly, his chest rubbing mine as he thrust, grinding into me, harder, faster.

My legs wrapped around his waist, tightening as the pressure built.

I felt myself clenching around him right before I lost it, my head pushing back into the bed, a rough, desperate cry escaping my lips, as I came.

I knew that he followed me as his mouth latched onto the pulse in my neck, his breath escaping in a raw gasp of a noise, his hard length grinding right into the end of me and holding himself there, wedged deep, his length pulsing with his release.

"You feel so good, sweetheart. I swear nothing's every felt better in my whole fucking life."

I felt my body go limp as the powerful tremors eased, and his words made me literally melt. I had the oh so stupid girl thought that if I could just have Tristan, I'd never need anything else, not ever.

I had the crucial and inescapable realization that I wanted him. Not just in bed. Not just as a friend, but all of him. Every piece of the puzzle. I'd never wanted anything so badly in my life.

CHAPTER TWENTY-THREE

He left me briefly, presumably to take care of the condom, but I didn't even lift my head up to look. For what I mused was the first time in my life, I felt well and truly sated.

I'd never come with a man inside of me. Hell, before yesterday, I'd never even had an orgasm with a man in the same room. Tristan always liked to joke that he had magic hands, but I was beginning to lean towards the idea that he had magic in *every* part of his body.

Turned out, feeling sated made me talkative, and so I found myself spouting out revealing little confessions between bouts of sex.

"That's the first time I've ever come with a man," I told him as I felt his weight on the bed. My eyes were closed, and I didn't think I'd moved even one inch since he'd left me.

His hand went to my belly in a light caress. "You want to tell me what that's all about?"

My breath trembled out in a long sigh, and I very deliberately didn't open my eyes. "Do you really want to know? I'd hate to unload on you if you don't feel like hearing my life story."

His hand went still on me, and my eyes shot open, going to his face.

He was glaring, and it made me flush. "Please tell me you

know me better than that, Danika. Seriously. That hurt my feelings. Of course I want to know. Tell me."

I just nodded and closed my eyes, not wanting to look at him while I spoke.

"Sex…didn't start out good for me. In fact, it was pretty horrible." My voice was almost cold as I told it. Just stating facts, I told myself. It was the old you. Nothing to cry about now. "I was," I searched for the right word, the word that made me sound less like a victim, "coerced."

"Coerced?" There was already clear rage in his voice. God, the man could get worked up in a heartbeat.

"There's a bit of a backstory, but it's boring—"

"Danika," he said darkly, censure in every syllable. "You know me better."

I did know better. He'd always been a great listener, a great friend.

"My mother disappeared on me and my sister when I was about fifteen. We tried to hide the fact that she was gone. We were good at covering up for her. I can't remember a time when we didn't have to, for one reason or another. She was an addict. Hardcore. Opiates had her basically bedridden for my entire childhood. She wasn't a functional person; she probably didn't even know what that was." I'd spent a lot of time trying to forgive her for that, but it hadn't been easy, and I still wasn't sure some days if I even knew what real forgiveness was.

"When she wasn't bedridden, she was gone, doing God knows what."

He'd grabbed my hands, rubbing the stress right out of them as I spoke. It helped. It felt good, distractingly good, which was what I needed. I hadn't told this story in a long time, and it wasn't an easy one to tell.

"We hid it for about a month before social services got wind. I suppose it was with good intentions that we were placed together into a foster home. It wasn't much of a home, it was a trailer actually, and the family we were put with was…not ideal. It was an older couple, poor as dirt. The wife worked. She was gone a lot. The husband wasn't."

His hands tightened on mine briefly before starting up again.

"There might be people with good intentions that help with foster care, but that system is broken. So broken that it puts young girls with old perverts without a qualm."

"God, Danika."

My voice was calm and steady as I continued, just stating facts, "We weren't there long before he started…coercing me. He knew which buttons to push, as predators tend to. Lucy told me that. She's helped me work through it."

"He told me that he liked young girls, younger than me, in fact. My sister Dahlia was the perfect age, he told me. But he could be nice, he said. He'd let me be a good big sister and take her place, and if I cooperated, and didn't tell, and didn't complain, or cry out, or scream, he'd leave my baby sister alone."

"How long did this go on for?" Tristan asked softly, something dreadful in his voice. I was thankful that dreadful thing wasn't for me, but it still made me shiver to hear it.

"It felt like eternity, but it was just over a year. It happened often. In the middle of the day, in the kitchen, anywhere he wanted. He loved to pounce on me in the washroom. He'd bend me over the washer a lot, and I couldn't make a peep."

I couldn't believe that I was telling this to him while I was lying on my back naked, but I didn't feel the need to cover up, as though I just trusted him *that much.*

"Long story short, my sister walked in on us. I wasn't fighting him, in fact I was cooperating, so she thought it was something I'd wanted. That ugly confrontation revealed that he'd lied about not touching her. He'd pulled the same routine on us both. I was a shitty big sister, and I'd failed miserably at protecting *either* of us. She ran away, haven't spoken to her since. No idea where she is, but I know that she hates me for what happened to her, and what she saw. She was pretty clear about that. I tried to explain myself to her, but she didn't want to hear it."

"God, Danika…"

"He didn't hurt me."

He made a choked noise in his throat that told me he took strong exception to that statement.

"Well, what I mean is, he didn't *hit* me or anything, but it *did* hurt. It was horrible, in fact. It's hard to describe, but when someone takes that choice out of your hands, even takes away your choice to struggle, well, it kills something important inside of you. I'm still struggling to find that something I lost. I struggle every day with it. To feel whole. To feel a sense of self-worth that Lucy tells me everyone should have. It colors every little thing I do, if I'm honest, but one of the most obvious results of that ugliness is that it's important for me to feel in control."

"I got a boyfriend when I was about seventeen. He said he loved me, seemed to mean it, and I was so ready to love somebody that I fell for him hook, line, and sinker. I probably rushed into the sex part of that, but it was actually my idea. I wanted to get it over with, especially doing it with someone my own age. It was never about liking it. It was about…enduring it, and feeling like it was *my* choice. My next boyfriend was a slight variation of pretty much the same damn thing."

My voice had stayed steady, my breathing even, as I told the embarrassing mess of a story, but Tristan's wasn't. His breathing was uneven, and messy, and spoke clearly of temper.

"Where does he live?" Tristan asked very, very quietly.

"Who? The old man?" I'd never say his name, not ever.

"Yes. Where does he live?"

"What? You making plans to go kick his ass?"

"Or kill his ass." He sounded so deadly serious that I opened

201

my eyes to study him.

"He died of a heart attack when I was seventeen. Been in the dirt for years now. No need for murder."

I was teasing him, but he didn't look amused. He looked troubled, and it was the kind of trouble that didn't go away with teasing.

"I didn't mean to kill the mood, but that's it, that's why I think sex hasn't been good for me." My tone was flat, but I felt so vulnerable, so open, and ready to be wounded again, and I strongly suspected that wound would come from whatever his reaction might be.

Words seemed to pour out of me in a jumble, as though I couldn't say them fast enough, because I'd clearly rather wound *myself*, than have it come from someone like Tristan, who could really do some damage. "Probably not the sort of thing you want to hear about someone you've slept with. I'll totally understand if you don't want to do anything else with me. The things I've done are…disgusting. Believe me, I know that better than anyone."

He was on me, angry and domineering, before I'd finished speaking.

He slanted his mouth over me, his movements angry, but his kiss so soft. When he pulled back to speak, his words were soft too. "You could never be disgusting, sweetheart. Never. I'm *so sorry* for what happened to you. You deserve so much more than what life gave you, and I wish to hell I could go back in time and kill that sick old man before he ever hurt you."

"Thank you," I told him, my voice thick. He'd hit all of the right nerves with a few short statements, *soothing* my wounds, instead of inflicting new ones. I should have had more faith in him. "But I really will understand if you don't want me anymore."

His answer was to move down my body with soft, feather light kisses, the contact sweet, his intent just the opposite.

He buried his face between my legs, eating me out with enthusiasm and skill. Skill and...talent. He had me gasping out his name, just on the edge, before he pulled back, turning me onto my stomach.

He pushed my legs out and up, until my knees were bent, my thighs spread. I tensed as I felt him positioning himself on my back.

He rubbed my lower back, and murmured soothingly. "Relax and arch your back for me a bit. I'll make it good, sweetheart, I promise."

"Are you putting on a condom? I can't see."

I felt him sigh against me. "Yes, of course I will. You made your wishes very clear. I wouldn't take that choice away from you."

I relaxed. He'd grasped that situation quickly.

The old man had never used a condom, never given me a choice about it, and I'd hated that *so much*.

"Thank you."

I heard a foil packet being opened. "Tristan," I said quietly.

"Yes, Danika."

"I trust you. It's really nice."

"It *is* really nice. Thank *you*, Danika."

His fingers moved between my legs, slipping between wet folds to plunge into me. He started up a steady rhythm with those magical fingers. He only pulled them out when I was on the edge again, panting and twisting against the contact.

"Danika, sweetheart?" he rasped.

"Yes, Tristan?"

"I'm done being sweet, if you don't mind. I need to fuck you really hard now, if that's okay."

The way he said it had me smiling, almost giggling.

"I'll make it good," he promised

"Yes," I breathed, closing my eyes, submitting to the act as I could only seem to do with him. As strange as it seemed, this was just what I wanted, what I *needed*, after that confession. There was no better way for him to show me that it hadn't changed the way he felt for me.

He worked himself in slowly, the pressure different, more intense, at this angle. He had to drag himself slowly out, then push back in a few times, adjusting the slant of my hips, before he began to pump into me in earnest.

My hands fisted in the sheets, my cheek flat to the bed, as he worked me from behind, his breathing heavy and harsh, loud enough to be heard even over my own uneven pants.

He worked me so hard that his hips began to slam into me, making a slapping noise against my ass.

I was a little shocked that there was no pain, only a pleasure building that was so big I wasn't sure I could handle it. It was coming over me like a tidal wave, the sensations overwhelming.

"It's too—too much, Tristan," I stammered, trembling with it.

"No, sweetheart," he panted, still driving into me, not even pausing. "Just let go. Let go for me, Danika."

I closed my eyes and let go. I let go of that thing inside of me that always wanted to cling to every ounce of control, and just let the waves of sensation wash over me, seeping into every pore.

I went over the edge trembling, gasping.

"Tristan," I nearly shouted.

"Danika," he said softly, that one word full of intensity.

He rocked deep into me twice more before he came inside of me, shaking against my back, and repeating my name raggedly.

I loved it.

He lay on my back, his weight pushing me down. Softly, and oh so sweetly, he kissed my neck.

That weight on me, at one time such a terror, was now just a solid reassurance. It was absolutely flooring what trust could do.

CHAPTER TWENTY-FOUR

"I want to suck your dick," I said into his ear, deliberately crude.

He stiffened.

I should have been worn out. We both should have, but we couldn't seem to get enough of each other. A few bouts of the best sex of my life had only made me hungry for more.

"Not in the cards tonight," he whispered back, confirming once and for all that he had superhuman control, since I could see that he was clearly hard. Again. "No more selfless acts from you. I couldn't stand it if I realized at the end that you were just suffering through it…"

I smiled as I pulled out my winning hand. "I've never done it before."

He went absolutely still, not moving or speaking for a solid minute. "Excuse me?" he finally said, pulling back to look at me.

I licked my lips slowly, drawing his attention there. "I've never sucked a cock before, and I'd like to suck yours. What do you say?"

"How is that possible?"

"The other…we just didn't, and the two guys I've dated didn't do oral, so I've never done it either…It only seemed fair."

"That's making the whole thing seem pretty fucking

calculated."

I shrugged one shoulder. "Am I wrong? Why should I do something they weren't willing to do?"

"I wasn't talking about that. I was talking about this right here, with us. Are you only offering because I've done it for you?"

I shook my head slowly, my eyes never leaving him. "I want to. I want to know what you taste like. I want to feel you coming in my mouth. I want to make you feel good. You were upset with me earlier, when I got you off with no thought to myself, but I love doing that for you. It's almost as good as when you do it for me."

"You swear you want to do it? This isn't some power play?"

Part of me hated that he knew me well enough to act like that, to know just the way my mind worked, but another part of me loved it. There was something so comforting in the certainty that someone knew about your biggest flaws and was still willing to stick around. "I swear it's not. I'd like to try it." I smiled my best siren's smile, and I knew by the heat in his eyes that it was a good one. "Pretty please, may I suck your big cock?"

He couldn't hold back his smile. "Now, how could I turn that down? You said pretty please, so I'm pretty sure I *have* to let you now."

"True story," I agreed.

I was still smiling as he came to his feet on the side of the bed, his own smiling face turned serious and harsh with intensity in a flash.

"Get on your knees," he said thickly.

I did, curious and puzzled as to what he planned, but very content to let him do the planning.

"Come here."

I moved to him, which brought my face very close to his erection, and meant that his plan wasn't all that complicated.

He fisted my hair, moving his velvety hard tip to rub along my bottom lip.

"Open," he told me, his breath hitching when I obeyed.

He pushed the tip in, and then a little more, filling my mouth. I started to tense as he reached the back of my throat, but his hand stroked over my hair, and his voice was soothing as he instructed me. "Relax. Just breathe through your nose and relax."

I calmed, his reassuring, confident tone all it took for me. My mouth was so full of him that, even with my mouth open wide, I still felt my teeth scraping against him as he pushed into the back of my throat.

"Careful there, sweetheart, I don't mind a bit of pain, but easy on the teeth."

I pulled my lips over my teeth as he pushed himself in deeper, my mind distracted by the idea of him not minding a bit of pain.

He pulled out and stroked into my mouth, and I was amazed at how much of him I could take, though he was careful not to gag me.

He didn't let up with the dirty dialogue for a second, his voice low and gravelly with need, which I found that I loved. "Your mouth feels so good. I'm not gonna last two minutes watching those gorgeous lips on my cock. Yeah, that's it, take it deeper. Suck, baby, that's right, suck it hard."

He dragged one of my hands up from the bed, gripping it hard at his thick base. "Stroke me. Hard. Jack me off into your mouth."

He paused, panting hard, as I obeyed, gripping his thick base hard, loving the feel of the hard smooth flesh in a way I'd never thought I could.

"I won't forget the sight of you like this, on your hands and knees, your mouth filled with my cock, for as long as I live. You're the hottest fucking thing on the planet, Danika."

My name turned to a moan as he came in my mouth, warm liquid shooting down my throat.

He didn't pull out until he'd given me every shiver inducing spasm, but the second he did, he was pushing me to my back, his mouth burrowing between my legs, his magical hands busy everywhere.

Tristan was the opposite of a selfish lover. Whatever he got, he gave back in spades.

"You're loud," he told me, when he'd wrung another glorious orgasm out of my system.

I tried my best to muster up a decent glare. "So are you. You talk the *whole* time, when your face isn't buried in my…"

"Pussy? You draw the line at saying pussy?"

"Shut up."

"And yes, I talk the whole time. Quietly. Or at least, I'm not shouting loud enough to bring the house down."

"Shut up," I told him again, blushing.

He just grinned, pushing down until his bare chest was rubbing against mine. "You tired, boo? Do you need some rest?"

My eyes widened. "Don't you?"

"Sure. Eventually…"

"What does that mean? We couldn't possibly…not again!"

He hitched up one muscular shoulder in a shrug, circling his hips to let me feel that, unbelievably, he could.

"How?"

"I just ate you out for ten minutes. It's hard to stay unaffected by that."

I hooked my legs around him, grinding against him. We were skin on skin, him teasing at my entrance, and it felt amazing.

I moaned loudly as he pushed in that first perfect inch.

He pulled out just as quickly, going for another condom, having to dig through the covers to find one. I watched him roll it on like he did it every day, which he probably did, which I didn't let myself think about.

He moved back into position, easing into me, whispering

rough, dirty, sweet things to me all the while. "You feel so good. So fucking tight. I'll let you rest after this time, but don't be shocked when you wake up with my dick inside of you sometime in the night."

I gasped, my only reaction to his words, since I wasn't coherent enough to actually speak as he rocked in and out of me, the strokes long and perfect, and so smooth, considering he stretched me with his every movement.

He pounded into me, harder and harder, not letting up, proving to me that I *did* like it rough, if Tristan was doing it.

"I'm coming. Are you close?" he demanded, pulling up to look at me, his face pained.

"Mmmm," was the closest thing I had to an answer.

He reached between us, his finger finding and circling my clit with unerring accuracy. It was impressive, how familiar he was with the female body, and impossible to get upset about how he'd gotten so familiar as he rocked my world, yet again.

I came, a gasping, toe curling orgasm, and he was right there with me, biting my lower lip, and then moving to growl rough compliments into my ear that made my whole body flush with pleasure.

Unfortunately, I didn't wake up with Tristan inside of me. We never got the chance, as tiny fists started beating on the locked door of my bedroom before six a.m.

I sat straight up, my eyes immediately shooting around the room, looking for clothes. I was decent by the time Tristan sat up, sheet falling to his waist, leaving his drool-inducing torso bare.

"I've got this," I told him. "You can go back to bed. I just need to go make the boys breakfast, and turn on a show."

I rushed into the bathroom before he could respond.

I exited the bathroom through the rarely used hallway door, being considerate, in case Tristan had already fallen back to sleep.

He hadn't, and no sooner had I found a TV station with cartoons than he was in the kitchen, starting in on breakfast.

I got Mat settled, and approached the kitchen. I leaned a hip into the counter as he got about thirty ingredients out of the fridge, going all out as usual.

He set the eggs near the oven, strode to me, grabbed me by the hips, and lifted me onto the counter.

He cast a quick glance in Mat's direction before slipping his hips between my legs. He pressed against me, and dipped his mouth down for a long, hot, drugging kiss.

He pulled back when we were both out of breath, straining hard against each other. "First chance I get," he rasped into my ear, "I'm going to bend you over the nearest piece of furniture, and make you lose your mind again."

I leaned back on my hands, eyes closed, as I let myself process that. So this wasn't over. There was more to come...

He went back to the food, a grin on his face that would have been completely infuriating if it wasn't also totally irresistible.

"Nothing to say to that, boo? No witty comebacks?"

"Good luck finding that chance," was the best I could manage with my brain a messy puddle on the floor. "I've got the kids all day."

"You want to bet me that I can't?"

"Not really. You become completely unreasonable when you get a challenge in your head."

"I'll take that as a yes. What do I get if I win the bet?"

I couldn't think of anything, so I just stared at him until he came up with something of his own.

"Restraints," he said, very very quietly. "That's what I get if I win. You come to my room, my bed tonight, and I get to use restraints on you."

I should have been more alarmed at the prospect, considering my history, but I searched myself for the fear, and only came up with anticipation.

"And if I win, Tristan in a bikini, right?" I shot back, just as quietly.

"You've got a deal. I can't fucking wait. Keep an eye on the stove for me. I need to go talk to Jerry."

I glared, my mouth dropping open. "You dirty cheater," I told him, outraged. "If you're doing what I think you're doing, that is *cheating...*"

He shrugged, heading down the hallway that led to Jerry's room. "We didn't set up rules. Don't be a sore loser about this, boo."

He strode back into the kitchen less than two minutes later, a shit-eating grin on his face. "Change of plans. Bev and Jerry are taking the boys to Shark Reef after breakfast. Family day."

He flipped a few things on the stovetop before moving to me, pushing his hips between my knees to whisper in my ear. "I can't decide whether I'll bend you over the couch, and fuck you hard from behind, or take you right here, on this counter."

CHAPTER TWENTY-FIVE

Bev and Jerry had the boys out of the house within two hours.

I eyed Tristan up as I heard the door closing behind them. "What did you say to Jerry to get him moving so fast? I haven't seen him up that early in years."

"I promised to let him organize something for the band in a few weeks. Dean doesn't want a manager. He thinks he can do it himself. He can't. He's too shiftless to get things done for us, but I've been letting him find that out on his own. Jerry will be great at it, so I'm giving him a shot. Dean won't be happy, but it had to happen sometime."

"Dean seems like a douche bag."

He just smiled. "Still mad at him for calling me the other night?"

That was only part of it. He was just one of those people that you only expected bad things from. I didn't say that to him, though. Dean was his friend, and I really didn't know enough about the guy to dislike him as strongly as I did.

He didn't seem to expect an answer, as he shooed all of the dogs out the back door, closing and locking it with finality, before turning to me.

He approached me, his intentions crystal clear.

He backed me up against the arm of the couch, a wicked

smile on his face all the while.

"Turn around," he ordered softly, his face bent down to mine.

I turned, and he used a firm hand at my shoulder, to push me, face first, over the high arm of the couch. I was nearly upside down in that position, and as he pulled my shorts and panties off without a word, I began to worry. I was wet, but his size, and this position, seemed like a bit much for me.

"Tristan," I began, as he peeled my top off.

"Don't, Danika," he warned, unclipping my bra, and slipping it free. "Don't start over-thinking again. Just close your eyes and enjoy the ride."

I tried to listen, I really did, but I was still biting my lip, wondering how this was going to work.

Of course, that changed as he took his mouth to me from behind.

There was no warning at all, just his hot tongue pushing at my clit, his access perfect with the angle.

He gripped the insides of my thighs, pushing me up and thrusting his tongue deep inside.

I writhed, my nails raking at anything in reach, finally snagging at a throw pillow.

He pulled back, but a quick rustle of clothes later, and the very distinct sound of a foil packet being opened, and he was back, but not with his mouth.

He worked his thick length into me slowly, pushing deep, squeezing in so tight at that angle that it felt like he was taking me over. The pressure was so intense, just with the filling of me, that I had to bite the little throw pillow to stifle a scream.

He dragged himself out in an agonizingly slow pull that rubbed against every sensitive nerve that I possessed.

I whimpered and clawed.

He kept up a steady, filthy dialogue the entire time. It was official; he was a talker. He wasn't loud, his voice low and gravelly, and when his breath would catch mid-sentence, or go unsteady with his lust, I thought it was hottest thing in the world.

"I can feel your inner muscles working on me, sweetheart. You squeeze me with every move. That feels so perfect. I knew it would be this good with us. So fucking good."

His voice grew rougher and rougher as he increased the speed of his strokes, and at that extreme angle, every stroke was a shock to my system. A good shock. An incredible shock.

His hands were gripping my hips firmly as he worked at me from behind, and when one hand snaked down to rub my clit, I couldn't hold back my cries, or the orgasm that was building up like a storm inside of me.

"Say my name, Danika. Say my name when you lose your mind."

I did. I practically shouted it as I came hard, the orgasm hitting me like a punch to the gut. I felt myself squeezing him as tremors shook me, and I knew the second he followed as he shouted my name.

His cock shoved deep inside of me and held, jerking with his release. I could feel every last twitch with the angle, and I adored it more than I'd ever thought I could adore something like this. Apparently I could handle rough sex, if the circumstances were right.

He bent close to my back, and I could feel how his breath shuddered out of his chest as he kissed the back of my head. I shivered from head to toe in pleasure.

I had the strongest, stupidest urge to tell him how I felt, but I held it in. Just barely. My brain felt like an emotional puddle of mush, and I had to say *something* about that. It wasn't in my nature to keep quiet.

After he'd pulled out of me, and straightened, one of his hands absently rubbing at my lower back, I pushed myself to my feet, turning into his body.

I threw my arms around his neck, shoving our bare, sweat slick chests together.

I placed an exuberant kiss on his chin, the only thing I could reach. "Thank you for making sex so good for me, Tristan. I didn't even know it could be like this," I told him, meaning it.

He bent, finding my mouth with his in a quick, wet kiss, though he didn't say a word, and his expression was blank to the point of inscrutable.

He grabbed my hand, pulling me with him to my bathroom, starting the shower and ushering me in, still without a word. We washed each other, still without a word, just soft, lingering touches, and a few brief kisses.

"Any other plans today?" I asked him as I dried off.

He shot me a look that could only be described as indecent. "More of the same. We still have hours to ourselves."

After the way we'd spent our day, I didn't imagine he'd even want to collect on his end of the bet that night, but I imagined wrong.

We went out, did our usual party routine, but we wrapped it up early, and instead of heading home, we headed to his new place. I felt almost breathless with anticipation. I didn't even know if what he'd suggested was something I wanted to do, but I knew that I trusted him, and I knew that he made a habit of making me feel good.

He tugged me through his apartment, not even turning on any lights as we made our way to his room. Even that I didn't get to check out, as he led me directly to the bed, and the first thing he did was cover my eyes with a small sleep mask. I could still make out light on the sides, but not enough to know what was going on.

He tugged my clothes off, doing it quick like he was in a hurry. I couldn't imagine why. I didn't think he could be that hot for me again after how many times he'd taken me already that day.

"Tristan—" I began, but he shushed me, and somehow, that time, it worked. Probably because he'd begun to pull my arms above my head, and that had me distracted. Distracted and squirming. And wet.

He used something soft on my wrists, first one and then the other, tying them above me and apart. I couldn't tell what he used to bind me, but I tugged against it once he'd tied me to the headboard, and it seemed unbreakable.

He pushed his weight down on top of me without warning, and I gasped at the contact. His low, rough, raspy voice in my ear had me trembling. "We're going to do this nice and slow. All I want from you is your surrender. Beyond that, you don't have to think about a thing. Understand?"

I did understand. I understood perfectly, and I thought he was the most wonderful man in the world right then for taking the time, for caring enough, to understand, too. The intoxicating bliss I'd found in his arms had come from trust, and this was taking that feeling of losing myself in the moment, of relinquishing control, to a whole new level.

He moved off me. I heard the faint sound of him slipping out of his clothes, then the louder sound of him ripping open the packet on a condom. He was bare and hard as he slid over me. I shivered at the feeling of skin on skin.

He took my earlobe very softly in his teeth as he parted my legs and slid between. His thickness pressed against me, teasing at my entrance, and I moaned, somehow already ready for him.

"I can't give you all the time I need tonight to show you how good this can be for us, because I know you have to watch the kids in the morning, so just consider this a *taste*."

What the hell did that mean? I didn't know, and was afraid to ask. It seemed too much like asking about the future, and I emphatically didn't want to do that.

I didn't worry about it long, that was for sure. In fact, I didn't worry about a thing as he took his mouth to my neck, and his hands to my body.

He took me over that way, owned every cell in my body. I

surrendered, and he took me with hard, smooth strokes, and rough, sweet words. It was an experience I'd never forget as he taught me that I could put myself completely at someone's mercy, and come out of it with no wounds at all. Instead, I felt more whole with the experience, as though the parts of myself that had been broken and lost weren't so lost anymore. Under his touch, in his care, I felt more complete, like a newer, brighter version of myself.

We became passionate lovers and stayed the best of friends, but we didn't talk about it. In fact, we treated the topic like the land mine it was. Almost week passed like that.

We just lived in the moment.

In a way, it was completely wonderful for me. I'd never been able to live in the moment, and here I was, living every second like I never wanted it to end. I didn't think about the future. I didn't *want* the future. All I wanted was now.

I wasn't even inside of my body most days. I was still living in our last embrace. I would go through my chores, do my usual routine, but my mind was back in my bed, giving myself to Tristan. He owned me there. I was his, and I savored that ownership. There was no question that I wanted it to last forever.

We were inseparable, even more so than before, which was saying a lot.

A few careless comments brought it all crashing down, though it was bound to happen, one way or another.

The morning it happened was kind of horrible, and kind of wonderful.

Tristan was sweet as could be, cooking breakfast, making me keep him company in the kitchen. He touched me constantly, with his hands, his mouth, his smile.

I was on cloud nine until he spoke.

"I'm glad this worked out like it did. I didn't think we could manage to have sex, and it not turn into a thing."

I shot a glance at the boys, who were happily watching TV, but they were oblivious to him having said the word 'sex' in little more than a whisper. I was also trying to distract myself from what his words implied.

"Hmm?" I asked, going for oh so casual.

"I thought we couldn't just be friends after something like that. I was afraid you'd start to develop, you know, romantic feelings. I love that it didn't turn out awkward. Who says having a fuck buddy is a bad idea?"

I tried not to visibly flinch, but didn't quite manage.

He caught my expression out of the corner of his eye, sending me a rueful smile. "I know girls don't like that term, but what else would you call it?"

"How about we just not talk about it?" I suggested, making a last ditch effort at averting the fallout that I felt building up in my chest like a scream that just had to escape.

"My bad. That's probably a very solid idea. I was just saying…I like this. This has been…nice."

I stewed about that all day. I tried to hold my tongue, really I did, but by bedtime I was in a state, the words 'fuck buddy', and '…nice' just rolling around in my head, looking for Trouble.

We'd made plans to go out late, and I found Tristan getting ready in my room.

"Can I just say something?" I began, my tone already on its way to angry.

Tristan finished shrugging into a thin T-shirt before giving me his full attention. "Yeah. What's up?"

"I'm pretty sure you're already aware of this, but I am not a *casual* kind of girl. I've only been with a few guys, and both of the ones I was with willingly, were in a committed relationship with me. Before you, I'd never slept with a guy who didn't tell me he loved me. It goes without saying that I take exception to the term fuck buddy."

He didn't look sorry, his brow arching at me, his eyes getting a little hard on mine, which I wasn't used to, not from him. "I'm sorry I used that term. I was stupid to even bring it up. We going out?"

"Let me finish. You think I haven't developed any romantic feelings for you...but that's just not true. I have a hard time keeping things to myself—"

"You don't say."

"Let me finish," I said again, through gritted teeth, mad now, just from the look on his face, and the sick feeling in my gut that I knew just how he was going to react to what I was about to tell him. "You're fooling yourself if you think I don't have those feelings for you, Tristan. I've fallen in love with you."

I felt my jaw clench as his gaze turned insolent.

"Bullshit," he said softly.

I'd never seen his mean side, and with just a taste, I was certain I couldn't handle it.

"Wh-what do you mean? Did you hear what I said?"

"Oh, I heard you. I just don't believe you."

"Why would I lie about something like that?"

"Prove it. Tell me why you fell in love with me so fast. Tell me how."

He was very helpful at getting my hurt to turn to fury in a heartbeat.

"It was actually very easy, you *ass*. I couldn't help it. Being around you, I couldn't help myself. You're just too easy to love. Going by your reaction, though, I see that I'm *not*."

"Don't guilt trip me, Danika. That shit feels manipulative."

"I'd rather be manipulative, than be a heartless jerk."

"You keep making these statements about love. You say I'm the heartless one, but you've got this relationship thing down to an emotionless science."

"What the hell is that supposed to mean?"

"Everything is never and always with you, like you've done it all before. You *always* do committed relationships. You *never* have sex without love. Do you know how mechanical you sound when you say those things? It's become nothing more than routine for you. You make it sound like any man could have you, if he just agreed to those two things. You play so hard to get, but two easy lies could get you into bed."

"Don't be an ass."

"I'm not being an ass. I'm not saying this because I *don't* care. If I didn't give a damn, I would just say those words. Don't you get that? I don't make promises because I'm honest, and most damned promises are a lie."

I felt my lip quiver. He'd done it now. I wouldn't hold back on him. I felt how ugly the words were before they'd even left my lips. "You think you're such a perfect guy, just because you tell women the score, and they love you anyway. You think your dad was any different from you? You think your mother named you after him because he was a bastard? He was probably *just like you*, just as charming, just as fun, just as irresistible. Your worst nightmare is to become like your dad, but what would you do if some woman came up to you tomorrow, and told you she was pregnant?"

"I always use protection—"

"Which doesn't always work. You're dodging the question. I'll answer it for you. You'd run away. Just like your dad."

His jaw clenched, and he shook his head at me, looking pissed now. "That was low."

I knew it was. I felt low for saying it, but I didn't take it back.

"If you'll recall," he bit out. "This was just as much your idea as mine. Remember when you promised me that this wouldn't ruin our friendship? Was that a lie?"

I couldn't answer that. I didn't know how, and the idea that he'd *allow* our friendship to end just broke my heart.

He cursed, a long, loud, fluent tirade. "We should have stuck to our don't list."

I felt my face turning red with temper. As though that asinine list had magic powers, to keep us from making stupid mistakes.

I exploded. "It wasn't a don't list, you douche bag, it may as well have been a fucking checklist! Your fucked up mind just saw it as a challenge!"

His eyes were so cold as he studied me. It was a new experience for me, watching that warm golden gaze that I loved shoot ice at me. "I'm leaving. How about you give me a call when you grow the fuck up?"

I blinked, feeling almost numb as he started to gather his things, shoving them into his large duffle with short, angry movements.

I sat heavily on the bed as he just continued to pack without a word.

"Tristan," I said once, a soft plea in the word.

He ignored it. He ignored *me*.

In fact, he never uttered another word before he walked out.

CHAPTER TWENTY-SIX

The next week was more hellish than any breakup I'd ever been through, which scared the shit out of me, because it wasn't even a real breakup.

He was never even yours to lose, I told myself, at least a hundred times a day.

He didn't call, he didn't text, and he didn't come back to the house.

The one ray of light that seemed to appear as a result of the fallout was Frankie.

Two days after Tristan left, she started calling. Calling, and texting, and just showing up.

Frankie was good company. She was funny, and irreverent, and just plain easy to talk to. I had no idea why, but she'd decided that we were fast friends, and so we were. Between her and my usual nanny duties, I should have been adequately distracted.

Too bad that still left the nighttime for tossing and turning, and rehashing all of the stupid things I'd done and said.

I told Frankie as much one day over the phone. Her response was to take her distraction campaign into the evening hours, and we so we started hitting the clubs.

She was so persistent about monopolizing all of my free time, that I started to worry she might be *interested* in me.

"You know I'm into guys, right?" I asked her one night, on the way home from a great dancing my way to distraction session.

She laughed. A lot. And then laughed some more.

"I know what happened between you and Tristan, so yeah, I figured."

"Okay. Sorry. I know I sounded like an idiot. I just didn't want to be a tease or anything."

She was driving, but she was laughing so hard she had to pull her car over to the side of the road. "Fair enough. I wasn't offended. That just surprised me. I didn't realize that you thought I was hitting on you."

"I didn't think that. I just wasn't sure..." I cleared my throat, uncomfortable. "Do you know Tristan very well?" I asked her.

"Yeah, I'd say I know him pretty well. I called you the other day because I saw him the night he left here. The way he was acting just...worried me. I could tell he was angry, no, furious, about something, and when I asked him about you, he got worse. And then later, he hooked up with some chick, and ended up getting into a fight with her boyfriend. I know he has a temper, and he's been in plenty of fights, but I hadn't seen him quite like that...He was lucky he didn't get arrested."

I barely heard the rest of it. After she'd mentioned him hooking up that night, there was a twisting pain my chest that sort of blacked out my ability to hear or concentrate.

"Did Tristan tell you what happened between us?" I asked, when I could speak again, still feeling utterly sick to my stomach.

"Not in so many words. I pieced together that you'd had a falling out because he refuses to talk about you."

"I swear to God, I'm never getting involved with another man for as long as I live. Especially if it's a *fuck buddy* scenario. Fuck that."

That put a huge smile on her face. "You let me know when you're ready to play for the other team, sweetie."

Unaccountably, I blushed.

She laughed, pulling back onto the street. "Sorry, I can't help it, when you give me an opening like that. What are your plans tomorrow night?"

"My boss Bev has this weekly thing going on at the house. We call it 'Fuck Anonymous', because it's a friend/group therapy session. I can't miss it, since I dodged it last week, and I know that the longer I avoid it, the more shit I'll get for it later."

"Sounds like a steaming hot mess. Can I come?"

I laughed at the description. It was apt, to be sure. "Yes! They'll love you. It'll be a match made in heaven."

"Perfect. What time does it start?"

"Eight-ish is when the talking starts. Drinks and appetizers are out a good hour before, though."

"Okay, then. I'll be there at seven. Any hot chicks?"

"Yeah. Several, but none of them are technically single."

"Fair enough. Have you thought about that tattoo that you wanted?"

I grinned. "I have. I think I want to do it."

"Will you do it on camera? It's not a requirement, but I'd appreciate it. The producers are always looking for some sex appeal."

"Why the hell not?"

She fist pumped the air. "Yes! Score! I can't wait. You just tell me when, and I'll get some of my cherry blossom designs ready for you."

"Soon," I said vaguely, torn between wanting to do it right that second, and wanting to feel like it wasn't an impulse decision, especially an impulse decision based on the fact that I was trying to stay distracted from the disaster that had become my love life.

Bev had to have known what was going on, when Tristan and I had gotten hot and heavy, but she hadn't tried to stop me. She had touched my shoulder a few times in passing, saying things like, "If you need to talk about anything, honey, I'm always here," or "I hope everything is okay…"

And then after, when it had all so obviously gone to hell, she'd gone out of her way to be there for me.

I never cried. I had always been good at keeping the tears in, and the mess with Tristan was no exception.

But Bev bought gallons of ice cream, and was even sweet enough to stay up late several times to eat it with me.

I'd confessed everything to her, every hot, ugly detail. She'd been as wonderful about it as she was about everything, telling me that it would be okay, and that no, I wasn't the stupidest girl alive.

"My man picker is off," I'd told her forlornly.

She'd patted my shoulder comfortingly. "Aw, sweetheart, it really isn't. I saw what you were dealing with. There isn't a girl alive that could turn down a guy like Tristan, with the way he was laying on the charm. Just take a lesson from it, and it won't be a waste."

I knew it was good advice, and I promised myself that I would tuck it away for future use.

Fuck Anonymous with Frankie was a riot. She monopolized the entire thing, going on and on about several of her latest disastrous relationships, and some of her unorthodox sexual preferences.

She told every story with so much humor that all of us were laughing for most of the session, and I was particularly grateful, because she'd deflected any attention off me for another week.

When she went into detail about her lifestyle as a dominatrix, I think she shocked most of the women, but I was fascinated, especially with all of Tristan's talk of restraints.

"So you're *always* dominant?" Candy asked, clearly tantalized by the idea. She'd been flirting with Frankie all night.

Frankie nodded. "Some people switch, but that doesn't work for me. I have a *very* specific fetish. There are very different ways to practice BDSM, but my way is full speed ahead *hardcore*, which isn't for many, even in the scene. I can only think of one other person, who shall remain anonymous, who takes it as far as I do."

Sandra looked more shocked than anyone else about Frankie's lifestyle, just staring at her, open-mouthed, as she went into detail about strap-ons and spreader bars. I got the feeling Frankie could have talked about strap-ons alone for hours.

"I work in the Cavendish Casino," Sandra told Frankie, her eyes still a little wide in shock. "I work over in the art gallery, which isn't far from your tattoo shop. Sometimes I see the camera crew when I go out for lunch. It's all very exciting."

"You got any tats?" Frankie asked her with a smile, clearly convinced that she didn't.

"Just a tramp stamp," Sandra said, which startled a laugh out of several of us, including Frankie.

"A tramp stamp is no joke," Frankie told her. "So you work on the property. You ever seen the big man on campus?"

Sandra needed no other excuse to start in about James 'the dreamboat' Cavendish.

"We think she should make a pass at him," Candy piped in, after Sandra had been going on for a solid five minutes.

Frankie looked dubious. "My advice would be not to. He's actually one of my closest friends, and if he's interested, you'll *know* it."

Sandra looked crestfallen, as though she'd really been planning to make a pass at one of the richest, most beautiful men on the planet. I admired her confidence.

"I met him at a club kind of recently," I added, when there was a brief pause in the dialogue. "Sandra has talked about him exhaustively for years, and I have to say, I wasn't at all disappointed. Those eyes..."

Frankie nodded. "He's to die for beautiful. He doesn't do relationships, but you couldn't ask for a better friend."

"Why would he?" Harriet asked, sounding a bit bitter. "Filthy rich, male, and gorgeous, he can stay single forever. He'll probably knock up some nineteen year old when he's eighty, and call it a day. Men have it so easy."

Frankie laughed. "Getting a bit ahead of things, aren't you? I can't say what James will be doing when he's eighty, I'm just telling you that the best you could hope for nowadays is a casual fling with the guy, and if he's interested in you, you will *know it.*"

"Well, fuck," Sandra pouted, "that messes with all of my workplace fantasies about him seducing me in my office."

My eyes widened. I honestly couldn't tell if she was joking or not, but she didn't crack a smile, so I was leaning towards thinking that she wasn't.

I didn't think it could be healthy to be that obsessed with your boss, but I held my tongue.

Lucy stayed late that night, lingering when everyone had left except for her and Frankie. I'd known she would. One sympathetic look from her and the tears finally came.

She gathered me up into her arms, and I told her every little detail about the last few weeks, leaving out nothing.

It was Frankie's first time hearing it all, and she looked surprised at some of it, like his reaction to my declaration of love.

"That *asshole*," Frankie said succinctly. "That's got to be Twatalie baggage, for sure, but that doesn't make it okay."

Bev and Lucy were fascinated by this.

"What on earth is a Twatalie?" Bev asked.

That made me laugh, even through my ugly tears.

"Not what, but who," Frankie explained, her tone wry. "Twatalie is his gold-digging ex. It's a long story, but she fucked around on him with some rich men, and he just didn't see it coming. Been a man-whore ever since."

That brought on a fresh bout of tears. That's what I hated most about crying. Once I started, it went on for a long time.

"He—he's already slept up with other girls. He went out and hooked up with someone the night we had a fight."

Frankie grimaced. "I'm sorry. I should have kept that to myself. I didn't realize the extent of what had gone on with you guys."

"I'd rather know. It hurts, but I needed to hear it. I have to get over this. I'm *so stupid*."

The three women rushed to reassure me that I wasn't stupid, but it was hard not to feel that way, when I knew that I was still in love with Tristan, and he was probably sleeping with some random woman that very night.

CHAPTER TWENTY-SEVEN

It was almost two weeks after the big falling out when I got an excited call from Frankie. She was bursting at the seams hyper, I could hear it in her voice.

"They're going to perform at Decadence! Can you believe it? Their first gig in months, and they get to rock at the Cavendish property on a Saturday night!"

I knew, of course I knew exactly what she was talking about, but I asked anyway. "Who?"

"Tristan and the guys! Can you believe that? Jerry is a miracle worker. We're *going*."

I felt sick to my stomach. "I don't know. I doubt I'm invited. And I'm not sure I want to see Tristan, like, ever again."

"And what about Jared? He told me that you promised him you'd come to his next performance."

"It was more the other way around. I made him promise to tell me when there was one, and he didn't. You did. I really don't think Tristan will want me to be there."

"Well, you're really wrong. Just come with me. We can watch from the back, then slip out right after they finish. No one will even know we're there."

"I know you. You don't want to slip out right after they finish. You'd want to stay for the party, and I don't want to be the downer that makes you leave early. And I certainly don't want to go by myself."

"Just stop it! You're coming. I'm driving you. Be decked out in the hottest thing you own by eight p.m. Or else."

"Or else what?" I asked, honestly curious, now that I knew about her dominatrix alter ego.

"Don't question the or else! Just be ready in your best, 'I'm hot and Tristan can eat his heart out' dress."

In the end, I barely even considered backing out. I wanted to see them play, and I knew that Decadence would be crowded enough to keep things from getting awkward.

I wore a tiny white dress that didn't cover up a thing in back, *barely* covered up a thing in front, and showed off most of my legs. It was risqué, so risqué that I'd only worn it once before, to go out with Tristan. He'd told me it was the sexiest dress he'd ever seen, and so I didn't even consider anything else. It was a clear choice for 'eat your heart out, Tristan' attire. My sexy red heels were another no-brainer, as I was well aware that they drove him crazy, since he'd told me that on more than one occasion.

Bev helped me curl my hair into thick ringlets, and even sat and watched me put on makeup, throwing out suggestions all the while. That was the best thing about Bev; she was unconditionally supportive. I knew she didn't think I should be going out to see Tristan, but if I was, by God, she'd help me look my best for it.

I went heavy with the makeup; smoky eyes and blood red lips, the combination bringing out the paleness of my skin and eyes.

It was pouring rain outside. It had been all day. But in the midst of a Vegas summer, it was still steaming hot. Still, I didn't want to get wet just going from the house to Frankie's car, so I found the biggest umbrella in the house, and made a mad dash for it.

I managed to slide into her car still mostly dry.

She grinned when she saw what I was wearing. "That's a fucking perfect dress for making someone eat their heart out. Good job, girl. Gonna give him a heart attack."

"I just hope he's not mad that I'm there. He'll probably think I'm a stage five clinger for showing up."

"No. Stop worrying about that. He knows that you're coming, and he's not mad at all. All of the guys will want you there."

I didn't get a load of what Frankie was wearing until we were getting out of the car at the valet station. My eyes widened.

I'd known that she was fond of half-shirts. She worked them like nobody's business, so much so that I'd found myself trying the style, just hoping I could pull it off half as well.

She'd taken the half-shirt to a new extreme, with a ripped up black shirt that showed a hint of under-boob, black leather shorts that showed more than a hint of butt cheek, and some kick ass black combat boots.

Nearly every piece of skin that she was strategically baring had ink.

"I forgot to tell you something," she said, looking mischievously happy.

I smiled ruefully, knowing it was going to be something crazy, just from the gleeful look in her eyes. "What?"

She pointed behind me, toward the doors that led into the casino. I turned to see a camera crew converging on us, already obviously taping.

I rolled my eyes.

"I had to get this on camera. It's good press for the band."

I saw her point, but still glared at her for the ambush.

She was impervious, grabbing my hand and pulling me with her into the chaos.

I thought wryly that maybe I should have counted my blessings, that she hadn't subjected me to any camera time before, considering all of the time we'd been spending together lately.

"Who is this new hottie, Frankie?" one of her production guys called out.

"She's Danika!" Frankie called back, not slowing down.

"Is she your date tonight?"

Frankie just laughed, and I felt myself smiling ruefully. "She's just a friend. Try to keep up, guys."

It was the strangest thing, but I did find myself forgetting that the cameras were even there, especially as we made our way into Decadence.

The club was more crowded than I'd ever seen it, but I'd never been there on a live music night before. The enormous, once spacious dance floor had been converted into a writhing mass of humanity, and the guys hadn't even taken the stage yet.

There was one useful thing about being followed around by a camera crew; people got out of your way.

We moved to a spot about five rows from the stage. The ideal spot to see without being right at the front.

I was surprised when Frankie started bossing the crew around like it was her job.

"One camera on us. You won't want to miss Danika dancing. I know I don't. The rest, get on the stage. Get a good spot right under the lead singer."

The all male crew was quick to obey.

I sent her a sidelong glance. "I knew you had your own show, but I didn't realize that reality stars directed the crew."

"That's not the norm," the one camera guy still on us muttered.

Frankie just grinned and shrugged. "They did it, didn't they? They'll thank me later." She looked at the camera guy. "Tell the truth, Rodney. Have I ever steered you wrong?"

"That you haven't."

"See. If you know what you're doing, people listen to you,

whether it's your job to boss them or not. I'm just trying to get the best footage possible. They know it, so they listen to me."

I laughed, because though I wouldn't have thought of it, she had a point, because they hadn't hesitated to follow her orders.

"I've found that often the quality you see in successful people is knowing when to take the initiative, and being quick about it. I've never sat around, waiting for someone to tell me to take charge. I just do it."

I considered that, filing it away. I wanted badly to become successful in life, at *something*. I doubted there was anyone who'd grown up in my kind of chaos that didn't.

The dim lights suddenly went dark, the camera's light all that was visible for a long, pregnant pause. The crowd went quiet.

"Dim that light, Rodney!" Frankie said in a loud whisper. "We don't want to take attention away from the show."

Proving her words yet again, the camera's light dimmed.

A spotlight shone onto the stage, illuminating a scantily clad girl with hot pink hair.

My nose wrinkled. "Is *she* in the band?" I asked Frankie.

"Nope. She must be the opener. The guys must be hooking her up, because I've never seen her before."

More lights went on the stage, illuminating the rocker chick's band. She started belting out a screaming rendition of some old metal song that I kind of recognized, though I couldn't have named it. I liked metal, but this wasn't good metal.

"Is this the kind of music they play?" I asked into Frankie's ear. It wasn't what I'd been expecting, at all.

She shook her head, swaying to the ear-splitting noise. "Not at all. She must be fucking one of them, because she is not a good opener for their brand of rock."

That made me feel slightly ill.

She grimaced. "I'm sorry. That was insensitive. It just slipped out."

I shook my head that it was fine. She was probably right.

The hot pink haired chick sang three very similar songs before ending the set. I had the thought that I wasn't enjoying myself. This had been a bad idea.

The lights dimmed again, and I felt sick to my stomach as we waited for the band to come on stage.

Tristan walked on last, though he wasn't dramatic about it. He simply filed on after the others, taking his place at the front with utter confidence.

The spotlight hit him, and he grinned at the crowd. They cheered loudly, the women's screams markedly louder. And that was before he even sang a note.

When a hard drumbeat started, the guitars bled in, and he actually began to sing, the crowd went wild.

Watching him like that on stage was like seeing the puzzle pieces all shifting into place. He was perfect up there, and it wasn't any one thing that made him that way. It was *everything* about him; the proud posture of his broad shoulders, his confident smirk. He'd been my buddy, and then my lover, but watching him onstage made me see just how powerful he was, what a force of nature his very presence was. Part of me loved it, loved him like this, in his element, and part of me hated it. It was terrifying, because deep down I knew that you could never hold onto a man like this. He would become too big to live a normal life. It seemed inevitable.

His voice was deeply melodic, the song almost romantic, and the emotion in his voice matched the lyrics, which floored me. I'd never seen that side of him. The idea that he had that in him, but I'd never seen it, left a pretty deep wound in me, and it began to sink in that he really only saw me as a friend. He wanted me, yes, or at least he had before our falling out, but not like I needed him to, not like I wanted him. If I'd kidded myself for a moment that my feelings weren't one sided, those hopes were dashed as he poured his soul into the song.

I'd fallen for him, but he just hadn't fallen for me. Seeing him up there, getting clued in to all of the pieces of his puzzle, it hit me like a truck. We hadn't just had a fight. He hadn't just left because he was angry.

He wasn't in love with me.

Growing up as I had, especially in my teenage years, had always made me feel a little lost. And I felt that now. Just lost. Who was I? Who was somebody like me even supposed to be? Nobody loved me. It didn't feel like anyone ever had. So where did that leave me? Going in circles, I thought. Looking for the wrong things in the wrong people. That's where I was. I wondered if somebody ever fell for me, like really fell, the way I did, if I would even know it. I only seemed to have guys that couldn't give a damn on my radar.

Still, I couldn't help but be happy for him, that he had something like this, something so big and special to show the world.

CHAPTER TWENTY-EIGHT

I'd gotten my strange wave of melancholy in hand by the second song in their set, which thankfully, wasn't another love song.

"He's like one huge pussy magnet up there," Frankie almost shouted into my ear.

She was right, and I hated it.

"He's one huge pussy magnet everywhere he goes," I replied.

She laughed, and I smiled unhappily.

I told myself that it was good to get a healthy dose of reality. It was the first step to moving on, and I needed to get past this insanity.

The band was good. Really good. By the third song, I was dancing.

Frankie started it, shaking her hips at me, jumping around like a maniac. I had never been one to turn down any excuse to dance, and killer live music mixed with good company was the best excuse of all.

I knew that Rodney the camera guy was taping everything, and I found that I didn't mind. In fact, I gave him a show, dancing playfully with Frankie to the heavy beat of the drum.

I loved a good rock song with some heavy drums. I closed my eyes and let the music take over, Tristan's deep, sexy voice washing over me. *How could you be so intimate with a person, and not know they could sing their heart out to a crowd of strangers?*

I told myself resolutely that it didn't matter.

They performed seven original songs, all different enough to be interesting, some edgy, some moody and emotional.

"There's some record producer guys here tonight. James Cavendish called them in. He should be here, too. We need to find him afterward, see what he thinks. Wouldn't it be amazing if they got a record deal?"

I nodded, my eyes wide. In my mind, there was no doubt that they would get one, they were that good.

When the set ended, the stage was overrun, mostly by women.

In a way, I was relieved, because I didn't have to worry about actually dealing with Tristan, or any of them, for that matter. I just wasn't up for it.

Frankie seemed to be of the same mind, tugging me in the opposite direction, out into the lounge, her eyes searching the room, before she pulled me past that too.

When she started to wander down a hall that clearly said employees only, I dug in my heels.

"Where are we going?" I asked her, eyes narrowed.

"I told you. I want to talk to James."

"This is for employees only."

"I work here. Kind of. Don't worry about it. What are they going to do? Kick us out?"

I thought that's exactly what they'd do, but I let her pull me along.

We wound up in a huge white room that I quickly caught on was for the after party.

"Frankie!" I rounded on her. "I told you. I don't want to see anyone. Why would you drag me back here?"

She ignored me completely, waving at someone behind me,

then rushing off.

I turned to see James Cavendish striding into the room, dressed for business but looking relaxed. And God, he was still as stunning as I remembered. In the brighter light of this room, even more so, his skin darker, his eyes brighter, than I'd realized.

He was grinning at Frankie, then hugging her, saying something quiet into her ear.

I approached them, feeling very out of place. I did not hang out with people like this, and I couldn't believe that Frankie did.

James smiled at me, holding his hand out politely to shake, and we shook. "Nice to meet you, Danika. Frankie has told me so much about you."

I couldn't have been more shocked, and I had to scramble just to make small talk with the intimidating man. "Nice to meet you, too. We met once before, actually. Some guy got kicked out of the club for being a creeper, and you came by to make sure I was okay."

His brows raised, and he gave me a killer smile. "I remember that. Wow, small world. I didn't make the connection. It's darker in the lounge, but I see it now."

"My boss has a few paintings from your gallery. Let me just say, I'm a huge fan of some of the artists you've discovered. Art is a passion of mine."

He looked intrigued, tilting his head to study me. "Well, thank you. It seems we share a passion, then, Danika."

Frankie seemed to catch his eye, and his grin widened.

"For art, Frankie. Relax. I wouldn't hit on your girl."

This baffled me, and I found my mind slowly trying to make sense of it when he turned his dazzling smile on me again.

"Who's the artist of the paintings? The ones your boss got from my gallery."

"Someone named Mallory. Jackson Mallory."

"Tell me about the pieces."

"One is an abstract, called Orchard. Bold, warm colors, emotional leaning towards moody. It's absolutely stunning."

He was studying me very intently. "I know the painting. I like that description. You have a flair for this, Danika. Tell me about the second one."

"It's untitled. A portrait of a woman. A redhead. Her features are very detailed and...sensual." I felt very embarrassed to use that word in front of him, but I couldn't think of a better one. "A semi-nude, though luckily the essentials are covered, since my boss has two little ones in the house."

"I remember that painting, as well. I'll tell you what, Danika. If you ever want a job in the art world, you let me know. You have a good eye, and a penchant for descriptions, which is very important. And most importantly, that passion."

I was stunned, and flattered beyond words. So flattered that I barely stammered out a thank you at the praise. I'd never considered working at a gallery, but I couldn't say why it hadn't occurred to me. There was no question I'd enjoy it.

"Whenever you're done trying to hire her, James, I want you to tell me what you thought of the band!"

He looked thoughtful. "They're good. Very good. That lead singer is an attention grabber. I'd be shocked if they don't get a deal soon. In fact, I think they're getting an earful about that already." He nodded across the room, and we turned to look.

I turned, my gut churning as I saw Tristan and the guys, engaged in an intense conversation with some men in suits. I saw that Jerry was with them, which I should have guessed. He'd been the one to put this whole thing together.

I turned away quickly, not wanting to look at Tristan, or notice all of the women waiting to get the band's attention.

I counted to ten, not letting myself look at him again.

"Does the casino have a magic act?" I asked James, a devil getting ahold of my tongue.

"Excuse me?" he asked, looking amused but baffled.

"Tristan, the lead singer. You said he was an attention grabber. You're right. He is. He's a great singer, but that's not even his biggest talent."

"Really? Do tell."

"He does card tricks. Sleight of hand that you wouldn't believe. I can't even describe it, it's so good. You should ask him about it. And you should think about getting a fresh, young magic act. There's enough old men with too much plastic surgery dominating that field. You should do something *different*."

James didn't blow off my suggestion, as I'd more than half assumed he would.

"That's a solid idea. Our current act is a walking heart attack, so I'll have to ask Tristan about this sometime. Ah, here he is. Tristan, Danika's been telling me..."

James trailed off as a hand grabbed my arm from behind.

"Excuse me," I heard an achingly familiar voice growl right before I was being dragged out of the room by a big hand that was attached to the person that I least wanted to see in the world.

TRISTAN

It was even worse than I'd anticipated, when I laid eyes on her again. One glance at her and I was lost.

We weren't alone, in fact it felt like everyone I'd ever met was crowded into the room with us. She was standing close to Frankie, their sides nearly touching. She was thinner than the other woman, but she towered over her, especially in those fuck-me heels.

Both of them had black hair, but that was about all they had in common, looks wise. Still, they were a striking sight, standing side by side. Danika looked like a supermodel, her lithe curves hugged perfectly in that tiny white dress that drove me out of my mind crazy, and Frankie could have been a pinup model, with her half-shirt exposing huge amounts of toned, inked up skin.

They were talking to James, in fact they'd gone directly to him, as though no one else was in the room. But of course, that wasn't the worst of it...

The part that made my gut twist hard was that she barely looked at me, just one quick glance and she looked pointedly away, as though she was afraid to meet my eyes, as though she didn't think I'd be happy to see her there.

That killed me, but I couldn't blame her. I'd been a bastard. Not only had I not called her for weeks, I hadn't even been the one to invite her here, hadn't even tried to reach out when I knew she was coming.

She was saying something to James that had her eyes flashing, her hands moving in small gestures to emphasize her point.

She was doing that adorable thing she did where she got so passionate about a subject that it turned into a rant. I loved it when she did that, and now she was doing it for James Cavendish.

And worse, James looked fascinated by her, interrupting her impassioned little tirade occasionally, his smile warm.

The guys had all been worried that our pink-haired opening act would blow our shot at a record deal, but I realized that I was about to do that, when I choked out James fucking Cavendish.

I was moving to them, approaching Danika from behind, before I could stop myself.

I overheard the last bit of what Danika was saying to Cavendish as I walked up.

"Tristan, the lead singer. You said he was an attention grabber. You're right. He is. He's a great singer, but that's not even his biggest talent."

"Really? Do tell."

"He does card tricks. Sleight of hand that you wouldn't

believe. I can't even describe it, it's so good. You should ask him about it. And you should think about getting a fresh, young, hot magic act. There's enough old men with too much plastic surgery dominating the game. You should do something *different*."

My chest ached, my vision going a bit blurry.

Cavendish smiled at her like she'd just said something brilliant. He looked up, said something in my general direction, but I barely heard him, I was so floored by the revelation that, while I'd been a complete bastard to her, she was promoting me like she was my damned cheerleader.

I didn't think, I just moved, striding to her, grabbing her arm, and dragging her with me out of the room.

She went along with me without much fight at first, but when she saw that we were leaving the club, she started to try to pull away.

"We need to talk," I told her gruffly.

"Now?! You think we need to talk right now? This is not good timing for you. I'm pretty sure you need to be back there, talking with those record guys."

"That's what Jerry is for. No reason for me to talk to them. Anything they wanted to know about me, they saw on stage."

She followed me rather sedately, for all of ten seconds.

"What the *hell*, Tristan? Have you ever tried to walk in four inch heels? I'm guessing not, but unless you want me to break an ankle, you had better slow down. And where are we going?"

I slowed, not looking at her, but listening to her, absolutely floored at how good it felt just to hear her voice again, even if she was yelling at me.

"I missed you," I told her quietly, as I punched the button on the elevator that led to the parking garage.

"You missed me?" she asked, her tone incredulous, as the elevator doors enclosed us. "You missed me?" she repeated, when I didn't respond. "Obviously. Because this is what you do when you miss somebody; you don't call, you don't text, *for weeks*, and you fuck around with random women."

I winced, suddenly feeling a little light headed. So she knew. Of course she did. *Fuck.* I didn't know if that was good or bad. At least I wouldn't have to tell her myself.

The elevator door opened and I tugged her out into the parking garage, practically dragging her to my car.

I opened the passenger door, just looking at her as she scratched at my hand like a wild cat.

"Let me go! What are you doing? Why would you think it's okay to just drag me to your car?"

I clenched my jaw, feeling completely out of control. "Get in the car. We need to talk."

She glared at me for a solid minute, my hand still holding her wrist. I knew I wasn't hurting her, but I wasn't letting go, either. Not until she got in the car.

She got in, calling me a few choice names as I closed the door behind her.

I got into the driver's seat, and just sat there for a long time, neither of us speaking.

I listened to her inhaling, exhaling, and thought again how much I'd missed just having her breath the same air as me.

"We need to talk," I repeated myself, yet again. "I missed you."

I didn't know why it was so hard for me to find the words I wanted to say to her, to find words to even begin to express what I was feeling, but that seemed to be the best I could choke out.

Something in my words, or maybe my tone, finally reached her.

She let out a long, resigned sigh. "We *should* talk. I'll start. You were right. About everything. We should have stuck to that stupid list. Friends was always our only option. I just lost my mind for a bit."

It felt like I'd been punched in the gut, only worse, because I'd been punched plenty of times, and it never felt like this, like some raw wound that I'd helped to cause, and that I might not recover from.

CHAPTER TWENTY-NINE

TRISTAN

I don't know how long I just sat there in a sort of stunned silence. I was not good with this shit.

I started the car, pulling slowly onto the ramp that led up to the top.

"Um, where are you going? This isn't even the way to the exit, Tristan."

"So fucking bossy," I growled, steering my car up onto the top floor, which wasn't covered.

Rain pelted the car, drowning out some of the tense silence that was driving me crazy.

I'd barely glanced at her since we'd walked out of the after party.

Where she'd torn my heart out of my chest.

By being my biggest supporter, when she had every right to hate my guts.

Finally, I turned to look at her.

She stared back steadily, her jaw firm, her arms folded across her chest. "So that's it then," she said, sass in every word.

"What's it?"

"We made a mistake. Let's forget it ever happened, and go back to friendship. I realized tonight—"

"I know what you taste like," I interrupted, my tone harsh. "I know how it feels to have you come against my tongue. What it feels like to have you clench around my cock while you lose your fucking mind. And you, you've tasted me. I've shoved my cock so deep down your throat I felt your tonsils, Danika. Are we going to forget all of that?"

She blinked at me, her mouth agape. Speechless. That was a first.

I leaned over and gripped her thigh. "How, Danika? Tell me how we're supposed to forget any of that?"

"You—you...It was all casual for you, Tristan. It didn't mean a thing."

"I've had my mouth all over you, my hands...my teeth. And your cunt has squeezed my cock so tight that my vision went blurry. Am I supposed to forget that, too?"

"Tristan!"

"And you said you were in love with me. Do you really expect me to fucking forget that?" I got out of the car, slamming it shut. I was drenched by the hot rain before I'd even made it to the passenger door.

I wrenched it open, pulling a shocked Danika out into the rain with me.

I shut the door behind her, pressing her against it.

I kissed her. She turned her face away, and I nuzzled into her neck before coming back to her mouth. I pushed my tongue between her lips, needing to get inside of her any way that I could.

She moaned, gripping the front of my shirt. I felt the moment she gave in, and my hands gripped her ass, dragging her up, grinding my erection against her.

Her legs wrapped around me, her dress so short that it rode up to her hips with the motion.

I wrenched my mouth away, sliding it to her ear. My breath was panting out of me, so I was breathless when I spoke. "I'm going to fuck you hard on the hood of this car, in the pouring rain. And. You. Are. Not. Going. To. Forget. It." I kissed the sensitive spot behind her ear between each roughly uttered word.

I felt her entire body tremble, and I shuddered against her.

I carried her to the front of the car.

I splayed her out, dragging her arms high above her head.

I straightened, keeping my hands on her knees, spreading them wide, and just looked at her.

Her dress had gone completely see-through, and it was more indecent than being outright naked. I loved it. I wouldn't forget the sight for as long as I lived.

Her breasts heaved, the nipples hard and pink against the filmy white fabric. Trails of eye makeup ran down her pale cheek, her pitch black hair wet and messy, trailing into her face, and I'd never seen anything more beautiful in my life.

I took my mouth to her, licking the rain off her skin, sucking at her through the soaking wet, paper-thin material of her white dress.

My hands got busy slipping off her tiny red thong, then unbuttoning my jeans.

I kissed my way between her legs, burying my face in her core, licking and sucking at her sex, the hot rain mixing with the taste of her, creating an intoxicating blend.

I didn't come up for air until I was sure that she had lost her mind.

I jerked my cock out of my jeans, moving over her, pressing hard against her as I guided myself to her entrance.

"You gonna forget this?" I rasped into her ear as I worked myself in.

Her answer was a nearly unintelligible negative. I eased in and out, my pace slow as I closed my eyes and savored that perfect feeling of being inside of her.

She clenched around me like the tightest little fist and I lost my mind.

My smooth strokes grew into hard jack-knife thrusts, harder, harder.

My hands pushed her legs wide open, wider, and I pounded in and out, in and out, telling her just how beautiful she was, how perfect she felt, my mouth at her ear.

Her replies came in the form of whimpers and moans, and I thought that I'd missed that the most; the sound of the most controlled woman I'd ever met losing her shit.

"Let go, sweetheart," I told her raggedly, so close to the edge. I reached down, finding her clit and rubbing it with the lightest touch, ramming hard.   One contact so soft, the other nearly brutal in its roughness. "Come for me. I need you to. Give me everything you have, every ounce of that control, sweetheart."

I felt her clenching me, the spasms that told me she was coming, and I rammed to the hilt and held, pouring into her.   It felt like I left my body and came back into it, it was that intense.

I started to pull out, but she was so tight, squeezing at my base, so wet, the tight glide inside of her so fucking smooth, that I found myself pushing back in before I'd fully pulled out, hard like I hadn't just emptied myself inside of her.

I bent down, sucking a nipple into my mouth as my hips circled into a rhythm that started out easy, but had my neck arching and turned into a full on hell bent fuck, my out of control need for her taking me over completely.

I made sure she came again before I sank deep, back bowed, and emptied myself inside of her. Again.

"I missed you," I said into her ear.   Maybe she'd believe me after *that*.

I shifted slowly out of her, shutting my eyes at the sweet pull of her on my cock.   I helped her straighten her dress, which made her laugh, which made me laugh.

She ran her hands over her may as well be naked torso, smiling.   "Am I all covered up?" she asked, pitching her voice loud over the still pounding rain.

"Get in the car, boo. If anyone else sees you like this, I may have to knock some heads together."

I glanced around, relieved to see that we were the only car on the roof level. I hadn't been in the right frame of mind to think to look before.

I handed her into the car, tucking myself back into my pants as I moved around to the driver seat.

She was digging into her tiny handbag as I started to drive.

"Where are we going?" she asked, as though she was surprised that we were leaving.

"I'm taking you home," I told her. "You can't walk around in that dress now."

She sighed, as though I were being unreasonable. "Well, I need to text Frankie. It was rude to ditch her."

"Frankie will be fine."

"It was still rude. And your fault."

"Yes. Just tell her that. My fault. Problem solved."

She played on her phone for a solid five minutes while I drove. I knew it was five minutes because I timed it, watching the dash and getting more rigid by the second, as she completely ignored me.

Finally, I couldn't stay quiet for another second. "We going to talk about what happened back there?"

I saw her stuff her phone into her clutch out of the corner of my eye. I couldn't see her expression, because my eyes stayed on the road, but I *felt* her glare. "Yes," she said bitingly. "Let's talk about that. You didn't use a condom, and you know how I feel about that."

That stunned me into silence, as I hadn't even thought of it. I did know how she felt about it, and I'd been so out of my mind, so mindless with my need, that it hadn't even occurred. I'd never done anything like that before.

I could remember the feel of her, skin on skin, how utterly

divine it had felt, and still, even while I was inside of her, I hadn't thought of the protection that I usually couldn't do without.

"Fuck," I said succinctly. "I'm sorry. I lost my mind. At least you're on the pill."

"At least. And it won't be happening again."

I felt my gut clench. "It won't?"

"It won't. No condom, no sex."

My lungs punched out in a huge sigh of relief. I'd thought she was saying no sex in general. I had one condom in my wallet. It was something at least, but I'd need to go for more in a hurry. It was debatable, even after coming twice, if one would be enough to take us until morning. I had missed her.

I gripped a hand on her knee, rubbing. I was getting hard again, thoughts of the near future taking over the now.

"I need your mouth, sweetheart," I told her quietly, meaning it.

"Excuse me?" she said, still full of that sass. Part of it was the fact that she was still rightfully pissed at me, and part of it was just her personality.

"You heard me. Suck my dick while I drive. I'll make it up to you later. As many times as you want. I've been dreaming about having that mouth wrapped around my cock for weeks." There was a definite plea in my voice, because I was desperate for the contact, desperate for her to perform a willing act on me just because I asked.

I was a little shocked and beyond relieved when she actually complied, shifting in her seat to grip me through my jeans. Her hot mouth moved to my ear, biting at the lobe as she unbuttoned, unzipped, and fisted me through my boxers.

I groaned as she jerked hard at me.

"Tell me again that you missed me," she whispered.

"I missed you, boo. Everything about you."

"Even my attitude?"

"'Specially that."

I took one hand off the wheel, gripping her hair and moving

her head down, as gently as I could manage.

"Suck me off, sweetheart. I need it fast. And now."

I helped her pull me from my pants, lifting my hips off the seat to free myself.

Her hot breath puffed onto my tip as she gripped me hard at the base. I pushed her onto me with a hand gripped in her hair. I was in no mood for teasing.

I felt her knowing laugh around my cock and I jumped inside her mouth. Her head bobbed up and down as she started up a rhythm, her tongue busy, her grip firm.

"Harder. Suck me off hard," I bit out, gripping her hair, jerking into her mouth, pushing far enough to feel her throat closing around me.

I was emptying into the back of her throat with a few short strokes, hand gripping hard into her hair.

She sucked me hard, wringing me dry, before she raised her head. Her hand still stroked me, with a lighter touch now, her nails scoring over my scrotum.

"I fucking love your mouth," I told her.

"You love fucking my mouth," she agreed, twisting the words.

I laughed, pulling her into my side, feeling a surge of such joy and happiness that she was even speaking to me. That joy seemed to be channeling itself into an urgent need to fuck her repeatedly. Luckily, she wasn't complaining.

CHAPTER THIRTY

She was already checking her phone again as I started driving.

"Frankie upset that you left?" I asked.

"Hmm? Frankie? Oh no. This is something else."

Just by the absent, slightly agitated tone of her voice, I knew who was texting her.

"Your ex," I guessed, feeling suddenly less happy and more violent.

She sighed unhappily. "He just won't get a clue. He thinks it's cute to be persistent, but I'm so over his crap."

I was pulling back over before she finished the first sentence. I grabbed her phone, ignoring her complaints, and started to read.

I was fuming almost instantly.

Daryl: I miss you. I'm at a party over at Dig's house. Come see me baby.

This text was followed by an address, which I assumed was Dig's house.

"What kind of a name is Dig?" I asked Danika, still scrolling through her texts. It was basically a variation of the same thing;

I love you, I miss you, come see me. There were several a day, all from him, none sent. From what I could tell, Danika had only responded once, a few weeks ago, and that was to tell him to leave her alone.

"It's a nickname, though I don't even know his real name. The guy's a loser. Even if we were still together, I would never go to a party at Dig's house. All of his party's just involve a bunch of skinny white boys smoking pot for days at a time."

That surprised a laugh out of me, but I came across a message that killed that quickly enough. In fact, I suddenly felt sick to my stomach.

I showed her the screen of her phone.

Daryl: I miss your sweet pussy, baby. Come over here. I need to be inside of you again.

"Does he say shit like this to you often?" I bit out.

She cringed, her cheeks flushed. "You tell me. You're the one reading all of my messages. And don't get mad at me about what he's saying. You think I have any control over that? I wish he'd forget I even existed."

"Well, you're about to get your wish. This is off Flamingo and Pecos, right?"

She was watching me warily. "Yeah it's close to there. You aren't planning to do something crazy, are you?"

I started driving again, the last words I'd read feeling like they were permanently scarred into my brain.

It was the most hypocritical thing in the world, but the thought of Danika having sex with another man, the idea of someone else being inside of her, even in the past, made me crazy.

"Tristan! You aren't really going there, are you?"

"I am going there. This guy is going to stop harassing you."

"Tristan!" She sounded genuinely distressed. "You're going to get yourself arrested!"

"Relax. I won't. I'm just going to talk to him."

"You promise? He's not worth getting arrested over."

"I promise," I told her, fully intending just to scare the shit out of the creep, but thinking that it would be totally worth it to get arrested to put the guy who'd been inside of her sweet pussy in the hospital. "I promise that I'm just planning to talk to him, but I'm going to need you to stay in the car. If he said some shit to you like he put in that text, I can't be held responsible for my actions."

"That's ridiculous! You don't even know what he looks like. How will you even find him?"

"I'll ask. Just promise me you'll stay in the car, and I will take care of this. I just need five minutes in there. Can you do that for me?"

She let out a noisy, frustrated breath. "I can. But you have to swear you aren't going to do anything crazy."

"I swear. Again."

The house was easy enough to find, once we got to the street. It was so crowded, some idiots had even gone so far as to park on the lawn.

"This Dig's house?" I asked Danika, parking several houses away.

"Yes. Be careful in there. He'll be surrounded by his friends. If something happens, you'll be outnumbered."

"I'll be careful," I reassured her, stepping out of the car. What I didn't tell her was that I hadn't lost a fight in my life, outnumbered or not. I was twice the size of most guys, and knew how to throw a mean punch.

"Five minutes," I told her before shutting the door.

I barely noticed how the rain pelted down as I went to the house, that text still bouncing around in my brain, making me crazy.

The house was not as packed as I would've thought, considering all of the cars parked out front, but the place reeked of pot.

There was a group of skinny white guys passing around a bong on a sofa in the first room, and that's where I started.

Lucky for me, there was only one Daryl in the house, and I was directed to the backyard by the group of potheads.

"Thanks," I called, knowing that just the sight of me had scared the paranoid bastards.

The second I stepped outside, I spotted a Daryl in the small covered patio, sheltered from the rain.

He was a skinny guy, covered in tattoos. He had one side of his head shaved, the other dyed black and styled emo. He had silver flesh tunnels in his ears, and a tattoo of a crow covering most of his neck, and he was wearing fucking skinny jeans. Somehow, I just *knew* it was him.

He was playing on his phone, and smoking a joint.

My hands curled into fists, and I strode right up to him.

"Daryl," I addressed him.

He glanced up at the name, reaffirming my suspicions. "Yeah?" he asked, his tone insolent. He had guts, for a tiny little thing.

I didn't beat around the bush, stepping close, lifting him up by the front of his shirt. I still towered over him. He tried to shake me off, but I barely noticed, letting him get a load of the look on my face. It was really easy to put murder in my eyes. I just had to think about that last text I'd read.

"We've spoken before. On the phone. I'm Danika's friend. Remember me?"

"Fuck you, man!"

He had a nerve, I'd give him that, but that's all he would get.

I turned, slamming his back into the house. He barely weighed a thing. "I seem to recall warning you to leave her alone."

"Who the hell are you?" he wheezed.

"I'm Tristan. I'm the guy that looks out for Danika, and I'm going to do you a really big favor. I'm not going to put you in the hospital tonight. I'm feeling nice, so I'm going to give you one more warning. Listen carefully, because I won't be telling you this again. Are you listening?"

I waited until he nodded.

"No contact. No calls. No texts. Nothing. If you do any of those things, you won't be hearing from me, you will be seeing me, and I won't be talking, I'll be putting your skinny ass into a body cast. Are we clear?"

"Why are you doing this? Are you fucking her?"

"None of your fucking business. But hear this, I see any of those dirty fucking texts again, that'll be a different story altogether. You'll be missing a pair when I'm done with you."

I dropped him to the ground and walked away, because if I heard one more word from him, I'd be breaking my promise to Danika.

DANIKA

I let out the breath I'd been holding when I saw him striding back to the car, five minutes later, as promised.

He got back into driver's seat, hands going to the steering wheel and clenching. I could tell he was upset by the tenseness in his posture, and that grip on the wheel.

When he spoke, his voice was low and hoarse. "Can you tell me why you stayed with him for so long? I met him for five minutes, and there's no doubt in my mind that you can do better. Worlds better. You're a smart girl. Why did it take you two years to figure that out?"

I didn't look away from him, but the answer to that question made me feel delicate. Still, I wanted to give him the real answer, no bullshit. "I guess I didn't want better. I wanted...just what I could keep. This probably doesn't make sense to you, since you have a family, but I wanted something like a family.

Even if he wasn't perfect, I thought he'd stick around. No one's ever stuck around for me.

"In the back of my mind, I guess I thought that if I aimed really low, things were more likely to last. I just wanted to belong to someone, and for someone to belong to me. It turns out, aiming low only brings you lower." I took a long, shaky breath. "I've learned that lesson a few times. I think it finally stuck this time."

His hand moved from its death grip on the steering wheel to softly cover mine where it was gripped in my lap. "I'll always stick around for you, Danika. I mean that. You're my best friend. No matter what, I'll always be there for you, if you want me."

That had me torn. Completely. My sweet side wanted to melt at those words, but my bitter side wanted to call him out, because he hadn't stuck around. Not even close.

My bitter side won out. "Like you've *been* sticking around? Taking off for two weeks, not calling, not coming by, not even inviting me to your performance. Is that what you'd call being *there for me*?"

"I'm sorry for that. I went off the deep end for a minute, but I'm back, okay? I, um, haven't had any luck with relationships. In fact, the only serious one I ever had was just *bad*. It makes my skin crawl to even think about how much of myself I put into that mess, and it just wasn't worth it."

"Twatalie," I said darkly, not wanting to talk about her; the woman he'd been willing to give so much more to.

He wasn't familiar with the nickname, and it surprised a laugh out of him. "Twatalie?"

"Frankie told me about her. If someone is named Natalie, and they're a twat, they automatically get downgraded to Twatalie."

He squeezed my hand, his smile big and warm and all for me. "It is fitting. And for the record, I wanted you at the performance, and I knew you were coming. I was a shit for not calling you myself, but I made sure that you knew about it."

"You told Frankie to tell me?"

"I didn't have to, but yeah I asked her to. She would have anyway, I see now. Frankie is good like that. Listen, I just need you to give me one more chance, okay? I won't pull this shit again. I didn't know…I didn't understand what a mistake I'd made, until I saw you tonight, but it's real fucking crystal clear to me now, that I shouldn't have done that."

I still had a million questions, and I was far from done picking this to death, but my sweet side won out for the moment. "So you want to call a truce?"

"Something like that. Whatever you call it that involves you letting me back into your life, and not hating me for being a bastard."

My breath shuddered out in a sigh. "I could never hate you, and you're already back."

He started driving, still holding my hand. "I missed you." He said it like he had each time before, as though he was just realizing it himself.

I let us into Bev's house quietly, going straight to my room.

Tristan was pressing himself against my back as I closed the door, his mouth at my neck.

"I need to be inside of you again," he rasped into my ear, his tone urgent, kissing me on that spot on my neck that drove me wild.

I loved his desperation, loved feeling like he couldn't get enough of me, and even if it meant something different to him than it did to me, I was going to savor it while I could.

He peeled my dress off me from behind, pushing me onto my stomach on the bed. I heard him working out of his own wet clothes before his hot body was pressing hard onto my back. He pushed until I was grunting under the weight of him, hugging me hard.

He eased off quickly, raising up to his knees, and using a hand on my belly to bring me with him. His hands on my hips had me on all fours, bracing for him. I heard him ripping open a foil packet before he was at my entrance, pushing just inside.

"Touch yourself," he ordered.

I reached down with one hand, rubbing my clit as his cock teased at my entrance, and his hands found my breasts, skimming over them with a light touch. I pushed back hard, working him in another inch.

He moaned, his fingers rolling my nipples, then tugging at them. "Work that clit faster, sweetheart. You aren't wet enough to take all of me yet."

"I am," I argued, twisting my hips towards him, desperate to feel him deeper.

He pulled out completely.

"You think so?" he asked, something in his tone making me crane my neck to look back at him.

"Yes. Feel me. I'm wet. I want you inside of me."

His fingers snaked down, slipping into me, proving my point with their slick entry. "So you are. Okay, then. Ask me for it."

I straightened, bumping into him until we were both on our knees, my back to his chest, his legs between mine keeping me wide open. My head fell back so I could look up at him. "What?"

"You want me inside of you. I'm telling you to ask me for it. Be specific, and say please. Also, use my name."

My first instinct was to tell him to go fuck himself, but something in his tone, some strange possessive thread, made me think he'd do just that, if I didn't ask. And something about that possessiveness, especially coming from him, just made me more desperate to have him buried deep inside of me.

"Please fuck me from behind, Tristan. Please bury your cock as deep inside of me as you can go, as many times as you can, until I lose my mind."

My tone was sarcastic, but it still did the trick. He pushed me down until my face hit the mattress, my knees still pushing my ass high, a position he took full advantage of, grabbing my hips and plunging into me with one deep thrust.

I stuffed a pillow in my mouth to keep from screaming as he went at it, rough with me as he'd never been before, his size making it nearly unbearable, it was so intense. And yet, I found myself building up to that pinnacle faster with his heavy, hard, needy thrusts.

He pounded deep, relentlessly bringing me over the edge. He lifted my hips higher as I clenched around him, grinding deep and, with a low groan, emptying inside of me.

He lay heavy on my back when he'd finished, kissing my cheek, and hugging me close.

I was so exhausted that I drifted off before he'd even pulled out of me.

I woke again sometime in the night. It took me a few disorienting seconds to figure out why.

Tristan's arm had tightened around me, squeezing the breath out of me. He was at my back, leg thrown over my thigh, arm over my chest. Somehow, I still hadn't woken up in fear. I slept so deeply in his arms, so peacefully.

His mouth was at my ear, his voice a deep, comforting rumble. *"Missed* you."

I shut my eyes, a wave of absolute contentment running through me. *I love you*, I thought. "I missed you, too," I said.

He relaxed against me, and we fell back to sleep.

CHAPTER THIRTY-ONE

I woke up alone. I had a small hope that he was already up, but a quick search of the house dashed that hope in a hurry.

My reaction to his absence was a strong one.

I started making breakfast for the boys, tears running down my cheeks.

I'd never been so emotional, and this one last thing, him disappearing before I woke up, made me realize what a mess I'd become.

I had it together by the time the boys woke up, but my composure was a fragile thing. The morning was torturous, and I had to struggle to be good company for the boys, when it usually came so easily.

After lunch, the boys helped me walk the dogs, a slow, disorganized trek around the neighborhood.

My heart tried to pound right out of my chest when we circled back to the house, and I saw Tristan's car, and moreover, Tristan leaning against the back end of it, arms folded across his chest, straining the material of his T-shirt rather distractingly.

He grinned as we rounded the corner, and everyone; the dogs, the boys, and me, started rushing to him.

He met us halfway, greeting the boys and the dogs with pats on the head.

His smiling eyes met mine, but the smile died when he saw how I was watching at him.

"What's wrong, boo?" he asked, sounding genuinely concerned.

I hitched up one shoulder in a self-conscious shrug. "Nothing. I just thought you'd disappeared on me again."

He straightened from where he'd crouched to pat the dogs, wading through them to move close to me.

He cupped my face with both hands, his eyes studying me carefully. "*No. No. No*, sweetheart, it wasn't like that at all. I just went to run some errands. You were sleeping so peacefully; I didn't want to wake you."

I opened my mouth to speak, but he bent his head down, touching his lips to mine, before I could get a word out.

In front of the kids, the dogs, the neighborhood in general, he kissed me senseless, and Lord could the man kiss. His hands stayed where they were, cupping my cheeks with a soft touch, but it didn't matter. He turned my thoughts into puffs of smoke with just his lips on mine.

When he pulled back he was smiling, and pandemonium surrounded us.

Ivan and Mat were both shouting questions at us. Embarrassing questions.

"Was his tongue in your mouth, boo?" Mat asked, sounding disgusted.

"Does this mean you're going to have a baby?" Ivan asked, sounding more disgusted.

"Did you just give each other cooties?" Mat asked, sounding less disgusted, and more fascinated, with that possibility.

"Do you have to get married now?"

All of these questions were accompanied by the dogs howling or barking. Loudly.

I looked up at Tristan, saw the twinkle in his eye, and started laughing. We both did.

We didn't stop until we'd herded the kids and dogs into the house.

"Did you already eat lunch?" Tristan asked, heading straight for the kitchen.

"We did."

"Oh," he said stopping, coming back to help me gather up leashes. "Any plans today?"

"Not really. Just watching the boys until dinnertime."

"Jerry's home. He was out late, but he should be up soon. I'll tell him to watch the boys while we go do some shopping."

"Shopping? For what?"

"Shit for my apartment."

"Boo, he said a bad word!" Mat shouted from less than two feet away, taking off his shoes.

"Fuck, sorry," Tristan said, heard himself, then smacked his palm into his forehead. "My bad. Boys, will you go see if your dad is awake?"

They took off for Jerry's room.

I waited until they were out of earshot to speak. "Shit for your apartment?"

"Yeah. You know, plates, silverware, pots, pans."

I wasn't sure I wanted to know why he didn't have any of that stuff already, considering he was in his mid-twenties, so I didn't ask.

"Come with me? You can come check out my apartment, help me get settled in."

"Sure, if Jerry doesn't mind."

"He won't," he assured me.

Jerry was a good sport about the whole thing. He usually was. He took the boys to play in the backyard, and Tristan started tugging me toward the front door.

I pulled back. "I need to change. I can't wear hot pink cheer shorts and a half-shirt to the store."

He glanced back, giving me one of his mind-shattering once

263

overs. "Yes you can. That outfit is fucking hot. Throw some flip flops on, and we're good to go."

I ran my hands through my messy hair. I'd washed it earlier, and hadn't even brushed it before it dried. I'd been in a bit of a state.

Now it was a messy tangle down my back.

"I'm a mess, Tristan. Give me ten minutes to make myself presentable."

He yanked me to him, pulling my head back by the hair to plant a kiss on my nose, his golden eyes smiling, dimples flashing. "You look drop-dead gorgeous. Most beautiful girl in the world. Perfect."

He pulled back, giving me a firm slap on the ass. "Now get those flip flops on, and let's go."

I didn't begin to know how to argue with that, and I'd be lying if I said that his flattery didn't affect me. It always had.

"Where are we going to get all this shit?" I asked after we were in the car, and heading out of the community gates.

"Costco over by the Galleria Mall."

"Costco?"

"Yeah Costco. You ever been there?"

"Yes, but I didn't know you could get all of that stuff there."

"Hell, yeah. You can get just about anything at Costco."

And so we spent the afternoon shopping for his new apartment. I had to admit I enjoyed myself. We spent hours in the warehouse store, looking at everything, from sofas, to vitamins, to books, to camping gear. We wound up shopping for food to fill his empty fridge, founds some nice square white plates, silverware, pots, pans, glasses, and even paper towels.

We went through every aisle in the place, just looking at everything. It was one of those moments where I realized how fun everything was with Tristan. I could enjoy spending time doing just about anything with him.

He grabbed a bouquet of pale lavender roses. They were

pale at the base, the color growing more vibrant at tips.

I smelled them, charmed by the unusual color.

"An exquisite flower for my exquisite girl."

I blushed, at the compliment, and the fact that he'd called me his girl. I was scared to read too much into anything with him, but it was hard not to hope.

"These are for me?" I asked him, smelling them again.

We were in line, five carts back, and he tugged me to him, stroking a hand over my hair, giving me a look that could only be described as fond. "Of course they are."

I felt myself having to blink back tears, calling myself a stupid girl as I glanced down at my feet. "No one but Bev has ever gotten me flowers before."

His hand clenched in my hair, and I thought it was involuntary, because he loosened his hold almost instantly. "That makes me want to kill somebody, sweetheart."

I didn't know what to say, so I just kept staring at my feet.

"Namely, someone who sports skinny jeans, and weighs about as much as one of my arms."

That made me smile. "Thank you for the flowers," I told my feet quietly.

He tipped my chin up with a finger, then slanted his mouth over mine. Right in the middle of Costco. I thought it was the sweetest thing in the world.

"Anytime."

"Why lavender?" I asked, when I re-gained the ability to speak.

"They struck me as different. Exotic. Like you. Just... unexpected. And of course, they were the prettiest flowers in the place."

I blushed. "You're such a flatterer."

His thumb skimmed along my cheek. "Only with you, sweetheart. I'm not like this with anybody else. And you have to know that I mean every word."

I didn't know whether to believe that, but Lord did I want to.

He took me back to his apartment. It was on the third floor in one of the mass-apartment communities that littered the valley. It took us several trips to get everything into his kitchen.

He didn't give me a tour of the place, explaining, "Dean is probably still passed out in his room, but I'll show you my room after I cook you dinner."

I put his things away, while he started making us spinach and parmesan pasta with marinara sauce.

"You're making us *frozen* pasta?" I asked, as he did just that. "Isn't that blasphemy? Aren't you supposed to like, make the pasta from scratch, and maybe squeeze the tomatoes into sauce by hand?"

He laughed. "Squeeze the tomatoes into sauce? Is that how you think it works?"

"Close enough," I said, as I laid out his new silverware.

"This stuff is good, and I'm too hungry to cook for two hours."

If he said it was good, that meant it was good. The man didn't eat inferior food. In fact, his food was so good that I'd gained five pounds while we were hanging out together, and hadn't even sweated it, because some enjoyment was just worth five pounds. It was that good.

Of course, I'd lost those five pounds and some extra in the weeks he'd disappeared, and completely broken my heart.

"Where's your restroom?" I asked him, after I'd put the silverware away.

"Use the one attached to my bedroom." He pointed, his back to me, still working at the stove.

I couldn't seem to help it; I snooped through his room. It was sparse, and he'd barely unpacked, so there wasn't much to learn from the endeavor. The only thing that really stood out to me were the myriad, half-empty bottles of liquor on his nightstand. I thought those said a lot about his lifestyle.

His bathroom was directly attached to his bedroom, with one

of the biggest bathtubs I'd ever seen. You could literally fit at least six people into it, which painted a picture that I didn't particularly want to dwell on.

When I came back into the kitchen, Tristan was almost done making the pasta, so I started to unpack his plates.

They were square and white, very elegant, especially for a bachelor pad. I had picked them out.

I had one of the plates in my hand when a topless brunette sauntered into the kitchen.

Topless was putting it lightly. She was wearing nothing but a nude colored thong and a smile.

She strutted, yes strutted, right up to Tristan and hugged him from behind, pressing her huge, fake, *naked* breasts against his back.

I wasn't prepared for this, so I just stood there, frozen, plate in hand, and watched the tableau.

Tristan stiffened at the contact, turned off the burner on the stove, then started to turn, looking as surprised as I was to have a naked woman in the kitchen. I couldn't even have said if she was pretty, I was that distracted by all of that naked skin.

His brow furrowed as he looked down at her, now pressed into his side. Or rather, one fake tit was plastered to his side, one to his front, just below his chest.

"Uh," he began, obviously at a loss for words.

The skank gave him a brilliant smile. *Dammit*, she *was* pretty. "I'm Kendra. From four nights ago. Don't worry about it. I didn't think you'd remember my name. We didn't do much talking."

I was gripping the plate so hard that I felt it dig into my fingers, and still, I gripped harder.

He grabbed her shoulders and pushed her back, until her implants where no longer making contact. "Okay, Kendra. But what are you doing here now, and where are your clothes?" He had the careful tone of someone talking to a crazy woman.

"I came here last night with Dean. I was hoping to see you again. I think I left my panties in your room. Will you help me go find them?" Her tone was all sleazy insinuation.

I quite simply lost my mind. The plate in my hand went flying, crashing into the wall above their heads. Another plate was in my hand and flying before anyone could react. Miss Fake Tits went running for it, but Tristan, the fool, started moving toward me, ducking plate after plate. I broke at least six before he made it to me. I didn't look down to check, but I was pretty sure that was all of them.

One look at his face showed me that he wasn't mad, which shocked me into immobility just long enough for him to get his arms around me in a hold that kept me from reaching out and breaking more of his things.

Why wasn't he mad? I'd just tried to maim him and a topless slut that he had apparently slept with four nights ago.

I didn't even speak. All that I'd had to say had been said with the breaking of six white plates.

He spoke, murmuring apology after apology into my ear. I found that so strange that I didn't even process it right away.

A shirtless Dean burst into the kitchen, with not one, but *two* naked skanks at his back, the one before, and a redhead. He started yelling as he took in the damage.

"What the fuck, man? I was sleeping, and you've got some chick breaking fucking plates in our kitchen? And Kendra tells me she tried to hit her with one!"

"Go back to bed, Dean," Tristan told him, sounding riled, which he hadn't sounded when he'd been talking so softly into my ear. "This is *not* your business."

"Of course it's my fucking business," Dean said. "This is my fucking place, too."

"What's your problem?" Topless Kendra asked, speaking to me, I assumed.

"Her problem is that she's my girlfriend," Tristan answered.

"And she was just disrespected in my home."

Kendra's lip shot out in a pout. "You didn't have a girlfriend four nights ago," she pointed out.

"We were on a break, but we aren't anymore. Dean, get them out of here."

"Fuck you, man. You get to keep that cunt around, and I have to get rid of *them*?"

I felt Tristan stiffen against me. His voice when he spoke was scary. "I'm only going to warn you once. You talk to her or about her like that again, we're going to have a fucking problem. Apologize, and then get the fuck away from me before I take your ass to task for what just came out of your mouth, and this ends with more than a warning."

Dean cursed under his breath, turned on his heel, and left the kitchen, muttering a very insolent, "Sorry," under his breath.

Slut one and slut two followed quickly behind him.

Tristan bent, scooping me up into a cradle hold, and carried me to his room.

He bent, laying me out on the bed. He lowered himself over me until he was pinning me down with his body, chest to chest, thighs straddling my hips. He pulled my arms up high, pinning them over my head with his hands on my wrists.

He brought his face very close to mine, his golden eyes gone soft. "I'm sorry."

I wasn't sure what he was apologizing for, and I thought I should probably apologize for breaking all of his plates, and trying to hit him with them in the process, but I just couldn't do it. The man made me lose my mind, and I was still upset about that.

Still, there was one thing, one question, that persisted, dominating my thoughts more than anything else that had happened.

"Why did you say I was your girlfriend? That was a lie. We were never together, not like that."

He took a deep breath, rubbing his chest along mine. I saw a flash of something cross his expression, and I thought it might have been pain. "It wasn't a lie. It was the way it should have been, if I wasn't so fucked in the head. I've handled things badly from the start with you, and I'm sorry for that. The way I feel about you...the way it's been between us from the start, I was an idiot for denying it to myself. I want to be exclusive. No just friends, no fuck buddies, no more avoiding commitment. I want to be with you. I've made it way more fucking complicated than it needs to be, and I want to un-complicate it. I've no right to ask it, but will you give me the chance to prove that I can be better than I've been?"

My heart was pounding about a million miles a second, in joy...and terror. He'd broken my heart before ever promising me anything. How much worse would it be, if he crushed me like that again, after I let myself hope for something more from him?

Unexpectedly, ridiculously, I burst into tears.

It wasn't a quiet affair. I let out big, gasping, ugly sobs, and once it started, it didn't stop.

It was the first time he'd ever seen me cry. A little sound of distress escaped from deep in his throat, a noise of deepest sympathy.

He nuzzled his face into my ear. "I'm so sorry, sweetheart. I'm so sorry I hurt you. I'd take it all back if I could, but I can't. I will try to make it up to you, though, okay? Please, just give me the chance. Please."

I was able to calm myself when I realized that the strongest emotion I was feeling was actually relief. The idea that I could fall so hard for him, that I could feel this *so* deeply, and have him feel none of it had just been so awful for me, and coming back from that feeling was an emotional breakdown.

R.K. Lilley

CHAPTER THIRTY-TWO

I never could keep my mouth shut. The good, the bad, the ugly, it all came out, and this was no exception.

With Tristan's weight on me, his soothing whispers in my ear, and the knowledge that he couldn't resist this thing between us any more than I could, had me spewing my heart out in minutes. I'd wanted to hold it in, because some confessions demand reciprocation, but my big damned mouth took the decision from me, as usual.

"I love you," I told him, my voice unsteady.

I knew he wouldn't say it back. I was prepared for that. But he did the next best thing, moving his mouth over mine in a ravenous, desperate kiss, his tongue invading my mouth.

I moaned against him, moving my body into his hard form restlessly.

He broke off, studying me. I moved my hips, trying to dislodge his uncompromising thighs. I wanted him between my legs, not straddling them.

"I want to be inside of you bare. I really am sorry about doing that last night. I lost my mind. But I swear to you, I've always used a condom. Always. You and I are exclusive as of now, and you're on the pill. The choice is yours, but I want you to consider it."

"Yes," I answered too quickly, too needy to say no to him. He'd just given me what I wanted most—himself, and I couldn't have denied him a thing.

He slanted his mouth back over mine, shifting just how I craved, his hips burrowing between my thighs.

He pushed his erection hard into me through our clothes, and my nails raked over his back.

He pulled back. "Don't move," he told me, moving down the bed. As he passed my hips, he took my shorts and panties with him with one smooth pull. "I got you something."

He went into his closet, coming back out with something dark clutched in one hand, and something that looked suspiciously like handcuffs in the other.

"What are you doing?" I asked him, squirming on the bed.

His mouth twisted into a smile. "Relax. You trust me, don't you?"

I swallowed, my jaw clenching, but I nodded.

He moved back to the bed, crawling to straddle me again.

He slipped my tank top and bra off, sliding my arms above my head with a feather light touch.

His lips moved close to my ear. "Close your eyes," he whispered.

"Tristan," I began, but he shushed me, pulling a black blindfold over my eyes, and tying it behind my head.

The world went dark, and I didn't understand the purpose of this until he began to touch me.

He kissed my neck as his hands moved up to my wrists. He cinched the handcuffs on very slowly, and as he tightened them, I realized that they were padded on the inside, to protect my wrists.

"Do you expect me to struggle?" I asked him, pulling lightly at my arms to test the restraints. "Is that why they're padded?"

"No, sweetheart. I expect you to submit. They're only padded because I can't bear the thought of so much as bruising you. I take the gift of your trust very seriously."

"I always knew you were kinky," I muttered. I felt him chuckle deliciously against my collarbone. With no sight, that small contact made me shiver from head to toe.

"This isn't for me, Danika. This is for you. To really let go, you need to give up control. All of it. Every bit." He punctuated every sentence with a soft kiss against my flesh, starting at my neck, to my collarbone, and moving down to the center of my chest, kissing directly down the center of me, across my ribs, into my naval, nuzzling there.

I writhed, my legs shifting in restless motions, trying to find his legs, wanting so much more than just his mouth on me.

He stilled me with a firm hand to the thigh, and I went nearly limp when I felt his chest press down against me, his lower body slipping between my legs, pushing them wide, then wider.

His hand gripped over my other thigh, sliding to my inner thigh to spread them farther.

I gasped as he pressed his lips to my lower belly, kissing, then licking, then sucking just hard enough to startle me.

He grazed over my hipbone with his teeth, licking over the crease that led into my thigh. He lingered at the spot just where my groin met my thigh, suckling there.

"Tristan," I gasped, bucking.

He lifted his mouth just enough to murmur against my skin. "Tell me, Danika. Tell me what you want."

"I—I want your mouth on me."

"Be more specific."

"I want your mouth on my, my…"

"Pussy. Say, I want your mouth on my pussy."

"I want your mouth on my pussy."

"Please," he prompted.

"I want your mouth on my pussy, please."

I swore I felt him smile against my skin, but finally, mercifully, he moved his mouth into the center of me, moving his clever tongue along my cleft and to my clit, making those quick, tiny little circles.

He did this, staying with single-minded purpose on that one spot, with that one contact, until I was just close enough to that fine edge to be frustrated.

"Tristan," I moaned.

He spoke against me, his voice so low and gravelly that it vibrated against me, teasing me further. "Did you need something else?"

"Your hands. I want your fingers inside of me, please."

The moment the please left my mouth, he was shoving two fingers inside of me. I was slick, and they slid right in. He pushed them deep, dragging them out, working into a rhythm, his tongue working those agonizing circles that drove me wild.

He had me where he wanted me, mindless, gasping, and letting go as I came, crying out his name, again, and again.

His weight left me briefly, and then he was sliding over me, skin against skin.

He lined himself up at my entrance, pushing in just the tip. He shocked me as he rammed in to the hilt, his size still so overwhelming. But there was no pain. He'd judged it perfectly. I was ready for him.

"I'm sorry," he rasped into my ear as he started up his hard, driving strokes. "I missed you."

"I missed you, too." I was too weak to deny him anything, even absolution. And when he'd driven me to the edge again, rocking into me, again and again, his mouth on my neck, I couldn't hold back those three devastating words. "I love you."

He came, pouring into me with a rough groan that formed into my name, bringing me with him in steady thrusts.

He said the pasta was unsalvageable, and had to make fresh.

He pulled on his jeans, not bothering to button them, and I threw on his T-shirt, which came to mid-thigh on me.

He tugged me into the kitchen, setting me on the counter for our usual kitchen routine, if in a different kitchen.

He set the water to boiling, and came back to me, cupping my cheeks, his eyes so soft. I didn't even want him to talk. His eyes were too perfect like that. They told me everything I wanted to know.

We made out like teenagers while he cooked.

He fit his hips between my thighs and took my mouth with slow, drugging kisses, his big hands cupping my face with the lightest touch.

He pulled back, touching his forehead to mine. "You're so beautiful. Most beautiful girl in the world."

"Oh, God, you're going to make me lose my lunch," an unwelcome voice burst out from the entrance to the kitchen.

Tristan straightened, shooting Dean a very unfriendly look.

"Get a room," Dean muttered, rolling his eyes. He strode to the fridge, grabbed a beer out, and twisted the cap off.

"Some privacy, Dean," Tristan ordered, his voice hard.

"Fuck you, man. This is the kitchen. You don't get privacy in the kitchen."

"You owe me, after that little scene earlier with your topless parade. Now give us some privacy."

"You'd already fucked both members of the topless parade within the past week. I really didn't think you'd be offended if one of them came to get me a beer without a shirt on. When did *you* turn into a fucking prude, Tryst?"

A few short sentences killed my good mood. We weren't exclusive *then*, I told myself. It still hurt. And I had to wonder if and when Tristan would hurt me like that again.

Tristan took Dean's words even worse than I did. He moved across the room, crowding the other man against the refrigerator. He stabbed a finger into the smaller man's chest. "Watch your fucking mouth, and listen carefully. If you disrespect my girl again, we are going to have a problem."

"Me? *I'm* disrespecting her? Would you say I've been more or less disrespectful than you when you were fucking everything in sight for the past two weeks? Does she know about that?"

I saw Tristan's hands clenching into fists, and I was moving before I knew I was doing it. I ran to him, hugging him from behind, and pulling hard.

He let me take him back, and back, until my butt was hitting the counter.

"Please don't," I whispered, my cheek plastered to his shoulder blade.

Tristan pointed at Dean, and his voice was shaking with fury when he spoke. "None of this is any of your fucking business, but I will educate you just this once. She and I weren't together then, but we are now. And if you can't behave properly in her presence, you know where the fucking door is. That's all you need to know."

Dean threw his hands up in the air, looking annoyed, just how he'd started, as though the entire exchange hadn't affected him a bit.

"Now give us some privacy," Tristan growled.

Dean left without another word.

Tristan turned into me, lifting me back onto the counter. His mouth came down on mine, hungry and hard. His hands were everywhere, one slipping under his shirt to grip my ass, the other slipping up to tug at my nipple.

I gasped when he slipped between my legs, and his bared erection slid along my wet cleft.

I turned my head away, breaking the kiss. "Tristan! We can't...not here. There's no privacy."

"He won't come back," he said hoarsely into my ear, pushing that first delicious inch inside of me.

"It's still—ah—the kitchen...oooh."

He shoved into me hard, pulling my hips to the edge of the counter for a better angle.

"Watch us. Watch my cock sliding into you, sweetheart. It's too perfect."

I glanced down. He'd lifted my shirt, and pulled his jeans down just enough to bare him. I watched his thick hardness pushing into me with breathless fascination.

His mouth took mine when he was seated to the hilt, but he ended the kiss abruptly, his eyes moving down to his cock dragging out of me. I couldn't help it, my gaze following his. I moaned at the sight and feel of that heavy pull.

"Feels so good," I gasped.

"Feels like heaven," he growled, taking my mouth again.

One of those magic hands slid down, rubbing my clit in perfect little circles that brought me over the edge.

He followed with a rough shout.

"There's no way Dean didn't hear that," I told him when I finally had my breath back.

He ignored my statement, pulling out of me. "Hopefully I didn't destroy another batch of ravioli. I'm starved."

That was a change of subject if ever I'd heard one. I watched him drain the pasta, trying to think a clear thought. He was so good at distracting me from absolutely everything but him.

He brought a ravioli to my lips. "Try it. You'll like it."

"I'm not a big fan of simple carbs," I told him, but I took a bite.

He gave my mouth a brief kiss as I chewed. He was right, they were good. Maybe not homemade Tristan good, but certainly the best frozen pasta I'd ever tried.

He made us one huge plate to share, tugging me into his room. He started a bath, feeding me pieces of ravioli between tasks.

He dragged off my T-shirt and his jeans, tugging me into the bathtub while we were still eating.

"Really? Pasta in the bath? I'm going to feel like a bloated whale when we're done."

He just smiled, popping another piece into my mouth. He

settled my back to his front, kissing my temple.

We finished the plate of food before he spoke.

"I know this is probably a sore subject, but I just wanted to explain myself."

"Okay," I said carefully, not sure I wanted to hear it just then. My heart felt very tender.

"I was a bastard after we fought. I...regret some of the things I did, and I'm sorry. I basically went on a two week binge. I don't think I had a sober moment. I thought I could get you out of my system, but I learned that it doesn't work like that. And I just want to be very clear about this. Now that I've made you promises, there is no chance that it will happen again. Okay?"

I nodded, the back of my head rubbing against his chest with the motion. "Okay," I whispered, feeling a little at sea. The way I felt about him, I had to wonder what I would do if he went back on his word. Would I have the strength to walk away from him? I honestly didn't know. I felt too wrapped up in him to ever walk away willingly.

CHAPTER THIRTY-THREE

We were nearly inseparable after that. He slept at Bev's house with me almost every night. He kept up his hard living, all hours lifestyle, and I was so completely obsessed with him, that I kept it with him.

We drank too much, slept too little, and had more sex in a two week period than I'd ever had in my life.

I was so infatuated that I fell asleep next to him, and still dreamed of him, as though being apart, even in sleep, just wasn't an option for my lovesick brain.

The curve of his smile, the shape of his dimples, the twinkle in his golden eyes, made my heart race, every single time. The way he looked at me, his possessive touch, the way we made love, had me wrapped around his little finger. There was no question—I'd never been so in love. In fact, the way I felt around Tristan made me question if I'd ever even been in love before at all. Loving him was like that; so out of control that it was hard to imagine there could be anything to compare.

He never said he loved me back, even though I said it all the time, but I felt more loved than I ever had before, and that was enough for me.

I'd never considered myself to be a jealous person before, but there was no doubt that I was with Tristan. Women noticed him.

Often.   And many weren't subtle about it.   That was bad enough, but what really made me lose it was the few times when we ran into women that he'd actually slept with.   When that happened, I turned into a nut job.   I knew that I did, and still, I couldn't seem to stop my knee jerk reaction.

We were at Decadence.   It had become our favorite club, because Cory worked there, and Frankie worked in the building. We'd been hanging out with her and Jared a lot, nearly every night.

I was chatting with Jared and Frankie.   We were ganging up on him, trying to talk him into making the band play more gigs. Yes, I'd started using the word gig.   When in Rome...

Tristan had made a trip to the restroom.   I saw him heading back to us.   The pink haired rocker chick that had opened for them at their performance stopped him with a hand on his arm.

We kept running into her.   Her name was Rosette, and she hit the clubs at least as much as we did, and I was almost positive they'd slept together just by the way she looked at him.

I glanced at Frankie, who always told it like it was.   "Have they slept together?   I mean before he and I..."

I could tell before she opened her mouth that she knew that they had.

"That's a question for Tristan.   I really can't say for sure, but he got around a lot...before."

I thought about how before was only a couple of weeks ago as Rosette clung to his arm, even to the point of following him as he made his way over to the rest of us.

He was smiling at something she said, though it did look like he'd tried to tug his arm away.

She wasn't budging, and my drunk mind took that very personal.   At least, I tried to tell myself it was the alcohol that made me so crazy.

I didn't go crazy right off the bat.   It wasn't quite so bad as all that.   Her hand on his arm was not enough to do it on its own.

It was her second hand, reaching up to grip his bicep, measuring it. She bit her lip and gave him what I thought was a very slutty smile. "You have the best arms, Tryst. So big. In fact—" she leaned into him, her chest against that arm, stood on tiptoe, and started whispering into his ear.

"You know he has a girlfriend, right?" I called out to her, feeling mad enough to spit.

She turned her head slowly to look at me, her eyes telling me clearly that she knew I'd been there all along. "I heard about that."

"So you just get a kick out of hanging all over someone else's man?"

"You've been dating for like two weeks, right? That has to be a record for Tryst. How far past breaking his own record do you think he'll get before he falls off the wagon again?"

Tristan shook her off, looking annoyed. "If you can't be civil to my girlfriend, you can fucking walk away." He pointed, as though to show her which way she could walk.

I loved it.

She didn't.

She turned a scathing glare on him. "Dean told me you were pussy whipped, and I didn't believe him. I see I was wrong." She made a whipping motion in the air with one hand, accompanied by the universal sound effect for 'pussy whipped'.

"Fuck Dean, and fuck you," Tristan shot back, going from annoyed to pissed.

"We already did that, honey." Rosette's voice was all sweet venom. "Lots of times, in fact. Does your girlfriend know about that? Does she know that we fucked right before I went on stage at our last performance?"

That had been the night we'd reconciled. So only hours before that he'd been with this skank...

One look at Tristan's wince, which told me she wasn't making it up, and I almost had another 'dish throwing' moment.

The only thing that stopped me was a well-meaning Jared.

He must have seen the murder in my eyes, because he grabbed me from behind in a gentle, but very firm hold.

"She's not worth it, sis," Jared said near my ear.

He'd taken to calling me that lately, and I secretly loved it.

As soon as Tristan and I had officially become a couple, the brothers' tension had seemed to ease where I was concerned, as though putting a name to it gave them such clear rules on how to act that it became a non-issue.

I adored Jared. He was the sweetest guy, and we'd spend hours talking on the phone some days. We could talk about nothing and everything, just how I could with Tristan, but the vibe with Jared had turned very brotherly, which I loved. He was one of those people that I couldn't sing enough praises about.

And yet, he worried me. It was a persistent but elusive sort of worry. Frankie and I discussed it often, how he was just a little too careless with life. He didn't take anything seriously, nothing at all. For instance, he was a horrible mess of a driver, and there was no drug he hadn't tried. I didn't see it first-hand, but Frankie had described his days long binges, where he'd reappear glassy-eyed and a little less himself.

He seemed to be completely himself tonight, and he always made good company like this, though I could have wished he wasn't quite so quick to hold me back from slapping a bitch.

I fought his hold like a maniac, especially when Rosette just smirked at me, her arms folded across her chest.

I'd never done it before, never even thought about, but my go-to move was to reach for a heel, throwing it at her stupid face.

Unfortunately, I missed.

"Come on, sis, we're taking a walk," Jared said, having to lift my feet off the ground to get me to move.

He had me out of the club and in the casino before I'd calmed enough to be set down.

"You can let go of me. I've got it under control now." I told him, when he just kept an arm around my shoulder.

I had to pull off my other shoe to walk, carrying it in my hand.

He patted my shoulder. "Let's walk. Talk about it."

"What is there to talk about?" I asked. I could hear the sullen tone to the question, and just hearing how whiny I sounded, helped me put it in check.

"Are you mad at him? That night she was talking about...I know that's the night you guys got back together."

I hitched up my shoulder in a shrug, finally giving in to his hold on me and leaning into him. It felt good to lean on him. He was just that kind of guy.

"I don't know. I'm...hurt, though that night was when we got together, not back together. Before that, things were...casual."

"Casual? Now that I don't believe. I didn't see it at first, but he's been crazy about you from the beginning. I've never seen him like this, Danika. You're special to him. He's fallen for you."

"I doubt that, but thanks for trying to make me feel better. You're a good brother."

Whatever Jared tried to say in response was interrupted by his big brother approaching from behind, and grabbing him around the neck, wrenching him away from me. Tristan took merciless knuckles to a squirming Jared's head.

"What was that all about, little brother? Why'd you take off with my girl?"

"You know why!" Jared choked out, finally wresting free of the bigger man. "Damage control. You should be thanking me."

Tristan had my other heel, and he handed it to me. I took it, backing away from him.

He followed me and tried to put an arm around me, but I was in no mood.

I jerked away, glaring.

"What, boo? You mad at me?"

"I don't want to talk to you right now. How about you give me some space?"

I could see he didn't like that by the storm gathering in his eyes.

"I don't like space. We can go home if you want, but I'm not doing space. If you have beef, that's no way to squash it."

"It is for me. Go hang out with Cory and Frankie. Jared and I want to take a walk."

His jaw clenched, and he looked like he wanted to argue with me, but he seemed to think better of it. He pointed at his brother. "Take care of her."

"Of course."

Tristan started to turn away, but suddenly turned back, and I saw a playful twinkle in his eyes as he looked at me again.

I saw his tactic. He was fond of using charm to get his way.

"He's *my* brother, so don't go getting him to take your side," he told me with a small smile.

In a way, his tactic worked. I'd gone from wanting to get a voodoo doll of him and stick pins into it, to wanting to tease him back.

"He's my brother now, too. Just ask him. He's started calling me sis." As I said the words, I realized how bad I wanted that, to be part of this family. It was an acute sort of yearning, and one I hadn't realized I sought with such desperation until I was staring directly at it. I'd always wanted a family, and I loved everything about having Jared as an adopted brother.

He seemed to agree, smiling at me, and moving close to take my arm. "Well, if I have to choose, I choose Danika. She doesn't pick on me."

Tristan waved us off, but his smile was big now, his dimples taunting me. "Fine. Go have your walk and talk about me. I'm going to go complain to Frankie about how crazy women are."

"Good luck with that," I called to him, Jared already tugging me away. "She'll take my side, too."

"Not if I let her give me another tattoo!"

"Ha! That's what you think. I'm letting her give me one, too, and I have no ink, so that's a much bigger thrill for her. And if I have to, I might show her a boob."

That had him turning on his heel and following us. The ink part more than the boob.

"What do you mean? You're getting ink? Where and what? And when did you decide this?"

I smirked. "Space, my friend. All good things come to those who give me space."

"I'll get it out of Frankie!"

"You won't. She's already been sworn to secrecy, and she won't risk me backing out just to appease your curiosity."

"You're an infuriating woman, you know that?"

I gave him the mature response for that one, sticking my tongue out at him as we walked away.

"Talk to me, sis," Jared began, as we finally lost sight of his brother.

I sighed, leaning into him again. "I'm just upset. It's not the kind of upset anything can be done about."

"So vent. You're a venter, right? It helps. Let me hear it."

I was a venter. I don't know why, but saying things out loud almost always made me feel better, even when the saying didn't change anything.

"What Rosette said back there, about the night of the performance. Well, obviously that stung. I mean, I had pretty much already guessed that they had a past together."

"I wouldn't call it that. She was a random hook up, Danika. That was his MO for a long time, but trust me when I tell you that he's completely different with you."

I nodded, giving him solid eye contact. "Well, I had already guessed about the hooking up, and he's always been painfully honest with me about things like that, and we weren't together when it happened, but later that night...we were, and I thought it

286

was a really special night, and now, thinking that it *so* wasn't, I just feel, I don't know, bereft. I love being with him. He's so great in a lot of ways, but he never expresses his feelings verbally, and so I have to take the special moments and treasure them. I just feel so sad, because I was robbed of one of the best ones. I feel like we lost something tonight, and I just need some time to process it. I just want to go somewhere and nurse my wounds, yanno?"

He nodded, his eyes so understanding that I felt myself tearing up.

I blinked those tears away, calling myself a stupid girl.

CHAPTER THIRTY-FOUR

Jared and I ended up at the casino's sports bar, betting on horse races, and drinking for free.

He was great at cheering me up, telling me funny stories about he and Tristan as kids, and just generally finding ways to cheer me up.

I was well on my way to a better mood, when he said something that had me stewing again, but for a different reason.

"If you need something stronger than a cocktail, just let me know. I can get you whatever you need within ten minutes."

I didn't respond for a while, thinking about that.

"Jared, you need to knock it off with that stuff. I'm not even sure what you were referring to—"

"Anything you—"

"No, thank you. Hard liquor is more than enough for me. You need to knock that shit off, Jared."

"We're only twenty-one, sis. Live a little. We can be responsible and boring when we're thirty."

"That stuff is bad for you, Jared. All of it. Alcohol is bad enough. You don't need to be trying every crazy thing that you come across."

He waved that off. "Don't worry about it. I like to party, but I know what I'm doing."

I sighed, thinking that it was impossible to talk a twenty-one year old out of being stupid. And I was the same age, so I should know.

He gripped one of my hands in both of his. "Listen. Whatever you think happened that night didn't change just because of what happened before. And Tristan may not express himself, but I know him better than anyone, and I can tell you that he's never been like this, not with anyone. He's fallen for you, and seeing it, I think it's the first time for him."

"He was *engaged* to Natalie." My tone turned resentful just thinking of that other woman.

"That was ages ago, and they were kids. Every guy in the world thinks he's in love with the first woman he has sex with... If anything, what you should take from Tristan and Natalie is that he is capable of being blindly loyal, maybe too much so. He made promises to her, and he kept every one of them. She's a piece of work for what she did to him, but that's not on him. If he was capable of being loyal to a woman like that, just imagine what he'd be willing to do for someone like *you*."

Tristan found us there hours later.

We were clutching hands and giggling, drunk off our asses.

We'd both gotten to the saying sweet things to each other' phase of our drunk.

"There's nothing I want more than to be your real sis, Jared," I told him, eyes wide. Somehow, in drunk mind, that was meant to emphasize my point. "I'd adopt you if I could. No bullshit."

He patted my hand, his own eyes getting crazy wide. "I'd adopt you back. No bullshit. But I have an even better idea. Marry Tristan, and it'll be legal. Wouldn't that be so awesome?"

We nodded together, slow, big nods. "Totally awesome," I whispered. "If I could have one wish in the whole world, that would be it. I love you guys. I want you to be my family."

He gripped my hand hard, his eyes and tone earnest. "I want that too. And we totally love you back. Tristan might not say it, but I know him better than anybody, and he totally does."

"I love you," I told him, feeling drunk, weepy time coming on.

"I love you back."

"Isn't this sweet?" Frankie asked wryly, from somewhere behind us.

I craned my neck and then whipped my head around to see where she was.

She and Tristan stood at our backs. She had her arms folded across her chest, a huge smile on her face.

Tristan wasn't smiling, but he also wasn't looking more than mildly annoyed, which was a good sign, considering I'd just been telling his brother how much I loved him.

"How many have you had?" Tristan asked sternly.

For some reason, that made us both giggle hard, clutching our bellies.

"Not more than eight," Jared said.

"Less than three," I said at the same time.

We looked at each other, and dissolved into giggles again.

"I've got Jared," Frankie told Tristan.

He nodded. "I've got my girl. Talk to you tomorrow."

Tristan came around my chair, kneeling down in front of me. He studied me, putting a warm hand on my knee.

"Still mad at me?" he asked.

I shook my head. "Not mad. Just hurt, but the hurt is numb now, so that's good."

He straightened, tugging me to my feet. He pulled me into his side as we began to walk, taking most of my weight.

"Hurt?" he questioned, sounding confused.

He's such a *guy*, I thought. "Yes. Hurt. That night we were together in the rain. I thought it was special, and it wasn't, and I feel like I lost something important when a night that was special to me lost all of its special."

His other arm came around, his hand snagging at the back of my head, then cupping, then caressing. "I'm sorry you feel that way, but you're wrong. That night was special, and whatever stupid fucked up shit I did before that can't change how special it was."

That made me warm all over.

I was so starved for any words from him that I'd take scraps and be happy.

"Jared was trying to tell me that. He's the best."

"He's the best," Tristan agreed, affection in every word.

"We never should have kissed. I didn't know he was my future brother at the time."

That had him stopping, his arms around me tightening.

"When was this?" he asked, his tone very, very careful.

"At the pool party, that night I went out with him."

"Did you...were you..." He didn't seem to know what to say, but his voice held a thread of something that had me tensing up, even in my drunken stupor.

"Was I what?" I asked.

"Are you attracted to him?"

I patted his arm. "No, no, no. It's nothing like that. Please don't get mad at him."

He rubbed at his chest as though it were sore, his eyes getting a bit distant. "I'm not mad. I just need to know what happened."

I waved my hand in the air in a motion that was supposed to be small, but turned big and sloppy. It reminded me just how drunk I was. Like drunk enough to tell Tristan some shit that he'd never needed to know. "We went out that one time. He kissed me. I let him, for like one minute.

"You kissed for a *full minute*?" He looked queasy, and he kept rubbing hard at that spot on his chest.

"I *wanted* to like kissing him."

"*What*? What the fuck does that mean?"

"It means that it lasted for a full minute because I wanted to like it. He's a good kisser."

His head dropped back until he was looking straight up. "I did not need to know that. That's so messed up. He's my brother, and you're my girl."

"Listen. He was a good kisser, but it didn't matter. I told him right then that we couldn't date. My feelings were too strong for you, and I let him know that. And that was that."

"Was his tongue in your mouth?" he growled.

My brows shot up at that. He was jealous, which I found to be the most hypocritical thing in the world. "Now *that* you don't need to know."

"Did he touch you anywhere?"

"Don't be an ass. I just told you everything, and you have no right to be jealous, let alone mad, Mr. Slutty McSlutFace."

That surprised a short bark of a laugh out of him, but it died a quick death.

He straightened, still rubbing at his chest. "I'm not mad. Really. Just hurt." He rubbed harder as he said the word hurt.

I put my hand over his, stepping close. It was crazy, but I actually felt bad, even after all of the things he'd done that had been so much worse than my one minute kiss.

"Is this what hurts?" I asked softly, caressing the spot he'd been rubbing. It was right over his heart.

He nodded, looking more miserable than I could stand.

"It hurts your heart that we kissed?"

He winced, but he nodded, and it was perverse, but I loved that I could affect him. He never gave me words of love, so any hint that I'd touched his heart had an impact on me.

"You know it won't happen again. You can trust both of—"

He cut his hand through the air in a dismissive motion. "Of course. I know I can trust you both. It just hurts. Probably because it reminds me how close I was to losing you, and how much I don't deserve for you to give me a chance. I should have given in to my feelings for you right from the start. I regret everything I did to push you away, and every time I lied to

292

myself about how I felt."

"Do-over?" I asked him, which drew a small smile out of him. This smile told me that he thought I was cute. I loved reading his smiles, and that I was learning what each one of them meant, day by day. He had the *best* smiles.

"Deal," he said softly, drawing me to him. "Let's start fresh, and forget about all the mistakes I've made."

"*We've* made," I chided, letting him pull me close.

We were in the middle of a casino, slot machines clinking in the background, and I didn't care. I let him kiss me. I'd let him kiss me anywhere.

It wasn't a light kiss. It wasn't a romantic kiss. It wasn't innocent, or casual, or appropriate for public.

It was a down and dirty, suck at my mouth kind of kiss, demanding, hungry, and perfect.

By the time he pulled back, I was clutching at his shirt, and shaky at the knees.

His mouth went to my ear, his voice rough and unsteady. "I need you. Now. I can't wait even a minute to be inside of you."

That had my brain go fuzzy as I tried to figure out what he could mean. He didn't keep me in suspense for long, pulling me into the nearest women's restroom.

It was huge, with marble floors and counters, and stalls with doors that went floor to ceiling, covered in opaque glass that frosted as you locked the door.

The stalls were so big, in fact, that they could accommodate a beast of a man like Tristan.

One woman gave us a strange look as she walked out, and we walked in, but luckily for us, she was the only one we came across before we were locked away.

Tristan pushed my back hard into the door of the stall.

I licked my lips as he worked himself loose from his jeans, his cock already huge and throbbing for me. He bunched my skirt up at the waist, running a finger over my cleft. He sucked in a breath when he found me wet.

He didn't even take off my panties, just shoved the thin thong aside, both hands pushing my skirt up, and lifting me. He pushed into me with a hard stroke, and a rough groan.

"If anyone comes in, they can see our shadows through this door, so I need to make this quick. *I need you.*" Each word he said was a rough pant into my ear.

I moaned, gripping at his shoulders as he ground into me.

He was in a hurry, but even then, he still saw to my pleasure with a soft touch on my clit, and hard thrusts into my core.

"I love you," I cried as I came.

With a rough cry, he followed me.

It was a hell of a walk of shame through the casino to the valet. "I need a shower," I muttered, tugging my skirt down as far as it would go.

He squeezed my hand. "We're just lucky it's so late at night that no one came into the bathroom."

"True. I doubt we could have pulled that off if it wasn't nearly four in the morning."

He kissed my hand, giving me his wicked smile. "We could have. We just would have gotten ourselves arrested in the process."

I rolled my eyes.

"I think I fucked the drunk out of you. I'll have to remember that little trick."

I giggled, because I was way more sober than I'd been when we'd started, so it was kind of true.

CHAPTER THIRTY-FIVE

My next jealous fit had a different start, but the same ending. Of course, everything between Tristan and I seemed to end with sex. Good sex. Great sex. The best sex.

A few weeks after Dean and Tristan moved into their apartment, they threw a huge house warming party. The place was packed, so packed that once I lost sight of Tristan, he stayed lost for a good thirty minutes.

I should have known something was up when Dean cornered me in the kitchen the second we were separated.

"Chinese and English," was how he began, reminding me once again why I didn't like him. I knew what he meant with the vague start, because I'd played this game way too often. It was the 'guess Danika's race' game, and I *loathed* it. One of my favorite things about the Vega brothers was that neither had ever played this stupid game with me.

"Wrong and wrong," I told him, my tone flat.

"Swedish and Vietnamese," he tried again with a greasy smile.

"Wrong and wrong."

"Why don't you like me, Danika? You're dating one of my best friends. You should try to be nice."

"Ditto."

"You never even smile for me. I smile at you all the time."

I gave him a forced smile that was all teeth. "Better?" I asked.

He nodded, not acknowledging my sarcasm. "Japanese and Norwegian."

I rolled my eyes. "Close enough. Japanese and Russian." It was always an awkward subject for me, since I'd never know the other half of that equation.

"That's a fucking hot mix, let me tell you. Between your body and your eyes, I'd say you got the best of both."

"Gee, thanks, you sweet talker."

"Sassy piece of work. My favorite kind. I bet you fuck like a wildcat."

He was crowding me into the counter, and I pushed on his shoulders, officially done with the conversation.

He didn't budge, just pushing closer.

"What is your problem? Why do you thrive on stirring up shit?"

His smile was huge. "Do I need a reason? Don't you ever like to light things up just to watch them burn?"

I shoved him hard, getting past him and away, troubled as to whether I should tell Tristan about how Dean had just acted. It seemed like a lose-lose scenario to me. Either it would get Tristan mad at his friend and bandmate, or at me. Lose-lose.

I found Jared passed out on Tristan's bed, Cory in the living room making out with some chick, and Kenny in the hallway chatting with people I'd never seen before. No one knew where Tristan was, and the apartment was not that big.

It didn't take me long to figure out that he had to be out on the balcony, or gone.

The balcony that attached to the apartment was small, and sat right off the living room. The blinds were drawn, making it look like no one was out there. I checked anyway.

Tristan was out there, and he wasn't alone.

I'd only met Natalie once, but I recognized her even from the back and with dim lighting.   Apparently she'd made an impression on me.

I stepped out onto the balcony oh so quietly.

Tristan's profile was facing me. He was leaning against the rail, drawing on a cigarette and giving his ex his inscrutable smile.

She had both of her hands on his chest, leaning into him, her voice low and earnest as she spoke quietly to him.

Her nails were bright red, and so it was easy to follow their movements as she stroked them over his chest to punctuate her words.

Her voice was soft, but I caught a bit of what she was saying.

"I saw your new girlfriend. What is she, like, sixteen? What the hell, Tristan?"

Tristan's mouth twisted into his bitter smile. "Well, she's not sixty, so I can see why you'd be confused."

She smacked his chest, lightly, and her tone was more playful than offended. "When are you going to get over that? And when did you start robbing the cradle?"

"Jealous, Nat?"

Every word they exchanged denoted a sense of their history. The fact that both of their voices held a strange note of affection amidst the catty things they said to each other told me a lot of things that I really didn't want to hear.

My heart twisted in my chest.

"Of course I am! We were each other's firsts, Tryst. That's not something you forget. Or do you?"

"Of course not, Nat." His tone was gentle, almost tender, and I thought I might be sick.

"So tell me what a sixteen-year old can do for you? You know I'm single again, right? Don't you miss me? I know you remember what *I* can do for you."

His wicked smile showed me that he was more than a little

drunk, but that was no excuse for his revealing reply. "I remember very well."

I couldn't bear to hear another word, and I was moving, striding to them, gripping a hand into her hair to wrench her away from him before he'd finished his sentence.

I used even more force than I intended, sending her sprawling somewhere behind me. I glared at Tristan, feeling jealous and hurt and betrayed.

He straightened. "Danika—"

"What is she doing here?" I asked him, wondering just how deep this went, but knowing that, even if it was shallow, it still *felt* like a deep cut.

"Dean invited me!" Natalie said, out of breath as she got back to her feet behind me. "You know I went to high school with them, right? That was about the time you were starting kindergarden."

"Fuck you, Twatalie," just sort of slipped out.

"Danika—" Tristan began, his tone annoyed. With me.

I exploded.

"You two can have each other! Have fun being whores together!"

I tried to storm away, but Tristan stopped me with a hug from behind. "Danika," he said again, squeezing hard enough to get my attention.

"Nat," he addressed his ex. "Give us some privacy, please."

She didn't say a word, just walked back inside, looking putout. That was fine with me. She was lucky that all she lost was a handful of hair.

Tristan's mouth moved to my ear, and I elbowed him hard in the abs. I didn't even get a satisfying grunt of pain out of him, which infuriated me, too. In fact, I didn't think there was anything that could calm me down just then, though I would have liked to throw some plates.

"Whatever you're thinking that was, you're wrong," he

explained very quietly.

A bitter laugh burst out of me. "You know who else said that to me? My ex, right after I caught some girl with his dick down her throat."

He squeezed me again, both arms pinned to my sides. "Don't compare me to him. I've never lied to you. I'm not a liar, and I'm telling you that was just two people who used to be friends talking."

"You're still in love with her," I accused, not keeping any of my pain at the notion out of my voice. "I could tell just by the way you talked to her. You wanted her to be jealous of me. Is that why you invited her here? To make her jealous, so she'd want you back?" My voice was shrill by the end of my little tirade.

His arms tightened again, his voice a frustrated growl in my ear. "You're being ridiculous. We were talking, and that was it. I don't have feelings for her. I haven't for years."

"You were flirting with her," I snapped.

He moved his lips to my neck, pressing there so softly that it made me shiver. "Maybe I was, but it was harmless."

"Harmless?" I tried to elbow him again, but my arms were locked down tight, so I tried kicking my heel back into him. He didn't even seem to notice when my shoe made contact with his shin. "How was it *harmless*? It wasn't harmless to me. It hurt like hell to see you *flirting with your ex!*"

His hands were on my arms, and he started stroking softly, a soothing motion, his face nuzzling into the spot just behind my ear. "I didn't think of it like that. I thought it was harmless, because it didn't mean anything to me, but I'm sorry if it hurt you. You're right, that's not harmless, and it won't happen again. Just understand this, even if we weren't together, I'd never go near her again, not like that. I know that woman too well to ever want to lay a finger on her, okay? And I don't need anybody but you."

I took a deep, trembling breath, finally convinced that what I'd seen hadn't been two exes that still wanted each other.

"But, sweetheart, listen carefully, when I say that I don't need anybody but you, what I mean is that I never have. *I need you.* I've never needed anyone or anything the way I need you. I need you in a way that would break me if I lost you. Being with you makes every part of my life better. Every second I get with you is the best second of my life. I'm not good at expressing myself, not like you are, but I treasure this thing between us. Don't think I don't."

I nodded, my heart racing. He'd never said anything so revealing to me before, and I savored every word like it was a feast. And I'd been starving.

His mouth moved back to my neck, kissing and biting at that tender flesh.

I gasped.

"I need you. Now."

"I think you might just enjoy it when I have jealous fits," I told him.

"I just might," he murmured, biting down on that tendon between my neck and shoulder. "But let's not pretend I don't want to fuck you just about every waking moment, regardless."

"Let's not," I agreed, almost laughing now. The man could give me serious mood swings.

"I need you right here, right now."

"*Here*, here?" I asked dubiously. "Here as in the balcony, in the middle of a party?"

"*Here, here*," he affirmed, his hands sliding down my arms, gripping onto my wrists, pulling them out from my body.

He nudged me forward two steps, wrapping each of my hands carefully around the top of the metal rail that ran the length of the balcony. Even his touch on my hands was a caress.

"Hold on," he warned.

I gripped hard, instinctively obeying the command in his voice.

It was a hot summer night in Vegas, and so I wasn't wearing much. He slid my little khaki cargo shorts and panties down my legs with one smooth motion. I stepped out of one leg, not bothering to step out of the other side of the shorts. Hell, I didn't even kick off my flip-flops. It wasn't that type of a fuck.

Tristan's hands ran up my body, starting at my ankles, up my calves, over my ass, across my naval, finally going to the front clasp of my bra to snap it open. He freed my breasts from their confines, but left my little white tank, and even the straps of my bra on. It wasn't that type of a fuck, either. This was a direct access, get at it as fast as you can kind of fuck, and I was right there with him.

His knee moved between my legs, nudging them a few inches farther apart, and I heard him unfastening his own shorts, and pulling himself free. He rubbed his bared erection along my already slick sex, over and over.

I stared over the balcony's railing, thanking God that it was dark, and that his apartment was facing away from the other buildings. We were on the third floor, but even in the daytime, I would have only been looking at a large concrete wall and the desert field beyond.

His mouth was at my ear, telling me in detail just how good I felt, as he worked himself into me. One of his hands slid up to pluck at my breast, his other moving to grab my hip hard as he seated himself to the hilt. We both let out a low groan as his hips made solid contact with my ass.

Balcony sex should have been a quickie, but it wasn't that. It wasn't a rough race toward the finish. He brought me over twice in a row, with his perfect strokes and his magic hands, and the sexy things that came out of his mouth. He took his time with me.

At some point, someone began to open the sliding glass

door.   The door itself was quiet, but the racket they made moving the blinds out of their way was loud enough to give us warning.

"Go back inside and shut the fucking door!" Tristan barked out, not even slowing his strokes.   Sure enough, that worked like a charm.

And strangely, hearing that rough command in his voice, that raised voice he almost never used, brought me over with a helpless little moan.

That had him moaning and jack-knifing into me, shouting out my name with his own release.   "You like it when I yell at people, huh?" he panted into my ear as he leaned hard against me, both of us recovering.

I didn't answer, didn't even acknowledge the question.   I wasn't sure what to think of it myself.

He nuzzled his face into my hair as he pulled out of me, doing it slowly, making me want him all over again just from the long exquisite pull of him.

I turned into his arms after he'd gotten loose, throwing my arms around his neck, and then, when he hugged me back hard, lifting me slightly, my legs around his waist.

I kissed his ear.   "I love you," I said, never able to hold back the words.

He squeezed me, kissing my cheek in the sweetest way. "Thank you for that, boo."

I tried not to let myself be hurt by that all too neutral response to my nowhere near neutral feelings.

CHAPTER THIRTY-SIX

The words he didn't say started to weigh on me more and more as time went by. I knew that I'd fallen way too fast for him, but as we approached the one month mark of our relationship, it started to feel like, if he didn't feel it yet, then he never would, and that thought *consumed* me.

I had seen how easy he was with his ex. The sort of careless flirtation, the easy affection he felt, just seemed so brutal to me the more I thought about it. I never wanted to be that to him—a woman who he'd owned completely and would never want again.

She'd cheated on him, and then he had moved on. I knew this, just as I knew that I would never do that to him, but I still couldn't shake the feeling that he could never love me like I loved him.

I became almost clingy in my affections, which I'd never been before. I'd get upset about being clingy, and become withdrawn, which drove *him* insane. Clingy, he could deal with, withdrawn, not so much.

We kept the crazy club hours, and I became worse and worse at my day job, which I beat myself up about often. I loved the kids, loved Bev and Jerry. They'd done so much for me, and had helped me out a lot with school and just general employment, and I knew that I was becoming a bigger flake by the day. Still, I couldn't seem to keep away from Tristan, not even for an evening, and the man couldn't stay home for one damned night.

The band started playing every other weekend at Decadence, and that was both heaven and hell for me.

I loved to watch Tristan on stage, the way his presence seemed to suck the very breath right out of a crowd.

If the place was so packed that the room got warm, he'd whip off his shirt, tucking it into his belt, and boy did that get a reaction. I saw him naked all the time, spent hours staring at his beautiful body, but even I was blown away by the sight of him, tattooed and huge and toned within an inch of his life, the cut of his abs even more stark when he was belting out a song. That was the heaven. That and his voice washing over the throng in deep, intoxicating waves, making me warm all over.

Like me, Frankie never missed a show. We went together, always watching the performance from a few rows back. Tristan told me he preferred this, since I tended to distract him, if he could see me in the crowd. I was torn on this, liking the way I distracted him, but wanting so badly to be front and center.

Rosette, the pink haired slut from hell, never opened for them again, but Tristan's female fans were nearly as bad. In just a few performances, I'd seen panties thrown on stage, a topless woman, and several with tops, try to grope Tristan, and heard things shouted at my boyfriend that no one should ever have to hear without a plate handy to throw. That was the hell.

I'd learned to focus on Jared when this happened. He was nearly as arresting as Tristan singing when he strummed on his guitar, a look of absolute bliss on his face. If the lead singer had been anyone but Tristan, I was convinced that Jared would have stolen the show. He was fond of taking off his shirt about halfway through the show, which the crowd always appreciated, showing that appreciation with screams and catcalls. How he was a relationship guy, and managed to stay single, I would never understand. Part of me wished I'd seen him first, like there was some chance that I may have been a different person before I set eyes on Tristan.

At the band's third appearance at Decadence, I got to see firsthand why Tristan didn't want me at the front of the stage, distracting him. In all fairness, though, there *were* extenuating circumstances…

Frankie had pulled me front and center between the opening act and the band coming out, spotting a friend of hers. It was a lovely Hispanic woman with an hourglass figure, and I saw right away that Frankie was interested in her. She'd told me many a time that this was her type.

We'd barely gotten introductions out before Tristan was filing on stage, the rest of the guys behind him. He'd spotted me before he even reached the mic. He sent me a slightly puzzled look, but that was all. He quickly looked away. He'd explained to me before that he needed to focus when he was up there, that no matter how many times he did it, it still gave him a strange bout of nerves, to the point where he couldn't handle the level of distraction I caused him with my presence.

I was nearly close enough to touch him when he started singing, and I loved that. He'd never sing for me off stage, and I'd asked a lot. This was the next best thing, and I swayed to the beat, my eyes glued to the man I loved. The man I adored. The man I'd become completely obsessed with.

The downside to being that close to the stage was that it was also the most crowded part of the room, bodies that I didn't know pressing up against me.

The band was on their second song when I felt big hands grip my hips, and a hot, hard body press against me from behind.

I stiffened. The bump and grind was a familiar element to the Vegas dance scene, but I usually managed to steer away from it, since I did *actual* dancing, and not the stand-up humping that some people *called* dancing.

The whole thing couldn't have lasted more than thirty seconds.

A greasy, unfamiliar voice whispered something suggestive in my ear, and I felt a strange erection poke into my behind. I didn't even have time to react, or even consider how I wanted to react.

My eyes shot to the stage as the singing stopped, though the music kept going.

"Get the fuck off of her!" Tristan shouted into the mic about a millisecond before he was jumping off the stage.

The creeper behind me was ripped away, and I did my best 'get the fuck out of the way' move, backing up three steps *fast*.

I saw Tristan gripping the man's shirt, saw him knee him in the groin hard, and saw him yell into his face.

That was as far as it got before security became involved, tearing the two men apart, but I saw the murder in Tristan's eyes, and wondered just how far he would have gone.

It was pure chaos after that. I don't think anyone knew quite what to do when the lead singer started the fight in the crowd, but needless to say, the performance was over after that.

Me, Frankie, and all of the guys ended up in the green room, and the strange perv from the crowd in another room, for obvious reasons.

It was a mess.

I was mad at Tristan, because it was a fact that he had overreacted.

Dean, the prick, was mad at me, even going so far as to tell me that it was all *my* fault.

That had Jared, Frankie, and Tristan all furious at Dean, though in all fairness, Tristan seemed to be mad at everyone in the world just then.

Tristan was in a state. He stood as far away from us all as he could get, staring at the wall, rage coming off him in waves of nearly visible hostility. He was a huge man, and when he was angry, he was scary to behold. Even the security guards gave him a wide berth the second we got into the room, and they were big men themselves.

We were waiting a good twenty minutes when I just couldn't stand it anymore. I strode up to the security guard, asking, "What's going on? Are we waiting for the police? Are they going to arrest him? Is that what's going on? How long are we going to have to wait here before we know what's going on?"

"We are waiting for answers, as well," the one closest to me said, sounding calm and reasonable. "All we were told was to sit tight while this thing is figured out. No police were called, as far as I know." The man put a hand on my shoulder as he said it. It was an innocent gesture. I knew that. Any sane person would have assumed that, as well.

But Tristan was not feeling sane. Sanity had left the building and he was striding across the room, shouting at the man to get his hands off me.

I watched him lose his mind, feeling a shot of fear at the sight, even knowing that it wasn't directed at me.

Thank God he didn't hit the man, just got in his face and started yelling like a maniac.

I had no clue what to do with him like this, so I just walked across the room to get away.

"Yoko Ono over there doesn't want to deal with all of this, even though she started the whole fucking mess," Dean said, his voice low and mean, but loud enough for me to hear.

I shot him a glare, but I wasn't the only one that heard him, and Tristan stopped yelling at the security guard mid-sentence, striding across the room, a finger pointed at his roommate, his eyes wild with his fury. "What did I tell you, Dean? What did I fucking tell you? Not one word. That's what I told you. Not one more fucking diss on my girl!"

307

I gasped, then covered my eyes when Tristan's huge fist made solid contact with Dean's face. I heard two more sickeningly fleshy thuds that meant a fist was hitting flesh, and then it stopped.

"I fucking warned you, you little prick!" Tristan shouted at him.

I was on the ground, curled into a little ball against the wall, not letting myself look. I hated fighting. I didn't understand it, and I never knew how to deal with it.

I felt Frankie sliding down next to me, her arm going around my shoulder in a comforting hug.

"It's okay. The guys pulled him off Dean."

"It's not okay. It's so not okay that he's acting like this. What's wrong with him?"

"I don't know," she said quietly. "But I'd be lying if I said it wasn't kind of fun to see him punch Dean in the face. The prick deserved it…"

I opened my mouth to respond, when the door opened, and James Cavendish walked in.

It was the strangest thing, how all of the chaos seemed to just calm in his wake. He walked directly to Frankie and me, nodding to the men as he passed, and giving Dean, who was holding his jaw and glaring at Tristan, a puzzled look.

He was wearing a dark suit and looking spectacular and polished, as ever.

He nodded at us, studying me intently. "Are you all right, Danika?"

I nodded automatically, though I wasn't quite sure what I was, just then.

"I heard you'd been assaulted again, and in my establishment, again. I can't tell you how much that displeases me."

"I'm perfectly fine. I'm more worried about what's going to happen to Tristan."

"That's what I'm here to work out. You see, I tend to think

308

that men who assault women on the dance floor deserve a hard knee to the balls."

Those words, coming out of the most sophisticated man I'd ever met, surprised a giggle out of me, which drew a small smile out of James.

"We've spoken to the man. He won't be pressing charges, though the downside to that is that we also will not be pressing charges against him. I wanted to get your approval before we go ahead with this decision, since you were clearly the wronged party."

I wanted to kiss him, I was so relieved. "So Tristan won't be arrested?" I asked hopefully.

"If this resolution works for you, then no."

"Yes, yes, it definitely works for me. Thank you thank you thank you."

He just nodded, smiling. He tilted his head toward Dean. "What happened there?"

I grimaced, and Frankie answered. "The band is having issues. Largely, that Dean is an ass. Don't worry about them, though. They've been friends forever. They'll be best buds again within twenty-four hours, I guarantee it."

James didn't look convinced. "I hope so. They have a good career ahead of them, if they can just keep it together."

"They will," Frankie assured him, squeezing my shoulder. "How bad was the aftermath? How big is the mess out there?"

James hitched up an elegant shoulder in a careless shrug. "It's manageable. They certainly made an impression. Don't think they won't have twice as big of a crowd for the next performance, though I wouldn't make a habit of kneeing people in the crowd, if they want to keep the place packed, and the record people interested. Excuse me, ladies, I need to go speak to Tristan."

My eyes widened as he strode right up to the walking powder keg, as though he had no fear at all. I wanted to shout, 'No, stop, he's liable to blow', but I just watched as James spoke quietly to Tristan, somehow, miraculously, managing to calm the other man in a few short minutes.

After James worked that little miracle, Tristan came over to me almost instantly, crouching down in front of me, his eyes concerned. He touched my knee. "I'm sorry about that. Are you okay? Did I scare you?"

I eyed him narrowly. "What on earth did James say to you to get you to calm down so fast?"

His brows drew together, another storm gathering in his eyes. "James? It's James, is it? When did you two get so close?"

"Tristan! Focus!" Frankie snapped.

He grimaced, his hand rubbing my knee comfortingly. "Sorry. He just told me that I was scaring you, and asked me if that was my intent."

"That was crazy back there, Tristan. *You* were crazy. I don't like this. It's not okay that you're attacking people, and I'm throwing plates, and shoes. I'm starting to think we aren't good for each other." Even as I said the words, I couldn't believe that they were leaving my mouth. I couldn't imagine ever letting go of him willingly, let alone encouraging the idea.

"Amen to that," Dean muttered from across the room.

Tristan started to turn, his golden eyes getting scary again.

"Tristan! Focus!" Frankie barked. It actually worked. Again.

I was watching him carefully when a slow smile transformed his face. It was evil. His sweetest smile, all for me. I was utterly powerless to resist.

He leaned forward until our foreheads were touching, and his smile was the center of my universe.

"Hey, now, boo," he said softly, rubbing my knee. "We both know that's not true. We *are* good for each other. In fact, I think we're just about perfect together. I'm sorry I lost my temper like that. I just saw him touching you, and the look on your face...I couldn't stand it. You looked frightened. I'd do a lot of things to keep you from having to endure someone's touch on you that you don't want. In fact, I think I'd do anything on earth to prevent that from happening."

I blinked rapidly, my eyes getting teary. It was just such a sweet feeling, to have someone looking out for me like that, even if I did know that it was crazy how far out of hand things had gotten as a result.

"Forgive me?" he whispered, still giving me that sweet, evil, irresistible smile. I felt like I was the most important thing in the world to him on the other end of that smile. The feeling was addictive.

I caved in a heartbeat, propelling myself forward, and throwing my arms around his neck. "I love you," I said into his neck.

His big, warm, perfect arms squeezed me tight, and in that moment, it was all that I needed.

CHAPTER THIRTY-SEVEN

The guys didn't only stick to gigs at Decadence. Unfortunately, there was no place to go but down from a place like that. Dean wound up setting up a few extra performances for them. I thought that he was only doing this to try show how they didn't need Jerry to manage them, but of course it only proved the opposite. Still, the guys were good sports, performing wherever they needed to, to try to drum up attention.

We wound up in a real dump of a club on a Tuesday night. It was one of those off the strip locations that probably wouldn't last a year. Frankie and I watched them play from the bar, since I'd learned my lesson about going anywhere near the stage, though this place was hardly packed. Tristan insisted that I was too much of a distraction when he was performing, and though I could have wished that it was otherwise, because I ached to be close to him when he was singing like that—I respected his wishes.

Still, as I saw some scantily clad bimbo try to climb on stage with him, I had the urge to do something crazy.

I stifled the urge, if barely.

Instead, I just drank. And drank.

Frankie was no help, ordering tequila shots. She was in a diabolical mood, getting me drunk with an unabashed smile on her face.

She was smiling at me for so long, and so intently, that I finally had to ask her why.

She just shrugged. "You're fun drunk, and I wanted to get some juicy gossip about stud muffin over there out of you. That's all."

I giggled. "Stud muffin," I repeated back, then giggled again.

"You're feeling pretty, I see." Everyone seemed to have adopted my phrase for being drunk.

I nodded, glancing once at the stage, which instantly made me a little sullen, since I had to stay so far away from him, when all I wanted to do was get closer.

"So tell me, is he the Dom I think he is?" she asked.

I shot her a startled look. "A Dom? Excuse me? Like S&M?"

She snorted. "A Dom is not all about the S&M, and I don't see that in Tristan. No, what I mean is, does he dominate you in bed? Does he take control of you like that? And is he heavy on the kink?"

I blushed, but this was Frankie, who'd always been beyond open with me about her own preferences, so I didn't even think about not telling her. "He is. I never thought about it quite like that, but he definitely takes control. I need him to, and he always knew it."

That had her brows shooting up. "So you'd say you're a submissive?"

I bit my lip, thinking that the term couldn't possibly apply to me, of all people. Except in that one thing... finally, I nodded. "I think I am, at least in bed."

She snorted again. "Obviously it's only in bed. What about the kink? What have you two tried?"

I pursed my lips, playing with an empty shot glass. "He's restrained me twice. I didn't think I'd like it, I thought it was for him, but the more I think about it, it was for me, and I loved it. I don't think it's his usual thing, but he's really good at it."

She nodded. "I think you two have hit a sweet spot. Miss control freak Danika could use a little escape into the land of submission. I'll talk to him about it, k? If anyone knows about this stuff, you're looking at her."

I nodded, shooting him a look. "I really...*really* like it. He's made sex so wonderful for me, but the restraints, and the blindfolds...it's like icing on the cake."

She laughed. "I agree. Totally. That's great. You know, the first time I saw him, I thought he could be part of the Dom club with us."

I studied her, wondering who the 'us' was. I was too drunk to keep such a curious question to myself. "Who is in the Dom club?"

She smiled, and it was pure mischief. "Well, it's me, and I would bet money that Tryst is about to join. And one other, but I have to swear you to secrecy before I tell you."

I was nodding before she finished talking. Who on earth would I tell?

"You can't even tell your fuck anonymous group about it. In fact, you especially can't tell them."

I nodded again, simply dying to know now. "I swear I won't tell a soul, not even Tristan."

"Well, him you could probably tell, because, as I said, he's about to join the club."

"Oh my God! Tell me now! You're killing me!"

She leaned in close, whispering into my ear. "James Cavendish."

I was floored. He was so rich, and polished, and sophisticated, and well, just plain beautiful. "Are you shitting me?"

She shook her head. "He's into the hardcore stuff, though, nothing you'd be on board for, trust me. He makes *me* look like a soft Master, and I am not that."

I rolled this around in my head for a good ten minutes before I spoke. I was fascinated by the idea that someone that high profile, could have such an unusual sexual preference and it not be public knowledge.

"That's crazy," I finally said.

She nodded. "I know. But doesn't it make him even hotter?"

I laughed, because there was no denying it; even to a lesbian, the man was hot. "I'm not sure. It really depends on what you mean by hardcore. I'm not into pain."

"Pain *is* what I mean. Yes, you can be sure that one is not for you. Though I do hear that he is *spectacular* in bed."

I let out a dreamy sigh, thinking of Tristan. "So is Tristan. Spectacular."

"Fan-fucking-tastic! Let's drink to that!" She signaled the bartender for another round of tequila shots.

"He's so *big*. Like huge. I never imagined I could enjoy a man with a cock that big. It was…intimidating at first. I mean, I'm small, how could he fit?"

Frankie was laughing so hard that she had to put both hands on the bar. "Oh my God! I love you so hard when you're tipsy!"

"Do you think he's, like, stretching me out? I mean, he must be, because we can fuck really hard now, and at first it took him a while just to work himself inside." I had the very lucid thought that I must be really drunk to be talking like this.

She was still dying with laughter, just shaking her head, again and again.

"Is that possible? Could that be where the term loose comes from?"

"I don't think it works that way," she gasped. "Babies come out of that thing."

I nodded, thinking fuzzily that she had a good point. "And he absolutely loves eating my pussy. Like, he could do it all day, he loves it so much. I didn't think a man could be like that, so into getting me off."

She was back to laughing hard and clutching the edge of the

bar. "Oh my God. I can't believe I'm not recording this. You are my favorite drunk *ever*. Let's drink to Tristan's oral fixation, because if anyone can appreciate going down on a girl, it would be me. Maybe he and I are like pussy eating soul mates, because I could eat a snatch all day."

I was giggling so hard that it took me three tries to grab the shot the bartender slid me. "You're so bad," I told her, dissolving into another fit of giggles.

We were both blitzed by the time the band finished their set. I cheered loudly as the small crowd went wild, then watched with longing as they left the stage, heading somewhere in back.

"I've only been fifty feet away from him all night, and I still missed him. Isn't that nuts?"

"Totally. It's also sweet. You've got it bad, huh?"

"So bad."

"Well, he's got it bad, too. Don't you ever forget it."

I just shook my head, unable to admit out loud that he didn't, or if he did, he sure wasn't telling me about it.

I felt someone kiss the top of my head, and swiveled around to see that it was Jared, not Tristan, as I'd been expecting. I grinned, nearly as happy to see him. I hopped off my barstool, giving him an exuberant hug.

"Good job! You guys were amazing, as always."

"Thanks, sis," he said, and I could hear the smile in his voice. He pulled back, studying my face. "You're sloshed, aren't you?"

I nodded. "It's you and your brother's fault. I'm trying to train my liver to keep up with your lifestyle. I need to shape up to stay in the picture."

He stroked an affectionate hand over my hair. "You don't have to change a thing. You're perfect just the way you are."

Even drunk, I could see that his eyes were glassy like they got when he was high, but I still thought it was the sweetest thing I'd ever heard.

The other four members of the band approached us just

moments after that touching scene.

Tristan was smiling, not at all bothered by the fact that me and Jared were having another love fest. "You telling my baby bro how much you love him again?" he asked. He wore his fond smile, and just then I thought I might love that one the most.

"I was getting to it," I admitted.

Tristan shouldered his brother aside playfully, moving until he was standing close, shifting his thighs between my legs. I was wearing shorts, but he parted my legs so wide that I was afraid I may have still been indecently exposing myself.

I opened my mouth to tell him that, but he buried his hands in my hair, and I quickly got distracted.

He leaned in close, his eyes smiling into mine. "I thought it was distracting to have you in the crowd, but I realized tonight that seeing you laugh at the bar while I perform is even more distracting."

I pouted. "Sorry." I pointed at Frankie, who was nursing a drink, and smirking at us. "It was her fault. She was making me laugh. Are you going to ban me from performances altogether now?"

"Don't be silly," he scolded, shaking his head at me, and using his hands in my hair to shake mine with him. "Of course not. I just realized tonight that I need your full attention on me, or it drives me *crazy*. I think I've thought up another solution."

I arched a brow at him. "Oh yeah?"

"Yeah. You need a bodyguard with you in the crowd, so I don't have to come down and break any nuts while we're on stage. I'll find somebody before our next gig."

I giggled, because a bodyguard sounded like a crazy idea to me. I opened my mouth to tell him so, but never got a chance, as he bent down, slanting his lips over mine.

His mouth was hot, and hungry, devouring mine. He always tasted so good. I could never get enough. His tongue slipped

317

into to my mouth, and I moaned, licking and sucking at him.

He pulled back briefly. "You taste like tequila," he said breathlessly. "Had a few, huh? I think I might be able to get buzzed just tasting you."

That made me giggle some more, and the giggling only stopped when he was kissing me again.

We necked like teenagers in the middle of a bar for God only knows how long. It was insane, and tacky, and wonderful.

His hands stayed firm on my hips as his mouth drank from mine, with long, hungry pulls. We'd never done this before, just kissed for what could have been hours. Our chemistry had always just been so crazy, our lust a race to the finish line that ended in ecstasy.

He pulled back at one point, panting into the top of my head. I turned, scraping my tongue across his stubble roughened jaw, begging for his mouth again.

He gave it to me, and we kissed like that for the longest time. We ignored all the calls from our friends of 'get a room', lost in our own little world of drugging kisses, and in my case, mad crazy love.

"You're so perfect," I murmured to him as we came up for air. "I can't believe you're all mine."

His laugh was rough and breathless. "I'm as far from perfect as a person can get, but I *am* all yours."

That warmed me down to my toes, as did the press of his lips on mine. He eased back from all out necking, and began to give me sweet, short kisses.

I tried to press my body to his, but he backed away.

"I can kiss you all night, sweetheart, but if we start dry humping in this bar, I'm liable to embarrass myself."

"I want you," I whispered, as his lips came back to claim mine. "I want you deep inside of me. For hours. I told Frankie how huge you are, how you stretch me you're so big, but I didn't tell her how perfect it feels to have you inside of me."

He pulled back, gasping out a laugh, his eyes finding Frankie. "You got an earful, huh?"

Frankie grinned, toasting the air. "Drunk confessions are the best. Tequila is like a truth serum, and she can't take any of it back."

"We could fuck in the bathroom, like we did in the casino that one time," I said into his ear, seriously hot for him now, so hot I didn't know how I could bear to wait until we got home.

He shook his head, smiling. "Not at this place, we can't. It's not four a.m. and deserted, like the casino was."

"Let's have sex in your car then," I suggested, trying to pull him flush against me.

He studied me, biting his lip. I tried to tug his head down to me, because I wanted to bite his lip, too, but he wouldn't budge. "That's a hard offer to turn down. It won't be comfortable, not that I give a damn about that."

I shook my head at him, my eyes wide. "I don't give a damn either. I need your cock buried in my pussy like ten minutes ago."

That has his eyebrows shooting into his hairline. "Aren't you in a mood tonight? Normally I can't pry the word pussy out of you."

"I do hate that word, but it's not bugging me so much tonight. Pussy, pussy, pussy."

"I love that word," Frankie mused, shamelessly listening to our conversation. "I love any word that gets a visceral reaction, every time you use it out loud. Pussy. Cunt. Fuck. Cock. Though it should be noted that the word cock is my least favorite of all of those."

Tristan turned his head to look at her, smirking. "How come that doesn't shock me?"

She snickered. "Here's all I'm saying, everything about a woman can be pretty, from her feet to her ears, but the same can't be said for a man."

Tristan threw his head back and laughed, his hands rubbing my hips. I loved his throat. The sight of it stretched like that drove me wild. I pushed up so I could lick it, and then suck hard enough to leave a mark.

"I can't argue with you there," Tristan told Frankie. "I'm right there with you; team pussy all the way."

I smacked his arm. "That sounds way too general for my taste."

He laughed harder, pulling my face into his chest. "Okay. I'm team Danika's pussy all the way. That better?"

I nodded, appeased at the conclusion to that ridiculous conversation.

"Go ahead, go screw in your car," Frankie told us, her tone wry. "Don't delay on my account. You've been making out in front of me for hours. Why get shy now?"

"Good point," Tristan said, taking her suggestion, and ignoring her sarcasm. "Excuse us. We'll be back in ten to fifteen minutes."

Frankie's grin turned rueful. "I wouldn't go advertising *that*. It's not exactly an endorsement."

"I've never had any complaints," was his parting shot as he tugged me out of my chair.

I felt giddy as we raced to his car, clutching hands and laughing.

"We're going to get ourselves arrested," Tristan muttered as he opened the back door of his car for me.

I just laughed harder, strangely uncaring of that possibility.

He crowded me into the car, and it was a tight fit, to put it lightly.

"Are you wet?" he asked, as he positioned me on my hands and knees, facing away from him. He began to peel my tiny jean shorts off.

"I've been wet since the moment you touched me."

"Good," he grunted, folding himself over my back, lining

320

himself up at my entrance. "Tell me if I'm too rough. I need to fuck you hard after all of that making out."

I moaned loudly as he worked himself into me, his breath hot on my neck, coming out in fast pants as he invaded me.

"I need you, Danika. I've never needed anything like I need this." Each word was drawn out and punctuated with a rough stroke. "I'll never get enough of you. *Never.*"

It wasn't his usual dirty talk, and his words fed so much more than my desire. I needed to hear these things, craved every little sign that he might be anywhere near as obsessed with me as I was with him.

His hands moved over the curves of my breasts, kneading softly at that aching flesh while pounding hard into the core of me. My nipples were puckered hard, and he pinched and then pulled them taut. It ached in a way that made me whimper in pleasure.

He rammed his huge, engorged length into me, hard and fast, keeping up an unrelenting pace that made me grip the door handle for dear life.

"Is it too much?" he rasped into my ear.

It was. It was so much, too much, his fast, brutal invasion stuffing me so full that I felt like I couldn't take it for another second, but I'd never tell him that, never let him stop with the wonderful filling of me.

The sensations were so intense that I wasn't sure if I was about to come or scream my head off.

Turns out, I did both.

CHAPTER THIRTY-EIGHT

Three days later, we found ourselves at a house party for some friend of Jared and Frankie's. It was a big house, and pure chaos, and the second we stepped in the door I wondered why I'd let myself be talked into it. I was tired. I hadn't had a decent night of sleep in I didn't even know how long, and house parties had never been my favorite. It always just tended to be the stoner way to party, since you had to hide that stuff in clubs and bars.

I could smell the pot smoke in the air the second we got in the door, and someone was actually snorting coke off a table in a room just right of the entrance, fully visible from the front door.

I was so over it.

All of that was bad enough, but about ten minutes in, as we made our way through the crowd, looking for Jared or Frankie or Cory or Kenny, I spotted my ex. Not Daryl the Dickhead. The other one. Patrick. The one that hadn't been a *complete* dickhead, though I'd dumped him anyway. He'd gotten too heavy into drugs for me to deal. And I'd fallen out of love with him. Though now that I'd found what I'd found with Tristan, and felt this crazy, out of control thing in my chest every second of the day, I had to admit that I hadn't fallen out of love, I'd just never fallen in.

I had a strange epiphany as I stared at Patrick's profile. I'd called it love, and looked for love, because that's what I'd wanted, but love was not a thing you could force yourself to feel, or, more importantly, it was not a thing you could keep yourself from feeling. Both realizations were demoralizing for me, a girl with control issues.

I was jolted out of my thoughts as Tristan threw an arm around my shoulders, pulling me close.

"What's up, sweetheart? You look like you just saw a ghost."

I grimaced. I very much wanted to avoid Tristan seeing Patrick and finding out that he was an ex, if at all possible. I just had a feeling that Tristan wouldn't take the meeting well. And that feeling was backed up by experience...For a former man-whore, he tended to be surprisingly jealous.

"Nothing like that," I finally answered. "I'm just not feeling this party. The chick snorting coke on the way in was a bit too hardcore for me."

He gave me his wry smile, rubbing my shoulder. "Yeah. This was not what I was expecting. Jared knows some crazy people, and Frankie knows everybody in town."

I started to make my way out of the room, heading to the backyard, when I saw Patrick spot me out of the corner of my eye. I knew it because he froze, and a second later, began to move toward us.

I grabbed Tristan's hand, trying my best to paint a very clear picture for Patrick. I didn't look his way again, and only hoped he'd gotten the hint.

We found Frankie and Jared out by the pool.

"Where are the rest of the guys?" Tristan asked them by way of a greeting.

"Hell if I know," Jared said, sounding put out about it. "They were supposed to be here hours ago. So were you, for that matter."

Tristan whipped out his phone. "Let me call 'em."

I was feeling antsy, and glancing around constantly, afraid that Patrick would follow us out. He didn't, not right away, but within five minutes I saw him coming out the back door, scanning the crowd. I knew, just knew, that he was looking for me.

It had been a strange ending with Patrick. It was almost like I'd just woken up one day and seen the situation for what it was; a relationship between teenagers who should have only ever been friends. What hadn't been sudden was my revulsion every time he'd wanted to have sex. And realizing that you didn't have to keep having sex with someone if you didn't want to had been an important lesson for me, though of course I'd had to relearn it with Daryl. The fact that Patrick had started doing some hardcore drugs had helped me to end it, as well, though I knew better than anyone that with my co-dependent streak, especially back then, I would never have left him for that alone, if I'd felt for him even a tenth of what I felt for Tristan now. I liked to think I'd gotten past some of those co-dependent leanings, but if push came to shove, I couldn't say with any certainty that I'd ever leave Tristan willingly.

Tristan still had his phone to his ear, and I squeezed his arm to get his attention.

When he looked at me, I pointed at the house.

"Bathroom," I told him, and took off. I assumed Patrick just wanted to say hi. I wanted to just get that over with, and avert any drama with Tristan.

I made it maybe three steps into the living room when a hand grabbed my elbow from behind. I knew instantly that it wasn't Tristan. The hand wasn't big enough.

I turned and looked into Patrick's steady gaze. "Hey," I said, giving him a weak smile. "How's it going?"

He studied me for a long time. "I'm okay. It's really nice to see you. You look...amazing."

"Thank you," I said, feeling flattered by the admiration in his tone, and unwillingly, enjoying it.

He was tall. Not Tristan tall, but he was close to six foot, with dark hair, a medium build, and some awesome tats. He was very handsome, in a boy next door kind of way. I'd forgotten just how nice his smile was, how sincere. And he still had enough dirty rocker in him to make my heart beat a little faster.

Even if it was only remorse, I was surprised to feel something, after all this time.

I hadn't been cruel about the breakup, which in the end, had been the most brutal thing of all. I'd drawn it out, to spare his feelings, and ended up hurting him worse.

"You're dating Tristan Vega," Patrick said, as though he was still processing it, and what he had learned didn't please him one bit.

"You know him?"

"I know *of* him. He's the lead singer of that band that James Cavendish is backing. He has a reputation…"

That was news to me. Not the reputation part, but the James Cavendish backing. I'd known he was introducing them to some record people, but I hadn't heard anything about him actually putting money up for them himself.

"A lot of local bands are really bitter about that. Their band hasn't paid their dues, and here they are, getting cash backing from one of the biggest names in town."

That had my hackles rising a bit. "And who gets to decide what dues you have to pay to make it? They're really good. Best I've ever heard live."

This was a bit of a dig. Okay, it was a huge, mean dig, because Patrick was the drummer in a local band that had been going hard in the live scene for years.

"Ouch, Danika."

I grimaced. "Sorry. That wasn't nice, but they're good, and I think it's bullshit to put your baggage on another band, just because they haven't been performing as long."

He nodded, chewing on his lip. "Fair enough. I might be a touch bitter, so let's just forget I said anything. Let's talk about you. What have you been up to?"

I shrugged. "School, work, nothing special."

"Anything going on with the dancing?"

"Not unless you count mad clubbing."

He laughed, and as I watched him, I saw a sharpness in his eyes that I didn't remember from before. I liked it. He seemed more present than he'd ever been when he'd been with me.

"You look great, too. How is everything with you?"

"It's good. I'm going on one year sober now, so that's a pretty big deal for me. The band isn't getting huge attention, but we still make the rounds, and we still love what we're doing."

I nodded. "That's great. I'm so happy for you, especially the sobriety part."

"Thank you. Hey, we should go for coffee sometime. Do some catching up. It's been so long...I'd love to reconnect again."

Of course, wouldn't you just know it, Tristan walked up just in time to hear that last part. He went full on caveman right off the bat, throwing an arm over my shoulder, and giving Patrick the look of death.

"You two know each other?" he bit out, and his tone, his very demeanor, just rubbed me the wrong way.

"We're old friends," I explained. Damage control.

"We dated for two years," Patrick countered. Opposite of damage control.

Tristan stiffened, his face getting a little scary as he just stared at Patrick for long, awkward minutes. Finally, he broke the awful silence, but what came out of his mouth was no improvement. "So you're one of the selfish pricks that fucked her, and never got her off."

I walked away, furious and hurt, before he'd gotten the last word out. The asshole. The complete hypocritical nerve of him, saying a thing like that, embarrassing me without a qualm.

I made it out the front door, and to the sidewalk in front of the house before Tristan caught me.

"Hey!" he called, grabbing my elbow. "I'm sorry. That was a dick move. It was a gut reaction to meeting that prick."

I had my own gut reaction right then, and it was to defend my ex, which said a lot about how angry I was at Tristan. "He's not a prick. Not getting me off doesn't make him a prick. You know, just because he didn't know how to get me off, doesn't mean he didn't try. *He* at least would tell me that he loved me."

That hit a nerve, and boy was I not ready for his gut reaction to that nerve getting hit.

"You really want to do this now?" he asked, his voice low and mean. My heart turned over in my chest at the question. This was going to be bad. I could tell with that one sentence that his claws were out, and I wouldn't make it through this unscathed. Still, I wanted to know. Whatever he felt, or didn't feel for me, I needed to know.

"You think because he said that to you, that what you had with him was better than this? Did him saying that somehow keep you two together forever? Love is just a word."

"Semantics," I said, my voice trembling. "If it doesn't mean anything, why won't you say it to me?"

"I don't say it back because I don't fucking believe you!" He was shouting, and my heart was breaking with every word. "When I hear you say I love you, what I hear is you keeping score, and I'm not playing that game with you. There is no score for me. There never was."

I couldn't speak, my mind racing to process his words, to try to make sense of them, to try to put them together in a way that I could accept, and not bleed out from all of the wounds.

"Love is nothing but the most flexible promise," he continued mercilessly. "You use it for your purposes, and it can lose its meaning whenever you feel like it. Don't act like you're more committed to us than I am, just because you like to say those words."

I shook my head, my eyes glued to him, my lip trembling uncontrollably.

"You've already thrown out the bombshell that you don't think we're good for each other. You think I don't know you well enough to know that's just the excuse you'll use on me when you break it off? You're building your case, even as we speak. That's right; I know you *that well.* Just like I know that, though you're very comfortable with the term I love you, you will be the one to walk away from this. Guaranteed. You think you love *me*, but you're in love with being in love."

"Don't try to tell me what I feel. Don't fucking do that. You have no right—"

"Don't I? I thought you loved me. Taking it back so soon? Or is this it then? Have you built up enough of a case to walk away yet? Because I haven't said three fucking words to you that you've taken the meaning out of?"

That broke me, because I'd let him see who I was, and all he saw was the worst of me. And even more painful, he seemed ready and willing to let me walk away.

He always said he didn't want to hurt me, but what he didn't seem to understand was, his rejection of my love was the *worst* kind of hurt.

I don't know if someone told them, or if we'd just been yelling that loudly, but the yard was suddenly filled with familiar faces.

Frankie approached me, trying to get close, to put her arm around me, but I backed away.

Kenny and Cory had obviously finally made it to the party, and they were surrounding Tristan, looking wary.

Jared clapped a hand onto his brother's shoulder, his eyes concerned. "Why don't we take a walk, bro? Let's cool off for a minute. You were shouting loud enough to wake the dead, and this entire neighborhood does not need to know that much about your personal business."

Tristan shrugged off his hand, striding down the sidewalk, his pace eating up the pavement until he was out of sight in the dark in just seconds.

Eyes wet with tears, my heart in tatters, I walked back into the house. I needed a bathroom, and a moment to regain my composure.

I found one, washing my face with cold water, then doing it again. I didn't want to think, and I had no idea what to do next.

I just felt...lost. Like life was a maze that I'd never be able to navigate, like everyone else had been born with a map, and mine had been forgotten, and I was destined to keep repeating the same painful mistakes, again and again.

I had a bona fide pity party for at least ten minutes. Some asshole pounding on the door was all that got me moving again.

I dried my face, and stepped out, my eyes on the ground. I had one goal—to find Frankie and get a ride home without another ounce of drama.

That wasn't meant to be.

I ran smack into Patrick's chest before I'd taken five steps.

He saw my tear streaked face, and without a word, just pulled me against him, running a hand over my hair. It was comforting. I had the brief thought that he was sweeter than I'd remembered.

That opinion didn't last long, though, as he dipped his head and kissed me, right smack on the mouth, and then didn't pull back.

I didn't react at first, stunned by what an insensitive prick he really was, to plant one on a crying girl. It wasn't until he pushed his tongue into my mouth that I shoved on his chest, wrenching away, glaring at him.

And, with the worst timing in history, once again, Tristan was there, catching enough of the kiss to put murder in his eyes.

I backed away as he cursed, and then charged, taking Patrick down to the ground with a tackle that I swore made the entire house shake.

I screamed, and screamed some more as he started punching the smaller man, right in the face, again and again, his massive arms faster than I'd have believed possible. Patrick struggled, he tried, but he didn't get one punch in before he went limp.

The sounds, the sickening thud of fist hitting flesh, and flesh giving to fist, made me nauseous, and I backed away, further and further, mortified by what Tristan was doing, what he was capable of.

Tristan kept hitting the limp man, his heavy fists brutal, and would have kept right on punching, if Kenny, Cory, Jared, and some guy I'd never seen before forcibly separated him from his prey. As it was, Patrick was out cold, his face bloody.

CHAPTER THIRTY-NINE

TRISTAN

It didn't even take ten minutes before I regretted everything I'd said to her, and moreover, the way I'd said it. Even the parts that were true shouldn't have been delivered like that.

I turned around, heading straight back, jogging now, panicking inside because I knew how she was, knew she would use my outburst to alienate us completely. I had so much more that I'd make her hear, though. I knew that I could change her mind.

I was at a dead sprint by the time I got back to the house. No one was left in the front yard, and I burst straight through the front door, searching faces. I went through three rooms before I ran into Frankie, who was looking, too.

"I saw her go into the house, but I haven't been able to find her since you left. You're in the doghouse, man. You better make this up to her. You better write some fucking poetry to make up for the shit you said to her."

I didn't respond, still moving, and looking, room to room, frantic to find her. I had the worst feeling in my gut, I knew that the faster I found her, the better chance I had of keeping this from turning into something that I couldn't handle.

I found Cory, and Kenny, and Jared, but still no Danika.

331

When I finally did come across her, I couldn't believe what I was seeing. I was so shocked, that I just stood there for a moment, frozen in place.

That piece of shit was touching her. No, not just touching her, kissing her. On the lips. With his mouth. His arms were wrapped around her, too, but all I could focus on was what I needed to do to his face.

Danika wrenched away from him suddenly, her eyes furious, the curve of her mouth disgusted.

I lost my mind, my last clear thought before I went ballistic being that I would destroy him. I would rip him apart, piece by fucking piece, for touching what was *mine*.

The next thing I remembered were cuffs snapping onto my wrists. I shrugged my shoulders, and the cops looked ready to Taser me for that small movement. I couldn't blame them. When men my size went ballistic, bad things happened, as evidenced by the guy being pushed away in a gurney.

I looked around, saw my brother, Kenny, and Cory, but no Danika, or Frankie.

"Where is she?" I asked Jared, digging in my heels when a cop tried to prod me forward. I'd move when I was good and ready.

"She left. Frankie took her home."

"Was she okay?" I asked, shrugging off the cop's hand on my shoulder. "Give me a fucking minute," I told the officer, turning to give him a hard look.

He swallowed hard, but set his jaw. If I pushed him much more, he'd Taser me to prove a point.

I turned back Jared.

Jared shook his head. "She was really upset, but she didn't get hurt or anything. You didn't touch anyone but that guy in the gurney."

I nodded, finally letting them lead me away. I knew I'd only made things worse by losing it, but even this second, when I thought of that guy touching her, putting his hands and his mouth on her, I wanted to pound his face all over again. And the fact that he was an ex, that he'd had sex with her at some point, that he'd been *inside* of her. *Mine*. Well, that made me want to *kill* him.

I was lost in my own thoughts to the point that I barely noted what was going on. I summoned up a smirk for my mug shot, but even through the booking, I wouldn't answer a single question that they asked me. I thought that if I talked about, even mentioned that piece of shit that had been touching her, I'd lose my mind again.

I was focused on one thing. "Don't I get a phone call?" I asked the officer that had been nonstop questioning me, growing increasingly frustrated when I just gazed off into space.

"You a fighter? You pro?" he countered.

I ignored that completely, even though I knew they were trying to trump up the chargers. "Phone call," I said stubbornly. I needed to call her as soon as possible, and start with the apologies. I was already fucked. Giving her more time to stew about it would only make things worse.

"Fine. You can make a phone call. Just answer some questions for me first."

I zoned out again, only hearing that he wasn't giving me the only thing I was interested in.

Nothing really got me out of my own head until I was being led into a room, and sitting at a table, was James Cavendish.

He raised his brows at me, waving a hand at the seat across from him.

I sat, eyeing him up suspiciously. We'd met several times now, but I still wasn't sure what to think about the pretty boy billionaire. My first inclination was not to like him, but he made that harder almost every time we talked.

"What are you doing here?" I asked him.

He gave me an enigmatic smile. "Frankie called me. You

had my dearest friend upset, which I take strong exception to."

"She's my friend too," I said defensively, "and I didn't mean to upset her."

"Yes. I see that. You went Hulk smash, and the rest is history, but let me get to the point here."

"Please do," I said tersely.

"I don't know if you're aware of this, but I've backed your band financially."

I sure hadn't been aware of that.

"I'm not even directly involved in that industry, but I'm not a man who sees a good investment and just watches it walk away. I've been working on a record deal for you, a solid one, but another incident like this, and you will tank all of your chances. This can't happen again."

I didn't mean for it to happen this time, I thought. "Got it," I said. I wouldn't blow it for the guys if there was a chance I could help it.

"Unfortunately, I'm not convinced. You see, I saw the other guy. I've posted your bail, and I'm paying all of his medical bills. But what you did to him...the injuries he sustained, those are not the actions of a man in his right mind. I hear they had to pull you off, or you would have kept going, but the damage was already very substantial, as it is. I'm not pleased."

"Join the club," I growled, because I was as disgusted with myself as anyone.

"I'm going to need some insurance from you that your behavior will change. My lawyers can get your sentence down to probation, they've assured me, but you will be attending anger management. You doing coke?"

I glared at him. "Excuse me?"

"Were you on something tonight?"

That was the sad part. I'd done coke before, and it hadn't made me act half as crazy as my jealousy had. I knew he was onto something, with the anger management. "Nada. Fine, I'll do anger management."

"I'll be happy to put you up in a rehab facility for substance abuse, if that is an issue, as well."

"It's not," I bit out, done with the conversation.

"Okay, then. I've posted your bail, as well, so you are free to go right after we discuss one more thing."

I glanced around, as though it was a prank. I knew for a fact that you couldn't do that to a guy, and then just walk out of jail that night. "Are you shitting me?"

"Not at all. I'll add it to your tab. I just wanted to talk to you about your magic tricks. Danika has told me about your sleight of hand. I'm asking unofficially, you understand, because I have my old act under contract for two more years. But when his contract is up, he's out. He just doesn't have his heart in it anymore. Sometime between now and then, I'd like to see some of your tricks. We are looking for something different, so keep that in mind as you prepare."

I nodded, totally stunned that, after all the time I'd spent at that, having nothing happen, now something huge was happening, and it was all because of Danika.

"Okay, that is all," he said, rising from his chair. "I'll send someone in to take your cuffs off and get you out of here."

I smiled at him, a purely ornery smile, because, in a purely ornery mood, I'd stolen one of the cops handcuff keys.

I unlocked myself with a few swift, quiet motions. This was the cheapest kind of trick, the kind where you weren't even doing a trick, you were just performing the unexpected, but I was in a mood, and I didn't really care that it was cheap.

I dropped my cuffs loudly on the table, and Cavendish gave me a very startled look, his eyes darting from the cuffs then back to me, again and again.

"How did you do that?" he asked, looking like he'd gotten a genuine kick out of it. That was good, because if he got a kick out of me phoning it in, I had a good shot at impressing him with

335

my more involved tricks.

I shrugged. "Magic," I told him.

He laughed.

I called Danika for five days, over and over, without a response. I finally resorted to leaving message after message, at first angry, then pleading, then sappy, then angry again, and finally, flat out desperate.

I told her I loved her, which I probably shouldn't have said for the first time in a message, but I was desperate. I called her a coward, then cursed her, then begged her.

I tried to go to the house once, but she only sent Jerry out to tell me that they would call the police if I didn't leave.

After that, I holed up in my apartment for days, and went into full on self-destruct mode. I was drunk or high or both every waking moment, denying to myself that this could possibly be it for us.

What if she never talks to me again? I tortured myself with that question. I didn't know what I'd do. I was filled with regrets. I hadn't opened up to her as much as I should have, and she'd complained about it often. I should have spilled my guts about everything, even if I did hate to talk about the crap she wanted me to tell her.

I found myself telling her everything about me in voicemails that she'd probably never even listen to. I was that desperate.

"I'm not good at this sort of thing, but I'll do my best. If you're hearing this, you know I'm trying here, and in return I'd just like to hear from you, to have a clue how you're doing."

I took a deep breath, trying to figure out where to start. "Fuck. Maybe I should be texting you this, or emailing, or something, but bear with me. I've never liked relationships. I've never thought that something like that could serve two people equally. I saw that from the way my mom was with one worthless boyfriend after another. She'd bend over backwards for them, and all they had to do was feed her bullshit lines and act halfway decent *some* of the time. I guess that's why I started to think they were kind of a scam. This belief was reinforced for me, over and over, as I watched her let men walk all over her for the sake of the 'relationship'."

"Nat was just sort of the icing on the cynical cake. We were just kids when we got together, and we made a lot of stupid mistakes. Nothing I did ever made her happy, and she had all of this emotional blackmail crap she tried to pull on me daily. Still, I stuck around, because I was young, and stupid, and I wanted so badly to be the opposite of my father, to be the guy that sticks around through thick and thin, that I was willing to put up with a lot, even being *miserable*, to prove that I was better than him, that I was nothing like him."

The message timed out, and I called again, waiting for the beep, and then continued right where I'd left off.

"Nat guilted me into getting her a ring. A ring I couldn't afford. She was relentless about it, said all of her happiness was tied up in it, and if I didn't make her happy, well, that was my fault, since her happiness was *my* job. She wore me down, and I busted my ass to get her a way too expensive ring. She told me it embarrassed her, because the diamond was so small. It was a three thousand dollar ring, so I had no idea what she meant, but that was how the relationship went. There were more bad times than good, more work than fun, more misunderstandings than communications. It exhausted me, and I was already fed up when I found out she was sleeping around."

It timed out. I didn't pause before calling and starting right up again.

"Nat pulled all kinds of jealous tantrums on me, always accusing me of cheating, when I wasn't. I think that's one of the reasons why it was so hard for me to stomach how she'd lied to me, again and again. I broke it off, and swore off relationships altogether, because she had taught me that I just wasn't good at them."

"I see now how wrong that was, how much power I'd given her, even when I'd been over her for years. I'm sorry for that. I'm sorry that you and I had a rough start, and part of it was because of baggage that didn't deserve the weight I'd given it."

It timed out again. I redialed again.

"I see now that I didn't know a thing about love before I met you. When it's right, like it is with us, it doesn't make your life harder, it makes your life *better*, even when it's hard. I've never been so happy as I've been with you, and I don't begin to know how to get past that. I can't stomach the thought that you could get over me, when I know I won't be getting over you. I love your smile, your honesty, your loyalty. I love your sarcastic sense of humor, and the way your eyes light up when you're giving me shit. I may just love that the most. I don't just love you, I *need* you, and I don't begin to know how that's *ever* going to stop. I guess this is a warning, in a way. If you think I'm letting you go easy, you're in for a shock. Buckle up, sweetheart, one way or another, I'm getting you back."

That was the last message I left before the waiting began.

I waited.

And waited.

Five more days passed, and I let the black moods take me again, but it wasn't because I'd given up. It was only that I couldn't bear how much I missed her, as I bided my time.

I thought that waiting was the hardest thing I'd ever been through in my life, but life was about to prove me very wrong.

CHAPTER FORTY

TRISTAN

I doubted anyone had ever had their worst nightmare come to life and not doubted that it was real. And so my first reaction to the news was denial. This had to be a trick. It had to be some sick prank. Jared couldn't be gone. He was my baby brother. It was my job to protect him. It wasn't possible that something like this could have happened to him on *my* watch...

My mother was sobbing endlessly, but the noise was always somewhere in the background, as though my brain was muting it, to soften the pain.

I didn't cry. I just sat, blank-faced and quiet, telling myself over and over again that this wasn't really happening.

A stinging slap to the face was what finally took me painfully out of my own head.

I blinked at my mother, who stood, furious and crying, in front of me.

"This is your fault!" she screamed at me. "It was your job to look after him, and look what's happened! You shouldn't have encouraged him to act so wild, you bastard!"

Her words hurt, each one inflicting a deeper wound, and some even opening old ones up wider.

I did the only thing I knew how to do under attack. I went on

Bad Things

the offensive. "Me?" I asked her quietly, a lifetime's worth of contempt in the short word. "Me? You were supposed to be our *mother*! You fed us pills like candy, you were drinking hard liquor and smoking pot with us by the time we were twelve! And you blame *me* for this? You blame me for the fact that he was a drug addict, when *you're* the one that got him hooked!"

She collapsed to the floor, sobbing uncontrollably, and I instantly regretted every word I'd said, even though it had *all* been the truth, if a hard truth to stomach.

I tried to comfort her, but she would have none of it, and I gave up quickly, going into a numb sort of stupor.

This isn't real.

This can't be happening. Not to Jared. He was the sweetest kid, always. Things like this didn't happen to kids that sweet. Bad things were supposed to happen to bad people, and Jared had always just been *good*.

He didn't fight like me. He wouldn't have hurt another person to save his own life. He didn't sleep around. He'd been waiting for the right girl to come along, for fuck's sake. Every shortcoming I had, he had been above, and I'd always taken a deep kind of pride in that.

People were talking in the background, though I couldn't have named them. I wasn't paying much attention to anything that was going on, so I only caught bits and pieces of what they were saying, little snippets here and there, and none of it made any sense to me.

Jared had died of a heart attack. A heart attack? A fit twenty-one year old didn't just have a heart attack. Did he? But of course that wasn't all of the story. Even in full on disconnect mode, I knew that. Drugs were the story. The only question was what, and how he'd miscalculated so far that he'd killed himself. Killed himself? No. No. *No.* That was wrong. Wrong. *Wrong.*

I was in my mom's house, though I didn't even remember

340

driving there. I remembered getting the phone call from Cory, and then I'd just been here, my mother's hysterical cries, her shrill accusations, just background noise.

I'd known lots of siblings that didn't get along. Dean had a little brother, and all that they seemed to do was rip into each other. Even mellow Cory and his sister hardly spoke.

That had never, *never* been the case with Jared and me. We had always been best friends. Even when we didn't agree on something, we respected each other, always, and respect went a long way. I didn't know how to accept the idea of his loss. I didn't know how to get past the denial, and face the absolute *horror*, the utter *agony* of it.

I only realized that Frankie was there when she knelt in front of me, her face tear-streaked and full of sympathy. She and Jared had been tight, and it alarmed me that she was so worried for *me*, because it made me realize that she was so right to be worried. I didn't have a clue how to handle this.

"You think it could be true?" I asked her, my own voice startling me with how it broke on the words. "You think Dean is pulling some shitty prank on us?"

She shook her head, black trails running, and running, and running down her face, her makeup in ruins. She didn't even wipe it off, as though she hadn't noticed. "No, Tristan. Cory saw him firsthand, and you know he wouldn't joke about something like this. Look at him. It's destroyed him too."

I couldn't. I couldn't look at anyone. I looked down at my hands, my shame almost as strong as my sense of denial. I knew that as soon as the first one caught up to the second, I'd be in for it. "This is my fault," I sobbed.

Frankie threw her arms around me, sobbing with me.

In the background somewhere, I heard my mother shout a loud agreement. She'd always instilled a sense of responsibility in me, to look after Jared, and I felt it like a stab to the heart. He'd been my little brother, and it had been my job, my *duty*, to watch over him, and while I'd been lost in my own depression, he'd slipped away, without me there to stop him, without me there to even hold his hand at the end.

That train of thought was pure masochism, and as I followed it, the denial left me, and the pain came, and I broke with it. I knew, absolutely, that I could die from this pain, that I could very well kill myself just to escape it.

I did the only thing I could in the face of utter despair. I reached out for a lifeline.

"Does Danika know?" I asked, pulling back.

Frankie shook her head, sniffling. "I haven't called her yet."

"Will you call her now? Will you tell Danika that I need her?" My voice broke again on the words. "She won't take my calls."

She patted my shoulder, standing. "Of course I will. I'll go outside to make the call. It's too loud in here."

I grabbed her hand before she could move away. "Do you know if she's listened to my messages?"

She squeezed my hand. "I don't think she has. She told me a week ago that her phone has been buried in a drawer. I'll have to call Bev to get ahold of her."

I nodded. "Will you tell her to listen to them, if she gets a chance?"

"I will. I'll be right back, k?"

I just nodded, looking down at my hands, watching my tears smack against them, surprised that I could actually hear them hitting my knuckles over the sound of my mom howling.

Frankie returned quickly, looking even more upset than before. "Bev said she'd tell her, but she'd taken the boys to run errands, and didn't have her phone, so she isn't sure how long that'll take. She said that, as soon as she returns, Jerry will bring her over."

I tried to be okay with that, but I wasn't. I couldn't cope with this for one more second without her, let alone some indefinite period of time.

I got up, then sat again, feeling totally lost.   Dark thoughts circled through my head, thoughts of guilt, and agony, and self-destruction.

I found my phone, and just stared at it for sixty-three minutes, while I waited in purgatory, counting every minute, because every minute felt like an hour.

When sixty-three minutes had come and gone, I knew I couldn't wait another.   I got up, threw my phone on the couch, and burst out the front door.

It was pouring rain outside, which I'd somehow failed to notice before.   I didn't care now, breaking into a run, running from anything and everything, intending to run until I literally dropped.

DANIKA

I knew that something was terribly wrong the second I stepped in the front door. The look of caring sympathy on Bev's face would haunt me.

It's strange the things that haunted you for years and years after a tragedy. The look on Bev's face when she braced to tell me the news, the tears in Jerry's eyes, a man who I'd never seen cry, the way the boys didn't say a word, as though clued into what was going on as soon as they saw their mother's face.

Some of it you'd expect; the last time I'd hugged Jared, the last time I'd seen him smile, the last time he'd called me for some silly reason, or for no reason at all. Those were a sweet sort of haunting though.

The bitter haunting came in the form of finding missed calls from Jared weeks later, calls that I'd missed because I'd been so wrapped up in my own problems, my own dysfunctions. The idea that I could have spoken to him again before he passed gave me the most acute sense of loss, because I'd thrown away something precious.   There was even one precious message

343

from him that I could never find the heart to erase. In fact, I kept that phone in a drawer by my bed, years after I'd upgraded, because I couldn't bear to let the sound of his voice be erased.

Hand in hand with the haunting, came regret.

As Jerry drove me to Leticia's house, I started listening to Tristan's messages, as he'd asked Frankie to ask me to do. As I listened, and realized that, while I'd been wrapped up in convincing myself that he could never give me what I needed, he'd been ready to give it to me, if I'd only bothered to listen.

I felt such regret then, because there was some chance, some strange persistent idea in my head, that if Tristan and I had made up faster, Jared might still be alive. He may have been with us, instead off somewhere without us, being reckless, getting hurt. *Losing his life.*

That regret taught me a lot about guilt, about how it supersedes all logic, and how it never really goes away, even with time.

All of the what ifs could destroy me, if I let them. That made me think of Tristan, and how, if I was feeling this unendurable, overwhelming pain at the loss of Jared, I couldn't even *imagine* what he must be going through.

I couldn't get to him fast enough. The idea that he was going through this without me, that he'd *asked* for me, and I hadn't already been there to hold him, quite simply tore me apart.

We pulled up to the curb just as he was tearing away from the house. I was out of the car, sprinting after him, before the car had come to a complete stop.

I screamed his name, but he didn't hear me, or at least he didn't stop. My flip-flops fell off, and my feet pounded bare against the sidewalk, but I didn't care. I wasn't going to let him be alone, not while I still had breath left in me.

I chased him in the pouring rain until I my lungs were on fire, a sense of desperation in every footfall that pounded hard against the wet pavement.

I screamed his name until my voice was hoarse, and I was too breathless to call out. But there was no way for me to catch him. He was too fast, and showed no signs of tiring, and so I found the breath to scream some more.

What finally slowed him was reaching a cul-de-sac, with nowhere else to go. There he paused for long enough for me to catch him with a wild, desperate hug from behind.

He stiffened, then turned, falling to his knees, his face buried in my stomach. He was as out of breath as I was, but that didn't stop his helpless sobs.

I gripped him tight against me, and his arms wrapped around me. We didn't speak for a long time, just clutched each other, and cried like the world was ending, because a sweet, irreplaceable part of it had.

When he finally spoke, his voice almost too soft to catch, it broke my heart all over again.

"I told you that I needed you. But now I need you to *survive*. Forever. I won't live through this without you, and I'm selfish for telling you that, but it's the truth. You're my rock, Danika. I can't ever lose you, or I'll follow Jared, I know I will."

The rain was pounding against us, soaking through our clothes, running down our faces, mixing with our tears. I barely noticed.

I bent down, crushing his face into me until I'd reached his ear. "You have me. I'm yours, and I'm not going anywhere, not ever again."

"I'm sorry. I was an ass. It was pure stubborn pride and jealousy that made me go off on you like that."

"Jealousy?"

"Yes. Jealousy. So much of it that I have dreams about pounding what's his name and skinny jean's into the dirt. I hated that you had a word for *this*. A word made cheap by using it on other men, and then throwing it in my face, like that should convince me to say it back. I don't have a word for *this*, because I've never felt *this* before. But I do love you. I just wish there was a way to explain to you that love is just the start of it, because it's turned into so much more for me."

It was the most bittersweet moment, a moment of finding something so perfect, right in the shadow of losing someone so precious.

EPILOGUE

I spoke at the funeral. Tristan and his mother were in no shape for it, and it didn't feel right not to have someone represent the family.

"Jared was just one month from turning twenty-two when he left us," I began. "Such a short life, but in that short time, he made such an impact on so many people."

Tristan had his head in his hands. He was still, but I knew he was crying.

I tried to keep it together as I continued, but my throat was so scratchy that I felt I might choke with unshed tears.

"I want you all to look to each side of you. Study those sitting beside you. I don't even have to ask, I can simply tell you with utter conviction that every person you are looking at adored Jared Vega. That is his legacy. Our love for him. He was the best of us, torn from us much, much too soon, but everyone who knew him had a life touched by his beautiful soul. Where there is love there is forever, and Jared will live forever in our hearts."

Leticia was sobbing loudly, and I had to take a few deep breaths to continue with any semblance of composure.

"Beloved brother, beloved friend, beloved son, you have left us far too soon, but our love for you cannot be measured in seconds, or minutes, or hours. It cannot be measured in years, or decades, or centuries. It is beyond the hands of time now. This love I feel for you can never die, will never fade, and cannot tarnish. It has become bigger than this life."

I had to stop and take three deep breaths as I heard the quiet sound of Tristan weeping brokenly into his hands.

I held up the black rubber wristband I had clutched in my hand. "You were all handed one of these on your way in. I want you to hold it in your hand, and study it. If you knew Jared, you know that he's had his arms covered in these for years. Since before he was fourteen, even before it was trendy, he sported at least one on each wrist. None of us will look at this little band again without thinking of him."

"Nothing could make us forget this sweet son, this loyal brother, this understanding friend, but let this also be our reminder of him. Often I will wear this on my wrist, or hold it in my hand and remember how he made me laugh, how I loved his smile, how he brought joy to all in his path."

I concluded by reciting Away by James Whitcomb Riley.

"I cannot say and I will not say
That he is dead, he is just away.
With a cheery smile and a wave of hand
He has wandered into an unknown land;
And left us dreaming how very fair
Its needs must be, since he lingers here.

And you-oh you, who the wildest yearn
From the old-time step and the glad return-
Think of him faring on, as dear
In the love of there, as the love of here
Think of him still the same way, I say;

He is not dead, he is just away."

As I finished my gaze happened to skim across Dean, who was down the row from Tristan. Seeing that even he was crying like his heart was broken had my eyes finally flooding with tears. I could only be relieved that I'd gotten through it before I broke down.

I approached Tristan on the bench, moving to sit beside him, on the other side from his mother, but they surprised me by moving apart, making a space for me between the two of them.

I took it without a word.

Leticia moved her face into my shoulder, sobbing piteously. I wrapped my arms around her, feeling so powerless in the face of her pain. I simply couldn't wrap my mind around how horrible this must be for her, when I'd only known Jared for a short time, and the loss of him had still shaken me to my core.

Tristan's lips moved to my ear, voice thick with tears. "Thank you for that. That was so beautiful, so perfect. It said everything that I wanted to say, if I could have found the strength. I'll never forget that for as long as I live; the way you were my strength, when I was too weak to even stand."

His face moved into my neck, and I found myself in the odd, and heartbreaking position of having an arm around both him and his mother as we all cried our hearts out.

It had been at Leticia's insistence that it was an open casket ceremony. I hadn't thought it was a good idea, and I'd been right. It was just too hard to look at him. I didn't think that anyone could feel better for seeing the body of a twenty-one year old man in his prime, pale and still in death.

Tristan and I went to see him together. He was clutching my hand so hard that it ached, but I didn't say a word.

I held my breath as I looked at Jared's still form, the air only escaping my lungs when I couldn't hold it for another moment.

I didn't know what to say. There were no words for this. His stillness, the peace on his face, it brought both comfort and despair.

Still, I tried my hardest to bring Tristan some bit of comfort with my own perspective. "I don't have a bad memory of him. I don't have a thing to say about him that isn't filled with affection. I know logically that no one on this earth is perfect, but to me, he was. There is bad in all of us, but I'll only ever remember the good in Jared."

Tristan hugged me to him, burying his face in my hair. "Thank you for that. It helps, to know someone else saw him how I did, that there are more of us to remember him like that."

"*Always*," I whispered in his ear. "I will *always* be here to remember him like that with you."

The day of the funeral seemed to last forever, well-wishers offering endless condolences to mother and son. It was so obvious to me that all of it was nothing but a strain on them both that it was hard to stomach.

I barely left Tristan's side, because that was where he needed me to be. He seemed to draw strength from me, and I was desperate to be what he needed, in the face of his pain.

His mother held a reception at her home after the ceremony. Friends and family brought food, and drinks, and no one seemed to want to leave, so it went on into the late hours of the night.

Tristan drank too much, stayed eerily quiet, and kept me close. It wasn't hard to talk him in to retiring early.

We shared his childhood room that night, clutching each other close on the twin sized bed. There were other places to sleep, more comfortable places, but I didn't even consider it. This was where he wanted to be, and I would be there with him.

"I love you," I murmured into his ear before he drifted off.

"I love you. So much. You're my rock, Danika," he said quietly.

Finally, for the first time in days, he drifted off into a deep sleep. I gazed at him with tender eyes the entire time.

Watching him sleep, feeling his heart beat under my palm, I could admit it to myself. I would love this man to the end of my days. I'd fallen too deep. Middle of the Pacific deep, with no land in sight. There was no going back. My heart was his forever.

BOOKS BY R.K. LILLEY
  IN FLIGHT (UP IN THE AIR #1)
  MILE HIGH (UP IN THE AIR #2)
  GROUNDED (UP IN THE AIR #3)
  LANA (AN UP IN THE AIR NOVELLA)
  BREATHING FIRE (HERETIC DAUGHTERS #1)
  BAD THINGS (BAD THINGS #1)

  TRISTAN AND DANIKA'S STORY CONTINUES IN
  ROCK BOTTOM (TRISAN & DANIKA #2)
  COMING SOON...

AN EXCERPT FROM *ROCK BOTTOM*

DANIKA

It had already been a shit of a day by the time I made it to Tristan's apartment. Shitty was really an understatement, though. It had been hell. Pure hell. Right in the fire of it.

I had too much on my plate, and my boyfriend was out of

town for weeks at a time, which just sucked. Knowing that I'd get to see Tristan at some point on a day like this was all that had helped me keep it together.

I had a key to his apartment, but I knocked first, out of courtesy. I wasn't that courteous, though, because I unlocked it and walked in before anyone had time to answer.

I saw right away that they wouldn't have answered, anyway.

It was three o'clock in the afternoon, but you wouldn't know it by the state of the apartment. Women were everywhere, slutty, groupie looking women, and I instantly felt my temper starting to boil.

Dean was lying, shirtless, on the couch. His jeans were undone, and some tramp had her hand down his pants, even as another bimbo sat hip to hip with him, sharing a joint.

Dean saw me and smiled, and I knew that this wasn't going to be a good visit. Just as I could read a different meaning into every one of Tristan's smiles, Dean's only ever meant one thing. Trouble. Not fun trouble. Just bad trouble. Ruin your day trouble.

"Hey! You come to join the party? I think your boyfriend is busy, but you know you're always first in line to suck *my* cock."

I walked through the living room, heading to the back of the apartment, where the bedrooms were. If I'd been thinking clearly, I'd have gone through the kitchen, but a few words out of his mouth and my brain was already too scrambled with my temper to have a mature interaction with him, if there was such a thing.

"You might not want to go back there. I believe he said he wanted privacy…"

I whipped my head around to give him one smoldering glare.

He just chuckled. "You know I think you're fucking hot when you're mad. I mean, I'd fuck you any time, but when you're mad, mmmm, now that would be a treat."

I stifled my first urge, which was to tell him to go fuck himself, because I knew he'd just turn it into a suggestion.   Instead, I settled for specific and childish.   "I hope you choke on one of your own used condoms, and die, you asshole," I told him, striding out of the room.

I heard him laughing behind me, and my fists clenched hard.

"Babe, I don't use condoms," he called after me.

"Disgusting pig," I muttered as I reached the closed door to Tristan's room.

I didn't knock, just opening the door quietly.   I figured girlfriend rights superseded some common courtesies.

I froze in the doorway as I took in the room.

Tristan was lying on his back on the bed, wearing nothing but his boxers, an arm thrown over his eyes, as though he were sleeping. By the agitated movements of his chest, I knew that wasn't the case.

A naked woman, some beyond trashy, slutbag blonde from hell, was straddling him.   Her hands were running over his chest, tracing his tattoos.

I was absolutely frozen, in fury, in hurt, in outright disbelief, which was all that kept me from reacting too quickly, which turned out to be a good thing.

"If you don't get off right this second," Tristan growled from underneath the naked tramp, his voice sleepy, and irritated, and just plain mean. "I'm going to throw you off. I told you, I have a girlfriend."

"She's not here now," the slut from hell purred, still running her hands over his chest. *My chest.* "I won't tell if you won't."

That was my cue to shout, yes, you bitch, I *am* here, but some devil kept me silent.   I sincerely wanted to see how this played out. I *needed* to see it.

"Well, then, since you apparently don't have an ounce of pride or self-respect, let me spell it out for you. I don't want you. I want you to leave my room and my apartment and never come back. I turned you down *three times,* and you still waited until I was passed out, and jumped me. How many times do I have to say it? I wouldn't touch you if you were my only option, which you aren't. Is that clear enough for you, or do you want me to try a different language now?"

He sounded mean, mean in a way I rarely heard from him. He was usually so amiable, bossy, yes, possessive, always, but usually just nice, and it was startling to hear his voice go pure mean.

Bimbo face seemed to get the hint, climbing off him with a pout on her face. "You're no fun," she muttered, "and I can tell that you wanted me. I got you hard."

"Don't take it personal. The fucking wind blowing gets me hard. Now get out."

She barely spared me a glance, but I had to stifle the urge to follow her and scratch her eyes out.

I stayed in the doorway, leaning against the frame of it while he sat up, rubbing his eyes. It took him a few quiet moments to notice me there.

When he did, he went white, as though he'd just seen a ghost.

He slid out of bed, moving to me, looking guilty as hell. If I hadn't just heard the whole thing with my own ears, that look would have been enough to convict him. It was a good thing I'd kept my mouth shut and let it play out. Still, I was spitting mad. I was sick to death of shit like this always testing us. It just seemed to me, that if you valued a thing, you found ways to keep it from being compromised. Groupies in the apartment had been a bone of contention for a while now.

He was in just a pair of black boxers and so it was impossible to miss the fact that he had a raging hard-on. That was the last straw for me. I just couldn't deal with this today, especially when I'd so been looking forward to a happy reunion, and not some disgusting groupie rubbing her naked body on him.

"I need to leave," I told him, already backing out of the room.

"I just can't deal with this shit right now. I have enough on my plate already."

He followed me, uncaring of the fact that he was practically naked, and sporting an obvious erection and the house was full of groupies.

"Danika, you have to believe me. Whatever you think that was—"

"I know what it was. I heard what it fucking was, and I don't care. I'm sick of this. If you cared about *us*, you wouldn't be putting yourself in positions where naked whores are rubbing on you in your sleep. Dean can have his groupies live here for all I care, but I'm out."

I turned on my heel, and strode to the front door. I had my hand on the knob before he stopped me, and he stopped me in the most Tristan way possible.

He pressed against me from behind, mostly naked, hard as a poker, and completely unmindful of the room full of people that must be watching us.

"I've missed you," he whispered in my ear, his hands moving over my hands, pinning them to the door above me. "You can't imagine how much I've missed you. I thought about you day and night. When I would text, and you wouldn't reply right away, I came so close to saying fuck it all and driving home to find you."

"I've been busy. I have classes, and I actually attend them pretty regularly. I always answered back as soon as I could."

"I know, but it's not enough. We should never be apart, not for any reason. I can't stand it. Come back to bed with me, sweetheart. I need you. Now."

The press of his body, that rasp in my ear, had me wet and ready and I wanted nothing more than to give in, but I didn't intend to just let this go. It had been too big of a problem for too long, and I was sick of it. I had enough shitty things going on in my life right now. Groupies humping my boyfriend in his sleep

356

was not going to be one of them.

"I need to leave. I'll call you later, but I really just can't deal with this right now. I'm too angry. I might say some things to you that I'll regret later, if I don't have time to cool off first."

He made a little sound of protest in the back of his throat, and of course that got to me. It had always been so hard for me to tell him no, and that had only gotten worse, the deeper I'd fallen for him.

"Please," he said, very very quietly, a word he almost never used. "I need you. Now. You can chew me a new one after. I can take it, sweetheart."

I wrenched my hands free, turning to glare at him. "It's not about chewing you a new one, you ass. It's about things that go on in this apartment when I'm away that I won't stand for. It's not about talk, it's about change—"

"Okay. Fine," he interrupted, looking earnest. "You tell me what you need and I'll see it done. Change away."

I set my jaw into a stubborn line, knowing that I was going to go down in the band's history for being a bitch for this. "No more groupies in the apartment. And wherever you're staying in L.A., for the recording, no groupies there, either. Girlfriends, dates, fine, but these sluts I see today, have got to go."

He gave a brief nod, turning his head to address the room. "New house rules. Any chick that isn't a girlfriend needs to leave. And since I know Dean doesn't have a girlfriend, that's all of you."

Of course Dean, who was still on the couch, had something to say about that. "Fuck you, man. This is my house, too. If you get to have your pus—"

"If you finish that fucking sentence, you know what's going to happen. Now, clear the room. The lease is under my name. If you have a problem with the new house rule, you can get the fuck out, too."

There was a lot of muttering and movement, but everyone

357

seemed to be obeying.

Tristan pulled me out of the way as the slutty parade started to file out. He watched for a moment, seemed to think it was settled, and turned back to me, moving against me until my shoulders hit the wall.

"Anything else?" he asked, but he didn't even give me a chance to answer before he was slanting his mouth over mine, hungry and hot, and just what I'd been waiting for. It had been weeks since I'd seen him, and I was kissing him back instantly, moaning as his tongue invaded me. He thrust it in and out, fucking my mouth.

He pinned my hands to the wall, sliding a thigh between mine, pushing it high, until I was riding it, my hips moving in circles to rub against him restlessly. It wasn't enough, and I hooked my leg behind his hip, every part of me working to bring his hardness into my core.

He groaned, working his hips between my thighs until we were fitted. Our clothes were in the way, but the contact was just in the perfect spot, and I worked against him, rubbing my clit against his cock, working to a fever pitch in seconds.

"Get a room," Dean said loudly.

Tristan ripped his mouth away, turning his head to bark, "Privacy! Now!"

Dean muttered something that I couldn't quite make out, but sure enough, he obeyed. I'd witnessed this exchange countless times.

The instant we were completely alone, Tristan started stripping me. He started with my tank top, peeling it off, opening the front clasp of my bra with one swift movement, and slipping it off my arms.

He went down to his knees to work on my jeans. They were tight, so he had to work them off slowly, taking my panties with them.

Being stripped was distracting, but not as distracting as his kiss had been, and as I became slightly less distracted, I found my mind moving to the thing that was bugging me, stupid as it was.

"You wanted her. You were hard for her."

He paused briefly, then resumed peeling. "Sweetheart, I was sleeping. That was morning wood, and for your information, I was dreaming of you when she interrupted me. I was expecting you, and when I felt someone get on top of me, that was the first thought that occurred. It didn't last but a second, though, before I realized that it was some strange woman."

That appeased me, but mostly because skanky groupies were now banned from the house, so it wouldn't be happening again.

The second he got my jeans free of my feet, he pulled my legs over his shoulders and buried his face between my thighs, effectively stopping any more thinking on my part. His tongue worked on me expertly, his big fingers delving inside of me, working into a rhythm that had me mindless and writhing against the wall, his shoulders pushing between my legs all that kept me upright.

He'd been growing his hair out, per my request, and I buried my hands in it, gripping for dear life.

"I love you," I cried out as I came.

"I love you, too, sweetheart," he said, as he freed himself from my legs, rising. He stripped off his boxers in one smooth motion, moving flush against me, and fitting himself between my legs. "I can't take these separations. I'm leaning towards saying fuck this record deal. You're my whole life. What's the point of it all, if I can't be with you all the fucking time?"

I couldn't respond, as he was wrapping my legs around his hips. He lined himself up at my entrance, pushing in that first perfect inch.

"Wait, condom," I said, not thinking at all. It was just sort of an instinct for me.

He froze. "Are you off the pill?"

I turned my face away, flushing. "No," I said, very quietly, wondering what can of worms I'd just opened.

He caught what my instinctive response meant instantly. He turned my face so I was looking at him, and the raw pain in his eyes just about undid me. "You don't trust me anymore? You think I'm screwing around on you?" His voice was devastated.

I shook my head, well shook it as much as I could, with my jaw held in his viselike grip. "I don't think that. We wouldn't be doing this at all if I thought that. I didn't mean for that to come out. It was just my instinctive reaction. I guess I'm feeling insecure."

He pulled my hand over his heart. "That hurts me. This is all yours right here. All of me. No one else gets a thing from me, you understand? I wouldn't do that to you. I wouldn't make all these promises if I didn't intend to keep them."

I nodded, blinking back tears.

He moved back into me, pinning me to the wall. His forehead touched mine as he gripped my hips, shifting his hips until he was poised back at the core of me. "I'm fucking done with this record deal if it means I'm losing your trust. This is forever for me, sweetheart. I want it *all* with you. You're the thing that gets me up in the morning, and lets me rest easy at night. I wouldn't have survived some of the shit these last few months if it weren't for you. You're my rock, Danika, and I *need you* to trust me."

I nodded again, then gasped as he thrust hard into me.

4442258R00203

Printed in Great Britain
by Amazon.co.uk, Ltd.,
Marston Gate.